Praise for

LAVASH AT FIRST SIGHT

"A beautiful story rife with food and family rivalry, *Lavash at First Sight* is smart and sexy, inspiring readers to go after their heart's desire. A dazzling romance."

—Ashley Herring Blake, *USA Today* bestselling author of *Dream On, Ramona Riley*

"I love Taleen Voskuni's voice so much—the way she can craft a beautifully descriptive sentence and then follow it up with a sly bit of humor. *Lavash at First Sight* is Voskuni at the top of her game with clever, flirty banter between Nazeli and Vanya even while they have to deal with the very real pressures from their feuding families."

—Alicia Thompson, *USA Today* bestselling author of *Never Been Shipped*

"A wonderfully lighthearted and loving look at family and identity, love, and the importance of staying true to oneself. I just ate it up!"

—Jenna Levine, *USA Today* bestselling author of *Road Trip with a Vampire*

"A heartfelt and dazzling love story that's good enough to eat . . . I devoured this fun, witty, and romantic book and can't wait for whatever Voskuni writes next!"

—Sarah Hawley, author of *Servant of Earth*

"A dazzling and transportive delight! Amidst family rivalry, clever competitions, and dreamy first dates, Taleen Voskuni expertly crafts a gorgeous love story that sizzles with heat."

—Courtney Kae, author of *In the Case of Heartbreak*

"Voskuni brings welcome depth to her latest romance with her keen focus on Armenian culture, along with descriptions of food that will leave your mouth watering . . . A delectable contemporary romance that revolves around family and culture."

—*Kirkus Reviews*

"After wowing romance readers with her splendid debut, *Sorry, Bro*, Voskuni is back with another fun and flirty rom-com that insightfully illustrates the importance of family and the universality of love while celebrating the food and heritage of Armenia and highlighting the joys awaiting visitors to Chicago."

—*Booklist*

"Voskuni brilliantly balances common characteristics of Armenian families (dare I say stereotypes) with exaggeration and comedy—the overly involved families, limited acceptance of difference, passion and pride for cooking and eating, and stubborn competitiveness, with a dash of elitism. I was pleased to see the acceptance from the families of their queer daughters, laughed out loud at their overbearing nature, and rooted for the parents to eventually see how they were more alike than different."

—*Armenian Weekly*

Berkley titles by Taleen Voskuni

Sorry, Bro

Lavash at First Sight

Our Ex's Wedding

Our Ex's Wedding

TALEEN VOSKUNI

Berkley Romance
New York

BERKLEY ROMANCE
Published by Berkley
An imprint of Penguin Random House LLC
1745 Broadway, New York, NY 10019
penguinrandomhouse.com

Title page art: Flower arch © Nadia Snopek / Shutterstock
Book design by Alison Cnockaert

Library of Congress Cataloging-in-Publication Data

Names: Voskuni, Taleen author
Title: Our ex's wedding / Taleen Voskuni.
Description: First edition. | New York: Berkley Romance, 2026.
Identifiers: LCCN 2025024401 (print) | LCCN 2025024402 (ebook) |
ISBN 9780593953648 trade paperback | ISBN 9780593953655 ebook
Subjects: LCGFT: Romance fiction | Novels | Fiction
Classification: LCC PS3622.O84 O97 2026 (print) | LCC PS3622.O84 (ebook)
LC record available at https://lccn.loc.gov/2025024401
LC ebook record available at https://lccn.loc.gov/2025024402

First Edition: January 2026

Printed in the United States of America
1st Printing

The authorized representative in the EU for product safety and compliance is Penguin Random House Ireland, Morrison Chambers, 32 Nassau Street, Dublin D02 YH68, Ireland, https://eu-contact.penguin.ie.

To Nicole and Jessica, my lifelong friends and members of the greatest group chat.

You are my lifelines, and I love you.

1

Ani

YOU'RE NOT DESPERATE. *You're a professional.*

Well . . . you're a little bit of both, but you can absolutely nail this.

Ani told herself these words as she stepped out of her car and took in the Tuscan-inspired winery before her.

So this was Ô.

Two weeks ago, when the email had hit her inbox, when Ani saw the bride wishing for a winery wedding, when she saw the massive six-figure budget, she knew her wedding planning business might be saved. And now she was here. Ready to make it happen, if she could calm her nerves.

Ani had seen photos of Ô online, but the Napa winery was far more breathtaking—and intimidating—in person. The stone villa towered over the plot, while well-manicured cypresses flanked the property like sentries, followed by miles of vineyards stretching out on either side.

The time was 11:20 a.m., ten minutes before her meeting with her prospective clients. Bab always said if you're on time, you're late! She wouldn't mind pacing the grounds, taking them in and using the meditative moments to relax her racing heart before meeting the new brides. The weather was perfect—mid- to high sixties—lucky for February, although not unheard of. She had painted her nails burgundy with a matching lip and wore her one silk shirt, pencil skirt, and heels. She hoped the look would bolster her confidence, bring out her inner 2001 J.Lo in the greatest movie of all time—*The Wedding Planner*, just like her—and, most importantly, wipe clean the memory of the last three months.

Then her phone rang.

Mom. Ani thought about not answering but then thought better of it and picked up.

"Parev, Ani jan," her mother's sweet voice sang.

"Hi, Mom."

"I am here, too!" her father chirped.

Naturally he was. Her parents were always together, constantly together. It was like they were allergic to being apart.

"Is today the day you are going to Ô?" her mother asked.

Ani had told them about the new winery wedding she was hoping to land, just as she told them about everything, usually.

But she did not, would not, could not, tell them about the debt.

"Just arrived, but I'm early, so I have a couple minutes," confirmed Ani, gravel crunching under her feet as she walked toward the open vineyards.

"I still cannot believe that Raffi Garabedian is the owner now," her mother mused. "I must ring Nora and get the details on how this happened."

"Raffi Garabedian," her father wondered aloud. "Was he not the doctor? Moushegh's son?"

"Yes, hokis," her mother answered, with that term of endearment she used most often for her husband: "my soul." "That is why I am wondering how he came to own a winery."

"Well," her father trailed, "his father *is* a member of the Armenian mafia, so if his son wants to abandon his Hippocratic oath and open a winery, he can."

"Mob business!" her mother cried, and Ani heard the smile on her mom's face. She could imagine her mother playfully slapping her father's arm.

But there *were* rumors.

Ani had wondered about the new owner, although he wasn't her main focus today. She'd heard about Raffi Garabedian all right. Her friend Nareh had warned her way back—it was about five years ago, before Ani became a wedding planner full time—that he was a total playboy skeeze despite his status as Northern California's most eligible Armenian bachelor. A fabulously wealthy and handsome doctor—what more could you want, the aunties would say. Her friend had said differently. He's gorgeous, yes, Nareh had told Ani, but vapid and misogynistic. Ani's sister, Talar, had warned her similarly, but now Ani couldn't remember what she'd said. She hadn't had time to catch up with Talar before the meeting today.

But one thing was clear: Raffi Garabedian was to be avoided at all costs.

Ani had seen him on the periphery at this or that banquet, and he'd even shown up at a family friend's wedding. Although she was mesmerized by his dark-set eyes, elegant height, and broad shoulders, she had kept her distance. The word of her crew was far greater than the pull of his hotness.

Today, however, she might have to interact with him. She

had no idea how huge the operation at Ô winery was—the grounds were vast, she realized, wandering through the bare branches of the winter grapevines. Maybe Raffi had staff to meet wedding planners and potential couples, so it was possible she wouldn't see him at all. She'd emailed the winery and someone had emailed back, setting up the time today, but it had been a generic welcome@owinery.com address. No name was signed. Despite Raffi's apparent unsavoriness, Ani was excited to go to the winery and support an Armenian business, even if the owner was a playboy and his father a possible mob boss. There were so few Armenian-owned venues, it was a bit of a treat to get to visit one.

Her mother's voice changed suddenly. "You must keep your heart open, eh, Ani?"

Ani's heart instead plummeted to the depths of her stomach. Not this talk, not now. The vineyard seemed to crawl on and on forever. Ani hadn't walked far, but she felt suddenly lost in a labyrinth.

"Mom—"

"Listen, tsakougus," her mother replied, using the endearing word for "my child." "It's been two years since Kami—"

A sharp pain pierced Ani's heart. "Mom—"

The name alone, *Kami*, made Ani shrivel up inside. She wished she had her drink, wished she could feel the ice-cold matcha latte flow down her throat and douse the embers Kami had left on her heart.

Her mother barged on. "We are worried about you. You have not dated one single person since then."

"I have," Ani insisted, trying not to get angry and failing.

"I've been on the apps and gone on dates, and they've all been terrible. Or nothing, bland. I don't feel anything for anyone." "Anymore," she wanted to add. Not since Kami.

"This is why I am saying," her mother continued, "meeting online does not work for everyone. You have a chance to meet this handsome man in person—"

"Maybe. I might not."

"—and charm him the way you do everyone."

Before Ani could say that she didn't *want* to charm him, she had to respond to the compliment, which was simply untrue. "I do not."

"You do. You are special."

Ani let out a sardonic laugh. Right. Her, special. The B student, the one who got stood up more often than not, the one who couldn't get her business off the ground and was instead running it into the ground. The one who got dumped by *the one*.

A crow cawed overhead. Ani snapped out of her spiral and checked the time.

"I gotta go. I don't want to be late."

"Okay, Ani jan, promise me. Open your heart."

Easy for you to say, Ani thought. Her mom and dad had been madly in love since they were sixteen. Giggling like teenagers and sneaking off on dates for forty years.

"Yeah, yeah, yeah."

"Listen to your mother. Bye, shakaruhs," her father added helpfully.

Ani stared at the horizon a moment in silence, then paced back to her car. When she arrived, her phone dinged twice and she saw two notifications.

One from her kick-ass assistant, Sanan, which read, Good luck today, boss!

The second, an overdraft fee notification from her bank. Goddamn it. She knew she shouldn't have indulged in that extra-large matcha latte, but Ani couldn't help it. The iced green tea always put her in the best mood, and lately she needed all the help she could get. She'd deal with the bank later.

Ani swiped away the tough-luck notification and responded to Sanan.

> Thank you! I'm here now, it's gorgeous. Hopefully I can close this.

Sanan responded: ✌️ Btw I googled Grace's IMDB page and noticed her latest credit.

Grace was the bride-to-be who had emailed Ani, filling out Ani's contact form and plopping in that jaw-dropping budget. From the sound of Grace's message, she was the one in charge of planning and wanted to surprise her fiancée, Mimi, with this venue. Ani and Sanan promptly Instagram-stalked their potential client and discovered that Grace was an indie movie actress originally from the Bay Area.

Sanan continued, Her new movie is in post-production and it stars . . . Robert De Niro! Granddaughter taking over the mob family business. Title? Mafia Princess.

A whole new flurry of both excitement and worry hit Ani. She was about to meet someone who had breathed the same air as Robert De Niro? Grace's expectations were probably going to be high. Ani needed to believe she could do a wedding of this caliber.

Mafia Princess! Ani texted back. Damn, I'd watch that. Gotta go now, I'll update you!

Two mob references in one day. Ani wondered what type of astrological retrograde caused that to happen. She also wondered if Mimi was an actress, perhaps someone Grace met on set. Grace's Instagram didn't include any photos of her fiancée, but she did have a picture of their hands holding, with eye-popping engagement rings on each of their respective ring fingers.

From inside her car, Ani grabbed her tote bag and her $47 (thanks, overdraft fee) drink.

She also gathered her courage.

Ani's discount pumps clicked on the pavement as she strode up to the winery.

Then, as she came closer to the villa, the thick doors at the entrance opened and out stepped the owner himself, the one she'd been warned about.

Raffi Garabedian.

Ani had seen him only in dim lighting before, with purples and blues flashing about at evening Armenian dances, and he was already unmistakably handsome there. But here? In the cool, filtered light from the Napa clouds, Raffi standing there in a white Oxford button-down, slacks, and polished black shoes, Ani had the thought, the actual thought, *I've never seen anyone this gorgeous in my entire life.*

He was tall, yes, but it was the way he held himself like an aristocrat that caught Ani's eye. Broad shoulders and long, long legs. The sharpness of his jawline stole her breath, as did his heavily lidded dark eyes. His hair, so thick and gelled to one side in a sexy coif. She wanted to run her hands through it.

Get a goddamn hold over yourself, akhchig, she inwardly muttered, *and remember what Nareh said.*

The way Raffi regarded her, though, didn't seem like he was eating her up with his eyes, slicing into a thick, juicy steak. And why would he, when she was just . . . fine-looking? Not a woman anyone would immediately read as hot.

And yet Raffi stared at her with what Ani considered to be interest, with curiosity, and she felt the tiniest surge of hope that maybe Nareh was wrong and he didn't suck, and her mother was right and she should open her heart—

That thought was interrupted by her heels crunching into gravelly rock at the threshold of the winery. Ani wobbled, trying to right herself. In one motion, Raffi bounded over to help, but Ani felt herself bobbing out of control as she kept attempting to find solid ground but was thwarted by the small rocks that had declared war on her patent pumps and seemed intent on knocking her down. Raffi reached to catch her right as she was about to face-plant but instead caught her arm, just as the contents of her extra-expensive, extra-large matcha latte smashed against his white shirt.

He did not immediately let go of her arm, even as he stared down at the damage.

Ani put her now-empty hand over her mouth because his Oxford was entirely soaked in green. It was so bad, but her brain still registered the curve of his pecs and the way the pressure on her arm where he was gripping her felt weirdly safe and good. *No, no it doesn't,* she tried to tell herself, remembering Nareh's warning words. He probably reached out not to help but because it was an opportunity to touch a woman. Gross. Still, the look on his face read "concern," not "sleazy delight."

Ani hopped out of her shoes in order to stand properly, and when it was clear she was able to balance, Raffi let go of her arm. She wondered if his gripping fingers had left a mark on her skin.

"I'm so sorry," she said. "These rocks, they—I mean, for anyone in heels, this is a total liability. Who put these here?"

By the look on Raffi's face, it was clear to Ani that it was him. He had put them there.

"This was YSL, you know," was his response, gesturing to the shirt, his voice as irritatingly deep and handsome as the rest of him. He appeared less in shock, more in disappointment.

Ani went from being apologetic to apoplectic at his snobby response.

"Such liberal use of the past tense. I could get that stain out in two minutes."

She was about to add that she was sure he could buy another one when her eyes were drawn to the clack of footsteps from above. A large older gentleman with thick eyebrows stood on the balcony of the winery, frowning down directly at Raffi. She barely made out the man's words in his low, growling voice. "Tun mart ches tarnar."

"You'll never become a man."

Ouch. That had to be Raffi's father, the mythologized mobster. Ani quickly averted her eyes. And speaking of ouch, she made her way barefoot across the craggy rocks, back onto the smooth concrete, mere steps from the massive winery doors.

She slipped her shoes back on, trying not to be aware of how intimate a gesture this was to do in front of someone she'd just met.

She stared at those blasted pebbles. "So were you going for, what, a moat around the property?"

Raffi drew in a breath sharply. "I thought it'd give the place a little something extra."

Ani gestured around her. "Believe me, this is already plenty extra. You should remove that unless you want a lawsuit on your hands." Then she caught his eyes, which appeared worried. "Not from me. From, you know, guests. Prime drunk patron stumbling block, right here."

"I thought wedding planners anticipated everything. Couldn't you tell your heels wouldn't make it?"

Ani was stunned. First, Raffi knew she was the wedding planner, not the bride. Had he . . . looked her up? Second, he was being combative, and this was not behavior she expected from supposed sexy, devil-may-care Raffi. Rude. And third (the one that made her blush), no, she hadn't anticipated it because she was too busy being distracted by his hotness. As annoying as he was, she couldn't deny his Adonis-like appearance.

Ani decided she'd give him the benefit of the doubt. She *had* ruined his very expensive shirt after all.

She stuck out her hand. "It's Ani, by the way, though I guess you already knew that."

She gave him a look like "Yes, I know you googled me." Okay, she couldn't help the snark.

Raffi chewed on his cheek for a quick second before relenting. He extended his large hand as he said "Raffi."

Then they shook, which was the second time they had touched in the span of two minutes.

"I have to change," he said gruffly.

"Of course," she replied.

Raffi disappeared inside. Ani took in a deep breath of the cool Napa air. Holy shit. What had just happened?

She could not stop poking at this guy, even though she was the one who had drowned his shirt in green liquid. His *YSL* shirt. What a prick. But he was the owner of the winery and still someone she had to at least be professional around. *Come on, Ani.* He might be a total snob douche, but she had to at least be civil to him.

And she was definitely not thinking about him changing out of that soaking wet shirt that clung to his chest. *Yes, yes, yes, he's hot*, she thought. *But danger comes in pretty packages.*

As if on cue, he waltzed back outside, donning a near identical fresh Oxford shirt. See? She knew that type of shirt must be a dime a dozen to someone like him.

Raffi turned to face her and cleared his throat.

"Listen, this winery means a lot to me. It's still in its infancy, and I'm"—he gestured toward the litigation rocks—"well, still getting the hang of things."

Oh. This was as unexpected as everything that came before. Was this an apology?

Ani frowned.

She attempted to decipher the meaning in his words. If he was saying sorry, he wasn't doing a very good job of it, although she couldn't help but be touched by how sincere he sounded about the winery. What was it, she wondered, that meant so much? He had been a doctor and then switched to running a winery—why? Raffi was too much of an enigma, which worried her because Ani absolutely loved solving puzzles.

"On that note," he continued. "Yes, I did look you up. I want to know everything about everyone who is going to be part of Ô."

Ani's breath hitched. She felt flattered and also maybe impressed by the extent of his research. Oh no, she was feeling intrigued by Raffi again.

"But I have to say, based on the work on your website—I have to be honest here—the types of weddings you've created in the past don't exactly line up with the vibe that Ô has. Your style seems more . . . quaint. And that worries me, because we are trying to achieve a type of brand here, and we don't want to tarnish it."

Red-hot heat rose up in Ani's face. Twin flames of anger and shame.

Anger, because how *dare* he.

Shame, because he was somewhat, almost right.

Ani had been a *good* wedding planner for the past four years, after she quit her paralegal job and made her childhood dream come true. But she hadn't landed any big opulent weddings. She was mostly unknown and had been doing cousin and friend-of-friend (and friend-of-sister) weddings, plus an extra one here and there when someone found her contact info and liked the low prices on her website. Because her couples didn't have the budget, she could only do so much, the photographs on her website could only be so impressive. Raffi had her there.

While she loved DIY-ing and working with any couple, regardless of budget, she also had to pay the bills. And luxury weddings paid the bills.

In theory.

Last year, she thought her big break had come when an Armenian couple—the now Avedissians—hired her to plan their bash at the Palace Hotel in San Francisco. Her parents didn't know them, and no one she knew was familiar with them either, which was unusual, but she took it as a sign that her reputation was skyrocketing. It was such a big wedding, she even made her first hire, Sanan. The couple kept asking her to pay the vendors and said they would write her a check at the end. Ani complied, wanting to put this wedding, with its orchids and ostrich feathers, in her portfolio, even though it meant opening a third credit card and signing a few IOUs with her trusted vendors. And finally, on the wedding day, after begging the couple for the check for weeks, Ani politely demanded the money, and the bride angrily scribbled her one for the sum that was owed: $49,700.

That check bounced, and the couple had disappeared from the face of the earth.

Ani had taken out a personal loan with a very high interest rate to ensure she could pay Sanan—who didn't know of her money woes—plus the priority vendors. The monthly payment had been breathing down her neck for months. Not to mention the credit card debt that was racking up. And now her account overdraft.

There was one person in her life who she could ask for a loan, but she never, ever would. She would not be the older sister who begged her younger and much more successful sister for money.

Ani hadn't put the Avedissians' wedding photos on her site. She had successfully planned one extravagant wedding, with all the bells and whistles—in this case, smoke machines and custom lighting. She'd steered the Avedissians' taste from the gaudy to the tasteful (leaving only mere touches of garishness to satisfy the bride). But she refused to showcase the con artist couple's wedding on her site, much less submit it to any magazines or blogs. She deleted the two photos she'd posted on Instagram as soon as the check bounced and Ani realized she'd been played.

So now, with Raffi doubting her abilities, it felt like someone had squeezed a full bottle of antiseptic on her very open wound. And not just anyone, but a man who was born wealthy, who likely never knew what it felt like to have a single caffeinated drink drop his checking account into negative numbers.

Ani felt a raging beast emerge from her chest at the injustice of *him*, in particular, making these comments about her work. After all she'd done this morning to build up her confidence. This man of ill repute thought he could try to take it all down. No. She wouldn't give in.

All thoughts of professionalism were suddenly crushed under her patent burgundy heels. Ani stared daggers at the spoiled playboy in front of her.

"Oh, that's new. A man who had everything handed to him on a silver platter doubting my abilities. Very original. Usually it's my parents, but you'll do as a stand-in."

Raffi balked, as if he hadn't insulted her work, as if he'd expected her to keel over at his criticism. She probably shouldn't have mentioned her parents, but it slipped out.

She wasn't done yet.

Ani took a step toward him, unafraid. "I built my business from the ground up with no help. It's hard to turn nothing into something, much less something big. Especially without any"—she looked around purposefully—"financial assistance." Ani crossed her arms. "Different from your story, I'm guessing?"

"I, I—" Raffi began, flabbergasted. His face steamed pink. Ani was pleased and definitely did not think about how cute his blushing was. It was not the reason she decided to continue her tirade.

"While we're taking shots," she said, shaking her head. "Where in the world are your manners? I've heard about you, you know. Slick, smooth. And I get I'm not the type of girl you'd normally go after, but wow. Didn't realize this was how you treated the rest of us."

Raffi shook himself. "I'm sorry, you *heard* about me?"

"You know exactly what I mean," she said, holding her eye contact strong. Now he knew that she knew precisely who he was.

Just then, a Range Rover drove up, gravel sputtering in its wake breaking Ani and Raffi's locked gazes on each other. Ani stepped back from him, remembering herself. The brides. She took a deep breath.

Raffi didn't matter; it's not like she had to work with him all that much. It was the brides whom she had to impress. They were the ones who would be paying her bills—if she was lucky—not him.

Don't think about Raffi, don't think about Raffi, she thought while thinking about Raffi.

The car's windows were deeply tinted, and almost as soon

as it parked, the driver's door popped open and Grace bounded out. The other bride remained inside, her back turned to them, seemingly on the phone.

Grace trotted over the danger-rocks in her kitten heels without a problem. Raffi gave Ani a "See, they aren't that tough to traverse" kind of look. Ani rolled her eyes in response while Grace couldn't see.

Grace gave her a quick hug, and Ani felt the bad vibes from her Raffi interaction melt away. "Ani, hi. So nice to meet you in person at last."

She was lovely, and true to her name. Taller than Ani would have imagined, willowy. She was, from what Ani had gleaned from her Instagram posts, half Chinese Malaysian and half white, with thick dark hair and striking features. She could see how Grace would star in a movie alongside De Niro.

"And you must be Raffi," she said, shaking his hand with both of hers.

Grace stared all around her. "I'm already in love with this property. I have to see more." Grace turned toward the car because her fiancée had not yet emerged, still chuckling during what must have been an amusing phone call. "Babe," Grace called to her.

Ani heard the fiancée's voice, muffled from inside the car, saying, "Okay, okay, yallah, bye." The voice sounded familiar, but it was hard to tell.

Ani started to relax and feel like she could do this. Wedding planning was her bread and butter, one of her greatest joys in life, and she'd give Grace an absolutely fabulous wedding.

Until.

A car door slammed, and from around the hood appeared the second bride-to-be, all curls and sleepy smiles, a face and a body as familiar as Ani's own.

It was her ex.

It was Kami.

And because Ani could look at nothing but the only person she had ever fallen in love with, she did not notice the shock on Raffi's face, too.

2

Raffi

RAFFI WAS HAVING a difficult morning.

First, that siren striding up toward him, the early stirrings of desire rumbling in Raffi's body, interrupted by her trip, when all he had worried about was preventing her from an awful fall. Then, his brother's shirt had gotten doused in mossy liquid, and in his stupor and fear about ruining an artifact of Sevan's, he had said the most idiotic words possible to her, this lovely girl who didn't deserve it. When she slipped her shoes back on, goddamn, he nearly lost his mind. He didn't think he was a foot person, but watching the way she eased the curve of her arches into leather turned his mind molten. Burgundy nail polish to match her hands. For some reason, he found himself liking that attention to detail.

He imagined that would be the end of the unfortunate events. A stained shirt—albeit, a sentimental one—the only casualty. But he was wrong.

Of course his father had to see the whole mess, comment on it, and not realize the woman he was with was Armenian and could understand.

The double humiliation of his dad's put-down and this woman witnessing it had been too much for him. But Raffi knew himself somewhat, and so he retreated indoors to gather his wits, along with the new shirt.

With Ani, he'd shared some truth about how much the winery meant to him, that he was still new to this world, and what did he get for opening up? A frown. Judgment from Ani for being a beginner. Well, she should know something about that.

What he hadn't expected was for her to fight back so hard. She had claws. She knew about him? Had heard about him? Not good, if they were to work together. Especially because he'd belatedly realized—thanks to her words and defenses—how badly he'd insulted her.

Raffi's brain had been scrambling for how to patch things up, or at least make things cordial again, but instead he'd been bowled over with a brand-new storm.

Raffi didn't like surprises. Not since he'd woken up in his parents' house a decade ago to learn that his older brother had died of an aneurysm at a party the night before. No surprise had been as horrifying since, not even close, but he did still get the full-body terror, his blood frosting over, whenever there was any sort of shock, however small.

Seeing Kami again, here, at his father's winery, engaged, wanting to say her vows on his family's property . . . it was all too much.

She bounded over to him, her jewelry softly jingling. Kami then threw her arms around Raffi, wrapping him in some rich jasmine scent, and planted a quick peck on his cheek.

"Raffi!" She beamed, light and airy and oblivious as always.

It had been ten years since he was with Kami. The two of

them had dated for a year around the end of their senior year of high school and first semester of college, to both of their families' great joy. The Garabedians and the Mardians merging? Two Armenian houses, similar in dignity, becoming more than friends? Their parents' dream. And Raffi, young fool that he was, thought he was in love. He'd only dated casually and not much, considering that he didn't finish growing until his senior year of high school. But then he'd had a bit of a glow-up, and Kami, who had been some version of a goddess all the years he'd known her, was suddenly interested. It was like a dream come true.

They went to different colleges, but he'd drive up to hers on the weekends to see her for a few hours—sweaty-palmed and hopeful, feeling like the luckiest guy alive when she opened her dorm room door wearing one of her lacy dresses and kissed him like he was the only person in the world.

Looking back, he could see it for what it was: high-gloss attraction dressed up as intimacy. Kami had this way about her—charming, magnetic, adding brilliance to every room she entered. It was easy to mistake that glow for closeness.

Kami had dumped him because she said she still had to "find herself." Then, two weeks later, Sev died, and all Kami did was send a text that read, "I'm so sorry about Sev. Sending you strength." After a year of dating! After declaring their love for each other—a first not only for him but supposedly for her, too. After their families kept joking-not-joking with them about when the engagement was going to be. After Raffi seriously considered what type of ring Kami would like. That perfunctory text was all he got. It confirmed to him that everyone had left and no one would be there for him.

He mostly avoided Kami at family-friend functions, and Kami was always traveling anyway, so he'd managed to escape her presence for several years.

And yet. Kami studied him now with a smile so full of kindness, like she was really, actually happy to see him again, that despite himself, he felt a little bit happy to see her, too.

"Bro," she crooned. "I haven't seen you in forever. And now I'm here, like this!" She stuck out her hand for him to inspect the ring. Emerald cut, approximately three carats, he'd estimate, thin band to fit her dainty finger, white gold or platinum. Very tasteful and, for her, modest.

Raffi appraised Grace in a new light, too. Grace, lithe and attractive, seemed slower moving, more thoughtful than the rapid rabbit beating heart of Kami. Probably a good combination, those two. Hopefully Grace knew what she was in for.

Something was happening, though; he felt the energy of it before he had a chance to visually take it in.

Kami's eyes widened as she took in Ani. And Ani? That girl who had held her own with Raffi moments before, fearlessly sparring with him, now shrunk in Kami's presence.

"What're you doing here?" Ani blurted, turning a shade almost as deep as her nail polish.

The statement was almost rude, accusatory, but mostly full of shock.

Kami flicked Grace's arm. "You silly, you didn't tell me you were getting *Ani* to plan the wedding, oh my God!"

Grace's eyebrows shot up. "Oh. This is *Ani* Ani? Oops. I knew it was a popular Armenian name, but I didn't connect the dots—are you okay with—?"

What did "*Ani* Ani" mean? Was this Ani famous? But then why was Grace apologizing? And why were Ani's shoulders hunched like that?

Inexplicably, Kami's eyes lit up in response to her fiancée. "Of course I am! No hard feelings, right? Besides, Ani, you're going to be *perfect*. You totally get me and my style."

Ani did not seem to return the excitement. At all.

Raffi gave a polite chuckle. "Not to be all nosy Armenian auntie, but I feel like I'm the only one out of the loop here. Mind filling me in?"

All three women turned to him.

Kami appeared delighted as she said, "We're exes, duh. Just like us."

What the—? Kami and Ani were exes, and everyone seemed all right with that? Well, he shouldn't say *everyone*. Ani was clearly not okay. Raffi was trying to put together the implications of this when Kami continued.

"Wait, Grace, you knew about me and Raffi, right? Except we barely counted, we were such babies back then. Little eighteen-year-olds."

Bile rose up Raffi's throat, and he had to hold it back. "Barely counted." That's what she called someone she had told she loved? "We barely counted." There. The proof he needed that he'd always been correct in writing off Kami. If only he could throw her off his property right now.

Except.

Kami's family were nearly billionaires. And she, ostensibly, wanted to have her wedding on his property. With her actress fiancée, who could bring publicity to the winery and potentially change everything for Ô.

Grudgingly, he decided to tuck away her comment and hear out her, Grace, and Ani.

Kami turned to Grace. "Seriously, babe, you okay with all this?"

Grace gazed at her adoringly. "Of course. We're adults here. I'm not bothered in the least, as long as everyone else is cool, too."

Raffi shrugged with a side smile—fine with him. Ani, seeming to realize she needed to respond, shook herself and gave two awkward thumbs-up.

The two brides then kissed—rather affectionately for a business meeting, Raffi might add.

The blood had now drained from Ani's face, and she turned pale, with a slightly green pallor to her skin. Raffi felt the need to comfort her somehow, even as the barbs from her earlier words still stung. He wanted to take away her pain—tsavt danem in Armenian.

Raffi coughed, then asked, "Should we get the tour started?"

Ani whirred to life. "Great idea," she said, seemingly relieved, her voice not nearly as bold as it had been when she'd accused Raffi of being an asshole. Which he had been.

Ani walked and began chatting, slowly coming back into herself, growing taller.

He noticed she was still holding the empty matcha latte cup. "I'll take that," he said, and regretted how haughty his voice had come out. He'd meant to sound helpful, but he'd ended up condescending. Still, he ducked into the building, tossed it into a trash can, and rejoined this motley crew.

Ani pulled her phone out of her tote bag, turned her back to Raffi—almost pointedly—and began taking photos of the grounds. In doing so, she had also given Raffi a breathtaking view of her ass, her pencil skirt hugging every last curve. The desire that overcame him when he first saw her announced itself again, loud and clear. God help him, he would not fuck the wedding planner.

Not that she'd ever want to, after the awful way he'd acted.

"Such pretty scenery," Kami cooed.

"I know," Grace said, admiring Kami in her flowy white dress, with a deep V cut showing a lace bralette underneath.

"The wedding would have to be outdoors," Raffi began, realizing this was the first time he was giving an aesthetic tour of the space and he was unprepared. Why hadn't he thought ahead? He had studied the science of winemaking as much as possible last year, and had given tours of the wine cellar and production area to vendors, but now he tried to envision the space as a prospective couple—his ex-girlfriend and her wife-to-be—would view it.

He continued, leading them toward the garden, the most stunning space on the property.

"The guests could walk this way after they park. Ample parking, too, so that's not a problem."

Raffi could feel Ani scrutinizing him, and he could tell that she could tell that this was his first rodeo.

The idea of hosting events at Ô hadn't even occurred to him until Ani inquired about the wedding. That's when he'd checked out her site and started to question whether her aesthetic aligned with his vision for the winery. He did regret his careless words, though. And not just because she had slammed him for it. His entire body had itched after his dad's comment, after Sevan's shirt was ruined, and he just . . . let it out. A dumb move.

Plus, Kami's glee in hiring Ani had to signify her confidence in the wedding planner. She obviously trusted Ani. So if Grace and Kami wanted to hire her, that was fine with him. He didn't want to pick linens. Well, okay, he kind of did; he didn't hate that stuff.

They approached the garden, where the air smelled faintly of rosemary, and someone among the three women gasped, probably Kami. "I knew your dad had bought the winery, Raffi, but this is even prettier than the photos." She sighed.

Raffi was especially lucky with the timing of this tour because the handful of cherry trees were blossoming, their pink flowers blushing on their branches and sprinkling the grass like confetti.

Grace turned to Raffi. "I wanted to get married at an Armenian venue since I know how important Mimi's Armenianness is to her, then your place popped up when I straight up googled 'Armenian wineries' and I had this feeling."

"It's going to be damn nice in the fall. Actual leaves on all the grapevines, turning yellow and red. You said in your email you were thinking of a September wedding?" he asked Ani.

"Yes," Ani and Kami said at the same time. Ani stiffened.

"What about catering?" Ani asked. "Do you have a kitchen that can support catering staff?"

He . . . thought so? He had no idea, honestly.

"Yes, we do."

"And your max capacity?" Ani asked, as if she already knew he had no fucking clue.

He knew the indoor capacity, because that was a fire code thing, posted inside. But outdoors, he'd have to eyeball it.

"Two—" Raffi started, trying to read Kami's and Grace's expressions to ensure "two hundred" fell within their range. He could probably fit two hundred here. Right? Neither of them seemed fazed, so he continued.

"About two fifty."

Ani glanced around skeptically. "About two fifty. I see."

He suddenly felt that the number was rather high. A breeze blew past, making him wish he'd worn his sports coat, and a shiver rattled down his spine as Ani studied him.

"That's fine," Kami said. "We want it more intimate. One hundred or so people."

"Tiny for an Armenian wedding," Raffi said, surprised, but also pleased because now that he thought about it, two hundred fifty people could definitely not fit comfortably seated in the garden.

"We want to do some traditional rituals, and some modern." Kami giggled, holding Grace's arm. "Obviously."

It did occur to Raffi then that the first wedding to be held at Ô would be a queer one. His father would absolutely hate that. But too fucking bad, Dad.

And with that thought, Raffi felt his father's gaze on him. He glanced up to see his dad on the balcony, presiding over the grounds like a malevolent landlord. Which, technically, he was.

Kami seemed to catch his eye, too. "Oh my God, parev, Moushig! Long time no see! This place is stunning, like actually magic."

His father nodded in her direction. He might disapprove of

Kami's choices, but her parents had still been important business allies to whom he was metaphorically indebted, and he wouldn't want to upset them.

Ani continued to grill Raffi with questions he had never considered before. What was the electricity situation like out there? Could they have hard liquor on the premises as well as wine and beer? Was there a noise curfew? Raffi swallowed and squirmed his way around each subsequent query she threw at him.

Ani seemed to have regained her composure after the shock of seeing Kami, although every now and then, when Kami nuzzled into Grace's hair or kissed her hand, Raffi would witness that green shade return to Ani's cheeks. It baffled him that she would choose to accept this job, grinning and bearing her way through it.

Once the tour was over, Kami and Grace said they needed a minute to chat. They walked into the villa, which left Raffi and Ani alone.

She stood there, and he could see her chest rise and fall as she breathed, while a gale of pink petals showered around this beautiful woman.

Then she spoke. "You've never held a wedding here before, have you?"

Raffi felt like he'd been slapped in the face. Had it been so obvious?

"Well," he countered, "maybe a wedding like this will be a first for both of us."

She straightened, turned her chin up slightly. "My portfolio is not up to date."

"Uh-huh," he said disbelievingly, and then once again he

instantly regretted letting his inner voice out. He was being a jerk, and her knitted brows were driving still more guilt into him. He had to turn this around.

"Listen," he began. "I feel like we started off all wrong. Let's try again. Lunch? My treat. No lawsuit rocks involved. There's a place nearby with these life-changing truffle fries."

Ani turned cold suddenly. Her eyes narrowed, and she folded her arms. "No, thank you. I don't date vendors."

Vendor! He had never been called such a boring, sexless descriptor in his life.

But he wasn't trying to ask her out. He really did want to press reset on their introduction. Still, the rejection was clear.

Raffi of the past would have taken her no as a challenge to amp up the charm and try to convince her, but not anymore.

"My bad," he said. "I didn't mean as a date. Just, you know, peace talks over truffle fries. But I fully respect and fully heard your no."

She didn't seem entirely comforted by his words. The look on her face, the tilt of her eyebrow, suggested she was confused.

Raffi didn't have time to piece together the meaning of her features because Kami and Grace had waltzed back outdoors.

Grace started. "We love the venue, we love that your and Mimi's families go way back, and everything is almost so perfect—"

"But," Kami picked up, "we were wondering if we could ask you for a teensy favor, just a couple additions."

"Uh, sure," Raffi said, knowing Kami had never asked for anything *teensy* in her life.

"I really do want this to be the wedding of my dreams, and I always imagined getting married under one of those, like, neoclassical domes. Brick or stone, big and romantic, lots of vines all over the place. Tons of flowers, too, we need more flowers. And also—"

Raffi was processing what this meant, exactly, when Kami hit him with more. "I've always, always wanted fountains and pools. There has to be water, the vibes are so pure, so immaculate, like holy water anointing the wedding, you know? So if you could build some kind of water feature to match with the dome and with the winery, of course, then we could have our wedding here."

Raffi was calculating the costs of everything, and he was seeing hundreds of thousands of dollars flash before his eyes. His father had money, yes, lots of it, but Moushegh had put Raffi in charge, and if the first thing Raffi did was go beg Daddy for a huge chunk of cash, he wasn't doing himself a favor. Dad hardly believed in him now, Stanford MBA or not. Raffi had strong-armed his way into keeping the winery alive, feeling like a little kid covered in glitter glue begging, "Trust me, Dad. I can do it!"

He chanced a glance at Ani, whose jaw had actually dropped. He caught the moment she realized it was open and shut it. Cute. So he wasn't off base, thinking this was an insane ask.

"The, uh, the cost—" Raffi began, keeping up what he thought was a professional, impartial tone. One of a *vendor*.

"Oh!" Kami said. "We'll cover the cost, obviously."

Raffi couldn't stop his eyes from widening, then he reined them in. He decided to go for smoldering instead, realizing this was the final sell. "Of course, this all sounds very doable," he said, completely clueless as to whether or not any of it was, in fact, doable.

Ani cleared her throat. "Um, we'd want to make sure the design of these landscaping features aligns with your wedding vision."

"For sure," Grace said.

Kami smiled hugely at Ani. "That's why we want you to oversee all the design and management of the project! We totally trust you. You've always had the best taste and sometimes know what I'm thinking before I even know it. And we'd pay you for it on top of the wedding planning. What did we say, Gracey?"

Grace replied, "My parents paid their landscape designer twenty K, so we felt that would be fair."

Kami clasped her hands together. "Please say yes, please say yes."

Raffi noticed that Ani gulped at Kami's comment about reading her mind. He was also processing this new development in the already new plan. Ani seemed to know a lot about the nuts and bolts of wedding planning, but he wasn't so sure about this design sense that Kami seemed to gush over. *Raffi* had good taste; everyone said so. Okay, maybe "everyone" was his mom and grandma, but they were women of discernment (with an alarming number of opinions about throw pillows). Besides, it was his winery—well, he was the steward of the winery, anyway. He couldn't have someone telling him what to do with it.

"Yes," Ani said, seemingly strained. "Of course."

3

Ani

WHEN KAMI AND Grace said their goodbyes, and Kami hugged her again, Ani barely felt it. Her body was stuck in some type of survival lockdown mode. Petals dotted the landscape, but she could hardly enjoy them. There was a *lot* to process.

- Kami was Mimi, the other bride for her new wedding.
- Grace called her Mimi? She wasn't sure how to feel about that.
- Grace was so statuesque and svelte and tall and calm and perfect—all the things Ani was not.
- Kami kept referring to how well Ani knew her. *Well then, why did you dump me, Kami?*
- Kami seemed barely fazed by Ani's presence, or rather, pleased by it. What did that mean?

- With all the PDA between Kami and Grace, Ani had fuel for nightmares for months.

- They wanted to create an entire fountain from scratch, plus a dome, which would require new flooring and altering the land—and they wanted this done in seven and a half months? And Raffi had said yes to it like it was no big deal? Boy was clueless.

- Speaking of him, what an absolute jerk and a half.

- He was also Kami's ex?! What? She didn't remember Kami mentioning him. Although . . . there had been that family friend she mentioned who she dated toward the end of high school. Kami hadn't said much about him. Still, this thing was getting far too incestuous.

- Did Raffi actually ask her out, or did she misinterpret it?

- And he backed right off, just like that? No fight?

- And finally . . . did she really need to take this wedding?

Ani could, after all, say no and walk away from it all. From Kami, from her expressions of love all over Grace, from this insane construction project, and from Raffi, who irritated her and confused her in equal measure.

She could decline, continue with her roster of weddings for the year, and slowly dig her way out of her money hole without Kami's help.

She'd prefer that. She'd like it, even, saying no to Kami for the first time in her life.

Raffi took a step closer to her, breaking Ani's doom cycle. "You look like you're about to either solve world hunger or pass out. Care to share which?" he asked.

Ani put her hands on her hips. She was not about to confide in him about her innermost thoughts, despite the cuteness of his joke. But she did have quite a few things to say to him. "Did you really say yes to the landscaping thing?"

Raffi shrugged. "Why not? They're paying for it. Would probably improve the place, make it more attractive for future weddings."

"Of course it will, but that timeline? I know Kami's taste. She's not going to want an out-of-the-box fountain from Wayfair; she's going to want a custom design, something grand and eye-catching and, most importantly, extremely time-consuming."

"Grand and eye-catching is my style," he said. She took in his expression of pride as he gestured around the winery and then himself. "Can't believe I changed out of that wet shirt. Nothing more eye-catching than a massive matcha stain."

Despite herself, Ani smiled. His tone didn't seem antagonistic; he was making a joke about what he'd previously been snippy about. Still, part of her wondered if he was making a reference to his hotness. Those high cheekbones were really something. She said, "Leave the designs to me."

Ani began to walk away, toward her car. The day was more than wearing on her. She needed silence to process everything. She didn't want to have to continue proving herself in front of this spoiled man.

"About that," he called, and she could hear him stepping quickly behind her.

"Ani," he said when she didn't turn around. She sighed. He sounded pleading and earnest, not demanding. And she really, really didn't want to admit that a tiny part of her liked the way he pronounced her name perfectly. Ani faced him.

"What about that?" she asked.

"This winery, you know, I told you, it's very important to me."

Her eyebrow began its ascent. "And?"

He shifted his weight from one foot to the other. He was actually nervous. "Do you, I mean—do you have the experience to take on a project like this?" he asked, finally. He had the good grace to look a bit embarrassed by his question.

"Do *you*?" she shot back.

He glanced away, a cheeky expression on his face, giving her a view of his jawline. So fucking sharp.

"I asked first," he said.

She didn't say a word, and there they remained in deadlock while the wind showered them in cherry blossom glitter.

"Aren't you a doctor?" she said at last, remembering this point. "Pretty sure I am more qualified than an MD for this particular job."

Now Raffi sighed. "I was a doctor. Almost. I was in my residency when I quit."

Ani was taken aback. She was not expecting this answer or the sad expression that briefly crossed his face.

"Another story for another day," Raffi said in a way that intimated he was not interested in sharing it another day, either.

"Sure, sure," Ani replied.

"I am one of those rare combinations of MD and MBA, though."

Ani couldn't stop her eyes from widening. "You have an MBA, too?"

"From Stanford." He smiled, as if knowing she wanted to ask. His teeth glimmered, a wolfish smile that made her breath catch. Just for a moment.

"You've been busy this past decade," Ani gibed.

"You could say that," he said, his eyes darkening, and Ani couldn't help but wonder what was behind them.

She decided to steer them back to the issue at hand. "So, what, you're going to fire me from the job Kami hired me to do? You think you, Mr. MD and MBA, know better than the Bay Area's most 'quaint' wedding planner?"

He groaned. "You ever considered getting into cooking? Your roasting skills are on point."

Ani put her hands on her hips again, trying to fight her smile. "Takes one to know one."

Raffi raked a hand through his thick hair. "All right, all right. Truce. I'm not trying to fire you. You can do the job. I'm just saying, I'm going to be around, is all." He stepped an inch closer to her. "When it comes to Ô, I want to have a hand in every brick that gets laid."

Ani breathed in sharply at his words. A man this stunning saying "gets laid." Unfair. It sent a hot zing through her body, she couldn't deny it.

"Sticking your fingers where they don't belong?" she chanced, and almost regretted it, until Raffi showed his wolf smile again.

"My favorite pastime. As you apparently know."

Ani gulped and had to turn away from him to stop the blush that she felt forming.

"I have to go. Another site visit," she lied. She gripped her tote bag and rushed off, hearing his "See you soon, Ani" in her wake, so slick the words penetrated her skin, try as she might to brush them away.

ANI MENTALLY BLACKED out the entire drive back to her apartment in Russian Hill, San Francisco. If she had thoughts, they were not deposited into her memory bank.

It wasn't until she saw the winter camellias blooming in her building's courtyard that she came back to herself. She needed to decide what the hell she was doing: take this wedding or not. And if she was, she had to debrief with Sanan. And potentially her sister and all of her friends.

Ani took the steps two at a time, and once she got inside her unit, she made a beeline for her room and flopped on her bed. Her roommate was a travel nurse with night shifts, so Ani often had the place to herself. Her sister, Talar, used to be her roommate until she got married and moved out. Since then, Ani had found roommates who were only temporary, because it hurt too much to replace Talar with anyone she could form a real connection with. The apartment, built in 1910, with creaky original hardwood floors and ornate but drafty windows, was hers and Talar's, since they first moved in together several years ago.

Ani pushed herself back, laid her head on the pillows, and stared at the small antique chandelier she and Talar had installed shortly after they moved in.

It was time to get serious. Would she take this job or not?

She knew she didn't want to, that merely seeing Kami on the regular would be painful. But to then have to plan Kami's wedding? The wedding she had envisioned for herself and Kami, the one they had even talked about during their year plus together? That would be torture. She wasn't a masochist, and she had no desire to put herself through that.

However.

They were going to pay her twenty grand for the landscape project and another ten grand for her wedding planning fees. That would cut her debt by more than half. She only wished she had quoted higher for her wedding planning fees, because she knew Kami and Grace could pay.

If she didn't take the job, she would likely have to lay off Sanan. The predatory interest rates with the credit card company and on the bank loan were simply too high to sustain. Even without paying Sanan, she would really have to hustle to get new clients. She only had three weddings booked this summer, and they were all smaller-scale affairs. Quaint.

She shook away Raffi's haughty voice and directed her anger elsewhere for the moment.

The Avedissians. Those fuckers. Leaving her in this position.

She'd tried every method of getting in touch with them, to no avail. Ani's only hope was that the bride, Knar, had an Instagram profile. She thought she had found her profile, undeniably Knar, with that severe brunette bob and curtain bangs. It was a private account, but the number of posts kept going up, so Knar was active. Last week, Ani had made a fake profile and requested to follow Knar. Now, Ani sat up and logged into her fake account again, but Knar hadn't accepted her request.

Maybe it was too obviously fake and Knar did not fool that easily. She'd need to find another way.

If Ani was able to get access to Knar's Instagram, she could maybe discover her whereabouts and show up and confront her. Or serve her with a lawsuit, if she had the guts for it.

But all that was hypothetical. What was real was an overdrawn checking account, two voicemails from debt collectors, and the one wedding she couldn't stand to plan that would, regrettably, pull her out of her miserable financial situation.

She couldn't afford to have pride.

It was depressing, but there was a part of her that felt invigorated by this opportunity. It wasn't just wedding planning. She was also tasked with turning Raffi's already lovely garden into a wedding paradise.

She would love to add landscape design experience to her roster. A really legit piece of experience. She had previously helped her parents redo their backyard, so she wasn't entirely clueless. Granted, it was a forty-by-twenty-foot space behind a humble home on a still humbler budget, but she'd created beauty, no doubt about it. She could do that in quadruple the size and with fifty times the funding. Right?

She'd simply harden her heart to Kami to make it work. And figure out a way to work with that pretentious ass who owned the place. It would be a challenge like no other, but Ani didn't shy from difficulty.

That's it. She'd take it.

Ani texted Sanan. Landed that new gig. Call me when you have a chance?

Then she sank a little deeper into her bed and called her sister because she was dying to spill about this insane venture.

Ani found an errant thread in her fluffy duvet cover that she wanted to tug when Talar picked up. "Ani jan, what's up? You okay?"

Talar was the younger sister, but there she was, acting like the older one. "Yes, Talar, I'm fine."

Then Ani assessed herself. Was she? No, she was not. "Health-wise, anyway."

"I had a feeling. You never call in the middle of the day. What's up?"

Her sister was a successful corporate lawyer overseeing mergers and acquisitions of tech companies and was always, always working. Ani thanked her lucky stars she had gotten out of the legal world. It crushed her soul, but it seemed to feed her sister's.

"You sure you have a second?" Ani asked, knowing that her sister was in the middle of her brutal workday.

"For you, of course."

Ani took a deep breath. "I got this new gig today. Kind of a big one, in Napa. And the bride, um—"

"Wow, good for you," said her sister with sincere pride in her voice.

But when Ani was on the precipice of spilling about the bride's identity, she could not bring herself to utter Kami's name. It was too embarrassing. She realized that if she told Talar that she had accepted the job of planning Kami's wedding, she would have to mention the debt, too. And that? That was a hard no.

Ani loved her sister, but Talar did everything better than Ani. Talar was prettier and taller, had gone to better schools, was more popular, and was more ruthless. While Ani had been a mere paralegal who sucked at her job, Talar was a lawyer at the most respected firm in the valley. And most crushingly, Talar got married first.

She could see the pity in the aunties' eyes when they said, at Talar's wedding, "Darosuh kezee." It was a well-wish that Ani would be blessed with the same luck as Talar. But she felt the whispers all around her, when she walked down the aisle, when she held Talar's bouquet, and when she gave her speech. "Such a shame she has no one." "Younger sister married first—that must be difficult for Ani." "I hear she is gay, that is why she is not married." "She seems sad, does she not? I can see the sadness in her eyes." It was all true except that she was bi, not gay, and that had nothing to do with her marital status. But the rest, she knew what they were saying, and it stung for months and months afterward.

Ani simply wanted to be the one not left in the dust for once. If she pulled off Kami's wedding, it could mean great things for her.

"The bride is kind of a diva. She wants us to build this whole water feature and a dome in the backyard of the winery."

Talar sounded incredulous. "And the winery is okay with that? That seems weird."

"They're a new place. I think they're trying to attract more weddings, so they're okay with it."

Every time Ani said "they," she thought of Raffi and felt a strange pull in her stomach. *Peace talks over truffle fries.* That was cuter than it should have been. She wanted to remember what her sister had said about Raffi. Maybe Ani's memory had overblown it.

"It's actually an Armenian winery," she added. "And the new owner is Raffi Garabedian. You know, the doctor—well, he's a former doctor. He told me today he dropped out and got his MBA instead."

"The mafia guy's son?" Talar asked.

"I don't think he's really in the mafia. I think. I hope. But yes, that's the one."

"Ani . . ." Her sister had caution in her voice.

"What?"

"Be careful, okay?" Talar said.

Ani turned indignant. Yes, she wanted to hear Talar's opinion on Raffi, but she did not like to be scolded, especially by her younger sister. "Can you not?"

Talar went into lawyer mode, her tone factual and confident. "I thought I told you. Total charmer, but he does not date. One and done. A few years back, he slept with my friend Lala—you know, the orthodontist?"

"Oh yeah." Somehow, although Ani knew in theory that Raffi had played the field with many women, hearing that sweet orthodontist Lala slept with him was like ice water being splashed in her face. She wasn't into Raffi anyway, but the whole "playboy" thing had felt more hypothetical until now. Lala was very pretty but a dainty-flower type, breakable, a total romantic. That last part was like Ani herself. She wasn't dainty, but she did, at her core, believe in true love and soulmates.

Because she thought Kami had been hers.

Talar charged on. "Lala was reluctant at first, having heard about his reputation. But he told her all sorts of lies about how she was special, asked her to let him take her to just one dinner. She eventually gave in, believing him. He was a perfect gentleman. Opened doors for her. Wined and dined her. Then as soon as they slept together, he never called her again."

Ani's face flared with anger. "That's so messed up."

"I know," Talar said. "So unless you're in it for a quick shag—"

"Ew, don't say 'shag.'"

"—you might want to stay away."

"Got it, got it. I'm not interested anyway."

Which was true. Especially now. The man had a smile that could swallow you whole, but Ani would not be swept up in it.

The only thing—the one little thing—that didn't compute was when she said she didn't date vendors and he didn't scoff or scorn her. He also didn't push or try to persuade her, like he apparently did with Lala. In fact, his response was incredibly mature. "I fully respect and fully heard your no." She had believed him. Still, it didn't matter. She'd work with him, only talk about the job when they were together, and keep him at arm's length otherwise. Seemed like the safe course of action.

After they finished the call, Ani trundled into the kitchen, looking for anything remotely filling and healthy to eat. She had settled on a cheese stick to tide her over until she could make some real food when a text came in from an unknown number.

It was a 415 area code, from San Francisco. And it was a link to . . . a Pinterest board?

Ani almost dismissed it as spam until she saw the preview. Fountains. Domes.

And then another text came in.

> Hey, it's Raffi. Hope you don't mind. Kami gave me your number.

Then another. Thought I'd get a head start. What do you think?

Raffi uses Pinterest?

When Ani tapped through to the board and saw how much thought had been put into the various pins, how they were pretty great comps to what she had in mind, and when she thought about him scouring the internet to work on this project and then taking the time to show his efforts to Ani, to ask her opinion . . . her icy feelings toward him melted just the slightest. Just a drop.

4

Raffi

RAFFI LOVED PINTEREST. He got a lot of his style ideas from the site, in fact. Luckily, his dad had never heard of it, so no chance of giving his dad more ammo for calling out Raffi on his lack of manliness.

Raffi sat at the laptop in the winery's office, feeling proud of his text to Ani, that he had shown initiative—and very good taste, he might add—and decided to text his book club group chat, MBD.

> You'll never guess, but Ô is hosting its inaugural wedding, which will be none other than . . . wait for it . . . the queer wedding of an indie movie star and my billionaire ex-girlfriend.

The dots began dancing almost immediately.

His friend Kennedy texted back. That sounds like some Hallmark Channel SEO wish list, not real life.

Riley jumped in. WHAT IN THE HOLY VELVET-SUITED HELL.

Is there a vibe board? Will tarot cards be involved? I NEED A GUEST LIST AND YES I WILL SIGN AN NDA.

Raffi chuckled to himself. Riley had more energy than the rest of the book club members combined.

Then Lana, in her signature quiet-snipe style, chimed in. I assume you're emotionally spiraling. Please let us know if you're okay.

Raffi: I'm fine. The relationship is ancient history. No spiral. Not even a corkscrew.

Kennedy: We're flattered you chose us as your emotional support coven.

Lana: Okay, reassured. Permission to roast?

Raffi: Wow, thank you all for these calm and reasoned responses. And Lana you know you have standing permission.

Kennedy: You're welcome. We contain multitudes. Mostly snark.

Raffi smiled down at the screen. God, he loved this group.

During his MBA program, he joined the club on a total whim. He'd always liked books when he was younger, fiction books, and then simply stopped reading at a certain point. None of his friends did, so he didn't either. Dad had actively discouraged it, on top of that. *You read business books, money books, not this garbage.* But when Raffi saw their club, titled enticingly Mad, Bad, and Dangerous Book Club, he figured he'd join. He hadn't realized it was a feminist book club, even though all the other members were women—he just figured, *chicks be reading*—and to be honest the nature of the club didn't dawn on him until the third text that was selected, another literary work dissecting the meaning of female identity. He didn't quit, though. He liked what was happening to his brain, being challenged into expansion. Slowly, over the next six months, he came to meeting after meeting full of questions after having read the work, feeling his entire worldview shift. Realizing . . . he'd been kind of an asshole to women for too long.

He'd watched a great deal of romance movies with Sevan, and there was often this notion of "fixing" a man. In his reality, it had been a whole group of women. His book club had an AA–like meeting where Raffi confessed, expressed a desire to do better, and his new friends all acknowledged his hopes and told them they'd be there for him. And they were. And he did do better. Not perfect, but better.

The final member of MBD, Maya, joined the group chat then. Sorry I'm late, a six-year-old tried to unionize the snack schedule. Did I miss anything? 😎

Raffi barked a laugh, the sound echoing through the quiet office—right as heavy footsteps approached from the hallway. His father lumbered in.

Raffi straightened, phone still in hand, thumb hovering over a half reply. But he set it down instead.

Dad's deep voice betrayed immediate disappointment. "What was all that about? You didn't tell me Kami was coming."

"I didn't know."

Moushegh clucked his tongue.

Raffi watched as his father gripped the wall and made his way closer to Raffi, one hunkering, uncomfortable step at a time. He could see the pain on his father's face.

Moushegh had always been an imposing man. Six foot four to Raffi's six foot two, broad-shouldered, and muscular, with eyebrows so thick they made jaws drop—he truly had the look of a mafioso, which didn't help the ridiculous rumors that had been spreading for years. But lately? His father had shrunk at least an inch, and his muscles had atrophied as his peripheral neuropathy attacked his body, particularly his legs and feet.

"So? Why was she here? I thought you were having a meeting about a wedding," his father demanded. Raffi could tell that his father was trying to hide how hard he was breathing. The walk over here must have been difficult.

"Kami was the wedding client. She's getting married, wants to have the ceremony and reception here, at Ô."

He could see his father doing mental calculations of who Kami was with, how the two women were arm in arm and canoodling like lovers do, because they were, in fact, lovers. Raffi braced himself for the bigotry tidal wave about to crash.

"To that woman?"

Lord, let him be patient.

"Yes," Raffi replied. "And I think it could be a great thing. They want to throw a lavish reception. Ô could be in magazines and get good press as Napa's hottest wedding destination."

"With . . ." His father's voice was low and dangerous. "A *gay* wedding?"

"Yes, Dad," Raffi kept his voice firm. "With a gay wedding.

Believe it or not, you can make it into *Vogue* as a same-sex couple these days."

"Leave it to you to reference a women's magazine."

Raffi scoffed. "That's because everyone knows *Vogue*. A shepherd in Anjar thirty years ago knows *Vogue*."

As grating as it would be to work with Kami, Raffi recognized this wedding needed to happen, badly. Not only, as he told his dad, would it get their winery on the map, but he also was honored to host a queer wedding, maybe do something good for a change. The general Armenian population's attitude toward queerness was so backward it angered him. Now he had a chance to showcase the wedding of the year. If they could celebrate Kami and Grace so openly and so luxuriously, it could be a major turning point for the Californian diaspora community. Five years ago, he wouldn't have fought his dad so hard for this, but now he knew better. Once again, thanks, book club.

"Why can't she marry a man instead? She should be marrying *you*, you know."

Raffi stopped short of rolling his eyes, which he knew would cause an outburst from his father about "treating him with respect." And he shoved away that brief feeling of deep hurt that pulled in his stomach, remembering his and Kami's talks about their future so long ago.

"Dad," Raffi said. "That's over. It's been more than a decade, and besides, she was the one who dumped me. I don't think she's interested."

"This is despicable, just despicable. We'll be the laughingstock of the entire community."

Raffi regretted his seated position; he wanted to be standing eye to eye with his father, to take a step closer to him. His heart was hammering as he prepared himself to fight this fight.

Instead, he leaned back in his chair, imitating nonchalance. "Dad," he said, "trust me on this. *We* say who's a laughingstock and who's not. If we're hosting this wedding, no one's going to point fingers. And—" He raised his voice somewhat as he saw his father open his mouth to retort. "I want to do this. It is a good thing to do, and it's going to be good for business. I'll say it again: Trust me."

Owning a winery had been his father's lifelong dream after decades of working nonstop running a wealth management firm. A winery, his dad thought, was the pinnacle of class. As kids, Raffi and his brother had been dragged to Napa constantly, although Sevan always found ways to make the trips fun, especially as teens when he would sneak Raffi glasses of the good stuff. Around that time, Moushegh built a massive wine cellar in his house. When guests came over, they received lengthy explanations about the various vintages that were to be paired with dinner. He was known as the wine and cigars guy, but mostly the wine guy. When the moment had come, Moushegh had big plans to make Ô thrive.

Unfortunately, it was also the year his dad's peripheral neuropathy ramped up and stole his mobility. His body couldn't keep up with the demands of the huge winery grounds, and he was too stubborn to accept any type of mobility device. Moushegh had been on the verge of selling the property after just a year of owning it, when Raffi stepped in and offered to run the day-to-day. His father would still be the owner, but Raffi would manage it.

And Raffi, right now, knew that he was not going to bend to his father's backward way of thinking.

Moushegh shook his head, disgusted, and turned away.

"I am too tired to argue. You want to run this place into the ground, make us the ridicule of the community, do it. See what happens."

Raffi crossed his arms. "Oh, I will."

THE TEXT FROM Ani was like a balm after the conversation with his father. Instead of fighting with him, she agreed with him. Raffi stayed in the cool, airy office, which carried the faint scent of oak barrels, overlooking part of the vineyards. In the distance, beyond the precise rows of dormant vines, low mist clung to the earth, curling over the land like a quiet whisper, making the whole valley look untouched, almost otherworldly.

She had said: Good start. I like this one.

Then she sent a screenshot of the dome that he also liked best.

That's my favorite one, too. Eye to eye, he texted back.

Ani replied: We should get started as soon as possible. Do you have time for a call?

He did. He couldn't lie that it sent a bit of excitement through his body when Ani asked him to chat. For fuck's sake, one of the last things she'd said to him in person had involved sticking fingers in places they didn't belong. She took her job seriously, and she also was feisty as hell. And she'd dressed him down multiple times. Color him intrigued.

"Parev, Ani."

There was the tiniest pause before she replied. "Parev, Raffi."

Speaking in Armenian didn't count as flirting, right? Maybe it did. Time to course correct.

"You wanted to chat? What's up?"

"Yes," she said, without skipping a beat this time. "If we're going to finish the brides' wish list in time, we have to get started ASAP. I'm working on designs right now, but I have to be honest that I don't know any contractors, so I'd just be searching around the internet and getting bids. I wanted to see if you had any contacts."

He sure did. "Oh yeah, I have a guy."

Ani responded quickly. "This is not the type of job where you can just 'have a guy' and it's some unlicensed family friend who can't even caulk a shower properly."

He tried to not think about her saying the work *caulk*.

"You seem to be speaking from experience."

"I might be. So? Is he legit?"

Raffi smirked. "You mean did he just build Thomas Keller's new personal residence by hand? Yes. He's legit."

He heard her intake of breath on the other end of the line, and it sent a small wave of pleasure through him.

"You're not kidding, right?"

"I would never joke about caulk work."

A frustrated sigh now. God, why had he said that? Then she replied, "And he'd be available?"

Raffi stretched out in his chair luxuriously, knowing he'd done well despite his stupid comment. "He'd better be; he's one of my best buds. Plus, he owes me a favor. And this would be a nice payday for him, too, so I'm betting he's in."

"Fine," she said, sounding slightly irritated. "Can we start on Monday? I'll come up to the site. Say nine a.m.?"

Raffi stopped himself from saying "It's a date" and instead went with "See you then. Have a great weekend, Ani."

Another quiet pause. "You too, Raffi."

5

Ani

ANI WALKED UP to the winery at nine that morning with Sanan at her side. As they approached the villa, Ani noticed a thin piece of plywood, painted gray with red outlines, sitting atop the death-trap rocks. And as they drew nearer, she read words that warned "Caution: Watch your step" printed in neat handwriting. *Raffi's?* she wondered.

"That's an odd choice for the winery," Sanan commented, not knowing the particulars. "Doesn't match the beauty of the rest of the place. I wonder if they already started construction."

"Oh, uh, that might have been my doing," Ani said as she stepped across it. The plywood held well and she did not go flying to the ground this time. "Long story."

"You got it, boss."

"Sanan . . ."

Her assistant was all about rules and hierarchy and doing things the right and proper way. Sanan had said her father was in the military and ran his household like an army unit. Ani had to continually remind Sanan that she had a more relaxed view of things. Part of her wished she had let Sanan in on the

Avedissians' actions before the wedding; she bet Sanan could have death-stared them into handing over the money. Too late now.

"Sorry, sorry, not boss."

The day was cold and Ani had worn her best wool coat for the occasion, figuring she wasn't going to get down and dirty today. They were just planning and measuring. It was long, loose-fitting, and plum-colored, and it made her feel like a million bucks. Just the right type of thing to wear around Raffi, to show him she wasn't impressed by all his YSL shirts, Gucci shoes, and seventy acres in Napa. She could hold her own.

Ani steered them to the side of the winery, toward the garden. There stood Raffi and his contractor friend, bro-ing it up among the cherry trees. Raffi slapped his friend on the arm and threw his head back in a laugh. No doubt talking about some weekend conquest, Ani thought. Well, she was just glad she wasn't one of them. And she would hold her ground, no matter how chiseled his jawline was.

Raffi's demeanor changed when he noticed Ani and Sanan. His smile softened and he stood more upright. Raffi was wearing a sports coat and button-down shirt at nine in the morning. His shoes were black and pointy. This guy had no chill.

"Ladies," he said, and Ani scowled at him.

"Raffi, this is Sanan, my amazing assistant," Ani said.

"Nice to meet you. Raffi," he said, extending his hand.

Raffi nodded to the man next to him. "And this is Chris, the lead contractor I told you about."

Chris shook Ani's hand, then reached for Sanan's, who seemed to freeze up a moment before remembering herself and quickly taking his hand. "Sanan," she said in a voice Ani had never heard before. Shy? Sanan was never shy. This Chris guy was pretty cute. About the same height as Raffi, beefier, most likely Armenian by the shape of his eyes and dark brows. Ani and Sanan were almost always all business and didn't discuss personal matters—not that Ani had any personal matters to disclose besides, you know, the debt—so Ani didn't know if Sanan was seeing anyone or if she was even into men. Guess this Chris guy was Sanan's type, though.

"I see you have a temporary fix over the lawsuit rocks," Ani said to Raffi.

"Careful, you're hurting the plywood's feelings," Raffi said, smiling. *Damn it, that was kind of funny,* she thought, while also thinking, *My god those teeth are sexy.* She didn't know she had a thing for sharp incisors.

"So you're telling me it *is* still going to be around for the wedding day."

"I figured it added a nice touch of 'abandoned warehouse' to the place. Too pretentious otherwise."

Chris chuckled. "C'mon, man. We were just talking about filling that space in."

Ani tried not to feel impressed by this. Raffi was just taking sensible advice.

"Well, that's good. Should we get started on the plans?"

"Definitely," Raffi said. He walked over to the part of the garden by the cherry tree grove.

"This would be the perfect spot for the Pinterest dream wedding dome. We've got the cherry trees, some vineyards, you've even got the villa in your view if you're sitting here as a guest. I know I'd be happy to watch a wedding from these seats."

Chris nodded with approval.

Ani took in his suggestions. She'd come prepared but wanted to consider all angles. "That is a pretty spot for sure, very lush, but I was also thinking . . ."

From her tote bag, Ani whipped out her iPad to share the digital renderings she'd created. She had spent some time playing with different design options, finding the best spots for the dome and fountain.

"Over here," she paced to the back side of the garden, "would give you the most symmetry. It has the best view of the hills and distant vineyards, and if you're thinking about the time of day when most ceremonies and receptions take place, the sun won't be in your eyes."

She walked back to where Raffi and Chris were standing and gestured around them. "Right now this seems great, but come four or five o'clock, in the late summer and early autumn when a lot of weddings take place, the sun is going to be blazing in your guests' eyes. And on top of that, photos will be ruined. In that spot there," she indicated back to the place she'd chosen, "you're going to get that perfect golden-hour glow brides dream of for their outdoor weddings."

On cue, Sanan flipped her phone screen to the mock-up she had made of the golden-hour light at a September wedding here on the property.

Raffi seemed irritated.

Then he took several steps toward Ani.

He was close enough that she could see the faint stubble

along his jaw and stripes of dark gold in his umber eyes. He looked at her intensely.

"Show me. Set me right on the spot where the dome is going to be."

Ani swallowed despite herself. God, his eyes, so smoky and dark. It was deeply unfair they'd been gifted to a guy like Raffi.

She caught a look on Sanan's face, one of confusion, as she headed toward the spot and Raffi followed like her shadow.

"We could build a platform right here," Ani said, drawing a half circle around them with her finger.

"That's doable," Chris said.

Then Sanan perked up and held out her hand. "Don't move, guys. Let me get this shot so you can see. You're standing right in the perfect position."

It was while Sanan was framing the picture with her phone that Ani realized she and Raffi were facing each other, like a married couple at the altar. They were just missing some vows and rings, and they'd be set.

"Should we hold hands?" Raffi whispered.

"Absolutely not," Ani hissed back, which only made Raffi chuckle.

The thought of holding hands with him made the back of Ani's neck sweat, even on this cold day. So she would not, she would absolutely *not*, do such an unprofessional, misguided thing.

"Got it!" Sanan cried. "Come see."

Raffi stepped away, leaving Ani behind in her cold sweat. She quickly followed and joined the huddle. She could smell

Raffi's cologne from here. Green and fresh, so clean and sharp. He didn't douse himself in it, either, as many Armenian men were wont to do. Just a touch, enough to be smelled up close.

Then she saw the photo. The way Raffi was looking at her made her pulse quicken. His eyes were . . . admiring, almost tender, and it threw her off-balance. After their clashes during their first meeting and the way she'd called him out so blatantly, multiple times, his look was . . . unexpected. That was strange. Maybe it was a trick of the light.

Ani dared a glance at Raffi to gauge his reaction. He was staring at the photo. His expression was soft, almost vulnerable, as if the photo of them together had stripped away his usual bravado.

Then he blinked and looked away and said, "I see your vision now, Madame Wedding Planner."

She straightened, crossing her arms as if to shield herself from the warmth that had briefly bloomed in her chest. Of course he'd deflect with a joke—this was Raffi, after all. The man who supposedly could make anyone feel momentarily special, only to leave them wondering if it had all been an act. She wondered if that was the charm she'd been warned about.

She let out a small, humorless laugh, more to herself than to him. "Please don't call me Madame."

"She doesn't like nicknames like that," Sanan added helpfully. "I try to call her boss all the time, and she always shuts me down."

"That's fair," Raffi said, eyes glowing. "I panic when people call me sir. A doorman called me that last week and I dropped my keys, tried to catch them, and somehow bowed? It was a whole thing."

Ani bit back a smile. The image of Raffi, all suits and smugness, bowing to a doorman like some flustered Regency gentleman, lodged itself stubbornly in her brain.

"Sounds dignified," she said coolly, but her voice came out softer than she intended. Her cheeks felt warm, and she hated that her body seemed determined to betray her good judgment.

Back to business.

Ani glanced around the garden, imagining where the seating would go. "This might be a bit much, but I think we should build flooring here. It can double as a dance floor later on and would look perfect matching the dome and the winery colors."

Raffi knit his eyebrows together. "How big?"

"Can I draw it?" Ani turned to Chris. "Got any chalk in there?" she asked, gesturing to his tool bag.

Chris checked. "Doesn't seem to be."

"We have some in the shed back that way. Used it recently for the, uh, rocks," Raffi said.

"Fine, I'll go grab it."

"I'll come with you," Raffi replied, already starting behind her.

"I don't need you to babysit. I can find some chalk."

"The door can be a little tricky—"

"I can handle a door."

Ani heard Sanan's voice behind her. "Shh, let's let them work it out." She glanced back to see Sanan with a hand on Chris's forearm. Well, not so shy anymore.

As twigs crunched under her boots, she realized it might be grimy in the shed and she would die if she got her coat dirty. So when she approached a bench, she swept off her coat and carefully folded it. Then, not wanting it to touch the bench, either, she set down her tote bag and placed her coat atop it.

"Getting warm?" Raffi asked.

"Don't want your cobwebbed shed to get my coat dirty."

"For your information, it is spick-and-span—it's actually quite new. But don't let me talk you out of it."

They passed by two guys carrying a barrel. Raffi stepped up to them and gave each that arm wrestling slap hug. "Jerry, Mike, my guys," he said, and they gave him friendly smiles.

"Cold one today, chief," the guy named Jerry said.

"But not frosty, so that's good for the grapes, right?"

"You got it."

The men walked on. Ani felt a shiver from the cold Jerry mentioned.

"Didn't you say it was right back here?" she asked.

"Nah, never said that," Raffi said, smiling. "Aren't you glad I came with you, though?"

"You're going to ax-murder me back here, aren't you?"

Raffi laughed loudly, throwing his head back the way he had with Chris. "I wouldn't use an *ax*. Do I look like a brute?"

"I'll have you know," Ani said, letting a smile peek out, "I am very well loved, and people will come to find me and exact their revenge."

She wasn't sure if the latter was true, but she did think, in the moment, of her parents and sister. Often pains in the ass, but always out of love.

"I'm sure you are, I'm sure you are," Raffi said softly.

Okay . . . He sounded sincere. She filed away yet another piece of the Raffi enigma.

Finally, they reached the shed, which was fairly large and,

from the outside at least, looked well maintained. Raffi entered a key code before opening the door and holding it open for her. "Opened doors for her," Ani heard her sister say, remembering the Raffi playbook.

In response to the memory, Ani put her hand on the door and declared, "I got it." Raffi shrugged and walked in first.

As he had promised, the shed was not a cobwebbed mess but meticulously organized and sparkling clean. She wondered if this was Raffi's doing or his staff's.

"Whatever you do, don't let the door shut," he said, right as a mouse darted out from behind a shelf, and Ani, despite her intentions not to be *that girl*, screamed—but then so did Raffi, a smaller, softer shriek. When the mouse ran toward them, Ani fled to Raffi's direction and accidentally rammed into him. Raffi stumbled back and caught her before they both fell. The heavy door slammed shut, and the mouse ran out of sight.

Ani caught her breath, her heart still racing, and she could feel Raffi doing the same against her. For a moment, she was acutely aware of how close they were—close enough that his windswept-desert scent was stronger now, while the solid weight of his arms wrapped around her. Her cheeks burned.

"Um, sorry about that," Raffi said, stepping back quickly, releasing his hold. "That was—" But he seemed to have lost his words, and he was turning red, which was almost endearing, if she didn't know better.

Ani gathered as much composure as she could scrounge, then asked, "So, what happens when the door shuts?"

He hesitated, meeting her eyes. Then he finally spoke. "It locks us in," he said quietly.

"You're kidding, right?"

Raffi shrugged. "Sadly not. It's a new shed, and it came with this dumb locking mechanism that we haven't had time to change yet. It's fine. We can just call someone to get us."

Then, for some reason, he looked toward Ani expectantly.

"So go ahead," Ani said.

"I left my phone in the office."

Ani's heart began to race. "Do you operate like it's 1980? A normal person always has their phone with them. It's called a mobile!"

He crossed his arms. "Well, where's yours then?"

"In my bag, on that bench, remember?" She began to pace. "Along with my water and snacks and all the emergency supplies a person could need. Oh shit, oh shit."

"Don't panic," Raffi said slowly, although his voice had lost some of its ease. "Sanan and Chris know we're here. They'll come soon enough."

Ani wasn't convinced. She strode to the door and pounded on it with her fist, the sound echoing loudly in the confined space. "Hello? Is anyone out there? Help!" She pressed her ear to the door, listening for footsteps or voices, but there was only silence.

"We're near the edge of the property—"

"I know, I walked over with you," Ani cut in.

Then she pulled at the door handle, confirmed that it was indeed locked, and let out a huge sigh.

"Can't believe I took off my damn coat," she muttered.

"Can't believe I screamed at the sight of a mouse," he mumbled, and she felt herself smiling despite her anxieties. "Don't tell anyone, okay?" he said with levity. "I have a reputation to maintain."

Right. His reputation. Well, she didn't have to talk to him. She'd act like he was part of the shelving.

Ani found a low round barrel; sat on it, hugging herself; and turned away from Raffi. She started to feel ice-cold, the type of chill that seeped into her bones and made her achy and sick. It was frigid in here. Technically above freezing, but only just.

Her makeshift chair was icy against her thighs, and an actual shiver released itself along her body. Ani closed her eyes and concentrated on being warm. A sandy beach in the tropics, rays penetrating her skin. Closing all the doors in a hot car.

There was some shuffling of feet and some moving around of objects on the shelves behind her. Raffi was no doubt grabbing the chalk.

Then, suddenly, she felt warmth envelop her shoulders and neck and she jumped the tiniest bit as her eyes flicked open. It was fabric, heavy and comforting. Smelling of verdant, rain-soaked herbs. Raffi had draped his coat over her shoulders.

Ani turned toward him and glanced up, half suspicious, half grateful. The coat was like a heated blanket, thawing her insides.

"Thank you," she whispered.

"Of course," he said.

Then, when she didn't turn away, he added, "Don't want your family to sue us if you drop dead here."

"Uh-huh," she said, and could feel a smile in her voice.

"Seriously, you okay?" he asked.

She nodded. "I'm good now."

She turned back around to face the door, thinking that the coat smelled way too decadent. She closed her eyes and took a deep inhale. Spiced air. Rich blue, green, browns. It didn't mean anything that this was possibly the best scent she'd ever encountered in her life. She was just a perfume aficionado.

"So. What do you like to do for fun?" Raffi asked, out of the blue.

Ani turned to face him and wanted to respond, "Wouldn't you like to know," but his expression seemed earnest. He was asking her about herself. She also detected a subtle shiver rattle his shoulders. He *had* just given her his coat.

She shrugged. "I don't know. Nothing out of the ordinary." *Just like me*, she couldn't help but think. "Hang out with my friends. Watch movies, the kind I'm sure you'd hate."

"You're sure I'd hate them?" Raffi questioned, the beginning of a smile starting.

She pulled the coat tighter around her body, felt the soft fabric against her fingers as they pinched it shut. "You know, frilly romantic stuff. Gallant men. Hijinks. Crosses over into my line of work, too, minus the hijinks. I guess most of what I do for fun relates to work. I brush up on flower arranging, photo editing, that kind of thing. I love making things beautiful for other people. I get to design a little corner of their lives that's just joy. I'm sure that sounds—well, whatever." Then, realizing she was talking too much, too fast—was she nervous?—she decided to change the subject.

Ani nodded toward him. "What about you? Is that outfit some kind of uniform you read about on a pickup artist forum?"

He seemed to always be dressed nicely. Two for two now. She was curious about why, and her question, although slightly mean, made sense in her mind. Also, if he was a PUA, she wanted to know for sure right off the bat. Any heady feelings coming her way from his excellent taste in cologne and sport coats would be quashed immediately.

He tilted his head. "What's a pickup artist forum? Is that like a mixed-media art thing? Finding trash on the streets or whatever?" He gazed skyward, considering. "But why would they wear suits?"

His confusion immediately made her feel guilty for asking. "You don't spend a lot of time online, do you?"

"Not really. Unless I have to do something for work."

"Lucky." She liked that; it was a healthy practice that she wished she could do more often. Unplug. Live in the moment.

"As for the suits—it's the way I want to look. I enjoy their feel. The seriousness of them. The subtle ways you can dress them up or down. I think I'm—I don't know—awkward and gangly in shorts and a tee. Doesn't feel like me."

Was that . . . a hint of insecurity? The idea of Raffi feeling awkward, gangly, and anything less than completely sure of himself didn't square with the image she'd built in her head: the untouchable, perpetually smug son of a maybe mobster, who seemed to glide through life like he owned it.

"So what do you do at the beach?" Ani asked.

Raffi stared at her and said with all seriousness, "I wear a full suit and then rip it off with one hand, revealing a neon-orange Speedo."

Despite herself, Ani laughed. There was something disarming about the way he leaned into the absurdity of his own image. "Why is that somehow so easy to visualize?"

Raffi caught her eye and smiled in complicity with her, sharing their joke.

"Well, you wear them well," Ani said, feeling like giving him a sincere compliment.

The edges of his smile softened, and for a moment, he looked at her like he wasn't sure if she was teasing him or being serious. His gaze dropped to the floor before flicking back up to hers. Eyes the color of sun-warmed cedar, dark and calm.

"Thank you."

Then he fidgeted with a button on his cuff, not catching her eyes. "I know the whole suit getup is kind of formal—not as strange as an orange Speedo—but they also just—" He paused. Shrugged. "I guess they make me feel stronger. Almost . . . protected."

Ani blinked, caught off guard. She didn't know what to say. It felt like he'd handed her a piece of himself, fragile and unguarded, and she wasn't sure where to put it. The air between them shifted, heavier now.

Was this an opening? The weight of the moment made her think that maybe he wanted to be asked. The question hovered on the tip of her tongue.

She took a breath and asked, her voice softer than she intended, "Protected from what?"

For a moment, Raffi just looked at her, his expression unreadable. Her heart sprinted, the audacity in asking that question catching up to her, but before he could answer, a loud knock on the window shattered the moment.

They both jerked toward the sound, their shared stillness broken.

"You guys okay in there?" Chris's muffled voice asked from outside.

And that was it.

Raffi blinked, his mask of coolness sliding back into place as if it had never slipped. "We're good," he called back, his tone light and easy. "Definitely no screaming about a mouse, all very normal."

Even as she heard the handle turning, Ani felt oddly unsteady, like she'd been yanked back from the precipice of something enticing.

When the door opened, Ani should have felt nothing but relief about being rescued from the mouse-ridden murder shed. But once they were outside and she approached the bench holding her belongings, Ani hesitated a moment longer than she should have when it was time to take off the coat and hand it back to Raffi.

THE FOUR OF them spent another half hour or so finalizing plans, which went surprisingly smoothly. As Ani and Sanan walked back to their car across Ô's parking lot, Ani received a text. It was from Kami. Ani gulped.

She, Sanan, Kami, and Grace had been emailing back and forth about to-dos, and Ani had sent out a very professional plan for them, trying her best to make everything as impersonal as possible. She also rejoiced when she got her first check for five thousand dollars, which was a nice reminder of why exactly she was doing this. But so far, their communications had been only emails, no texts.

"One sec, Sanan, got to read this," Ani said, hoping not to be rude as she was sure she was about to disappear into her own world.

Ani tapped to read it.

> Hey girl! So I'm having my first wedding dress try-on this Friday at Belle Bridal. Would loooooooove if you could come and give me your expert advice. I trust you more than Mom and Galia tbh. You know what I mean! Can you come? Pleeeeease? At noon. xx

Ani stared at the last letters of the text. Ex. Ex. *That's exactly right, Kami*, she thought angrily. *I am your ex*. Only once over, but thanks for the reminder. Kami was inviting her to something as personal as wedding dress shopping? This felt wrong. So wrong.

And yet Ani could not resist the pull of Kami, even after so long. Part of her wanted to see Kami again, to bask in the warmth of her attention, to feel that rush of being the person Kami trusted most. But another part of her—the part that had spent months, *years*, untangling herself from the aftermath of their breakup—knew better. This was a terrible idea.

Not to mention the family factor. Would Kami's mom even want her there? They always got along, and she adored Kami's sister, Galia, especially, but how utterly awkward. She could already picture the polite but strained smiles.

She sighed, her thumb hovering over the screen. She knew she should say no. But she was the wedding planner—the wedding planner who desperately had to keep her clients happy. And her bride, ex or no ex, needed her.

Sure, I'll be there, she typed.

When she pulled away from the winery, she spotted Raffi at the doors of the villa. He raised his hand in a small wave, and Ani felt a strange tug at the bottom of her stomach as she remembered the weight of his coat and the charged air between them not an hour ago. Then she waved back.

6

Raffi

RAFFI WAS AT home—a town house that was a recent build, modern and sleek inside—after a fabulous lie-in until ten. He was about to brew his first cup of sourj for the day to cure himself of the hellish hangover he'd gotten after a night out with Chris and way, way too many martinis. It was a few days after Ani and Sanan had come to the winery, and he and his father had gotten into one of their famous rows after his dad tripped but luckily caught himself—although Raffi had suggested, again that his father get a cane.

His dad must have been in a foul mood from something else because he lost it on Raffi, threatening to take back the winery and revoke his inheritance, blah blah blah. Raffi, not feeling like backing down, told his dad he didn't need any inheritance, could make it on his own, and as for the winery, he was running it beautifully, thank you very much.

The truth was, the wine itself was good, maybe even great, but no one had heard about Ô. They were too new, there was too much competition, and Raffi was having trouble selling bottles. Every trick he'd picked up from his MBA courses fell flat. All the retailers seemed to have their relationships with suppliers set. People said they'd look into it and call him back but never did. Raffi was, actually, panicking.

Thank God for the wedding, even if it was Kami's, Raffi thought as he scooped the finely ground Armenian coffee into the jezveh. He had enough runway that he could wait for the wedding to happen and hope for the PR to work its magic.

But he still wanted to do something else in the meantime. One of the main skills he'd picked up in his MBA program was how to party, although he had already been a dab hand at it. Still, his fellow business-degree earners loved to organize and throw parties of all themes. He should do that at Ô. Invite them all, his book club, too, of course, plus the more rager-y types who would guarantee the function wouldn't be a bore—and buy bottle after bottle. He resolved to get a date on the calendar and contact them.

As he watched the coffee begin to bubble, he remembered Ani saying something about picking out stone tile for the flooring.

He gave the wedding planner a call.

"Ani jan," he said, suddenly in a good mood, although he hadn't had his first sip of coffee yet.

He heard her voice over the phone's speaker.

"Raffi, what's up?"

The sound of her reminded him of the shed. The two of them locked in together, Ani shivering to herself, pretending she wasn't freezing her ass off. She'd been so shocked when he put his coat on her; it was like no one had ever done something nice for her in her life. That, or she thought so little of him that she couldn't believe he'd give up his warmth for her.

When she had handed his coat back, he picked up the faintest scent of orange blossoms. For some reason, long after she left, he kept catching the phantom scent of it.

"Today's stone-picking day, right?" he asked.

"Something like that, yes."

The coffee foamed, threatening to boil over. Perfect. Raffi lifted it off the burner, turned the stove off, and began to pour.

"You know I'm coming with you."

"Raffi, I am well qualified to select stone tile on my own."

"Ani jan," he said, privately reveling in adding that *jan*, that little appendage of admiration to her name, "I told you I need to approve every last nail, plant, and piece of tape that gets put up at my winery. I'm coming."

There was silence on the other end, and he wondered if he had pushed too far, reminding her of their first unfortunate interaction. He took the moment to sip his sourj. It was excellent, just the right amount of sweetness.

"Fine. I was going to go to a place near SF, but since you're coming, too, there's an even better warehouse just outside Napa. Richland Tile Company."

Raffi noted that he was still in his pajamas. A very fine silk set from Paris, a gift from his mother—the only type of love she bestowed these days, if he could even call it that. After Sevan died, Raffi's mother absconded to Europe and Beirut, where she stayed the vast majority of the year. She came back for Christmas and Nor Dari . . . sometimes. Always with bags and bags of presents, with smiles and stories of her friends, like she hadn't actually abandoned him. He'd tried to press her on it once, years ago, and at first she waved it off, saying she came back, didn't she? Raffi had his own life, and Moush was always working, so why couldn't she have a little fun? And when he pushed further, his mother burst into tears, saying her only remaining son hated her, why had God been so cruel? And on and on.

And Raffi agreed. Fate had been cruel, but his parents' responses to the tragedy . . . they could have controlled that. They could have risen up at some point, eventually, and noticed there was still another kid who was missing his absolute best friend in the world, who needed his parents more than ever. But they never did.

He plucked those thoughts from his mind and looked up this tile place. Fifteen minutes north of him. She'd have quite a drive.

"Why don't we carpool? It's far from you. I have this company van, and if we need to pick up any materials, we can throw them back there."

There was momentary silence.

"Fine. See you at the winery."

He hadn't meant that they should meet at the winery, but he was suddenly sheepish at the thought of suggesting she come to his place.

So they met at the winery.

Ani showed up looking fine as hell in a power business dress that clung to her every curve. Raffi tried not to think about any of them and focused on the task ahead.

She locked her gaze with his when they said hello, and he was momentarily awed again at the beauty of her large doe-like eyes.

"Shall we?" he asked, and held open the van door for her.

It was one of those white industrial vans for couriers or serial killers. A tad creepy but useful for hauling materials. One of his employees had convinced his dad that it was a necessary purchase. Certainly *not* the type of vehicle Raffi would roll in. No, he preferred the understated elegance of his vintage Jaguar. But again, he was here trying to exude professionalism, so shady delivery chic it was.

"Thanks," she replied, but it sounded like a curse.

"What should we listen to?" he asked, then answered his own question. "Harout, obviously."

"Nothing like the original Armenian pop star himself shuttling us on our way to buy tiles for the soon-to-be-greatest Armenian winery in Napa."

Raffi fiddled with the screen, scanning to find the perfect Harout song for this moment. The right vibe, something light and celebratory. She'd called his winery the greatest.

They listened to a collection of Harout's top hits and did not speak much on the drive over, Raffi finding himself strangely nervous and wanting to impress Ani.

"Have you seen him in concert?" he finally asked.

"Once, I think, at the Armenian school, such a long time ago."

"Weird, me too. I must have been at that same concert."

Raffi kept his eyes on the road, but he heard a smile in Ani's voice as she said, "Funny to think about little-kid versions of us jamming to Harout Pamboukjian on the Armenian school's dance floor."

"I went hard that night," Raffi said.

"Didn't we all?"

"Of course," Raffi ventured, hoping it wouldn't sound too braggy, "that wasn't the only time I saw him. Dad hired him to play at his fiftieth birthday party."

Ani rolled her eyes with a smile. "Of *course* he did."

"What Moushegh wants, Moushegh gets," Raffi said. Except for rerouting Kami's wedding elsewhere. This one? This is what Raffi wants.

"You guys, uh, close?" Ani asked.

He remembered now that she'd overheard Dad with his little comment about him never becoming a man. He cringed at the memory, shame prickling under his collar, and inwardly winced.

"Not really. But I don't know—I'm hoping with me running the winery, which was his dream, not mine, maybe that might change."

"I see," she said. Raffi wanted to ask her what exactly she saw, because he was afraid he'd shown too many cards once again and needed confirmation. What was it about this woman that made him divulge his thoughts, ones he believed he had kept balled tightly in his fist? She loosened his hold on them. To avoid further spillage, he kept quiet.

Then she unexpectedly said, "You know, there's this legendary nursery not too far from Richland Tile. Small family-run place that sells the most stunning blooms. I bet we could snag some eye-catching shrubbery for your winery. You interested in checking it out afterward?"

"Of course," Raffi said, sounding overeager. Ani nodded, seemingly pleased.

Soon after, they reached the tile store. When they entered, a statuesque brunette woman greeted them.

"Hello, welcome to Richland Tile. Happy to help you with anything."

"Great," Ani said, taking the lead. "We're looking for poetry stones for outdoor landscaping."

The woman clasped her hands. "Wonderful! Are you two remodeling your home? Newlyweds?"

"Oh, no," Ani said, with way too much horror in her voice.

"Oldlyweds," Raffi joked, clapping Ani on the shoulder. He wasn't sure what had gotten into him, but it may have been that look from earlier, the look in Ani's eyes when he opened the van door for her. The way she'd riffed off him in the van, the thought of their little selves dancing the night away to Harout so many years ago.

"Wow, you two must have gotten married young," the sales rep said.

"Sure did," Raffi said. "High school sweethearts."

Ani stared at him, a naughty smirk picking up. "I hated him at first. He was such a spoiled jerk."

The sublime curve of her neck. That smile.

Raffi decided to take a chance and put his arm around Ani. If he felt any signs that she wasn't enjoying it, he'd remove it, apologize, and stop flirting with her. He shouldn't be anyway. He and Ani were going to spend a *lot* of time together. What the hell was his endgame here? If they hooked up, it would be awkward for months. He filed away that thought for later, because then something wonderful happened.

Ani melted into him, getting closer, softer. And her enjoying it made him enjoy it even more. This was . . . interesting.

"Things changed, though," Raffi said, "when she got to know the real me."

He dared to look down at Ani, and she glanced up at him, an expression of curiosity coloring her face. God, those eyes.

The rep cleared her throat. "Well, if you wanted poetry stones, they're right this way."

Raffi removed his arm, sensing the moment was over. Ani smoothed down her dress, which was already quite smooth. They followed the sales rep outside.

After the two of them had checked out several types of stones, they agreed upon a style they both liked, which was a happy surprise.

"As for color," the rep was saying, "we have this sandy color, a terra-cotta, a blue-gray, and white with gray veining." She pointed to samples of the various options.

"White," Raffi said, at the same time Ani said, "Sand."

"Kami would want white," Raffi said. "White and green? Can't find a better bridal combination."

Raffi thought this was a salient point that was airtight, inarguable. He would not be convinced to choose *sand* when there was an option for white stone. It'd be so striking, like an outdoor Versailles.

"I know Kami would want white," Ani said. The way she said Kami's name reminded Raffi that he wanted, at some opportune time, to ask her what went down with her and Kami. Why had she shrunk like that in Kami's presence? And why the hell—if their relationship ended badly, which was his guess—was she planning her wedding? But right now, he had white stones to defend.

"Then what's the issue?"

"Have you considered the scale at which we're going to be covering your garden in this? White is going to be blinding."

The rep stepped backward. "I'll give y'all a moment."

Ani whipped out her tablet from that giant tote bag of hers, took a photo of the white stone, and began tapping furiously.

"What're you doing?" Raffi asked, hoping to catch a glimpse of her screen, but she shielded it from him.

"Give me a second," Ani muttered, eyes narrowed in concentration. Raffi watched her hands fly over the glass in quick, precise motions, and before he realized it, he'd leaned in slightly, as if proximity might help him understand her better.

"Okay, look," Ani said, handing him her tablet.

"That's your garden with white stone, and this"—she swiped to a second image—"is your garden with sand-colored stone."

It was all there, a photo of Ô's garden with the stones they'd been shopping for, tiling the ground in the image. And it was with deep regret that he had to admit that she had a fucking point. The white was way too much.

"What kind of sorcery is this?" he asked, still in awe of how she'd managed it.

"It's called Photoshop. The image isn't even close to perfect—"

"It's close enough. You pulled that off in two seconds."

She shrugged. "I've found it's helpful for my brides to be able to visualize the space with different linens or flowers or whatever, so I got good at mocking things up."

"You can say that again, damn."

She looked at him expectantly.

"All right, yes. The white's a disaster. I admit it. The sand looks better than I thought."

Ani seemed to allow herself the tiniest victory smile. "And it matches so beautifully with the color of the villa's stone."

He had to agree there, too.

A short time later, they left the store with an order for a metric ton of rocks, plus some of the building materials for the dome, which they were modeling after their mutual favorite Pinterest image.

On the walk back to the van, Ani said, "Not bad, right? Turns out trusting other people isn't the end of the world."

She gave him a winning smile—bright, a little flirty, and completely unguarded.

He returned an easy grin. "And turns out I'm more flexible than you thought. Right?"

Ani's cheeks went pink, then she said, with a playful glint in her eyes, "Not going to make the obvious joke."

Raffi strolled along, pleased. "Didn't even cross my mind."

The laugh Ani gave was so true, so tickled, that Raffi felt something shift between them, and then she inched closer, so that Raffi felt something shift between them. He didn't want to stop hanging out with her.

"So, any revised stance on those truffle fries? I'm getting hungry. Might be nice to stop and have a bite before going to the nursery?"

They reached the van, but suddenly Ani turned and stood in front of the hood. She chewed the inside of her cheek, as if holding back an entire conversation.

Raffi stopped a few steps behind her. The air between them went still. Her face was all control, but her fingers had curled into the sleeves of her coat, like she needed something to hold on to.

His stomach gave a quiet twist. "Everything okay?" he asked.

Ani let go of her coat, hands dropping to her sides. "Do you remember Lala? She's an orthodontist, Armenian, dyed blonde hair often in a bun."

Raffi's brows furrowed. Lala? They were talking about food; why was she bringing up someone named—

Oh.

That Lala.

His whole body stilled. One of the women he'd slept with five or so years back, really sweet girl. Did not deserve the Raffi storm coming into her life. A weight settled behind his ribs, bracing for the inevitable, and fully earned impact.

"Shit," he muttered under his breath. He asked Ani out to lunch, *again*, even though the vibes felt completely different than the first day they'd met. But she had not only heard rumors about him, she'd heard the truth. The part of himself he regretted the most.

Ani crossed her arms. "You remember, then. She's a friend of my sister's."

He exhaled sharply, dragging a clammy hand through his hair. "That was—that was years ago. I'm not that person anymore."

Ani let out a short humorless laugh. "So? Does that change the fact that you pursued her, slept with her, and never called her again?"

Raffi flinched. A sharp, clean, deserved slap. The way Ani was looking at him, like she'd confirmed every reason not to trust him, cut deeper than he would have expected.

He couldn't blame her, though. He hadn't even forgiven himself.

"I was an asshole," he admitted, voice lower now. "I—yeah. I did that."

He finally met her gaze. He continued, "What you heard, that was true at one time. But I haven't been that person for a while now. And yeah, I haven't been in a relationship lately. That part's . . . more complicated. But I'm not out there chasing hookups constantly. Not even close."

Ani shook her head. "Honestly, Raffi. If I didn't know a thing about you, maybe I'd go for those fries. *Maybe*. But I know people you've hurt."

Raffi blinked. The knowledge hit him low in the gut, heavy and bewildering. She might . . . like him? At least a little? But understandably, would *not* go there. Still, even though it was a rejection, her admission gave him the first flare of hope since this conversation started.

He nodded. "Fair. Fair." Then he rubbed the back of his neck, eyes on the ground. "I sent Lala an apology text about a year ago, by the way—not that it makes up for what I did."

Ani didn't speak.

"But I thought you might want to know how badly I felt about how I treated her. Still do."

Silence settled between Raffi and Ani, taut like the moment before a string snaps. Raffi didn't dare move. Ani stood still, too, her expression unreadable, eyes fixed somewhere just past him.

He swallowed, the sound too loud in their quiet. Then Ani spoke at last, her tone taking on a polite register. "Well. The errand at the nursery *would* be a lot easier if I had a van. Are you still up for it?"

He exhaled. *Yes, yes, whatever you want, Ani,* he thought. The sentiment came out much stronger, even in his head, than he'd expected.

"At your service. Direct me?"

She moved toward the passenger-side door. "Anshousht," she said. *Naturally.*

7

Raffi

ANI WAS RIGHT; this nursery was something else. Like a secret garden tucked into a forgotten enclave of Napa. He hadn't ever realized it was there, but once they entered, it expanded into a larger backyard, bursting with greenery.

He and Ani ambled through the various aisles. Beside him, Ani sized up the varieties, trailed her fingers over their fronds, even cupped a blue flower blossom between her fingers so it fit into her palm.

Then she stopped in front of a brilliantly green leafed plant, almost like a bush, with medium-sized delicate silvery-white flowers.

"This is a rare one. Moonlit Cascade. It blooms twice a year, right now and in early fall—just in time for the wedding. What do you think?"

Raffi took in the white blooms and joyful green leaves. "We'll get that green and white."

"Yes." Ani smiled. "Can't find a better bridal combination."

Hearing his words spoken back to him, her voice kind

instead of mocking, gave him a twinge of hope that their professional relationship wouldn't be doomed, even after the conversation they'd just had. He gave her a friendly smile.

Then, wanting to be helpful because Ani had basically done everything today, he said, "I'll check out."

"Okay, great. And, um, Kami is going to pay you back?"

Ani's posture had changed with her question. Stiff, like she was suddenly filled with anxiety.

He shrugged. "She said to send her and Grace the receipts or to let them know if we needed them to call in their credit card information."

Ani seemed relieved. "Good, you know, that they gave you options."

"Right," he said, unsure of what that was all about. The concern in her eyes piqued his curiosity, not for the first time. This Ani, so full of secrets. He thought again about what type of person would unhappily plan the wedding of their ex—besides him, who had very legitimate reasons. And anyway, as Kami had said, their relationship "barely counted." Ani's and Kami's? Even by Kami's lax standards, he had a feeling theirs probably counted.

Raffi had trouble finding the checkout counter, then realized it was a small shabby podium with an older man standing in front of it, glasses down to the tip of his nose, scowling at some paperwork.

"We'd like to buy all of those types of flowers." Raffi pointed toward the plants Ani was still standing by. "All that you have. Clean you out." Raffi flashed his winning smile.

The man raised his eyes painfully slowly and looked up at Raffi.

"Clean me out, eh? 'Those types'?"

His tone did not sound friendly in the least. In fact, Raffi would go so far as to call it unfriendly. Warning alarms blared in Raffi's head, but he wasn't sure what he had done to offend exactly.

"Do you know how rare that plant is? How finicky it can be to take care of?"

Raffi did not.

"Yes, sir. I've been warned about its prickly nature."

The man looked Raffi up and down. "You're lying."

Raffi wasn't sure how to respond. His heart rate jumped because the man *was* correct. Did Raffi stick to his lie, or did he confess? And how the hell had he gotten into this high-pressure situation where he had to convince the clerk that he was worthy of his wares?

Then he felt Ani's thick, wavy hair brush his arm, and she surfaced from behind him to face the spiteful seller.

She spoke with a soft smile. "Mr. Burdock, we'd be honored if you could sell us as many Moonlit Cascades as you can spare. I'm well versed in their maintenance and know about the seasonal watering changes, eggshell fertilizer that helps them bloom to their full potential, and their overwhelming sunlight needs. And I'll be overseeing their care. They would be the crowning jewel of our garden, if you'll allow us."

Raffi's brain was caught between Ani's deft words and her mesmerizing lips. And how, exactly, she was softening the curmudgeon before them. The man's eyes relaxed as Ani spoke, and although he didn't smile, his frown had disappeared.

"All right then, miss, if you'll be overseeing them. Take what you need."

"Thank you," she said, beaming. "We might need to take all you have today, if that's okay?"

The man paused, and Raffi held his breath.

"It's okay," the clerk proclaimed.

Was it just that she was a gorgeous woman, charming this guy? He didn't think so. If it was up to Raffi, they'd be leaving empty-handed, possibly after an unpleasant exchange of words.

Raffi simply stared in Ani's wake as she strolled back toward the plants. Then she turned around and caught Raffi's eyes, the slightest hint of pride in them.

"You coming?"

He didn't move, taking in the way the light played in her hair, the curve of her smile, the whole shape of her.

The seller spoke up. "Better get going, bucko. Lady's request."

That shook him. Raffi nodded his head in the man's direction and hurried to help Ani with the plants.

Together, they loaded plant after plant into the van, until every last bit of space was taken up, to the point where leaves were tickling their elbows when they sat up in front.

Now fully out of earshot of the picky purveyor of plants, Raffi shut the door and asked, "So how the hell did you do that? And what was his deal anyway?"

"Do what?" she asked innocently.

Raffi gestured toward the shop. "You were amazing in there. You came in like some deity who smoothed over the whole situation and told the guy exactly what he wanted to hear. How'd you even know all that?"

Ani blushed, which sent blood rushing through Raffi's

body. He wanted to see that blush again, traveling lower, painting more of her skin—if he could allow himself to dream. Which he wouldn't.

Raffi started the van and kept his eyes straight ahead.

"He's well-known for being sort of a jerk and overprotective of his plants. Doesn't like to see any of them die after all the work he puts into them. Sorry, I should have told you. I just got distracted—"

She didn't finish her thought.

"But how'd you know about those specific flowers?"

Ani shrugged. "I'm in the wedding business. I know plenty about flower varieties, and these back here, we actually grew one in my parents' backyard. When my family and I went to the nursery, the blooms caught my eye, but the person at the gardening center warned me how tricky they are to take care of. So I read up, tried those methods, and so far the plant has doubled in size, so I must be doing something right."

It seemed Ani knew *everything*. Who needed the internet when you had the world's most brilliant woman by your side?

They were taking a back road through Napa County, with massive bare oaks like sculptures erupting out of the earth and lush green wild grass blanketing the hillsides. It was beautiful out here. He was glad he'd moved to Napa. Yes, he liked flashy things, but he'd soured on city life. Give him a nice glass of wine on a quiet balcony overlooking the Silverado Trail instead of sitting in traffic on Van Ness behind the 30X bus belching its exhaust over his hopes, dreams, and freshly dry-cleaned blazer any day.

Then, Raffi's throat began to itch. He needed, very badly, to give a loud and unbecoming hack to clear it, but he wouldn't dare with Ani one foot away from him. He dealt with the discomfort.

"So, you know about rare flowers, sun and light, Photoshop, landscaping, how to deal with surly old men. What else?"

His voice sounded odd to him, strained, but he hoped it was one of those things that he noticed but she didn't.

"Nothing else. Those are my only areas of knowledge," Ani deadpanned.

"Uh-huh, don't believe that for one second."

Raffi smiled, but then it dropped immediately because his throat felt tight. Was he getting *nervous*? What was this? Oh God, was this what a crush felt like? It'd been years since he had a real, bona fide crush. Kami was probably the last—

Against his will, Raffi let out a choked cough.

Ani turned toward him, alarmed. "You okay?"

"Yep, fine," he said. *It's just a crush.* Oh God, his budding feelings for Ani were affecting his physiology. They didn't teach this shit in med school.

Then his windpipe constricted dramatically, and when he tried to breathe he could hardly draw any air, and his face itched like it was covered in hives. Oh no, this wasn't *feelings*; he was having a full-blown allergy attack. A serious one. What the hell—he didn't know he was allergic to anything. And the culprit? The fucking flowers.

He wheezed and began to slow the van, readying to pull over.

"Allergy attack. Flowers." His voice came out horribly, so weak and strained.

They were about twenty minutes from the nearest clinic

where they'd have an EpiPen. Way too far. If he pulled over and got out of the van, the allergy symptoms could subside, but he was really far gone, about to lose his ability to breathe, so leaving the flowers might not be enough. They could call 911 and the fire department would be here in about ten minutes, considering how far out they were from civilization. Hopefully he'd survive by then. Oh God, he was going to die on the side of the road. He, a doctor, totally unable to help himself. Death by flowers. God, his father would hate that. So unmanly.

He hadn't even made the winery a success yet, hadn't really accomplished anything in his life except half efforts. He saw that now, so clearly, how he had to—if he was granted another chance—do better.

Even with the fear of imminent demise hanging over him, Raffi managed to pull over to the side of the dirt road. He was about to get out and instruct Ani to call 911 when he saw what she was doing.

She'd unbuckled her seat belt and in her hand, like a warrior goddess, was the shining tube of an EpiPen. Her expression was completely focused on his thigh.

Then, because one of the many Moonlit Cascades towered between them, she stood, her back hunched, shimmied over, and then was straddling him—*straddling* him! He literally could not breathe anymore and he could feel his face purpling, but holy shit, this miracle woman was on top of him, arm raised, and then with a hard whack, she stabbed him right in the upper thigh and let the epinephrine flow into his bloodstream.

Within seconds, the pressure in his throat loosened and he could breathe again, great gasping breaths.

And he couldn't help himself; he put an arm around Ani and felt her warmth, her own breaths quick, up and down.

"Thank you, thank you," he said quietly.

"Of course," she replied, not taking her eyes off him.

It was then he allowed himself to feel her legs, and most especially, the heat *between* her legs pressing against his thigh. He swallowed and knew that if his body wasn't coursing with epinephrine, constricting his blood vessels, he'd be sporting a partial boner. He had a mental one, despite his body's suffering.

He was mute, his heart absolutely racing and mind jumping between physical agony and a surprising bliss. Also he was still coming to terms with the fact that he had nearly died and that this incredible woman had just saved his life.

"You okay now? Did it work?" Ani said while she climbed off him, his hand sliding along her back, and returned to her seat, careful to avoid crushing the flowers. He felt her absence acutely. If he was being really honest with himself, he wanted her back on his lap, wanted to grab the back of her head and kiss her.

He didn't realize until now how badly he had been suppressing his desire for Ani. Before the flowers attacked him, he could have lived with being totally professional and shoving away all sexual thoughts of her. But then she'd mounted him and saved his life, and now he didn't know how to act around her.

He would try to keep it simple for now.

"It worked." Raffi turned toward her. "You saved my goddamn life, Ani."

She seemed a bit shy. Maybe she did feel something when she was straddling him. Something good, he hoped.

"I come prepared. Do we need to get out of this van?

"Good idea."

Raffi tested his limbs before he hopped out, not wanting to crumple onto the road. He didn't need any further humiliations.

Ani came around to his side, which Raffi found very touching. He leaned against the van and felt a refreshing breeze ground him.

"So, you carry an EpiPen?"

Who knew that after almost dying, the thing he'd cling to for safety would be small talk?

"Not for me," she replied. "Part of the trade. After one wedding guest choked from a hazelnut allergy during the second wedding I planned, I decided to carry an EpiPen on me at all times."

Once again, Ani proved to be so much more than a run-of-the-mill wedding planner. He'd really misjudged her skills, and he felt embarrassed by that, especially after what he'd said to her that first day.

He noticed, then, that her hands were shaking. "Was this your first time using it?" he asked.

She bit her bottom lip and nodded. Ani had been worried, maybe scared, but she'd done it anyway. That was real courage.

Then a tiny seed of a thought appeared in Raffi's mind, growing larger and larger. He had intimate feelings for Ani—*that* he had established—but more than that, he was entertaining, for the first time in more than a decade, that he wished he could properly *date* someone. Not someone. Ani. Court her, listen to her hopes and dreams, get to know what really made her tick, introduce her to his friends. Maybe even introduce her to his father, and not as the wedding planner.

The only thing was, he didn't have a chance. She'd already completely shot him down, so it wasn't like he could ask her out.

She was off limits. Just his luck.

He was at a loss as to how to proceed, but he figured, for now, he'd just talk to her.

He looked toward Ani and caught her eye. "I'm glad you did."

"Me too," she said quietly.

Raffi tucked away those two words in his heart so he could revisit them again and again.

8

Ani

ANI WOULD RATHER be anywhere in the world right now, including the earth's lava-hot mantle core, than at Belle Bridal.

Her stomach dropped as the tall glass doors of the bridal boutique sealed shut behind her like a tomb. Rows of flouncy white tulle hung high on their racks, staring down at Ani. Unfriendly ghosts. Spirits of the dresses she could have been choosing for her and Kami's wedding. Around the corner, she heard the voices of women—among them would be Kami's family, who she hadn't seen in two years. She'd have to smile and chat and give well-informed opinions. With this wedding, Kami was pulling her out of so much debt, so she *was* indebted, almost literally. She couldn't run now.

Ani swallowed and caught a glimpse of herself in the mirror. She'd worn her wedding planner uniform of pencil skirt with white button-down shirt and went with a "no-makeup" look. She didn't want to appear as if she was trying too hard. What a lie.

The screech of an older woman brought her out of her head.

"Is that Ani Avakian?" Kami's very loud and boisterous Aunt Sima asked in Armenian.

"It's me," Ani replied in their mother language.

Then Kami's mom appeared behind the auntie and rushed toward Ani, kissing her on both cheeks.

"Ani, tsakougus," she exclaimed, using the word for "my child," which was usually such a sweet word, but right now it did nothing but depress Ani.

Kami's mom was as stunning as her daughter, only twenty years older. She'd always liked Ani, despite her family's very different station in life, and despite, you know, being a woman that her daughter was dating. Queerness was not openly accepted in most Armenian families, but Kami's mom had a bit of an artistic, rebellious streak—similar to Kami's—and wasn't one to bend to the staunch traditions of the elders. Besides, she was loaded and single, and she often said that allowed her to do whatever the hell she wanted.

"Is Ani here?" The unmistakable voice of Kami called out from behind the sage velvet curtain.

"I am," Ani said, while several women also answered in the affirmative.

Then the curtain flared and out popped Galia, Kami's younger sister. Galia and Ani had been close, and saying goodbye to Galia was yet another heartbreak that Ani had suffered when Kami dumped her. They could have stayed friends, of course, but it was too difficult.

Galia was shorter and spunkier than Kami. She had cropped hair with a magenta streak on one side, and she primarily dressed in black, in stark contrast to Kami's usual creams and whites.

Galia threw her arms around Ani and said, "God, I missed you. I can't believe you're here."

"Meeeeee neither," Ani wanted to say.

"It's so nice to see you again," she settled on. Which was true. But it all still just made her sad.

"Okay, who's ready to see dress number one?" Kami asked, still hidden from view.

Ani was not ready. She did not want to see.

Kami disregarded the adamant thoughts in Ani's mind, flung the curtain to the side, and emerged to gasps and exclamations from her family members.

Kami was dressed in a thick ballroom-style satin dress with a tight strapless bodice. And Kami was looking right at Ani, as if her thoughts were the only ones that mattered.

Ani's heart pounded, and she found that she had to concentrate on her breathing to keep it natural. She should not be seeing this. This was not for her eyes. How did Kami not understand that?

"Oh, this is lovely, so elegant, so classy," said Aunt Sima.

"Timeless," added her mother.

"It's a little boring, though," Galia said.

Everyone stared at Ani, awaiting her tiebreaking words. God help her, was this how it was going to go the entire hour?

"It's a lovely dress," she began, "but it doesn't feel quite 'Kami.'"

Kami's eyes lit up. "That's what I was saying, Mom!" she directed toward her mother. Then she looked at Ani appreciatively. "See, you always know."

"Then why didn't you choose me?" Ani wanted to say. *I always know, I have great taste*, she thought, but that wasn't enough.

Kami disappeared behind the drapes.

What were Kami's exact words? "We're just too different. You're never around on weekends, and you never will be, as long as you keep doing this wedding thing. I need someone to travel with, let loose with."

Kami had not been supportive of Ani's work, to say the least, so it was awfully rich that she was now being hired to plan Kami's damn wedding. True, Kami thought Ani was good at her job, but she didn't understand why Ani had to work so hard. It baffled her—the trust-fund baby who never had to work at all, who owned a variety of small vanity businesses kept afloat by other people. She would complain and complain when every single Saturday Ani was busy, when she was at site visits, when she did after-work-hours jobs for her brides.

Ani couldn't help but compare her position to Grace. Wouldn't Grace, as an actress, also likely be traveling a lot for work and gone on weekends? Ani couldn't say for sure, but Grace gave off the air of being moneyed, so maybe that's what was missing from Ani. That was what Kami meant by "too different." The people who had to work to survive versus the people who "work" for fun. Who "work," if it suits them.

Raffi was like that, wasn't he? Although he seemed to be taking the winery very seriously. He clearly wasn't indolent. And he had been a resident, a job well-known for being grueling, but he did quit that. Every time she saw him, she got the impression he was searching for something, working toward something she couldn't see.

God, she could not believe she'd climbed up on him in the van like that. But he was choking, dying. His face had turned puce, for goodness' sake. She was just trying to get the best possible angle, those flowers were in the way so she couldn't get to his leg from her seat without crushing the blossoms, and the van's spaciousness allowed her to get in that position. Pure action, no thought.

But then, when the scary moment had passed, when he'd put his hand on her back . . .

She'd felt a stirring deep in her core. That hand. He'd been so grateful, that touch was the touch of worship. Like he was feeling her to see if she was real, if the whole thing had been real. It sent heat straight between her legs. Which she had then realized were pressing against his thigh. She removed herself but immediately regretted it. It was the only course of action, the only sensible course, but some animal part of herself wanted to hop back on, take his prominent jaw in her hands, and see what would happen.

These thoughts were ridiculous. This was Raffi! He claimed he'd changed, but she knew anyone could dress up lies in pretty words. Even though he did sound sincere. And he didn't, for the most part, act like a careless playboy around her. Still. Still. She should not allow these lusty thoughts to enter her consciousness.

"Ani jan?" Kami's aunt asked.

Ani realized she had not been paying attention to any of the proceedings and that the pit of dread in her stomach had disappeared. Hmm. Maybe she could survive this after all.

"Oh, sorry? I was thinking about a work matter," she lied.

"Do you think sleeves or no sleeves?"

Ani shook herself and tried to answer impartially, as if she were not giving an opinion about her ex-girlfriend's wedding sleeve situation.

"Sleeves are in right now, but trends come and go. Kami should choose the dress that looks best on her and that she feels is . . . the one."

"See, Kami? You do not have to choose sleeve!" her aunt shouted past the curtain.

"I know, Tantig. Okay, check this one out."

Kami appeared, wearing an open boho lace number that tightly fit her body. Ani swallowed. The dress left nothing to the imagination, and Ani didn't need to imagine; she could just reach into her memories and see that body in all its glory. This dress was a stark reminder.

Before anyone could say anything, Kami gushed, "I *love* it."

Both her mom and aunt made clucking noises. Her aunt said at earsplitting volume, "Kami jan, it looks like lingerie!"

Her mom said, "You know I will love whatever you choose, but it feels so open. You don't want your grandfather and great uncle Varoujan seeing your outlines like that."

Kami turned around. It was extremely low cut in the back as well.

"It looks like an arrow pointing toward your butt crack," Galia quipped. She looked to Ani. "Tell me I'm wrong."

Ani pressed her lips together because Galia's assertion was unfortunately accurate—the back of the dress was practically a WELCOME TO THE CRACK billboard. Ani said carefully, "You could probably add some lace to the back to make it less of a plunge. And cups with extra lace to the front so it's not as sheer in the . . . chest."

"That would be an improvement," Kami's mom mused.

Even Kami's aunt seemed to consider it.

Kami stared down at the dress, inspecting the lace. "I love this pattern, so floral but not in a dowdy way."

"No." Her mom laughed. "No one would call that dowdy."

Kami glanced up again, inspired by something. "Oh my God, speaking of flowers, have I told you guys the flowers I'm thinking of for the wedding?"

She had not yet, and Ani was curious about this because it was part of the design she'd be working with to create one cohesive look for the wedding.

"I want lots of white, and obviously roses up the wazoo, but most importantly I want ranunculus in my bouquet and, like, everywhere. They're my absolute favorite flower."

Kami looked at Ani meaningfully at this last proclamation, and Ani practically stopped breathing. Ranunculus. In her bouquet. All over the winery grounds.

Their flower.

Ani was the one who introduced Kami to ranunculus; it was their thing together. They always got arrangements of ranunculus for each other. For special occasions or just because. Kami had become obsessed with the tight petals, the dark centers. Ani thought maybe Kami would have discarded her love of the flowers just like she discarded Ani, but no, apparently not.

Kami saying that ranunculus were still her favorite flower almost felt like she was saying Ani was still her favorite person. But she knew she wasn't.

And suddenly, this entire thing was unbearable. Kami in her wedding dresses, the outline of her breasts visible, her family missing Ani, everyone wanting her opinion, and the goddamn ranunculus that Kami had kept as one of her favorite things. Ani's face grew hot, almost to bursting, and she felt tears threatening to spill.

Ani gave a look of surprise, a show for everyone. "Oh my goodness, I'm sorry, I forgot I have to do something time-sensitive for work. You guys don't mind if I step out for five?"

It was weird of her, and this was work as much as anything else was work, but no one objected. Once Ani rounded the corner, she ran. She pushed the heavy glass door and stepped into the sunlight. The pressure behind her eyes built up, about to explode with tears. She slipped into a quiet alcove where she was sure she would be alone and let it out.

Ani cried hard. She cried for the way she'd come up short with Kami, for the way she'd been so alone ever since, for her inability to say no to Kami, for the fact that she'd never love anyone else the way she had loved Kami.

Every person she'd met since Kami had been a complete dud in one way or another. Two years, two whole years of not meeting anyone remotely right for her. It was a sign that she was destined to be unlucky in love her entire life.

She was wiping away the wetness on her face when she heard a voice ask, "Ani?"

A male voice.

She whipped around, away from her sad corner of concrete, and was met with the concerned princely eyes of Raffi Garabedian.

He was carrying a sleek leather briefcase in one hand and a wine carrier in the other, effortlessly commanding the space without even trying. He set both on the ground and approached her. He, broad-shouldered with a natural elegance, looking like a fantasy nobleman come to life.

She, a weeping mess. She hiccupped once and then wondered if a person could die from sheer mortification.

"Are you okay? Are you hurt?" he asked.

"Yes," she wanted to say. "I'm so, so hurt."

"I'm fine," she said, using the heel of her hand to push away tears. The way he was looking at Ani . . . was he genuinely worried about her? She wished she could melt into the concrete wall, dissolve into nothing, and spare herself the weight of his concern.

Raffi laid a gentle hand on her shoulder, and something inside her pulsed with delight. "You're clearly not fine. Can I help you somehow?"

Ani laughed helplessly, and Raffi removed his hand. Her traitorous mind thought, *No. Put it back.*

"Reverse time so I could somehow convince Kami to stay with me? Among taking back some other . . . mistakes?"

"I've been meaning to ask—" Raffi said, then cut himself off. He restarted. "I know you two dated, but it seems like things didn't . . . end well?"

Ani leaned against the wall and huffed out a big breath.

"I thought she was the love of my life. We even planned our wedding—what kind of music we'd choose, where we'd want it held, big or small. But neither of us actually proposed. Then, she dumped me. Two years ago. I hadn't seen her or talked to her since then, barring a string of embarrassing 'please take me back' texts I sent right after the breakup."

Around them, the stark lines of the brutalist architecture

loomed, the concrete walls and geometric shapes casting sharp shadows in the midday sun. Raffi seemed to be taking in her words. His eyes were engaged, and she could practically see his mind working. He wasn't dismissing her or mocking her. It wasn't a mistake telling him, that was a relief.

Ani continued, "And now I'm not only planning her actual wedding, but she invited me to watch her try on wedding dresses. I was just in there with her relatives, but I couldn't take it anymore."

Raffi visibly flinched.

"Don't go back," he said.

She laughed bitterly. "I can't do that."

"Sure you can." Raffi shifted around. "God, it's just like Kami to ask you to come to something like this. Kami's charming as hell, don't get me wrong, but she forgets that other people exist sometimes. That they have, you know, feelings. And that she might have to sacrifice her wants for someone else's needs."

He seemed to really know her, and his tone of voice made it sound personal, like they hadn't had a casual relationship, as she'd originally believed. There was something deeper there, something raw.

"Oh?" was all Ani said.

Raffi stiffened, then he changed his expression into one of coolness and brushed off her question with a dismissive wave of his hand. "I just know how she is. Always has to be the center of attention, always has to get her way."

Ani hadn't met anyone who had said anything like this about Kami before, and it was . . . refreshing. She wanted to press further, but she could tell he wasn't about to elaborate.

His voice had tightened just enough to betray him—he was not open to sharing whatever it was.

People in suits and business casual wove through the open atrium, their footsteps echoing against the hard surfaces, their voices blending into a low, steady murmur.

After a beat, Raffi exhaled, the tension in his shoulders easing as he flashed her a wry smile. "Which she did, once again. How many people can say they've got both of their exes planning their wedding?"

Ani laughed. "Kami really likes to keep 'em close." And then Ani realized this was the first time she had made light of their situation with Kami.

Raffi smiled. "Or, more likely, she just doesn't think about the fact that it's weird."

"It is *so* weird. I hope she'll be the only ex whose wedding I have to ever plan."

He tilted his head, studying her for a moment. "Why are you doing it then?"

Ani panicked. She could not, absolutely not, tell Raffi about her debts. Being Kami's weeping ex was bad enough; she couldn't also be the weeping ex who was not solvent. Raffi wouldn't understand that anyway. He'd think she was some idiot who couldn't manage money. And maybe she was.

"I can't say no to her," was what Ani said.

Raffi nodded, his jaw tight.

She felt an awkwardness in the air, so she asked, "So you dated her toward the end of high school?"

Raffi looked up sharply. "And first year of college. Why? She talking about me, spilling all my secrets?"

Ani chanced a half smirk. "What secrets do you have?"

He returned her smirk. "Wouldn't you like to know."

She would, actually. She found that she really, surprisingly would.

The way he was standing here, in the middle of uninspiring concrete shops, he was like a king. So tall and elegant, with his broad shoulders and dark eyes. He was in another suit today. Navy. And he was talking her down from her Kami meltdown, surprisingly successfully.

"Kami mentioned some family friend she dated around that time."

"Great things to say about me, I'm sure."

"Surprisingly, not much," she said. "But your families are close?"

Raffi shrugged. "In a way. They were business partners for a while. My dad managed the Mardians' money, invested for them, that kind of thing. They're one of his biggest clients, so he's always tried to maintain a good relationship with them. That's the only reason he's allowing this wedding on his property."

It took a second to understand what he was saying. "You mean a queer wedding?"

"Exactly. Ole Moushegh isn't exactly the most open-minded man."

Ani needed to know, so she asked it.

"And you?"

Raffi's stance relaxed, and he leaned back slightly, his hands sliding into his pockets as he gazed out toward the bustling atrium. "I'm glad we're doing it, barring the whole Kami thing." He turned to her fully then, his voice growing with conviction. "Show the Armenian community here that we can have a big fat gay Armenian wedding and it's okay. That the world doesn't end if we celebrate queerness. It makes us stronger, actually. What a concept!"

He wasn't just shrugging it off; he seemed invested in it. She didn't want to stereotype, but the typical Armenian man wasn't usually a champion of queer rights, so she figured Raffi was, at most, indifferent. But Raffi appeared enthusiastic. This part of him hadn't made its way through the rumor mill. Raffi Garabedian, playboy misogynist extraordinaire, and also a . . . proud queer ally?

She nodded in support of his words. Then she noticed, finally pulled out of her misery, that Raffi seemed happy to stand here and talk to her. His posture, his face, they were welcoming, like he had nowhere else in the world to be. Speaking of which, she did wonder what the hell he was doing at this shopping center in the Embarcadero.

She asked, "By the way, what brings you here?"

Raffi cleared his throat. "Our worlds collide again. I dropped off some of my wine with Kami's aunt earlier—"

Oh. She kept forgetting that Raffi's and Kami's families went way back, to the point where Raffi would be hand-delivering his wine to Kami's aunt. Ani also had been far too distracted to notice that Tantig Shoghig had wine bottles with her.

"Met her downstairs and loaded them into her car. Then, while I was in the area, figured I'd pop into some restaurants, beg them to buy our wine. It's going *great*," he said sarcastically.

"Shoot, that sounds tough."

"Got to keep trying."

Raffi picked up his briefcase and the wine carrier. "You good now? Or, you know, better?"

Ani gave him a small smile. "Definitely better."

He started to walk away, and Ani felt a sadness creep into her heart.

Then he turned and said, "Oh hey, tomorrow night I'm having a party at the winery. Small bites and all-you-can-drink Ô wine. Some friends, friends of friends. I know it's pretty far, but if you're around, maybe you'd like to come by? Sevenish." Reading her growing shock, presumably, he added, "Not a date. Just a party."

Ani swallowed. He was inviting her to a party with a bunch of his friends. Not a date, true, but it still somehow felt . . . she didn't know. Intimate.

"Um, maybe," she said. God, that sounded like a no, and she didn't want it to sound like a no. "It's far, but who knows, maybe something will come up on the site and I'll be there." That wasn't much better. She tried yet again, "Sounds like a great night. I want to come, if I can."

Raffi gave the tiniest smile. "Happy to hear it."

Then he walked away, and somehow Ani felt she could deal with Kami and the rest of the wedding dresses now.

She also thought she should make an important call to Nareh soon.

9

Ani

IT WAS SATURDAY afternoon, and Ani's sister, Talar, had one hour of time when she wasn't working, so the five of them (their parents, Talar, and Talar's husband, Nshan) gathered at their parents' house for an early dinner.

Ani was currently in full kid mode. Splayed on her parents' couch, eating manti. She had helped make them at least. She and her mother had cheated and used premade wonton wrappers for the dough, so they weren't as perfect as when her grandma Yiayia made them, but still, they ended up delicious.

It was a clear, cold afternoon, and the sun was setting, filling her childhood home with golden light. Ani had survived the rest of the wedding fitting with Kami and her family, and then she went home to work on more aspects of Kami and Grace's wedding the rest of the day.

The fitting. It had been on track to be a huge disaster, with Ani losing all sense of professionalism . . . until Raffi. He'd waltzed in like a savior, right when she'd needed him. She didn't know she'd needed him.

The way he listened to her, the way he continued to buck

every stereotype she'd imagined (besides the way he dressed, which was still, very much, to impress). There was something about Raffi.

That's why she needed to call her friend Nareh, who had originally warned her off the guy. Ani had Talar's secondhand perspective; now she needed Nareh's firsthand one. Really, she needed to confirm that the Raffi she knew was, in fact, the same person Nareh had cautioned her about. But that call could wait.

For now, she had one other unpleasant order of business. Ani still hadn't told her sister or family whose wedding she was planning.

Her mother hovered over Nshan, asking in Armenian, "Would you like more, my son?"

"Yes, please, that would be great," he said with a smile.

Ani bristled somewhat. Nshan was fine, always in a good mood, but he was just too . . . comfortable being doted on. He didn't so much as once put a plate in the sink. But Talar never said a single negative word about him, so maybe she was fine with it.

When her mom had refilled Nshan's plate and finally sat to eat herself, Ani said, "So, that new luxury wedding I booked. Did I, uh, tell you whose wedding it is?"

"No, tsakougus," her mother said.

"Someone we know?" Talar raised an eyebrow. Her parents might have been oblivious, but Talar, the lawyer, was not. She drank her tahn and kept her eyes trained on Ani.

"You could say that. It's actually a funny story. I didn't realize who had booked it because it's two brides, and I'd only talked to one of the brides. This actress, Grace."

"An actress! How very interesting," said her father. "Anything we know her in?"

"Not unless you're into indie films," Ani said.

"What is 'indie'?" Bab whispered to Mom.

Ani smiled, then continued. "But then I got to the venue and met the other bride and it was—well, it was Kami."

Talar choked on her tahn, and it appeared to go straight up her nose because she grabbed a napkin and coughed and blew. Her father jumped up to pat Talar on her back. Nshan surveyed the scene with mild interest.

"Who's Kami?" he asked.

Ani rolled her eyes. He had met Kami twice, a few weeks before the breakup.

"Her—" came Talar's strained voice. She coughed and appeared to regain her composure. "Ex-girlfriend! The one who broke her heart into a thousand pieces." Now she rounded on Ani, and Ani knew how opposing counsel felt standing across from Talar. "You're planning her wedding? Are you out of your mind?"

Mom and Bab jumped in at once, admonishing Talar for her harshness.

"But," Mom said, "Talar has a point. Why are you doing this, Ani jan?"

Ani, after some thought, now had a much better answer for this than "Because I can't say no to Kami," like she'd stupidly told Raffi. Or better than the truth, which is that she was in massive, crushing debt and needed the job.

"This is the only *true* luxury wedding I've ever gotten," she said. With the Avedissians, Ani had been so busy with the details of the wedding, she hadn't had time to show off to her family all that she was doing. And thank goodness, because look how that turned out.

"Hey—" Talar said.

"Tal," Ani said. "You told me—and I quote—'I'm going to be penny-pinching left and right,' then handed me a hot glue gun and wished me luck."

Talar gestured at her, sputtering, "You're amazing at DIY!"

"Thank you, but anyway," Ani continued, "the point is, my portfolio is lacking, and if I want to attract more high-end clients, this wedding, this massive budget and the vision they have . . . it has the potential to completely transform my career."

Her family all stared at her. Except Nshan, who kept eating.

"I don't want to say I told you so, Ani jan, but this is what happens when you quit your stable job in law and start your own business. You have to take clients you don't want to."

Ani's grip on the couch tightened, her knuckles white. Of course her mother would say that. Anytime Ani mentioned something remotely challenging about her work, her parents reminded her, explicitly or not, that she'd walked away from the safe, prestigious path they had dreamed for her. That she had chosen instability, stress, and, in their eyes, unnecessary hardship.

But what was the point of reminding them why she took the risk? Why she had decided to pursue a career that brought her joy instead of a more stable one? It would only lead to another exhausting debate, another round of sighs and tsks, eventually melting into passive aggression.

So she swallowed the anger rising in her throat, let it simmer under the surface, and forced her voice into something calm, measured.

"She's a client, Mom," Ani said carefully. "That's all."

Her mother squinted at her, calling her bluff. "You're doing okay? Your heart is not . . . hurting?"

But Ani wouldn't let her have it. "Yes. God. I'm fine. I can handle this."

"Well . . . if you are okay with it," her father said tentatively.

Talar shook her head at her sister. "I don't believe the craziness of this situation, but if you think this is a career move, then damn, go for it."

"I don't need your blessing," Ani said. And wanted to add, "little sister." She didn't like the way her family treated her like this poor soul, this fragile thing. She supposed she had been devastated—for years—because of Kami. But still. "I promise I think it's a good move."

"All right, all right," Talar said. She stood up. "I'm getting more tabbouleh, anyone want?"

Nshan responded, "Me!"

ANI WAS DRIVING back home, thinking that in a few hours, it would be time for Raffi's party. Which she still hadn't fully decided whether or not she should go to.

She needed to talk to Nareh. Maybe Nareh wouldn't even pick up. They were friends who saw each other twice a year or so when their friend groups aligned. Ani really liked Nareh; she just hadn't had the chance to get close to her yet. Still, Nareh was always the sweetest, and Ani knew she'd be honest with her.

Screw it. She'd call. Ani used voice command to dial her friend, and Nareh picked up after a couple of rings.

"Ani! Hi!" Nareh's voice was perky and excited.

"How're you doing?"

"Good, good. We're just at home, prepping some dinner."

Ani heard another woman's voice, deeper and slower, ask, "Is that Ani? Tell her hi."

"Erebuni says hi."

Ani knew about Nareh for years but didn't say much other than "Hey" until she found out Nareh was getting married to Erebuni, another Armenian woman. Another queer Armenian woman in her social circle? Amazing. Ani was still a paralegal when the other two got married, but she was thinking of making the switch around that time. In fact, it was Nar and Erebuni's wedding that gave her the final push to quit her job and make her wedding planning dream come true. Ani had helped them with their invitations and assisted in the day-of coordination of their lovely wedding. She envisioned one day planning another queer Armenian wedding from the ground up but doubted it would ever happen. She never thought she'd be planning *Kami's*.

"What's new?" Ani asked.

"Oh, you know, working and finishing up this round of fertility treatments. Feels like it's never going to happen . . ."

Erebuni's voice cut in. "It's been so hard. But I'm still hopeful."

"Thank God for Erebuni, honestly. There is no way I could get through this hellish process without her."

Ani's heart clenched. She loved what they had—it was unshakably tender—and she yearned for it. She thought she had had it with Kami, but Kami thought differently.

Still, she felt for them and could only imagine what it must be like to want to be a parent so badly but not have it happen for so long. And they really would be such wonderful parents.

"You guys are the best. Sending you all the good vibes," Ani said.

"Thanks, jan. So, what's up?"

The freeway was mostly empty right now as Ani sped down it. "Well, kind of funny. Uh, I'm planning this Armenian wedding and it's going to happen at an Armenian winery."

"Wait, wait, pause—Armenian *winery*? I need details," Nareh said.

"It's called Ô. Stunning property. I'm helping do some landscaping work for them, too."

Nareh stayed quiet on the line, most likely waiting for Ani to get to the point. "And, uh, the reason I'm calling is that Ô is owned by the Garabedian family—you know, mobster-y dad. And his son . . . Raffi is running it. So I've been working with him a lot."

"Wait. Raffi Garabedian?"

"Yep."

Nareh's voice grew sympathetic. "Oh no, I'm so sorry. Is he hitting on you nonstop?"

"Um, actually, not really. That's why I wanted to call. You told me about him a few years back, and I want to confirm that it's the same person. 'Cause he's been, well, great. Easy to work with, hasn't pushed any boundaries."

Nareh did not sound convinced. "Raffi Garabedian, like blue-velvet Gucci shoes Raffi Garabedian, right?"

"The very same," Ani said, her voice sounding shaky.

"Isn't he a doctor?"

"He was, but I guess now he runs a winery."

Nareh appeared to be thinking, and Ani imagined her staring up at the ceiling as she tapped her memories. "I mean, he wasn't the *worst*. He wasn't handsy or anything, but he was just so corny. He called me 'reporter girl' and said I was old-fashioned for wanting to go on a date first. He talked way too close, invaded my space, and just, like, assumed I would want to hook up with him. So arrogant."

Raffi had asked her to lunch twice, but the first time she believed it was simply to make up for their early interactions. The second time, well, they'd been having such a beautiful morning together, she was even borderline flirting, so it didn't feel inappropriate. Even when he was pretending they were a married couple, it felt fun, not gross. And his arm around her? That had felt more than fun. It had been . . . exhilarating.

Ani responded, "Damn, sorry. I just wanted to remember what you had said about him. It was a while ago, right?"

"That whole thing at Explore Armenia? That must have been about five years ago. Right 'Buni?"

"Five and a half, yes," came Erebuni's voice.

A long time ago. Raffi had alluded to many things changing since that time, that a lot had happened. She wanted to hope.

Nareh's words didn't align with the Raffi Ani knew, although he'd shown hints of it here and there. She wanted to hear from Raffi himself, *how* he went from that Raffi Nareh had met at Explore Armenia to the one Ani was working with now. Though . . . should she? He said himself he hadn't been in a relationship in quite some time and didn't elaborate. Maybe he wasn't pushy with women anymore, but it's possible he was still a one-night-stand man. And Ani wasn't about to waste her time on a man who was allergic to commitment.

Ani thanked Nareh and Erebuni, hung up, then exited to take Van Ness up to her apartment.

She needed to make a decision. Raffi's party. She shouldn't go; she really shouldn't. The prudent thing to do would be to stay home or call up Sanan or one of her other friends and go out with them here in the city. Definitely not put on a little white dress and platform sandals and drive up to Napa. That would not be a good idea.

Right?

10

Raffi

THE PARTY WAS in full swing. Raffi had a baller playlist that filled the space with uplifting, sexy vibes; the food he had catered from a local chef was bomb; and his friends had come and brought even more friends. His biggest partier buddy, Devin, had shown up with an entire ream of counterfeit wine-ratings stickers, and after he sipped each, he declared it a winner and slapped a 99 on the bottle. Raffi turned around and gave all the wine-related compliments to the workers, who actually knew what the hell they were doing. All he did, he said, was provide moral support and not get in the way of the smart people who ran things.

And yet Raffi himself was not happy. Ani hadn't come. Maybe she forgot. Maybe she was still so hung up on Kami there was no way she even saw him as anything other than a pesky *vendor*. He thought they'd had a moment, with the flowers and the EpiPen, but maybe he was wrong. After he invited her in person, he hadn't followed up via text or anything because he didn't want to come off as desperate. But maybe he should have. The invite was too casual. He hadn't given her enough hard details; he should have—

"Raffi!"

Before he saw them, two pairs of arms were thrown around him. Riley and Maya, the two most boisterous members of Mad, Bad, and Dangerous Book Club, squeezed hard and then unwrapped themselves from him. Lana and Kennedy were close behind, giving him quick hugs and smiles.

They were all Stanford MBAs doing impressive work just a few years after graduating. Kennedy and Maya, who also had master's degrees in education, cofounded a progressive elementary school; Riley had landed a job in health care, vowing to create change from the inside; and Lana had invented a way to turn landfill trash into building materials and had just gotten her patent approved. And he was . . . putzing around a winery.

Riley shouted over the music. "We're so proud of what you're doing! Iconic behavior, Raffi. Utterly iconic."

MBD Book Club met twice a year, down from their monthly meetups while they were in school, but they still kept it up. Seeing everyone outside the walls of their book club was a treat, and he basked in the warmth of old rhythms.

Maya beamed in his direction, waxing nostalgic. "Remember when he read his first Carmen Maria Machado? How his mind was so blown? Look how far he's come."

Kennedy added, "Or when we read 'Cat Person' and he was like, 'Wait, why didn't she just go home?' So sweet and innocent."

Raffi waved them off. "Okay, okay. We don't need to relive Raffi's greatest hits of becoming a feminist."

It was true, though. He owed them so much.

Riley glanced toward the counter where various vintages were being uncorked. "Seriously, though, this place is impressive. Now excuse me while I grab a glass and chat up that cute pourer."

Lana nodded appreciatively toward Justine, who Riley made a beeline toward. "She *is* attractive. Not anyone you're dating?"

"No," Raffi said, jarred by the thought. Justine was nice-looking, but first of all, Raffi would never date or hook up with someone who worked for him, and secondly, he simply never had those kinds of thoughts about her.

There was only one person that piqued his interest. One person who was hung up on her ex and *not* interested in him. "Still single over here."

Kennedy rolled her eyes. "Hopeless!"

Lana said, matter-of-factly, "No, no. There's always hope."

Raffi scratched the back of his head. "Fill up as much as you want, by the way. On the house."

His friends took the invitation. He downed his third glass, surveyed his party, then decided to get another.

As he was getting his refill, the song changed to *the* one everyone loved, this winter's number one hit, upbeat and celebratory. Shouts and whoops filled the air. His friends, acquaintances, and people he didn't know created a dance floor in the middle of the winery, swaying, shaking, and two-stepping.

Riley grabbed his hand. "C'mon, Raffi, let's dance."

Raffi shook his head. "Nah, I'm good. You guys go on. I have host duties."

"If you change your mind, you know where we'll be," said Maya, and she pranced toward the newly minted club in the middle of Ô.

Raffi watched them, as sadness so profound filled his body he thought he might vomit. He was glad for everyone, pleased they were having a good time and that the party was successful, but he felt so starkly alone in that moment.

His father refused to come tonight, saying he didn't want to see what went on at one of Raffi's wasteful schemes, a stupid attempt at drumming up business. His mother was in Monaco, escaping the harsh winter and likely asleep at this hour. His brother was dead.

They had always been two brothers, a whole thing that had been severed.

Sevan should have been here, not just tonight but the entire time. Advising Raffi against med school because it was so obviously a bad fit for him. Helping him figure out girls, women, instead of the debacle that was his love life. Swapping clothes, playing ball, doing stupid childish things in their twenties like crushing cans on their foreheads and hiking Half Dome in the middle of the night. Sevan should have been here for all of it.

Riley motioned yet again for Raffi to come hit the floor as she attempted a daring take on the lawn mower move and somehow pulled it off. But he felt no desire to join.

Raffi did not dance. Not anymore. He used to, and in fact, he'd had a bit of a knack for it. His mother had secretly put him into ballroom dancing classes, which Raffi found he loved. Mom had told him, "You can move. Everyone can learn and get better, but there's also God-given talent and you have it. Let's not waste it."

The Argentine tango had been his favorite. He'd won several regional competitions, which his mother and Sevan had attended, clapping him on the back, hugging him tight. They'd both been so supportive. But then he quit the hobby completely. His dad had never found out, so he wasn't the reason he stopped.

Raffi had dropped his classes after Sevan died, had quit dancing altogether, and most of the time being around music and other people dancing was fine. But sometimes? It was unbearable.

Raffi took advantage of being the proprietor of this winery by topping off his glass a quarter inch from the brim.

He was holding this glass, inspecting it and calculating how stupid it had been to fill it that high while wearing tailored wool, when Ani floated in.

The music faded to a muffled throb while he took in the sight of her. She donned a short white dress and high platform heels. The soft lighting caught in her hair and shimmered against her skin, like the room had saved its glow just for her. And she was searching the room.

She had come. That was the thing.

It wasn't just how stunning she was—and make no mistake, she was st-uh-nning—it was that her presence somehow took him from crying under a metaphorical bridge with a not-so-metaphorical bottle of wine to feeling like this night was suddenly full of possibilities. He didn't care to analyze why; he just wanted to get high off the sensation of it for now.

Ani found him and strutted over in those heels.

"You came," he said, and realized he sounded far too excited. No game, Raff, no game.

"I'm just checking out the lighting after dark," she said, obviously lying.

"In your finest workwear, I see."

Ani looked down at herself, and he detected a pinkening of her cheeks. "This old thing? I happened to have it on when it crossed my mind that it would be a good idea to see how your venue handles night lighting and sound." Her eyes darted around. "Very well, I must say."

Raffi fake bowed. "Thank you, Miss Wedding Planner. I live for your accolades."

A smile tugged at the corner of her lips, and she seemed to be fighting it.

"Miss Wedding Planner would like a drink," she said. "What've you got?"

Now it was Raffi's turn to hide his blush. Hearing her use his nickname for her gave him a rush of blood in places unmentionable. Then he had to snap himself out of it because getting a visible hard-on at your own party was not cool. Nor anyone else's party, except maybe those elite Silicon Valley orgies he kept hearing about and not getting invited to.

"We've got a bunch of local IPAs, Guinness, every classic cocktail you could think of, but absolutely no wine. Gross, hate the stuff."

"Totally. Grape corpse water," she said, again with that smile.

"So, cabernet? Or are you a chardonnay type?" he said, turning toward the counter, thanking his lucky stars that his wine was actually good and he'd have a chance to impress this incredible woman.

"Sauvignon blanc, actually," she said. "Steel barrel aged is my preference, but I go for oak, too."

"Maybe I should be calling you Miss Wine Spectator instead?"

Ani shrugged. "Had a period of time when I went to wineries a lot."

Based on the way her expression dropped, Raffi suspected that period of time coincided precisely with when Ani and Kami had dated. He decided not to pursue that avenue of conversation. But also? A bit of his optimism slumped.

What the hell was he doing, when Ani was so clearly still hung up on her ex? Her ex who she had to see constantly, for whom she was basically on-call emotional support staff? His interest in Ani was all kinds of stupid, and he would not continue flirting with her. After handing her the wine, he would walk away and mingle.

"Lucky for you," he said, "all our whites are steel aged."

Raffi reached over the counter, giving Ted, one of the pourers, a wink like, "I got this, thank you. You can see I'm doing this to show off to a girl, right? Sorry for getting in your way." He grabbed his nicest sauv by the neck, poured Ani a decent-sized glass, and handed it to her. Then he picked up his own monstrous red again and was only now mortified by the *screams-alcoholic* size of it.

Ani raised an eyebrow when she caught sight of his glass. But Raffi, undeterred, decided it would be rude to walk away now, so he lifted his absolute unit of a goblet and spoke his benediction in English and Armenian.

"To the woman who saved my life, cheers."

Before they could clink, before Raffi could fully take in that pleased expression on Ani's face and the slight flush to her cheeks, their quiet moment was toppled on its head.

Riley, seemingly smashed on free wine and high on her

favorite music, bounded over to Raffi, grabbed his face in both hands, and kissed him on the cheek, which was a very Riley thing to do. Always physically lovey-dovey after a few drinks. But today, the force of her affection caught Raffi by surprise and bumped him in a way that the entire contents of his Incredible Hulk–sized cabernet sauvignon erupted from his glass and soaked Ani's very white dress.

Ani stared down at the damage. It was worse than the matcha latte she had pegged him with, and Raffi felt so horrible, he did the first thing he could think of, which was grab a flimsy napkin off the counter and rush to blot the stain. He turned back toward Ani while Riley caught up and gasped at the entire display, saying a string of words he couldn't quite hear, and he must have been a little tipsier than he thought, because his hand headed straight for the heart of the stain, on Ani's chest. He reached for the stain, nearly at his target, when—oh, *no*—the napkin slipped right out of his grasp and his hand landed on something soft and warm and oh my God that was a boob. Hand on the boob.

Raffi caught Ani's eye, her sheer horror, and he removed his hand as immediately as the apologies began to flow.

But he shut up as soon as Ani's mouth opened and she started to speak. "This was . . . This was . . ."

This was what? She seemed to be referring to the dress, by the way she stared down at herself. Had he ruined a priceless family heirloom? What if it was some vintage sixties creation her parents had brought over from Lebanon and now he'd destroyed it?

". . . a mistake," she finished.

With that, she turned and stormed away, toward the doors. Any bit of hope he'd had at a great night, all that optimism, was crushed.

Devin, his party animal buddy, chose that exact moment to drape his arm around Raffi and say way too loudly, "Don't worry. Plenty of other hotties, right? We know how the ole Raffi G operates."

"Bro," Raffi said angrily—much more angrily than he had expected to become at that statement—but it was too late. The doors had shut behind Ani.

Now he could finally hear Riley. "I am SO sorry. I let the music and the vino get to me. She looked wrecked. You need to go after her, like, yesterday."

"Aw, c'mon, this man doesn't chase anyone. Women chase him."

Riley put her hands on her hips. "While that may be true, Mr. I Buy Up Hospitals and Chop Them Up Into Parts—"

"Hey! Wait, do I know you?"

"Devin. We were in Operations Management together. Riley?"

"Oh. Your hair is short now, I—"

Raffi didn't hear the rest of their conversation. He rushed out of his own party into the night.

The chilly evening air sharpened his senses and made him feel far less drunk as he searched for Ani. It wasn't difficult. A car door slammed and an engine ignited, along with bright lights. Raffi ran toward them.

A part of him wondered if maybe the accidental wine spill followed by the accidental grope were all for the best. He shouldn't be pursuing Ani. They still had well over six months of working closely together. Maybe that was fate intervening in the form of a whopper wine pour and a careening Riley. Telling him to *stay the fuck away.*

But the thought of her leaving, sopping wet in a wine stain of his doing, driving off alone and possibly even *crying*, created a leaden feeling in his stomach. He couldn't allow that.

God, what had gotten into him? A woman hadn't made him feel this way in, well, ever. He didn't need to think about that now, though, because he had reached her car.

"Ani," he shouted, lightly slapping the rear passenger door twice just as the vehicle began to reverse. Raffi jumped back in a move of self-preservation—at least he still had good instincts, even three heavy glasses in. The car stopped suddenly, lurching forward from the abrupt halt.

He heard swearing from inside her car. She shut it off and swung open the door, and despite Ani's obvious anger, he couldn't help but feel relief that she hadn't simply ignored him and left. He had a real chance to apologize.

"—do you think you're doing? I almost ran you over!"

"You didn't. My survival skills are top-notch," he said, feeling a goofy grin spread across his face.

Ani unbuckled herself and got out of the car, slammed the door shut, crossed her arms, and stared at him. "What do you want?"

Raffi took a deep breath. The sight of her infuriated face was intoxicating. He could feel the anger rolling off her in waves, and he wondered what other types of emotions she could elicit with that intensity. Then he told himself to put the testosterone on mute and turn on his brain instead.

"Listen, I needed to give you a real apology for destroying your dress and—" How should he phrase this? "The napkin slip."

"A slip, was it?" she said, sneering. "Or getting bold and handsy after a couple drinks?"

Raffi planted his feet firmly on the ground and looked straight into Ani's eyes. He needed her to understand. "I promise you, I would never touch someone without their consent. Ever. I know some of what you've heard, but that? That was never me."

Ani let out a breath, defusing. She seemed to believe his truth. He felt the blood pumping through his body at the sight of her chest rising and falling and remembered how soft and warm she was. He couldn't help himself. Raffi took one step closer and lowered his voice. "And if I was touching you in a place like that, on purpose, believe me, you would *know* it was on purpose."

Raffi watched her swallow, the tiny bump on her throat bob up and down. He'd pushed, possibly too far, but Ani wasn't running.

"Apology accepted," she whispered. Then, somewhat louder but still sounding unsure of herself, she said, "I—I need to go. Get this stain out. The sooner the better."

An idea hit him then, and it was delicate, so he needed to make sure he didn't sound like the scallywag she suspected he was. "Why don't you take care of it here? In the kitchens. We probably have whatever cleaners you need."

Ani raised a skeptical eyebrow at him. "And what would I wear in the meantime? Bra and panties?"

Now Raffi visibly swallowed. He didn't know how she'd

take this, but it was the best idea he had. "We have T-shirts. Men's XL would fit like a dress on you."

Ani appeared to consider it, looking away from him. "Fine. Do you have salt? Dishwashing liquid?"

His spirits lifted. She was going to stay. "Check and check."

She followed him back to the office without a word. The bass of the music from the main room pumped against the walls while Raffi crouched down to open a box of Ô T-shirts he'd had made. He dug through until he found a men's XL and handed it to Ani.

She was a sight in the bright lights of the office, arms crossed over her stained dress, made up to the nines, those chunky high heels making her legs look so taut. He wanted to get back down on his knees and—

No, no, he wouldn't let his mind go there. Too tempting. Too much wine. He had to restrain himself.

Ani eyed him and shook her head slightly.

"What?" he asked.

"You're going to stand there while I change?"

Yes, preferably.

Raffi truly had to stop himself from blurting, "Is that an invitation?"

"Right, my bad."

He stepped outside the door and waited, listening to the music and hoping his guests were all fine without him. He had no desire to go back out there. The only room he wanted to be in was the one with Ani. He was being a tutum kloukh, the soft insult his grandma would lob at anyone who did something silly. "Pumpkin head." Hollowed out of all its guts, just an empty gourd making stupid decisions.

Honestly, he was still feeling honored that Ani had showed up at all. His winery was an hour plus away from San Francisco, where it seemed she lived. He wondered about it. Was she in an apartment? Did she live at home? What neighborhood? What were her favorite restaurants and shops? What did she do in her free time? Was she currently seeing anyone, casually dating, or what? He'd need to tap his Armenian gossip network to find out. Or stop being a coward and just ask her.

He'd distanced himself from the Armenian community somewhat once he started his book club transformation. The Hyes had seen too much. He realized how much of a bad rep he'd given himself after years of sleeping with the hotties of the Bay Area Armenian scene and not calling them back. *Lala*. He'd sent other apologies in addition to hers, but it still didn't feel like enough.

The door opened a crack and Ani peeked out. "It's a little shorter than I expected. Is anyone out there?"

"Not a soul." Translation: Please come out so that I may see, for my eyes only.

"Okay. Let's do this fast."

She appeared in the hall, a white Ô printed on a long black shirt that skimmed her mid-thighs. The baggy shirt and her platform heels were quite a sight. He may have been a pumpkin head, but he was a pumpkin head who was currently leading a deadly sexy woman wearing only a T-shirt through the halls of his winery, so he considered that a win.

Ani had spread her burgundy-splotched dress over the countertop, and Raffi struggled not to imagine her in that dress, splayed across the stainless steel. He helped her straighten it out, and their fingers grazed for the shortest moment, which sent a rush through his body. He was really far gone. Every moment around Ani made him feel high out of his mind, in the best way. He didn't want it to end.

Ani said, "Thanks for this. I don't know if we'll get it all out, but attacking early is our best shot. I really love this dress."

Raffi was curious to see if it was a vintage or super valuable item he'd destroyed. He was slightly relieved to read ZARA on the label, but then supposed it didn't matter since Ani clearly adored it.

"I'm going to use a lot of salt. That okay?" she asked, almost as a challenge.

"Use the whole bucket if you need to."

Before he could stop her and grab the container himself, she stood on her tiptoes to reach the salt on a high shelf, the bottom of her shirt lifted up. So high. Panty skimming. He could almost make out a color, possibly blue . . .

Heat climbed up his neck. He forced himself to look away, then grabbed a discarded dish towel and began folding it into a tidy trifold. He was a bit of a neat freak, yes, but more than anything it was crucial to have something, anything, to do besides stare.

Ani's heels clicked back over to the dress. "Good. I'd be bummed if I ruined it. I spent way too much money on it at a time when I really shouldn't have."

"Oh?"

Ani made a face, like she realized she'd said something she shouldn't. She smothered the stain in salt. "It's fine, though. Everything's fine."

That did not make it sound like everything was fine, but he

honestly had no idea what she was talking about and he was still a little dizzy from that view of her thighs, so he kept his mouth shut.

"Dish soap?" she asked him.

Raffi was grateful for a task that would tear his mind and eyes away from the oversized T-shirt that had somehow become the sexiest thing he'd ever seen. He roamed the unfamiliar kitchen like it was uncharted wilderness, locating the sink, then a bottle of dish soap.

He returned to Ani and presented the bottle like a prize.

She snatched it from him, no time for their fingers to meet. Good. Wise. Probably for the best.

He shoved his hands into his pockets so he wouldn't do something stupid, like reach for a paper towel just to get closer. He was a grown man. He had willpower. He had degrees. He had intimate knowledge of the 1855 wine classification system of Bordeaux. He could absolutely survive a woman in a baggy shirt and heels.

Still, he averted his eyes with monk-like determination and muttered, "Let me know if you need anything else."

Ani glanced up from her work and regarded him. He caught the flicker of a smile tug at her mouth, like she could see right through him and was generously pretending not to.

He rubbed the back of his neck and took a big, possibly unnecessary step back. Just in case she was also psychic.

"I'm good for now," she said. Then she busied herself with the dress again. "So, uh, was that a girl you're dating?"

Raffi's brain had to work fast, which was difficult at this stage of inebriation and horniness. A girl, a girl, which girl?

"Uh—" was what his mouth put forward.

Ani looked up from her dress with a skeptical expression. "The one who kissed you?"

He had been kissed? Oh!

"Riley? Oh God, no. We're just friends, and I'm not her type anyway. No man is. That's just her personality—excitable at parties, always kissing people."

"Oh," Ani said, shaking the salt off her dress with genuine surprise on her face. That was good; he could see the wheels turning and they were moving in his favor. This was, he realized, the first time Ani had shown any verbal interest in him in that way. He didn't even know for sure if she was interested in men, although the way she had melted into him when he hugged her at the tile store, pretending to be a married couple, suggested she might be attracted to him. Was part of the reason she had run off so angrily not just because of the dress but because she thought he was hooking up with Riley?

Feeling brain cells returning to him, Raffi thought he should explain further. "She's part of my book club, Mad, Bad, and Dangerous. I joined not realizing it was a feminist book club and—"

Ani froze, her hands buried in soapy water, her dress half-draped over the edge of the sink. "You joined—" she started, then stopped, pulling her hands out of the water and shaking them absently, droplets flying everywhere. "Wait, you are *currently* part of a feminist book club?"

Raffi was suddenly excited at the prospect of sharing about MBD. He loved having discussions with Riley, Lana, Maya, and Kennedy, having brand-new thoughts awaken. It was like he could feel himself growing, and he wanted to explain this to Ani.

"Sure am. Our latest was *Sister Outsider*, which—though I don't say this lightly, even as someone who tends to be a generous reader—was genius. I'm trying to commit some quotes to memory. There's one that's been echoing in my head: how sometimes we're blessed to be able to choose the manner of our revolution but most often 'we must do battle where we are standing.' I mean, damn. During the discussions I usually listen more than I speak, but when it comes down to it, I just love a good fucking sentence. A powerful sentence."

Raffi had to stop his recap because Ani was staring at him open-mouthed and he was worried a fly had landed on his face or some other such horror.

"Who . . . are you?" she asked.

Raffi shrugged. "I like reading."

Ani squinted at him, her head tilting slightly as if that might help her see him more clearly. She wiped her hands on a towel, her movements slow and deliberate, like she was buying time to process what she'd just heard. "Yeah, but shouldn't you be reading books like *Rich Dad Poor Dad*? Or if you're into fiction, like Ayn Rand or H. G. Wells?"

"Never really got into sci-fi."

"You know what I mean!"

"Honestly, I stumbled into it. I didn't realize what kind of book club it was, but the members, now my friends, were so patient and just plain kind to me. I felt like I could learn all this material without being judged. So I did."

That had made all the difference. He was incredibly thankful for their gift of compassion.

Ani seemed to shake herself out of her momentary stupor,

then soaked the stained fabric in detergent. "Interesting. That's . . . really unusual. In a good way. I mean, people don't always—they're not always—open, I guess."

She scrunched her dress together, rubbing the soap all over.

"I got lucky," he said. "A good group of people can change everything."

Or one person. One incredible person.

She gave a tiny nod. "Yeah," she whispered.

Ani turned on the cold water tap and watched it douse her dress.

She glanced at him. "You're missing your party."

Raffi stayed where he was, on the other side of the kitchen. *Be cool, be cool.* "They're fine without me."

After a moment, Ani lifted the dress and surveyed her work. The stain was almost gone, but the fabric still appeared discolored.

"It's the synthetics. Harder to get stained, but once one seeps in, much harder to get out." Ani sounded defeated, and Raffi felt really fucking bad for ruining her dress. He had done this, put that look on her face. He should figure out a way to—

"I should go," she said.

Damn it, the moment was over. What kind of dish soap did they have in this place? Maybe it was too eco-friendly, wasn't grease-cutting enough. And it had just blown his chances of getting closer to Ani.

"Sure, whatever you like," he said, trying hard not to betray his disappointment over the fact that she wanted to leave.

"Can I?" She motioned down to the T-shirt.

"Of course, it's yours."

"I can find my way out," she said at the kitchen door.

Aka "Don't follow me to my car." Okay, noted. He followed her just into the hall, since that was where he was headed, too.

"Drive safely," he said, like an Armenian mom. Good God, his game was crushed.

But that got her to turn around and give him the tiniest smile. "Thanks," she said. Then, "Pari kisher."

He returned her "good night," then reluctantly rejoined his party.

11

Ani

ANI STOOD IN the floral studio of Napa's premier florist, Tilde, a place whose work she'd seen in *Brides* and *Martha Stewart* and even *Architectural Digest*. A place she never thought she'd be working with to create the floral concepts for her clients' wedding.

She was surrounded by works of natural art in every corner of the bright space. The air smelled like lavender and fresh soil, and the soft hum of classical music played in the background. The celebratory aspect of the moment was only dampened by Kami, who was hanging all over Grace, sending complicated feelings to the pit of Ani's stomach. But for some reason, Ani didn't feel as horrible as she had at the bridal shop. Maybe she was starting to get over it? Or maybe she was simply numbing to Kami's presence.

Or maybe it was that she couldn't stop thinking about Raffi. Raffi, stepping close to her, saying in the most casual offhanded manner, "If I was touching you in a place like that, on purpose, believe me, you would *know* it was on purpose." How her body responded, so quickly, so intensely, to his words.

How she wanted to step right up to him and dare him, "So do it." She wanted to see what those hands could do, what that gorgeous mouth could do.

But that's probably how it started with every woman and Raffi, wasn't it? He'd whisper some such sexy thing, and boom, they'd fall into bed together and that was the end. Despite his unreal, Disney-prince level of handsome, and despite all the experience he'd supposedly had, she'd always assumed, before two nights ago, that he wasn't all that good in bed. Not a generous lover, a taker, fast and selfish. But after what he'd said to her, the tingles it sent all over her flesh, she thought her assessment could have been wrong. Maybe he was incredible in bed.

But why was she pursuing this line of thought at all? She wanted a great love; she didn't want a great fuck.

Well, she wanted that, too. But the love! The love was far more important. A necessary ingredient without which she was uninterested—mostly—in the sex.

"I'm Madison, nice to meet you."

The hand of a tall, pretty brunette woman came into view and interrupted Ani's dangerous musings. She was not the main designer, Ani knew from research, but that was fine. She doubted Jeannie, the woman who had started it all, would be taking unknown clients personally at this point in her career. Ani wondered if she'd ever get close to that type of success. A household name in wedding planning. Sought after. Exclusive. She highly doubted it.

"Ani, and these are my clients, Grace and Kami."

The two of them did make a pretty picture, she had to admit. And they looked like they belonged here. Ani felt a little out of place and wondered if Madison could tell she was wearing discount rack shoes and a cheap belt. This place, smelling of fragrant florals, also smelled of money. A clear DO NOT ENTER sign for anyone who had to wonder if this place was in their budget.

She needed to steel herself and begin her pitch. And for some reason, Raffi's words floated into her head. "You were amazing in there. You came in like some deity who smoothed over the whole situation. You knew exactly how to placate him." The awe in his voice. Like she did something he never would have been able to pull off, not in a million years.

"Grace and Kami are envisioning a neoclassical design for their wedding florals. Invoking classical antiquity. Lush arrangements with an abundance of white and cream flowers, roses, peonies, hydrangeas, and"—she did not swallow, she did not choke, when she said the next word—"ranunculus, complemented with olive branches and laurel leaves. We're talking urns overflowing with florals, delicate garlands filling the space. The venue is a new winery. I'll show you some images in a moment so you can get an idea."

Kami's eyes lit up. "Oh my God yes, yes, yes, that is exactly it! I would just die if all that came to life."

Grace smirked. "Please don't, though, Mimi. Because I'm pretty sure this team"—she motioned at Ani and Madison—"is going to pull it off and I don't want to invoke the ''til death do us part' too soon."

Kami giggled and kissed Grace's cheek. "Don't worry. I've got the strongest lifeline my tatik has ever seen."

Tatik. Kami's sweet and stern grandmother. Ani missed her, although she supposed she'd see her at the wedding.

Then Grace stood up straight and dug into her bag, pulling out her phone. Her eyes got large when she read the name on the screen. "Got to take this, one sec."

Grace stepped outside. Without her, Kami came close to Ani. Too close. Ani did not like it.

Madison was talking about her vision, about gold accents, while Kami gasped. At one point, Kami touched Ani's forearm, caught her eye, and smiled like they had a secret together. She said, "I can't believe we're doing this. I'm so thankful you're here helping us."

"I—of course."

How Ani wanted to tell her so, so many other words. To please back away, not touch her like they were still lovers, not bring her head so close to whisper like that. Because all it did was bring back memories of when she and Kami were together.

They had been good, they really had, or so Ani had thought. She and Kami met at a wedding Ani was planning. Ani was so busy running around she hadn't noticed Kami until it was time for the bouquet toss, and Kami had risen from it victorious, holding her flowers in the air like a trophy. Ani had admired her liveliness, and her beauty, obviously, and *then* Kami locked eyes with her, walked straight over to Ani, and asked her to dance. Ani had taken it as some kind of sign. She was the one. And they were destined to be together.

Ani loved the way Kami was always thinking of absolutely wild things to do together. Like on an ordinary Tuesday night, she'd call up Ani and declare that they were going to go nude bathing at Baker Beach. What? It was allowed, she'd say. And not only that, she would get Ani away from her work planning and boring life at home, get her up and actually do the thing.

Once they got so drunk at a party in the financial district they ditched it, stumbled to a skyscraper next door with an outdoor courtyard, and, because it was night and the place was abandoned of its daytime workers, proceeded to have sex right there, out in the open. Kami felt like armor. She was so sure of herself, of getting away with *anything*, that Ani had enjoyed being protected by it. Rules didn't apply to Kami, and when Ani was with her, rules didn't apply to Ani, either.

But now, this overly familiar Kami was grating on her, but since Kami was her client and the only thing stopping Ani from folding her business and moving back in with her parents, she allowed it.

At this thought, she heard a man's voice. "Ani? Kami?"

She spun around. It was Raffi. It was Raffi?

Standing there in Tilde, looking like Prince Ali in a tailored gray suit, complete with a new set of shiny Gucci shoes.

She couldn't keep the shock out of her voice. "What are you doing here?"

Kami spotted him now. "Raffi! Oh my God, did you know we were coming?"

Raffi shook himself and responded curtly. "No, I did not."

Wow, he really did not care for Kami. He had never, not once, spoken to Ani like that. Even when she'd spilled an entire extra-large matcha latte on him.

He looked at Ani. "I'm here to talk flowers for a VIP event I'm holding," he said, his tone lighter.

Now Madison perked up. "Oh, you're working with Andrea. I'll go get her."

But before she went to do that, Madison took a good slow look at Raffi, up and down, and Ani felt a great green monster grow in her. *Stay the hell away, Madison*. Followed by shock at how possessive she felt. That was not expected. At all.

Luckily, it seemed Raffi had not noticed Madison's assessment, or if he had, he was choosing to ignore it. He looked, instead, at the flower displays before them, just as Kami was doing beside them.

She hadn't seen Raffi since the night of his wine-tasting party. Wearing that extremely short T-shirt. His hand on her chest. His apology outside, so sincere. Then his flirtation, his words she had thought of for two nights since, over and over, imagining the scene that would take place afterward, had she kissed him instead of leaving.

Ani took a deep breath. "Nice surprise," she said.

The side of Raffi's mouth quirked up, and his eyes shone bright. "It sure is."

Oh no, she died a little at that adorable half smile, one that he reserved for her. He ignored Madison, scorned Kami, but she got that cute smirk.

She pretended to keep looking at the flowers while Kami oohed and ahhed over different arrangements. Ani was nodding half-heartedly at Kami when Kami asked, "Hey, babe?" and Ani instinctively answered, "Yes?"

Oh no, *no*. She did not just do that. Unbeknownst to her, Grace had returned and sidled up to Kami. Kami's actual babe, not Ani. Duh. DUH.

But hold on, her ears were just catching up. Then her brain. She had heard a man's voice also say "Yeah?" at the same time as her response to Kami. A man's voice to her right. She turned to look at him in horror. Raffi had his hand clamped over his mouth and was now coughing. No. Way.

Kami cocked her head at both of them and then went, "Awww. I'm touched."

Grace had a somewhat amused expression on her face, and Ani wanted to spontaneously combust rather than hear what she had to say next because she knew Grace was getting ready to address it.

"Well," Grace said. "This is awkward. But it shouldn't be. We talked about it when we met, right? And if it makes you feel any better, it's not just Kami with her exes. My ex Cassie is going to be a bridesmaid—we had a bit of a friendcest group back in college—so this is not exactly uncharted territory. Ani, you really don't have to look so uncomfortable. It's fine."

Ani shifted her expression, realizing she was probably still wearing a look of horror. Then she gave a feeble laugh.

Grace continued, "Couple more exes, and we could start our own intramural volleyball team."

To this, Raffi and Kami laughed. Ani wanted to—it was funny—but she was frozen in fear at the topic of this conversation.

Grace looked very specifically at Ani. "I know Kami trusts your opinions and style and, therefore, so do I. It's all good, okay?"

Ani nodded fervently.

"It's not like you're still in love with her or anything."

Ani laughed, definitely a little too loudly. Raffi shifted his weight from one foot to the other.

Kami put a hand on Ani's shoulder. "It's okay, everyone's a little in love with me."

What the heck was that supposed to mean? Kami knew that Ani still felt something for her but thought it was natural because that was the way she went about the world? Ani's companions' reactions were reassuring, though. Raffi rolled his eyes. Grace did, too, but in a loving way. "You have the biggest ego, I swear. But for good reason."

Kami smiled along. "That's right, for good reason."

Ani felt like she was on some kind of nightmare game show, where everything everyone said made things worse and there was no possible way to converse her way out of this situation. Everything that came out of her mouth would dig her hole of mortification deeper and deeper.

So she said nothing at all and kept on smiling, surrounded by living works of art. Everything was fine.

"By the way," Grace was now saying to Kami, "they need me to go to the studio this Tuesday. Filming some promo thing for the movie with Robert."

"Oh my God! Can I come?" Kami's voice was bright and eager, and her hands clasped together like a kid asking for dessert.

"Of course, I'm sure that'd be fine with Bob."

"You are so amazing, babe. I'm so proud of you. My Mafia Princess."

And this time no one besides Grace responded to the "babe." Ani wasn't looking, but she could hear that the engaged couple were now kissing. Lovely.

Ani was saved by Madison and another woman waltzing in. Ani had never been so happy to see two hot women stride toward her, which was really saying something.

The moment was crushed, however, when the woman, Andrea, greeted Raffi, slicing him out of their group. She whisked him out of the room, and he turned only briefly to give a small goodbye wave. Ani felt a sharp tug in her stomach.

Just then, she got an alert on her phone and looked down to see a reminder to pay her credit card bill. Ugh, she had been putting it off, hoping for another influx of cash before the due date.

She looked around at Kami and Grace, blissfully unaware that their wedding planner was deeply in credit card debt, while they ordered six figures' worth of flowers. Kami. Fuckin' Kami, nearly impossible to be around. But she'd have to swallow it and take it because of things like this alert. Otherwise, she would have run far away. To spare herself any more Kami-related embarrassment and whatever strange feelings she was having toward Raffi.

Raffi! Who just wanted her body, who was likely only interested because he wanted to sleep with her, despite what he said. She still felt there was a very high probability that if they slept together, the next day he'd leave. Or apologize with some supposedly soothing words but make it awkward for the rest of their months of work together. She had to be more careful, guard her heart, not fall for his little tricks.

But that smile he gave her felt so genuine . . .

No!

She was Ani the wedding planner, and she was going to pull herself out of debt and keep her heart intact if it was the last thing she did, goddamn it.

12

Raffi

ABOUT A WEEK after running into Ani at Tilde, Raffi rolled up to the work site that was once his winery's garden to find Chris and his crew already there at nine a.m., cutting stones and laying them out. The sand-colored stones Ani had picked were looking fantastic, just as she had predicted. Ani. He wondered if he could find some excuse to call her over to check out the progress.

Then again, he had seen how Ani reacted when Grace said, "It's not like you're still in love with her or anything." Ani's laugh, plus the confessions she'd spilled at the Embarcadero, definitely implied Ani was, in fact, still in love with Kami. He was such a fool, pining after someone who was hung up on someone else.

And *yes*, he, too, had answered affirmatively to Kami's "Hey, babe?" It was like some ancient artifact came loose and tumbled out of its place on the display shelf. It had been instinct, to answer her call, at one time. Kami did have a certain power, he'd give her that. She had presence and charisma and apparently the ability to summon up a ten-year-forgotten "Yeah?" to the question "Hey, babe?" But that was the end of it; he wasn't melting in Kami's proximity otherwise. Unlike Ani.

"Hey, man," Chris said and walked over for a handshake/low five combo.

"It's looking great, bro."

"Good. I wanted to make sure it was still going according to plan. I guess Sanan is coming over anytime now to assess."

Chris ran a quick hand through his hair when he mentioned Sanan, and Raffi's heart skipped a beat. Sanan, Ani's assistant, was coming? Might that imply . . . ?

"Is Ani coming, too?" Raffi asked.

"Don't know. Why?"

"No reason."

Chris stared at him. Raffi stared back.

Raffi cleared his throat. "I'll keep an eye out."

"You do that, man," Chris said, and went back to work.

Raffi swept into his office to see if any progress had been made on the sales end of things. They'd had slightly more wine tasters come by and a slight uptick in wine club members, but the enterprise sales were not going well, and without those, or a massive upswing in individual members, their run rate was looking grim. He had about seven months of cash flow before he'd have to put his tail between his legs, go to his father, and admit he had failed.

Which was simply not an option.

Raffi made a few more calls, left more messages, and hoped. The wedding was five months away. He couldn't depend solely on its presumed success and had to keep acting in the meantime.

He peered out the window to see Sanan's slim figure as she chatted with Chris. She tucked her hair behind her ear, and Chris leaned in just a little too close during their conversation. Then they laughed like they were sharing a private joke. Maybe Ani was just out of sight.

He walked out of the building into the garden, looking this way and that for Ani's long, thick hair and her huge eyes, but she didn't seem to be around.

"Hi, Sanan," he greeted from afar, and she greeted him politely.

She walked over. "Ani wanted to check up on the design but couldn't make it. She's picking linens and flatware with Kami today—"

Sanan said a few words after that but Raffi didn't catch them, imagining Ani simpering after Kami, hearts in her eyes. Kami was being so flirtatious with Ani, anyone could see it. How could Grace not? Or maybe Grace did and was simply not bothered. Kami had a flirty personality, so maybe Grace knew exactly who she was marrying. It never bothered him when he was dating Kami, after all.

Still, it irked him how Kami laid it on so thick with Ani and how Ani ate it up. "She's getting married," he wanted to tell Ani. "You have to get over it . . . and, you know, possibly consider who's right in front of you. Me. I'm talking about me."

"Let me know if you need anything. I have to make some calls," he told Sanan, whose visible task list seemed to be all contractor related anyway.

In truth, he had a text he wanted to send. One text, two motivations.

> Ani jan, how are things going? I'm here with Sanan. Everything seems fine, but I want to make sure this wedding goes perfectly. Can I help in any way?

First, he wanted to remind Ani of his presence, especially since he knew she was with Kami, or would be shortly. Secondly, he did *need* this wedding to go well and would do anything in his power to get it there. If it was as high profile as Ani was making it out to be, if he could book more weddings, if it could get Ô on the map, he'd have a chance at showing his dad he could keep his dream alive. And that Raffi did it his own way.

She texted back shortly, which ignited a flare of hope in him.

Raffi jan—his heart leapt. That was the first time she'd said it. *Said it back.* She mirrored his endearment term. For a moment he couldn't read anything else, couldn't see anything but stars. *Raffi jan.* He tried to hear it in her voice, smooth and confident. His entire body felt light, taking it in.

When his vision had resumed, he continued reading, pretending like he hadn't just been knocked sideways by a single word.

—all is well. Getting the work done as soon as possible is the priority. We should do a photoshoot after it's set, for my portfolio and your winery.

Check this out, he texted, and sent her a photo of the stones he'd snapped.

Perfection!! Damn, he's quick, she replied.

And I assure you, still meticulous.

I can see that, Ani responded.

Raffi then asked, What's next?

She responded, We need to figure out the fountain. Can we meet this week and nail it down?

Yes, he certainly could meet this week.

Definitely. Let's do it. Wednesday?

Two days from now.

Perfect, she replied.

"I can't wait," he wanted to reply, but of course he stopped himself.

Meet me here, 10am, I'll drive us. Then he texted her his home address. It'll be easier. A risk, sure, but it made more sense for them to meet at his place first.

There was a brief pause before she texted back. Hmm, maybe she realized it was a condo, not the winery, and was worried about meeting at his place. Then her text came in. Sounds good, she replied.

Nothing would happen. She wasn't interested in him. They were going to figure out the fountain situation, and Raffi would get to spend some time in the company of a beautiful and brilliant woman. Simply bask in her radiance, that was all. That was normal to want, right?

While he was not ready for the conversation to end, he heard a lumbering outside his door. His dad entered, his perpetually unimpressed expression wearing down his face.

"Dad, here," Raffi said, moving to grab a chair.

"I'm not an old man, I can pull out my own chair."

His dad waved him off, but as he did, the man lost his balance and began to topple to the floor. Raffi dove toward him and broke the worst of his fall. He was holding his dad, who was quite heavy, in his arms. The son carrying the father. It felt all wrong. His dad, evidently, thought so, too.

He spat, "I was fine. I would have caught myself if you didn't do that!"

His dad wrenched out of his position, got on all fours, and was about to get up but clearly couldn't. Raffi, now standing, extended his arm. His father reluctantly took it and pulled himself into the chair.

"Dad. Come on, can we please talk about it? It's time for a cane. At the very least."

"Dghas," his dad said, meaning "my boy," a loving phrase he almost never, ever used. Raffi leaned in, shocked, wanting to hear more. His dad's voice was low. "I would rather die—*die*—than be seen with a cane. Do you understand me?"

Raffi drew back like he'd been slapped. He didn't answer right away.

Instead, he glanced at his father. Shoulders still broad, but hunched now with pain and age, eyes still sharp, but dimmed around the edges. He looked like a fortress crumbling from the inside out.

"You don't have to prove anything," Raffi said. "Not to me or anyone else."

Moushegh gave a bitter laugh. "That's what young men say. Until they're the ones sitting here."

Raffi tried to find the words, something that didn't sound like pity or rebellion. But nothing landed.

Moushegh filled the silence. "One day, when you are old, you will understand," his dad said. "And if God blesses you with sons, you will understand further."

Raffi looked at his father, this man who had built everything through grit and force and willpower. His dad still believed that strength meant silence. That asking for help was defeat.

Maybe Moushegh would never change. But Raffi could.

And if he ever had sons, he'd show them that being a man meant more than swallowing your fear. It could mean tenderness. Vulnerability. Joy.

Moushegh crossed his arms. "But the way it's been going, it appears I will be cold in my grave by the time any grandchildren come around, if they ever do at all. When was the last time you brought a woman around, eh? Think you're too good for them all, do you? Well, you're not. Women are worth fighting for, making ourselves better for. I don't understand why you treat them with such disrespect."

Raffi was taken aback. First, his dad was giving him love advice? He really must think the end was near. Secondly, his dad had noticed anything at all about Raffi's dating life?

"Dad, I don't treat women disrespectfully. I'm very transparent—"

"Bah." His father waved. "Sure you do. You never bring a woman home. That is disrespect."

Dad knew about Raffi's past dalliances? Gross. He supposed word did get around the Armenian community, but still.

"No, I just haven't found the right—"

"Then look around! All your friends are married. Aram Vartanian is married, Daron Chamlian is married, even that little runt Penyamin is married, and to quite a beauty I must add. Open your eyes, son. Do you think there's anything more important than family?"

"Um—" Raffi stammered. He didn't know his father felt this way at all. He hadn't exactly invested much time in his. And he, his mother, and his father were hardly the picture of a close-knit family.

"Fooling around, satisfying your every desire, do you think that is manliness?"

Raffi suffered severe whiplash. Just moments before he was disgusted by his father's definition of manliness, but now? This addendum sounded surprising.

Because his father wasn't entirely wrong.

It wasn't about needing a wife, that wasn't the issue.

It was how Raffi had been moving through the world the last few years, mistaking honesty for decency. Even though he'd been hooking up less and less, he must have been subconsciously realizing that telling women he didn't want a relationship didn't automatically make his intimacy with them harmless. What if those women had felt something spark—like the kind of current he felt around Ani—and he'd walked away without even noticing? That part stung.

Because with Ani, the draw was undeniable, and they'd barely touched. *Ani.*

He wished he could tell his dad: "Yes, I did find someone I wanted to bring home, but she turned me down, so that's that."

"I mean . . . no."

"That's right. *No,* you jackass." His father swore in Armenian. "It is to make sacrifices for your family."

Maybe it was because he'd just held his father in his arms,

broken his fall, and stopped a calamity that Raffi felt emboldened to talk back, something that had previously always terrified him. "Like you made sacrifices for ours, working endlessly so you didn't have to see any of us?"

"Ungrateful boy! How dare you!"

"You didn't have to work *that* much. No one doe—"

"Who would have built the Garabedian empire otherwise? You say that, sitting pretty here in this winery I purchased, living off the life I made for you."

Raffi shook his head. His dad was right in a way. Although the winery was in trouble and Raffi was stressed, he would take this role over any job he'd ever previously had. Especially the one he was most recently in, management consulting. If he never had to hear the words *value chain* or *agile methodology* ever again, it would be too soon. So yes, his dad had set him up with that.

"Fine, Dad. Thank you for working yourself nearly to death for us."

"I don't need your thanks. Get me some damn grandchildren to run around and break some of our finest vintage bottles, that's what I want."

His father had a hint of a smile at his own joke, and Raffi couldn't help but smile sadly at it, too.

"Noted. After I pull this winery out of the red, I'll work on it."

His father grumbled as he rose painfully from the chair and shambled out of the room.

Raffi sat and stared blankly at the computer screen in front of him for several moments. That was possibly the most personal conversation he'd ever had with his dad. Must have been the fall. His dad had come face-to-face with his mortality and felt the need to impart wisdom on Raffi. Not all of it bad.

But there was something else—something that kept tugging at the edges of his thoughts during the talk with his dad. In the back of his mind, coming in and out of visualizations, were the gorgeous cosmic eyes of Ani.

It was a hopeless situation, but still. Wednesday could not come soon enough.

13

Ani

ANI GOT TO the address Raffi provided at ten a.m., like they'd planned. It was a rustic area with several rows of modern low-rise condos dotting the landscape. They were fairly close to The Parker, one of the famous luxury hotels in the area—where she would love to plan a wedding one day—and she wondered if the condos were also owned by the hotel, as they had that same air of contemporary country resort.

Raffi was already waiting outside the buildings in his signature navy suit, white button-down, and a pair of sunglasses that made him look like a celebrity ready to make his Cannes entrance. Not like a guy about to hop into a van and do fountain recon.

Ani, however, was not in her flirtatious best. She'd decided on a shapeless black dress that hit her knees and surely would prevent Raffi's interest. However, she couldn't help herself and decided to pair the boring sack with red heels. They were a classic style, not too flashy or too high, but they were still . . . red. She needed *something* to not feel frumpy, and the heels were the perfect antidote.

She parked, popped out of the car, and felt for the first time like maybe they should hug? But that seemed wrong—they were colleagues—so she decided instead to take advantage of their distance and gave a wave hello. There, it was done and over with.

"This your building?" she asked.

"Home sweet home," he said.

It was *very* nice, no doubt about it. Everything felt brand-new, and it melded with the landscape well, intentionally designed.

"Is this part of The Parker or something?" she asked.

He nodded. "Kind of. It's owned by them, but there are twenty or so condos. We do get access to the pool and spa, though, so that was the selling point for me."

The Parker pool was a legendary hot spot, the type of place where Napa's elite lounged with their thirty-dollar cocktails and wore sunglasses so expensive they probably came with their own insurance policies. Ani imagined Raffi lying back in a chair, women gawking over him, striking up conversations with him . . . She felt an uncomfortable twisting of jealousy in her chest. Jealous of women who might not even exist. She blinked, startled by the intensity of it, and silently scolded herself. She had promised herself she'd guard her heart, not get envious over hypotheticals. She needed to calm the heck down.

"Cool if I drive?" he asked.

"Of course."

She followed him toward the small parking lot.

"I actually have something in the car for you," he said, almost sheepish.

Ani stopped walking for a second. He had something for her? What could that possibly be? She racked her brain and came up with: an iced matcha latte, some bottles of wine, a photo of the progress being made at the site? She truly could not imagine anything else.

They stopped in front of a forest green convertible that looked both old and modern at the same time. Since they were on the side, she couldn't peep what type of model it was, but she did know it was a stunning vehicle.

"This is what you drive?" she asked.

"Shockingly, not the creeper van," he replied. "This is more my everyday. The van's just for special occasions."

Ani smiled while Raffi popped the trunk and pulled out a nondescript black bag.

"An apology gift," he said, handing it to her.

Ani looked up at him before taking the bag, but his eyes were hidden behind those dark glasses, so she couldn't read how he was feeling. "Oh . . . kay," she said.

"Go ahead, let me know if it's the right one."

So she did. Ani opened the bag, and inside, folded neatly and wrapped in tissue paper, was the exact white dress that had been forever destroyed by a cabernet splotch. Her brain could hardly compute.

"Did I get it right?" he asked, seemingly nervous.

"Raffi, oh my God, yes. How did you . . . ? You didn't have to, you know."

She stared at the dress in her hands. What the hell? He was gifting her something, something so thoughtful. She had loved that dress, but considering her situation, there was no way she was going to buy a brand-new one. Now she had one.

He shrugged. "I totaled it. This was the only right thing to do."

"But your YSL shirt—I mean, I ruined that one, and I didn't, I can't—"

He waved her off. "That was different. It wasn't the brand, it was sentimental."

"Oh God, that just makes the matcha stain so much worse."

And she also wondered how that shirt was sentimental. Was it from an ex? Kami?! Or something else?

He took off his sunglasses and rubbed the bridge of his nose. "No, it's fine, it's fine. It's just a shirt."

Ani heard the lie.

"Is it?"

Raffi glanced down, his hands fidgeting with the sunglasses he'd removed. "Well, no. I'll tell you about it sometime."

They caught each other's eyes, and Ani hoped she was able to impart the full meaning of her words. "I'd like that."

He half smiled. Then turned his attention back to the open trunk. "There's something else. It's stupid. I wasn't sure if that dress was the right one or not, so I got something else, too, and I can't return it anyway so just keep it, and if it doesn't fit you can regift it, I won't mind."

He rambled as he handed her a box. A black box that said Balmain Paris. She hoped, she desperately hoped, this was one of those times when you put the gift in a box it didn't belong to. Her family had a couple running Nordstrom boxes they kept recycling and using for Christmas and birthdays year after year.

She opened it, and inside was perfectly pressed tissue paper sealed with a Balmain sticker. Balmain was not a normal designer. It was Kardashian-level pricey. Unobtainable. Not even worth dreaming about.

"Raffi," she said dangerously. "What did you do?"

"What?" He shrugged, genuinely clueless.

"I can't open this."

"Yes, you can. I got it for you," he said, then immediately inspected some gravel by his shoe, as if too embarrassed to look at her.

She took a deep breath, gingerly peeled off the sticker, and lifted the tissue to reveal a black-and-white short-sleeved tweed minidress, which was, indeed, designed by Balmain, and the single most beautiful article of clothing she'd held in her hands. The stitching on this thing, the silk lining . . .

"You hate it?" he asked. "Tweed was a risk, but it's in fashion right now and also sort of timeless, so I thought it could last a while."

Her voice came out a whisper. "Raffi, are you fucking kidding me right now? You bought me a very, *very* designer dress? You can't do that."

She felt that was true, but she also felt . . . spoiled, in a good way, in a way she'd never been before. Kami had been fabulously wealthy but never bought her lavish gifts, which Ani didn't even know she would want. Until now.

"Sure I can. I destroyed your dress and wasn't sure if I got the exact same one, so I bought a backup."

"Balmain is not a backup!"

Raffi shrugged. "I love shopping, so sue me."

Ani breathed out. "My God. I can't accept this."

"But do you like it?"

"I love it!" she shouted, and although she was mildly abashed by her outburst, she caught his widening smile. "But this is insane, you realize that, right?"

Raffi huffed. "Just accept it, please. It'll make this all less awkward. I didn't mean the dress to be a huge thing, just a nice gesture. A please-forgive-me type of gesture."

She started laughing. "Okay, Raffi, yes, all right? I forgive you. Wholeheartedly. You've more than made up for it."

He nodded. "Thank you."

Ani tucked the dress back into the box. "What the hell am I supposed to do with this now? I can't just tote it around Napa in the back seat of your convertible. I sure as hell am not leaving it in my car. Civics are the most likely car to get broken into. I learned that the hard way."

"Sucks," he replied with actual sympathy in his eyes. "Leave it in my trunk, then."

"Okay, yes," she said, and handed over the two dresses to Raffi, who nestled them safely away.

Ani shook herself. "What were we doing today, again? I have no clue."

This time Raffi laughed. "Well, sweetheart, we're going to see about some fountains."

Ani had been on her way to the passenger-side door when she froze. *Sweetheart*. Oh, she loved that. The word sent shivers through her body. Fancy gifts, pet names. Raffi was pulling out all the stops, and Ani was going to have a hell of a hard time trying not to fall hard and fast for him.

She didn't understand why he was bothering with *her*, though. Why her? She was just . . . Ani. Even her name was plain. She wasn't particularly pretty ("Bug eyes, bug eyes," she heard the chant of her middle-school bully) or smart or accomplished. In fact, in everything she was sort of a B+, which also, not coincidentally, matched her 3.3 GPA in both high school and college. Raffi could have *anyone*, yet he seemed to be pursuing her. Was it just because she had turned him down? But surely others before her had turned him down. He wasn't everyone's type just because he was handsome. She wondered if this was the same type of game he'd pulled on Lala, her sister's friend. Or if this was something different. She wished she could just ask him.

She willed herself to keep moving. And reply, she had to reply. "Right, fountains."

Raffi slid into the driver's seat. "You were telling me that my vision for a Trevi-like fountain was ill informed and a huge liability and would mess with the overall vibe. So we're going to DePietro Winery to see who's right."

Ani moved to open her door and stepped in. "Thank you for the recap. Helpful." The sage leather of the seats hugged her. The weather was nice today—finally not cold and no chill in the air—so a convertible ride through Napa sounded like a good idea. *With a Balmain dress in the trunk!*

Raffi started up the car, which she now saw was a Jaguar, and for which the buttons, dials, and lack of any music technology prior to 1970 indicated that it was actually an old car. Interesting. She'd have pegged him for a BMW M series type of guy, not a vintage Jaguar. Then again, she was discovering more and more that all her preconceived notions about Raffi Garabedian were, in fact, wrong.

Raffi revved the engine, which was quite loud at first, more than a modern car, and they drove off. Raffi appeared light, happy; even without the obviously large smile, she could feel positive energy emanating from him.

"How'd your VIP event go?" Ani asked, thinking this might be the reason.

"Eh, fine. Probably not as well as it should have gone."

"Sorry to hear it." So, not that.

Raffi tapped on the steering wheel with some urgency. "Honestly, I hope this whole Kami renovation makes a difference, because no one seems to have heard of or care about Ô, no matter what I do."

Ani put her arm up on the bare windowsill, enjoying the breeze tickling her arm. "Have you booked any weddings besides this one?"

"Weddings? God no. People barely come for tastings."

That gave her an idea. "Wait, let me see something."

Ani pulled out her phone, searched two of the major wedding venue databases, and found nothing about Ô.

Ani waved her phone at Raffi, although he was driving. "Well, no wonder. Your winery isn't getting booked because it's not in any of the big wedding venue registries."

"I hadn't even thought of— Can you, I don't know, message me their links?"

"I can do you one better. I can add Ô for you."

"You don't have to—"

"No, it's no problem. And that's just one thing." She found herself sitting up straighter, facing him to talk, filled with a sudden effervescence. "You need a full page of your website that showcases your venue for weddings, with the information potential couples would need to entice them to send an inquiry. Not too much, not too little. Oh, definitely add the architect's renderings of the new space; people will eat that up and start booking after October." As the wind whipped through her hair and the golden hills of Napa rolled by, Ani's face lit up with yet another idea. "Ooooh, add a wait list. That'll really get people salivating."

She was getting such a thrill out of helping Raffi, it almost shocked her. Like she was ready to head back, bust out her laptop, and set all these sites up for him. She wanted to help an Armenian business succeed, of course, but maybe she wanted Raffi in particular to succeed?

"Okay, Miss Wedding Planner, I obviously need to hire you for PR and marketing."

Ani blushed, the warmth spreading from her cheeks to the tips of her ears. The first time he'd called her that, it had almost felt like sarcasm—like he was surprised that she actually had a good idea. He'd said it again at the wine-tasting party, and in that context, she hadn't hated it. But now, hearing it again, she realized it wasn't condescending or overreaching; it was playful, teasing in a way that made her feel like they were in on the same joke. And when he complimented her skills, it wasn't flattery; it felt genuine, like he actually saw her as someone who knew what she was doing. For once, she didn't feel like the B+ version of herself she'd been carrying around for years.

"Should we maybe make some time after the fountain assessment to work on it?" she asked.

Raffi said, "I'd like that."

Ani hardly had time to take that in because her phone rang. It was Kami. She didn't want to talk to her right now, especially as the momentum between her and Raffi was only growing and she didn't want to hit the brakes on that. But Kami was, in truth, her most important client.

She turned to Raffi. "Sorry, gotta get this."

"No problem."

Ani slid her finger across the screen to answer. "Hey, Kami, what's up?"

Kami's voice on the other line was frantic. "I'm having second thoughts."

Ani sat straight up in her seat, her heart whirring. "What?"

She felt Raffi's gaze on her. This would materially affect him as well. Oh God. She had to handle this. Was it because she had been too flirty with Kami, too amenable? Did Kami want Ani back now? This was all her fault.

And thinking about it, if that was what Kami was calling about, why was Ani filled with a sick, roiling feeling in her stomach? No hint of excitement at all. Panic, in fact.

Kami's words came through the phone like a flurry of feathers, high-pitched and rapid, each word tumbling out faster than the last. "About the iridescent crush color we chose. Did we dismiss the cashmere velvet too quickly? Like, I'm obsessed with iridescent crush, don't get me wrong. But is it too trendy? Cashmere velvet is so classic."

Ani relaxed in her seat and blew out a long breath. This was about the table linens. Second thoughts about the table linens! Not love. Not regret. She almost cried, she was so relieved.

And there were two lines of thought that washed over her. The first was that so much was riding on this wedding—more than she realized until she thought it might be snatched away from her.

The second was a shift she felt in her body, deep and tectonic. A shift so immense she had to shove it away in this moment and address Kami's actual question.

Ani drew herself back into professional mode.

"Cashmere velvet is definitely classic, but we decided it wouldn't be as stunning, as memorable. And you are going for out-of-this-world memorable. That's what you get with iridescent crush. It's undoubtedly the right choice."

Kami seemed to calm on the other end of the line at this reasoning. "Right, you're right. I just needed reassurance, you know? I knew you'd have the answer. So this is definitely the way to go."

Ani filled her voice with a confidence she reserved for clients—even as something unsteady flickered beneath. "Without a doubt. You're going to love it."

"Oh my God, Ani, I don't know what I'd do without you. Thank you! Ciao!"

And she hung up before Ani had a chance to reply.

Ani kept the phone to her ear, frozen, processing what had happened. Not about the linens. Not even about Ani's momentary anxiety that the wedding was being called off.

Something bigger.

For two years, she'd lived with the ghost of what she and Kami had been. She had turned over in her mind every lingering thought of Kami, hoping, perhaps, that it was all a mistake. That Kami would come back to her. But sitting here, the phone warm in her hand, breeze cool on her face, she felt it—the astonishing lightness of not wanting Kami back.

It was a grief and a liberation in the same breath.

Ani put down her phone.

"What was that about?" Raffi asked, somewhat gruffly.

Ani blinked, as if waking from a dream she hadn't realized she was still in. She put a hand over her heart and told Raffi only what he needed to know. "Kami started off the conversation saying she was having second thoughts, and I nearly died on the spot."

"There we go, I was wondering what had you so anxious. I almost pulled the car over, but then you were talking about velvet crushes and everything seemed okay."

"Yes, she meant she was second-guessing our color and texture choices for the tablecloths."

"And she needed to call you for that?"

Raffi merged onto the freeway but kept a slower speed so the wind wasn't unbearable. Ani rather liked it, whipping through her hair.

"She was panicking. Sometimes in a wedding, brides or other wedding party members will focus on one detail and freak out over it like it's a make-or-break, because of all the stress. There are so many balls to juggle at once, it gets overwhelming. I don't know the psychological term for it, but they seem to concentrate all that anxiety into, say, the choice between chicken piccata and chicken Milanese as a coping mechanism. Something they can control and perfect. I see it every time."

"Hmm," Raffi said. "Guess I could see that. Well, whatever you said worked. That magic touch again."

Ani turned away slightly to hide her blush. "Uh, yeah, I'm lucky Kami somehow trusts my judgment. That's not always the case."

Ani expected a flicker of satisfaction in saying this. Instead, all she felt was a quiet, comforting truth: She didn't need to be the person Kami turned to anymore. It wasn't the burden it used to be. She was fine being there for Kami in a professional sense, but nothing more.

She let the wind take the rest of those old feelings and toss them behind her like something no longer worth carrying.

Raffi didn't say anything. She could let him sit in silence, but his irritation at Kami was something she wanted to bring up, and now she had a chance.

"You're not the biggest fan of Kami, are you?" Ani asked.

"Huh?" He seemed to be stunned out of his line of thought. "Why, are you?"

Ani answered somewhat defensively. "I mean, not really. I was. I used to be her number one fan, but it's clear I was in love with some kind of fantasy."

As she said it, Ani shocked herself with the truth of it. She had clung to the heartbreak for so long, convinced it was proof of something real. But maybe she hadn't lost a great love. Maybe she had only lost an illusion.

The memories shifted in her mind, no longer golden and untouchable, but something more fragile, human. The fights they had sidestepped, the times she had ignored the gut feelings that whispered Kami wasn't all in, the way Ani had always been the one to smooth things over, to give more, to believe harder. She had told herself they were meant to be, but had Kami ever truly made her feel safe? Had she ever really been chosen?

And now, here she was, speaking the truth of it aloud—not in some dramatic breakdown, not in the heat of an argument, but in a car with Raffi, the road open and seemingly endless, a reminder that forward was the only way to go.

She'd just confessed like that, as if it was another ordinary thing to say. To Raffi, of all people.

But he wasn't "of all people"; he was taking in her words. Eyes fixed in concentration.

Highway 29 slowed down into a comfortable road with wineries dotting the landscape, and Raffi took his time, seeming to enjoy the pace.

"I get that," he said. "Maybe I felt the same way, too, once. I had a lot of hopes for us, and we ended things amicably. But then—"

Ani didn't say one word. She could tell he had something big he wanted to share, and she was not going to interrupt.

Raffi continued, "A week after, my brother died, it—it shattered my whole world. And Kami, she was one of the people I was closest to. We had told each other—well, the usual things couples say. And yeah, we'd broken up at that point, but it still hurt. She sent me this one little text. 'I'm so sorry about Sev. Sending you strength.' And that was it. That was all she ever said. I didn't expect her to get back with me or come over and nurse me back to health or whatever, but—we were so close at one point, just weeks before, and that was all I got. My brother died. *My brother.* A lot of people pulled away from me around then—maybe I was shitty to be around, I don't know. But I haven't—I just—everything between us, how I felt about her, changed after that."

Oh. Shit. Ani had no idea, none, that Raffi's brother had died. When he was twenty or so? How had no one told her? Poor Raffi. Poor young Raffi, newly adulted, newly dumped, newly made an only child. She really fucking felt for him. And suddenly all the hooking up, all his flashy clothes and bravado, seemed to make sense. He was hurt, badly.

Then she remembered his father's words to him. "You'll never become a man." God. After all that, to not even have your father on your side? She hoped he was close with his mother.

And the Kami revelation, well, it made a whole lot of sense, how ice-cold he was with her. It hadn't really been Kami's fault, she was nineteen or twenty as well, and they were broken up. Maybe she felt her text was what was appropriate considering they weren't together anymore. But Ani still didn't blame Raffi for how he felt about Kami.

Processing all of this, she felt like she had been struck in the chest.

"Shit, Raffi. I didn't know. Any of it. That must have been horrible, to feel so alone. You didn't deserve it."

Raffi's jaw was tight. "Maybe I did. Why else would something like that happen?"

Ani sat up straighter and faced him, although his eyes were on the road. "No, that's not how it works. Tragic things happen all the time, for no reason at all. Not as punishment."

She was speaking like she had any idea, but still, she believed it. Tragedy hadn't touched her in the same way. Ani hadn't grown up with abundance like Kami and Raffi, but she had two loving parents and her sister. This conversation also really made her want to spend some actual one-on-one time with Talar, who she'd grown apart from since her sister got married. That was a shame, and it was on her to right it.

"If you say so, Ani jan."

"I do."

Raffi visibly swallowed, and Ani wished she could hug him.

"That shirt, the first day, the YSL one—it was Sevan's, my brother's."

Ani's body instantly surged with guilt, thinking about how she had destroyed it. She had thought it was just a shirt. Just a stupid, expensive shirt.

She had been so caught up in her own indignation, she'd never considered there was more beneath the surface of Raffi's irritation that day. Never questioned why a man who otherwise seemed indifferent about so much had looked genuinely wounded when she'd ruined it.

"Raffi, no . . . Oh God. I can't believe I did that. I am so sorry. Sorry doesn't even cover it—"

But he waved her off. "I meant it before. It's been ten years. I'm not saying I need to get over it—I'll never be over Sevan's death—but I need to change how I react to memories of him."

Ani wanted to respond but wasn't sure how to, then Raffi continued. "That's why I said that ridiculous thing to you. 'This was YSL.' Or whatever the exact words were. I freak out about everything related to Sevan, and the fear of missing him is so intense I guess I—sometimes I lash out. You didn't deserve that. So actually, *I'm* sorry."

Ani shook her head. "You don't have to be. Not at all. I understand you."

He didn't speak. His eyes shone.

Then he seemed to shake himself. "Enough sad topics for one drive," Raffi said. "Can we talk about crushed velvet again?"

Ani made sure her voice carried the weight of her words and said, "Raffi. You can talk about this anytime. I mean it. It doesn't bother me at all and I—I want to know more."

"All right," he said in a soft voice.

Then, he reached over and took one of her hands in his.

Her breath caught. His hand was so big, enveloping hers, warm and smooth, and his touch lit up her whole body, sparked up her spine.

He gave a light squeeze. "Thank you."

Ani brushed her thumb against his and felt lightheaded at her boldness, stars dancing at the edges of her vision. Desire pulsed through her, want and hunger growing.

But then he released her hand, and the moment was over. Her skin felt cold in his absence, achy without him. She desperately wanted to touch him again.

She exhaled slowly, trying to steady herself. Her heart was still racing, ridiculous and unchecked, like it hadn't gotten the memo that the moment was over. She forced herself to focus on the familiar rhythm of her breathing, the way her body fit into the leather seat, the coolness of the air slipping in through the edges of the car.

They didn't speak again, and she wondered if Raffi was undergoing a similar unraveling. Both silent while burning below the surface.

Soon after, they arrived at DePietro Winery.

Conversation started up again as soon as they pulled into the long driveway. She began talking about its landscaping, the front entrance, the benefits of a smooth driveway versus a crunchy one—comfort versus rustic. Ani latched on to her words, forcing her mind into the details, the logistics, the work. She needed to anchor herself in practicality, in things she could measure and define.

Raffi parked and hopped out. "Shall we go see about a fountain?" he asked.

"Let's," Ani said, and pretended that her skin didn't still tingle where he'd touched her.

14

Ani

DEPIETRO WINERY WAS extravagant. The Vatican of wineries. That was its gimmick, with Roman columns, Donatello replicas, and an imposing fortress of Italian cypress trees.

Ani and Raffi cut through the winery building toward the back garden area, where the fountain was that Raffi had his heart set on. He didn't want an exact copy, but the overall feel was supposedly what Raffi had in mind. And Ani knew it was a terrible idea.

They reached the monstrosity in question, a massive, deep fountain set against a wall, with statues and sculptures growing out of its every surface. A couple of the designs nearly grazed Ani's head as she poked around the place.

"DePietro must have taken out so much insurance against this fountain. Look at this thing."

"You're always talking about liability. Were you a lawyer in a past life or something?"

Ani flushed, because she wasn't exactly. Her sister was the lawyer, corporate and successful. Ani had been the lawyers' servant and whipping boy, and her office was a rundown, badly managed firm that dealt with complex litigation, usually in the torts realm. So yes, she was always thinking about liability and how to avoid a nasty lawsuit. In her line of business, it was good to think that way. Weddings were full of potential disasters, beyond just the groom unexpectedly smashing cake into the bride's face. Put a bunch of people in a room with an open bar and candles and wine glasses and sparklers, and injury is imminent.

"I was a paralegal, actually."

"What? But you're a wedding planner. *The* wedding planner, in my mind."

Ani smiled at that, warmth blooming in her cheeks. "*The* wedding planner." His words settled onto her like embers, small but glowing, sneaking past her defenses before she could swat them away. "Thanks, but yeah, I really was. Broke away from it four years ago and started the wedding planning business from scratch."

Raffi regarded her with something like awe. "That's a huge change."

She shrugged. "You know a thing or two about huge changes."

"But I was always in school, and school was always being paid for. And the winery? I didn't start it from scratch. It was handed to me." He shot her a look, one brow slightly raised. "As someone may have pointed out to me the day we met."

Ani's stomach twisted. God. Had she really said that? To his face? She cleared her throat, suddenly very interested in the stitching on her sleeve. "Ah. Yeah. That . . . may have been me."

Raffi smirked but didn't push. "You, meanwhile, took an actual risk."

"Maybe," she said, ducking her head slightly, hiding a smile.

Then, grasping for a shift in conversation before her embarrassment could fully settle in, she looked around and asked, "Speaking of risk, do you see the potential pitfalls here?"

He waved off her concerns, peering over the edge of the fountain. "We won't make it as ridiculously deep, and we'll raise the wall so guests can't tumble in." He gestured to the low, very trippable wall. "It'll be great. Distinct from DePietro's but in a similar style."

"Sure, but think about how it's going to look overall. It has to be backed up against the winery, and it's going to distract from all the other elements in the garden. You want something that flows—literally—with the rest of the garden's vibe."

"If we're building a fountain anyway, shouldn't we make it as showy as possible?"

"You are so Armenian."

"And you are so Americanized."

Ani smirked. "Hey, my entire career is to make one day of everyone's life as opulent as possible."

"Touché," Raffi conceded.

"I don't need my house to look like Versailles, though," Ani continued, "and you don't need your winery to, either. Come, look at these."

She directed Raffi toward a separate water feature, where the fountains flowed alongside the walkway, forming a path.

"I was thinking more like these, but around the ceremony area where the dome is. Could make it really stand out and delineate it from the rest of the garden."

He seemed to consider her words, when a woman's voice rang out. "Raffi? Is that—yes, it's you!"

A slender blonde woman in a tight-fitting, cleavage-showing power dress rushed toward him and embraced him in a way that made Ani's blood pressure rise.

"Oh, hey," Raffi said, his body going a little too still, like someone bracing for impact. He gave a half-hearted pat on her back, the kind that suggested he wasn't sure how long this was supposed to last. His huge sunglasses still covered his eyes.

"I haven't seen you since that mixer at the Langstons'. You know . . ."

Raffi coughed. "That was a while back."

"I know! Where have you been hiding, mister?"

That "mister" was when Ani strode away. Clearly, this was a woman Raffi had slept with. Model pretty, bubbly, the drip of money all over her. The type he went for.

A cool breeze cut through the warm April afternoon. Her stomach twisted, tight and cold, a slow-spreading ache she hadn't braced for.

He'd been kind today—sweet, even. Thoughtful in a way she hadn't expected from someone like him. And maybe that's why it stung more than it should.

And the dresses he bought her. They had felt meaningful. But now, with that woman's easy laughter still ringing in her ears, it felt cheapened.

Unknowingly, Ani was making her way back toward the gaudy fountain. Walking without a destination, only wanting to put distance between herself and him.

When he handed her the gifts, though, he seemed embarrassed, not suave and debonair, not dashing in a con man sort of way. He was nervous. He wanted her to like them. He wanted to get it right.

But. *But*.

She didn't know what to do. She found herself drawn to Raffi, felt that the man she'd come to know was different from his reputation, but—

That was when her shoe caught hard against something solid—a hidden ledge? A loose stone? She didn't have time to figure it out before her legs lurched violently out from under her.

She was weightless for a moment, then the impact came, sudden and merciless.

The shock of cold water punched the air from her lungs, biting through fabric, skin, bone. It took her a moment to register the icy grip seeping into every inch of her, the way her clothes clung to her like dead weight. She'd fallen into the goddamn liability fountain.

Her first instinct was to scramble upward, but something was pulling her down.

Standing up shouldn't have been a problem, except the water was heavier than it should have been, except—

Suddenly her back and butt slammed into something hard, the jarring force rattling through her bones. It was so dark and murky in here, she couldn't see a damn thing. A deep, mechanical whirring hummed beneath her, vibrating through the water. A pump.

Shit.

Ani twisted and tried to push away, but her limbs slipped

uselessly on the algae-slick bottom of the fountain, her pulse hammering faster now, her chest tightening like a vise. At some point, she'd lost her shoes.

The hem of her dress was stuck and being sucked into the pump more and more. She yanked hard—nothing. Shit, shit, shit. Ani got to her knees, which were still slipping along the bottom, and she just barely broke the surface, gasping—yes, air!—but she then slipped again and swallowed a mouthful of foul, grimy fountain water. The suction continued to pull at her dress, pinning her underwater. Panic surged through her chest. How many more breaths could she steal like that, how much more water could she swallow before, before . . .

15

Raffi

RAFFI WAS PROCESSING seeing . . . what was her name again? Kylie? Kayla? Kyrie? K-woman was talking to him a mile a minute about all the changes in her life, about her new workout routine and her spiritual healer telling her to go for things she'd previously shied away from, and huh, was she talking about him? About trying to ask him out on a date? They had hooked up one night when he was new to the Napa scene. It hadn't meant much at the time, but now he saw it for what it was: a careless moment that had ripples he hadn't considered.

He wished, more than anything, that Ani didn't have to witness this—that she wasn't seeing this version of himself he was doing his best to reform. Wait. Wasn't she here a second ago? Where had she gone?

His former fling touched his arm, and Raffi was about to come up with a polite way to tell her he wasn't interested when he heard the loud splash. His head snapped up to the fountain, but he couldn't see what had caused the noise. It was a significant splash, so not a twig or an acorn from the trees on the property. As he scanned the area, he saw it. My God. A single red heel sat splayed at the base of the fountain, as if it'd fallen off unexpectedly.

Ani.

His blood ran cold. Oh no. No, no, no.

Raffi rushed over without thinking. The fountain was far from where he was standing—how had she wandered off so quickly? But surely she'd emerge any minute, right? By the time he got there, she should be out of the water.

Instead, the water agitated, like something was fighting under there, so Raffi ran faster, ripping his jacket off and throwing it to the ground. This shouldn't be happening. Something was terribly wrong. He knew if he didn't get over there as fast as humanly possible and wrench her out of the water—if anything at all happened to her, he'd never forgive himself.

There were a couple of people nearby, peering toward the disturbance, but no one was doing anything. No one! They were all sitting around, staring, sipping wine while letting a woman drown—what the hell was wrong with people?

Raffi approached the fountain, spotted Ani's thrashing arms just under the surface, and without another thought, jumped in. Oh fuck. He shut off his brain from the full impact of seeing her fighting for her life and concentrated on getting her safe as fast as possible. No matter what, he would not fail.

The icy water stabbed at him and his clothes dragged with heavy weight as he submerged himself to try to figure out what was wrong. He couldn't see much, but as soon as Raffi put his arms around Ani, her jerking settled a bit. He pulled her up, but something resisted.

Following the area of tension, his fingers found where she

was stuck, the fabric trapped, tethering her to the bottom like an anchor. Her hands suddenly joined his and together they yanked, not caring about anything except getting her free.

And then—release.

He surged upward, hauling her with him, breaking the surface with gasping, ragged breaths.

She began coughing—*thank God*—eyes squeezed shut with the effort, her body shuddering against his. He pulled her, soaked and cold, into his arms while she coughed and coughed and he clapped her back. She was breathing. She was breathing. And then he realized he was, too. Big, heavy breaths of relief.

"Ani," he asked gruffly. "Can you hear me?"

She made a series of gasping squeaks. Not good enough.

This wasn't like when one of his former patients was in a life-threatening situation, a hair's breadth from dying. That was blind duty. This was personal. And his eyes felt wide open for the first time in a long time.

He didn't just have a crush on Ani. He was falling for her, hard.

Her brush with death had grabbed his little crush by the throat and thrust it into deeper territory.

Raffi rubbed her cold cheek with his thumb. "Ani, I've got you. Can you talk?"

One shaky hand rose to his chest and squeezed the placket of his shirt. "Why—" he thought he heard her say, but he wasn't sure. But still, his heart leapt. She could breathe and she could talk; this was all pointing to her being okay. He had no idea if she'd hit her head or what had happened underwater, or if there was the possibility of brain damage—his heart stopped for a moment just thinking about it—from the combination of contusion and near drowning.

"What's that, Ani jan? Can you try again?"

He cradled her head in his arms, swept a wet lock of hair off her forehead, then stroked her soaked hair near her forehead and temples.

". . . Y . . . S—"

Was that a combination of English and Spanish? *Why es?*

". . . L?" she asked, voice hoarse.

Raffi threw his head back in exasperation. Making jokes? She was fine; she was going to be just fine. And his heart filled. "Jesus Christ. No, it's—who cares? You can talk. Asdvadz . . ."

He hugged her tight and planted an impulsive kiss on her forehead. Professionalism be damned, she almost *died*. Then a second later the rush of oh-shit-what-did-I-do? hit him, and he studied Ani's reaction. But she had a serene smile on her face. She didn't mind. She maybe even liked it. And she was *alive*.

They were both wet, head to toe, and she was shivering in his arms, so he held her tighter.

"How are you feeling? Tell me anything that hurts."

He reached for her wrist, pushed his two fingers against it, and counted. Elevated but not out of control.

She kept the same smile on her face. "I was stuck down there. Terrified when I realized what was happening, panicked, couldn't get myself free. But I felt someone pulling me, and I knew everything would be okay. I was so happy—so happy it was you."

Raffi tried not to let himself get overly excited about that.

He still had a diagnostic to perform. "You feel faint or anything?"

"I'm not—I'm not sure."

Raffi popped his head up and for the first time realized there were people around, surrounding them, talking among themselves. "Hey—" he shouted. "I need a blood pressure cuff, stat. Can anyone here help with this?"

"I'll do it," responded a woman he couldn't quite see.

"Thank you. Towels, too, please? And everyone please back up, give us some space," Raffi ordered. "She's going to be fine."

Having worked in emergency hospital settings and seeing how the team banded together so seamlessly to dispense care, it did shock him how, in the case of an unexpected event outside a medical facility, no one took charge. It was fine, though; he was all too pleased to take control here.

"Ani, lav es?" he asked, checking in again on how she was doing.

"Better and better," she said.

Ani lifted her head slightly, glancing around.

"You're soaked, too."

"Doesn't matter," he replied.

"And you ruined your fancy shoes—"

"Sh, sh, it's okay. Don't worry about them."

He found himself stroking her face again, near her temples, and she leaned into his touch. His heart raced, still ridden with adrenaline but also something else. Something warm and pleasing.

A young woman wearing a DePietro badge appeared by his side and handed him a blood pressure cuff.

"Thanks," he said. "Appreciate your help." Raffi was less

afraid now and feeling less irritated and more charitable toward the crowd.

He wrapped the cuff around Ani's pretty arm—or tev, in Armenian, which also meant "wing" and felt appropriate here. He pumped and took her reading. She sighed in his lap, a content sigh.

"Normal enough," he reported. "Surprising after that scare."

"I don't feel scared anymore," she said, looking up at him. She was breathtaking from this angle. "You were so far away. How did you make it in time?"

"I ran."

"Oh." Ani smiled to herself.

Oh. Because of him? Maybe. He invited hope into his heart, liked the way it nestled in there.

"Let's see if you can stand and get you out of here."

Raffi propped her up while getting into a kneeling position himself. He held her hand while the other was wrapped around her waist. Together, they rose.

He was quite a bit taller than her, and he loved the way she tucked into his chest.

"How does it feel?"

"Great, actually."

"Not like you almost drowned?"

She shook her head. "Not at all."

Then a shiver passed through Ani, and as he held her, he felt the tremble of her body, top to toe.

"We need to get you warm."

A lot of good he was doing her now, soaking as he was. The air, which had previously felt pleasant, now hit as cold.

Luckily, as they walked toward the entrance, that same

employee from before rushed toward them, holding out a DePietro-branded blanket.

"Not quite a towel, but this should work. It's on the house. We are so sorry."

Raffi narrowed his eyes. That was the least they could do, but she seemed to be a young employee, possibly new, most likely not management. He would be coming back and demanding blood. But not from her, and not today.

Raffi grabbed the blanket and draped it over Ani. He reached over to grab her red heels, then carefully fitted each on her feet. She pinched the blanket tightly at her chest.

"What about one for him?" Ani asked.

The employee shifted nervously from foot to foot. "We don't have another. I'm so sorry."

"Ani, I'm fine. Can you walk?"

In truth, he was touched that at this moment, after what happened to her, Ani was thinking about his well-being. She'd nearly drowned, had been trapped underwater, had faced the kind of panic that could break a person apart. And yet here she was, worrying about whether he was warm.

Something about that lodged deep in his chest.

He didn't need a blanket. He was fine. But he wouldn't say no to Ani's concern for him.

"Yes, and in fact . . ." She opened up the blanket and invited Raffi inside her cocoon.

"I really don't—"

But when the warmth of the cotton, and the warmth of her body, pressed against his skin, he acquiesced. He pulled it around himself and put an arm around her to bring them closer so they'd both be wrapped.

"This okay?" he asked.

"Yes," she said, breathlessly.

She was soft, still so wet, but her body was warming from being cloaked.

He could hardly help himself as they walked; it took every ounce of his willpower not to pull her in all the way to his body, tilt up her chin, and kiss her.

Instead, he directed her toward his car. They both stared at the vintage leather interior for a moment.

"This is totally going to ruin your seats, isn't it?"

If Raffi was alone and happened to be fountain-soaked, he would have simply taken off his clothes and driven in the buff. That wasn't really an option here.

"Okay, here's what we're going to do. I'm going to put the top on, bump the heat all the way up. You keep the blanket, I'm—"

"I don't want to completely ruin your seats. Just take off your shirt. Maybe even your pants. I won't look."

He raised an eyebrow at her while his pulse skyrocketed. "You won't look?"

She shrugged.

He hesitated. "You can look."

"I can?"

"I mean, if you— It won't, you know, it won't embarrass me, is what I'm saying."

"Right, right," she said quickly.

"All right so, let's get to it."

Raffi exited the blanket, and the press of her body, the windy Napa air freezing him immediately. He worked to set the roof of the car in place and snapped it in.

Ani swaddled herself and slid into the car, looking snug, he was happy to see.

Now his part. He unbuttoned his shirt and had the distinct thought that this was not how he wanted to be undressing in front of Ani. He had imagined a more intimate scene, not the parking lot of the DePietro Winery, free for any tourist to see.

Ani kept her eyes forward as he undressed, studying the dials and switches of his car. Raffi placed his hands on his pants waist, then felt terribly embarrassed and decided he'd rather destroy his car's interior than sit in his wet Calvin Kleins in front of Ani. If he ever got the chance to take his pants off in front of her, it was going to be on his terms, not dictated by the delicacy of his car.

"I'll get you back to your car so you can go home and rest," he said.

"Thanks," Ani said.

He slid in, Jaguar gods forgive him. Then, true to his word, he turned the heat on as high as it went.

"Would you be okay if I did a more thorough exam when we get to my place? I mean, right before I send you off? I just want to make sure you're okay to drive."

"Of course, that'd—"

She cut herself off, staring at him for the first time since he removed his shirt. He felt her gaze blazing hot on his skin. Raffi kept himself fit. Sure, he was no beefy Moushegh but he was muscled, and weights and cardio were a part of his daily routine. He was vain enough to want, achieve, and maintain a six-pack. That was a bonus, though. Working out had been the only way he'd stayed sane in med school.

"You kept your pants on," she said. Why did she sound almost disappointed about it?

"It was too amot," he replied.

Amot, the Armenian word for "shameful" that ruled behavior. Ensure you don't do anything amot. Don't say anything amot.

"And being shirtless wasn't?"

"It's certainly skirting the line, but I figured my medz would forgive me for losing my shirt. Not the pants, though."

"Fair."

A moment passed, thick with something between them Raffi couldn't quite pin down. Raffi gripped the steering wheel, flexing his fingers against the leather, trying to ground himself. Ani was right there, wrapped in the blanket, close enough that if he just reached out—

He exhaled slowly, forcing himself to focus on the road ahead. She had almost drowned today. That was what mattered. Yes, she had been giving him looks, real interested looks. Yes, she had that flicker of disappointment in her voice when she realized his pants were staying on. And yes, his body had reacted, heat unfurling low in his stomach despite the cold air still clinging to his skin.

But he knew now was not the time to make a move. He exhaled, shifting slightly in his seat, trying to shake off the feeling.

Instead, he wanted to ask her something real, but not too heavy. Something that would let him hold on to these moments a little longer, to keep her in this new, pleasantly strange space they had wandered into.

So he asked, "When you get home, what are you going to do? What are your, I don't know, comfort things?"

It was casual, but the answer mattered. Because after everything, he wanted to know what steadied her, what made her feel safe. He wanted to know her.

Ani smiled, that private smile again. He loved it, and he wanted to put that on her face every single day.

"Well, I'll probably take a bath with some eucalyptus salts."

"Very nice."

"It's not that nice. The bathtub is probably from 1950, and who knows what previous tenants have done in it. I usually just shower."

Please, go on describing the details therein, he thought.

"But then I'll probably get in my giant towel robe and watch *The Wedding Planner* for the zillionth time."

Raffi almost slammed on the breaks. *The Wedding Planner.* Of course she loved that movie. She *was* J.Lo's character personified.

"You really are a modern-day Mary Fiore," he said, a knowing grin on his face.

Ani turned her burritoed body toward him.

"Excuse me?" she asked. "You pulled that deep-cut character-name knowledge out of your head? What is going on here?"

"I love that movie. I've probably seen it about six or seven times."

"Six or seven! You?"

He put a hand over his heart. "You wound me, thinking I wouldn't love a masterpiece like that."

"It's not that, it's just—" She paused. "No, you're right. You've done nothing *but* surprise me, Raffi."

"Hopefully in a good way."

"Definitely in a good way."

He wanted to see the expression on her face but felt it would be too significant, and he wanted that but it also scared him, so Raffi kept his eyes forward.

"My brother introduced me to it," he said. As soon as it was out of his mouth, Raffi couldn't believe he'd said it.

He never talked about Sevan. Never. And now he had twice with Ani.

Not only that, but he felt like he was dying to go on. Raffi explained, "He was completely infatuated with J.Lo and would make these outrageous statements like 'This is J.Lo at peak beauty. Utter perfection.' So we'd sneak around and watch it together, commenting on it like we were sportscasting, cheering when they kissed, all that. We had to make sure Dad was out of the house before we put it on. He'd hate that we were watching it. Only action movies starring men in our household. I've seen every single James Bond movie. Not that I don't love those, too."

Ani gestured around her. "And were possibly influenced by his style?"

He smirked. "Possibly." Yeah, he couldn't say he hadn't wanted to be just like James Bond, the womanizing and all. But even Bond must have grown tired of that life, never attaching himself to anyone. 007 dying alone. Raffi didn't wish for that.

"What about you? It's your comfort movie?"

"I watched it when I was ten or so and realized that was exactly what I wanted to do. My sister and I were always marriage obsessed—" She cleared her throat. "You know, in a kid kind of way. The romance of it all. I'm not, I mean—things have changed there. But I was always kind of a romantic. And always pretty organized. So the idea of getting to plan other people's weddings seemed like a dream. I wanted to be just like Mary Fiore, just as professional and calm and competent."

Why, when she mentioned *marriage obsessed*, did Raffi not freak out but instead get this gooey feeling inside? That was pretty unusual, even for an intense crush. Right? He didn't really know; this was uncharted territory.

"Well, you sure are. Every time I've been calling you Miss Wedding Planner I've had J.Lo—Mary Fiore—in mind."

"That's . . . really sweet. Too bad I don't also have her success."

Raffi cocked his head to the side. She was ambitious, he liked that. "Well, maybe after this wedding you will."

"Put us both on the map."

And generous. He was wishing her success and she came right back and brought him into it. This woman, this woman!

They arrived at his home far too soon, and Raffi did not want their time together to end. He also was legitimately worried about all she had been through, and how her driving an hour and a half back home could be a terrible idea. But he didn't want to seem like he was keeping her here in some kind of domineering, possessive way, especially if she didn't want to stay.

Raffi parked and got out of the car. The shift from being soaked and stuck to the seat to standing upright in mossy fountain wetness was miserable, but he didn't want to keep Ani waiting. He wasn't about to duck inside, change, then tend to her while she was wrapped in this blanket, quietly dripping on the sidewalk.

"Okay, let's check you out," he said.

She came near him, and he became acutely aware of how shirtless he was.

"I have kind of a headache."

"Did you hit your head when you fell?"

"No. More like a regular headache." She pointed to a spot on her head. "Here. It's not so bad, though."

"Would you be okay if I felt around the area? Just in case."

The rise and fall of her chest seemed to deepen slightly. Maybe it was his imagination. Maybe it wasn't. "Yes, that'd be fine," she said quietly.

Raffi weaved his fingers into her hair in the area she indicated, pulling back strands, and looked for bruising, cuts, or any other signs of impact. Her hair was so thick, it fell heavy along his fingers.

"Let me know if anything I'm doing hurts you."

"Okay," she breathed. "It doesn't, so far."

He kept lifting locks but found no signs of impact. He arrived back at the area she had pointed to.

"I'm going to press gently. It might hurt a little, but tell me what it's like on the pain scale."

She nodded. He pressed two fingers against her scalp. "Anything?" he asked.

"No, I don't think so. It's hard to tell. I guess I'm a little, uh, distracted."

Raffi reddened and was glad her head was turned away from him. If there was any legitimate pain, she would have noticed. That was enough to stop his worries and concentrate instead on his joy.

"Oh?" he asked.

"I mean, I'm face-to-face with your pecs. Let's not pretend you don't have—I mean, you know. You know how hot you are."

He honest to God did not think she felt that way. Raffi took pride in his appearance, but Ani seemed, first, preoccupied with Kami, and when that abated, she seemed to be utterly focused on her work. And in their interactions, she called him out, joked with him in ways women he was attracted to didn't. He thought it was possible she didn't find him to be her cup of tea physically, which was fine. Not everyone did.

And now she was telling him how *hot* he was? Standing mere inches from him, his hands wound in her hair.

He decided to run his fingers through, all the way to the ends, and her eyes closed in what appeared to be pleasure. He wanted to do the same.

"Thank you," he said softly. "I've never enjoyed a compliment more."

"Stop," she said, laughing.

He put a hand lightly on her shoulder. "I mean it. It feels truer, coming from you."

A car drove behind them then, blasting an eighties ballad Raffi knew but had forgotten the name of, soundtracking their moment. He should kiss her, right? This was the moment. He could just lean in and touch his lips to hers.

Suddenly her eyes grew huge, huger than normal, which was quite a sight.

"The band!"

He stepped back, feeling the moment was over. He was also curious about what this important band was that could interrupt their quiet, private moment. "What band?"

She closed her eyes in embarrassment. "I can't go home. I

completely forgot. With all the, you know, near-death experiences and all. In a couple hours I was going to check out this band, The Six Intentions, for Kami and Grace. They're supposed to be the best wedding band, but I wanted to see them play live to get their vibe. Music can make or break a wedding, especially one like our brides are planning. When I emailed, they said that they were playing an engagement party tonight and that the family said I was welcome to stop by and listen."

Raffi smiled inwardly. Well, this could work, too.

"That's perfect then."

"No, it's not, look at me!"

Raffi gestured toward his home. "You can do your eucalyptus bath and comfort movie here. I have everything you need to get ready."

She still seemed a bit worried. "Yeah, but I don't have anything to w—"

They looked at each other as she remembered.

"Yes, you do," he said.

"Raffi, God. Did you have this planned?" She laughed.

"Did I make DePietro trip you into its ridiculous fountain? You were right, by the way, about the liability, and I'm never doubting your judgment again."

She smiled, tucking her chin. "Fine, thank you. Okay. I'll stay. But I'm going to wear my normal white dress, not the—"

"You can't wear white to an engagement party." Raffi laughed at himself. "Why am I the one telling *you* this?"

Ani froze, eyes widening slightly as the realization hit. "Oh. Shoot. I—"

"Wear the Balmain."

"I can't—"

"Wear it," he said gently. They stared at each other intensely. Then he added, "It'll be perfect for the party. Assuming it fits. Doesn't hurt to at least try."

She did not break his gaze. "Fine, I'll try it. Show me in."

With that, Raffi scooped up the two dresses from the trunk in one hand, his wet shirt in the other, and led Ani toward his front door.

16

Ani

RAFFI'S HOME WAS ridiculous. It may have technically been a condo or town house or something, but it had a secluded, almost retreat-like feel—despite being attached to neighbors on the east. Two stories, with sweeping views of Napa Valley's hills and vineyards. Floor-to-ceiling windows flooded the space with golden afternoon light, stretching over sleek oak floors and a sprawling sectional that looked like it had never been lounged on. Everything was brand-spanking-new, top-of-the-line, in a style she might call "warm minimalist luxury." It even smelled like a hotel; the air was scented faintly with cedar and something clean, like fresh linen. But as she glanced around, there was so little about his home that felt personal. No framed photos. No knickknacks. He did have a full bookshelf, though, which, given their discussion at his party, didn't surprise her. At least that detail felt real, lived in.

Raffi—still shirtless, chiseled as a statue of Adonis—ran about, straightening pillows, ushering cups and plates toward the sink, and apologizing for the mess. It really, really was not messy. Ani kept a spotless home herself and could not help but think that they were compatible in this way. If they lived together. Which was *crazy*, right?

But the past two hours had been crazy. Ani had stepped into this day knowing she had some budding feelings for Raffi but determined to keep them at bay. And instead, he had showered her with lavish gifts, then saved her goddamn life and took care of her afterward, and her feelings had turned into an actual bay. An expansive, glittering gulf that seemed to only be growing.

They had been standing so close, and she took the plunge and said it out loud. That he was unbelievably hot. She had held back, honestly, from the full range of words she could have used to describe his looks. But he was shirtless—*shirtless*! And holy six-pack, his body. He already looked good in clothes, but she wasn't expecting him to be *cut*, too. Like, chiseled male-model body. My God. And a man who looked like that, who had pulled her out of a death fountain and held her close, almost kissed her.

He had put his hand on her shoulder and Ani knew it was about to happen, she absolutely wanted it to happen, but she was terrified. She hadn't actually kissed anyone since Kami. Two years of dating on the apps and not feeling a spark of chemistry with a single soul. She was afraid she'd forgotten how to do it. Raffi would be getting rusty Ani. And if they kissed, she worried she wouldn't be able to stop, and they'd sleep together, and what if he changed his mind and decided he wasn't that into her? They still had months of working together. She couldn't do that to herself, having Raffi and Kami both trampling all over her heart, and working with both of them on a daily basis. She had to protect herself.

So when that car drove by blasting Spandau Ballet and she remembered where she was supposed to be that evening, Ani could have suppressed it and let the kiss happen. But she ruined it instead.

And now she somehow found herself wrapped in a blanket, warm but damp and uncomfortable, in Raffi's unreal home. About to take a shower. Or a bath.

"Let me show you to the bathroom," Raffi said.

"You have a lovely place," she said.

"Thanks. I feel pretty damn lucky to call it home."

Raffi showed her down a hall, scrubbing a hand over the back of his neck like he wasn't sure what to do with himself. "Here's the guest bath, and there's a bedroom right here if you want to use it for changing or, I don't know, napping? Whatever you want to do."

She nodded, biting back a smile, relishing his awkwardness.

"I was, uh, thinking—" he said.

"Dangerous pastime."

He laughed, and she felt a warming glow at his genuine enjoyment of her little joke. "Really, though, this is kind of awkward but—you have a dress to wear but not the, uh, undergarments." His hand lifted slightly like he was about to gesture, then he thought better of it, shoving it back down to his side instead.

Ani instantly blushed and knew he could see it. "Right," she said. Then tried to distract from her embarrassment. "You mean to tell me you don't have forgotten women's underwear lying all around your home?"

Raffi placed a hand over his heart, feigning deep offense. "Ani, please, I always give back the skivvies. I'm not a heathen."

He dropped his hand, losing the teasing tone as he shifted back into practical matters. "Seriously, though, why don't I just wash your clothes while you're in there. I can do a speed cycle in ten minutes—"

Oh God, he was going to launder her clothes? He was going to touch them. The thought turned her on but also gave her that feeling like, oh God, this was so amot, so very amot.

"Wow, fancy washer-dryer?"

"The speed cycle was why I got it."

The thought of Raffi doing any laundry was, puzzlingly, doing it for her.

Raffi continued, "I was thinking if I start it now they should be dry in less than an hour, so you could even still wear your same outfit. I've got a robe for you in the meantime."

He was so meticulous in his planning for her comfort. She loved it. "The dress can't go in the dryer. Lay flat to dry."

"So, I guess you'll, uh, wear the new dress?"

"I think I will."

Then, there was a moment when they both stood, bathroom door looming larger as it beckoned Ani, neither saying a word.

"I'll just . . ." she said, moving toward it.

"Right, then toss me the clothes. I'll pop them in, then shower off myself."

Ani gulped. He would be holding her sopping-wet, dirty underwear and bra in his bare hands.

She watched his chest rise and fall, and he seemed nervous about it, too, not titillated. She realized she trusted him.

Ani crept into the bathroom—spotless, with a smattering of dark manly face and bath products.

"I have some scented bath salts in the bottom right drawer," he called.

So thoughtful.

Ani had wanted a bath at home, but now she didn't think she could possibly relax, *naked,* in a bathtub while she knew Raffi was out there, handling her dirty clothes, then puttering around the house. And *not* being in that bath with her.

There it was. She could admit it to herself. She wanted Raffi to join her. To continue his nakedness, strip off his pants and boxer briefs, and climb into the bath with her. She wanted to kiss him, to feel his bare skin against hers. Everywhere.

Shit.

She had a feeling that if she invited him in, he wouldn't say no.

But, but. Protecting herself was paramount, far more important than some fleeting lust. Which might not just be lust, but at the moment, lust was dominating her thoughts.

"I might just . . . shower, if that's okay," she called out.

"Doesn't matter to me. You do you."

Ani faced herself in Raffi's bathroom mirror. Her hair was pasted down, mostly wet, although some of her flyaways had dried. Lovely. She wasn't exactly a sight to see.

She shrugged off the blanket, revealing her previously shapeless bag dress tight and clinging to her body. She peeled it off. She saw herself in the mirror in her bra and panties and couldn't help but think that she was inches away from Raffi. In his home. Soon to be naked. And the thought sent a zing of pleasure right between her legs.

She worked off her bra, then her underwear, and put all of her clothes in a neat pile. For modesty's sake, she tucked the undergarments into the dress so they weren't out in the open. "Shnorkov aghchik," she heard her mom's voice say. "Proper girl."

Ani, buck naked, inched toward the door and opened it a crack, feeling a mix of incredibly vulnerable and thrilled at once. With her clothes balled in her hand, she stuck them outside, but when Raffi tried to grab the heavy, wet pile, it teetered and fell to the floor.

"Oh God, I'll—" Ani began.

"No, I'll get it, don't worry. Just get in there and relax. I'll take care of everything out here."

Well, the man said to relax, so she supposed she would.

Leaning into the shower, Ani turned the knob and a waterfall showerhead sprayed, and the room started to steam within a minute. She stepped in and let the warm liquid rush over her. She lifted her face toward the spout and let the water run all along her body, drenching her in its heat but absolutely not purifying her of her thoughts. If anything, when liquid dripped between her thighs, she imagined Raffi's large hands there. She wondered how he would touch her—would he be gentle, or would he be rough? And with him, she realized she wanted both.

Come in, come in. If she just willed him hard enough, maybe he could hear her plea and enter the bathroom. She wanted to hear the turn of the door handle, see his tall frame tower into her vision. She was burning with need for him. But of course, he wouldn't come. He was being nothing but gentlemanly, nothing of the Raffi of Yore she'd heard about.

Oh God, this was not off to a good start. But it didn't matter, she reasoned—thoughts were one thing, but action was quite another. She would be good. She would not kiss this sexy, kindhearted man who had saved her life.

Because there was a distinct possibility that if they kissed, if they did more than kiss, he would never call her again. She couldn't get her hopes up, put her heart out there on the line, only for it to be stomped on once again. That was what she needed to focus on.

Ani finished up her shower, sadly not having enticed him to join her with sheer telepathic powers but having successfully not delved too deep into her Raffi fantasies. She wrapped herself in his extra-plush towels, the fabric still carrying the faint warmth of the heated rack.

When she'd finished blow-drying, she found the robe Raffi had mentioned, pulling the soft weight around her shoulders with a sigh. It was the kind of robe that made her want to curl up and never take it off.

Then she checked herself out. Now this was a look. Her hair turned out glossy, bouncy—thanks to Raffi's unfair talent in picking out hair products. Her makeup was mostly gone, but a touch remained so she had a nice, natural look going. And wrapped in that robe, which skimmed the top of her feet. She cinched the belt tight, the material smooth against her skin—a reminder that she was entirely, completely naked underneath.

She opened the bathroom door and stepped into the hall. At first she didn't see Raffi, but then she caught him in the kitchen, arranging food on plates, concentration and a touch of panic painting his face. He had gotten them sandwiches, it appeared, and salads in the time she'd spent washing up.

"I didn't know if you ate meat," he said as if in mid-thought. "So I got a turkey and a vegetarian from The Parker's room service, but you can have either."

Ani's heart swelled, and a low, steady heat glowed in her chest. It was such a simple thing, really. A sandwich. But the fact that he had thought about it, thought about her, made something settle inside her in a way she hadn't expected.

She also hadn't realized how hungry she was until now—for food, sure, but maybe for this, too. For someone noticing the small things.

Then he looked up at her and froze, taking in the sight of her freshly showered. His eyes sparked with appreciation before he blinked it away and turned back to his preparations.

Ani pretended not to notice, leaning casually against the cool counter. "Turkey sounds good to me, unless the vegetarian happens to have a big slab of mozzarella? Can't say no to that."

Raffi's smile grew. "It's your lucky day. The veggie special today was mozzarella pesto. Kind of jealous, to be honest. I should have gotten two of them."

"We can switch."

Raffi scoffed. "You kidding me? Miss Wedding Planner, my guest, gets what she wants. Whatever she wants."

Crimson crept to her cheeks. *Whatever she wants*. He was a spoiler, my God, and she liked it.

"Speaking of," he said. Then he gestured toward the TV in the other room. On the screen was the opening frame of *The Wedding Planner.*

"All queued up and ready to go."

She closed her eyes a second longer than a blink to take it in. "This is really sweet, Raffi. I just want you to know . . . I appreciate it."

He did the thing where he paused again, his hands stilling on the counter, as if needing a moment to soak up her words. Then he said, "After the morning you had, I figure it's the least I can do."

He shifted his weight, reaching for a bottle on the counter and running his thumb along the label in an absent motion. "Wine? Or is it too early?"

Ani didn't drink much, but somehow, a glass of cold wine sounded lovely at the moment.

"Only if it's Ô," she said. "The rest of the stuff in Napa is trash." She couldn't even say that without breaking, and her smile caught on Raffi's face, too.

"One sauv blanc, coming right up."

Raffi poured for both of them, then brought the plates and drinks to the coffee table in front of the TV. Ani followed his lead, taking a seat on the beige couch. The cushions rose around her, pulling her in with a slow give. The whole scene felt strangely domestic—easy in a way that made her stomach tighten.

He flipped on the movie, and Ani took a long sip of her wine. Cool and refreshing, with a little fruitiness that lingered on her tongue. Ô really did have something special here. She took a renewed interest in helping out Raffi with his marketing. It was funny, she wasn't so great at marketing herself, but touting someone else's product came much easier to her.

The opening credits rolled and the familiar music of

up-tempo early 2000s soft pop began as Ani took her first bite of the sandwich. The flavors hit all at once, and she had to voice it. "What the hell is in this?"

Raffi sat up straight, alarmed. "What? Is there something wrong? An allergen? A fingernail?"

Ani laughed. "I meant 'what the hell' in a good way. Is this God's pesto? I've never tasted anything like it."

He put out his hand. "Okay, you can't call it 'God's pesto' and not give me a taste."

She raised the sandwich toward his mouth, pushing into inappropriate territory. "Be my guest."

She was feeding Raffi Garabedian a mozzarella sandwich.

She watched as his teeth sank into the bread, and she had several impure thoughts about what else she'd like those teeth grazing against.

Then he moaned, which only intensified her visions of his mouth against her. After a couple of chews, he said, "Damn, I've got to order this next time."

Ani concentrated on slowing her breathing and distracted herself by watching the little-kid version of J.Lo carefully arranging Barbies on the screen.

When the camera panned to the little girl holding up the bride and groom dolls, Raffi pointed to the TV and said, "Hey, that's you!"

Ani shrugged, but she couldn't help the way her smile grew. "Honestly, not too far off."

They ate and watched, and Ani relished how much Raffi was getting into the film. She had it memorized, too, and enjoyed overreacting to the big moments and character introductions.

Then, in the scene where J.Lo and Matthew McConaughey met at a San Francisco outdoor movie and the mood was quiet and romantic, Ani felt her eyes growing heavy. They closed once, then fluttered open as the couple on-screen shed their jackets. Raffi murmured, "You know this is fiction because no one would willingly remove their outer layers in Golden Gate Park. Can't even look at them without a secondhand shiver."

"Mm-hmm," she agreed, her voice soft with drowsiness. Her eyes fluttered shut, and she instinctively leaned into the nearest source of warmth—solid, steady, and impossibly comfortable.

When she woke, McConaughey was smiling like the happiest fool in the Civic Center, realizing Mary wasn't married. Why had Raffi fast-forwarded . . . ?

And then, Ani realized she was pressed up against Raffi, his arm draped around her. She felt cocooned, safe, and absurdly comfortable. But also, holy shit, she'd fallen asleep on him?

She rubbed her eyes. "Oh my God. Sorry, didn't realize how tired I was."

Raffi turned toward her, his voice thick and soothing. "It's okay. I wanted to keep you upright, just in case. I hope you don't mind . . ." He rubbed her arm quickly once with his hand.

"I don't at all. It's, um, comfortable."

"Yeah. Comfortable," he said, although she could hear him swallowing.

Afraid to break the spell of Raffi holding her tight, Ani didn't move a muscle or say another word, and they both quietly watched the climax of the movie, as Matthew McConaughey rushed through San Francisco in search of his one true love. When the two main actors embraced and shared their kiss at last, Ani had to focus extra hard on not moving, and she felt Raffi stiffen, too.

She wanted it, though. If Raffi were to swoop in and kiss her, she'd do it. She'd kiss him. Caution be damned, she wanted this man. That was the moral of the movie, right? You can't fight your true feelings.

But Ani was also a little coward and could not find it in herself to make the first move. So instead she sat there, frozen, Raffi's protective arm around her, while the two of them watched a different couple make out on-screen.

If they weren't going to kiss, maybe they could talk, because Ani needed to know something.

"Do you believe in this stuff?" she asked.

"What? Leaving your fiancé at the altar is a good idea?"

"No, you know. Love. All that." Ani's voice cracked only the tiniest bit when she said *love*.

"I never did. Life seems too random and cruel for something so pure. Like if you skip ahead ten years, J.Lo is going to be throwing vases at Matthew McConaughey's head and he's going to be doing that crazy smile-shout thing back at her, making all kinds of accusations."

Ani blinked at him, torn between laughing and being slightly horrified. "That's . . . kind of terrible?"

"Well, that's the example I've seen."

"Your parents didn't get along?"

He laughed, an actual loud, scoffing laugh. "That's an understatement. They always fought, but after my brother died, they said some pretty unforgivable things to each other, so my mom just . . . left. She spends most of her time in Europe, Armenia, and Lebanon, and if we're lucky, she'll come around once a year for the holidays."

That. Was. Horrible. She couldn't even imagine. His brother died. His father maligned him, and his mother abandoned him. She felt this sinking feeling in her stomach for Raffi, for his loneliness, for his years of pain.

"Jesus."

"Yep. So, I don't know. Tough to believe in the power of love after that. It skipped my household anyway."

"I don't even—I'm so sorry."

He squeezed her once. "Don't feel too sorry for me. I have plenty. I'm grateful for it, too."

"Yeah, but *love*. Kind of important."

"Well, what about you? Do you believe in all this?" He waved at the screen.

Ani exhaled, glancing at the rom-com still playing, at the sweet ending where everything wraps up neatly in a bow. Did she believe in it? The grand, all-consuming, meant-to-be kind of love? "Not that particular story necessarily, although I'd like to think Mary and Steve were still having mind-blowing sex ten years on."

He laughed, a happy, surprised one this time. And she liked it. She wanted Raffi to laugh like that instead of the sad, angry version.

Then she continued, "I'm kind of the opposite. Lifelong romantic, lover of all things pretty and dreamy. Grand romantic gestures, the whole shebang. Until recently. Realized that's pretty unrealistic. Most people don't get lucky that way. There are no grand romantic gestures in real life."

She stopped herself from mentioning Kami. Somehow, she didn't want to bring up her ex anymore. It didn't feel right.

"Kami," Raffi said. Ani groaned. "She really did a number on you. What happened?"

Ani sat up more, and unfortunately she was farther from Raffi this way, but he kept his arm around her while she faced him.

"First off, I want to tell you this honestly. Since working on her wedding the past few weeks, I don't know, it's like the Kami spell has been broken. I see her more clearly. Sort of how you see her, although not as critically."

"Really?" he asked, a tone of hopefulness in his voice she clung to.

"Yes, seriously. The things she demands of me, her total lack of regard for me. It got to a breaking point. I mean, she's still my client—my biggest client, by far—so I'm bending over backward for her, don't get me wrong. But it's not really *my pleasure to serve* anymore. Or, I don't know, I'll serve her, as her wedding planner, but not with this wistful *it should have been us*. I get it. We would not have worked out. We didn't. And that's how it was supposed to be."

Raffi nodded thoughtfully. "For a while you thought breaking up was a mistake?"

"A long while. An embarrassingly long while. She just— I stupidly thought she was the one. She's so fun-loving and spontaneous and brought me out of my shell. She'd say all of these insanely complimentary things about me, building me up, to a point where I was convinced that was love. But looking back, sometimes it seemed like they were just words. Not much else. Like, for example, when we had plans to meet on a

Friday night but hadn't settled on where or what time exactly, she'd just drop off, not answer my calls or texts for hours. And then at like nine p.m. or something, she'd ask me to meet her at a bar where she was with some friends. That would make me feel so shitty, but then I'd get there, and she'd introduce me to everyone as this style and design genius and her beautiful girlfriend, and I'd sort of forget about it. If I ever brought it up, she'd apologize profusely and then start making out with me. And this wasn't just one or two times. This happened *all the time*. That's—I mean, that's not the worst. But it's not really considerate, right?"

His fingers drummed once against his knee before he shifted closer, his body angling toward her. "No, it's not. Ani, you deserve so much better."

"Ha, I don't know about that."

His gaze held hers, steady and unflinching. "You do. You're an incredible person. And words only go so far. You need those words, don't get me wrong. You should be told how special you are, but you also deserve the actions to back them up. Someone who's there for you. Who takes responsibility for their mistakes."

She wished she could ask, "Someone like . . . you?"

The way he was looking at her now, the darkness in his eyes pulling her in, closer and closer. She could practically feel his body buzzing with electricity. He glanced, in a heartbeat of a moment, toward her lips, then back up.

Ani turned away shyly, suddenly burning from his eye contact. "Well, thank you."

"But I'm glad," he said, "that you're seeing Kami more clearly."

"You are?"

"Yeah, I am," he said quietly. "Why?" she wanted to ask, but she couldn't get her mouth to form the word. Ani started to feel so incredibly awkward, like it was on her to push him toward a kiss, but she just couldn't do it. It was not her way.

Ani took charge in many areas of her life. She quit her job she hated; she started a new business; she alone made herself responsible for the debt she got herself into. In her work, she directed, she led, and she was happy to march forward when brides needed a guide.

But in her love life, she was different.

She wanted others to make the first move, to have them press themselves upon her (metaphorically and literally). It was as if she needed confirmation she was wanted, but that wasn't all. To let someone else drive, for once—that was what she liked. Not with everything all the time, but for a first kiss especially? She couldn't put her finger on why; she just knew that was the way she was.

In fact, now that Ani thought about it, that had been one area in which she hadn't been totally content with Kami, although she pushed aside her feelings and pretended it wasn't a big deal. Kami had kissed her first, and she would sometimes initiate in unexpected moments, but in general, Kami wanted to sit there and be admired. And because there was plenty to admire, Ani wasn't all that conscious of the fact that she herself was often left unsatisfied.

Ani wasn't going to make that same mistake again. She simply could not kiss Raffi right now, and he was refusing to kiss her, so there was only one choice.

She sprung up.

"You know, we still have a bit of time before we head over.

I brought my laptop. Do you want to get started on some of that Ô promotion?"

Raffi gave a weak smile, and Ani wondered if that was a sign of disappointment at her abrupt subject change. "Good thinking. Let's see what you got."

And so Ani spent the next hour and a half side by side with Raffi on her computer, showing him the various websites, asking him information about Ô, and adding it to the wedding venue registries. Then she mocked up a version of the page he needed to add to his site. It was time well spent, but also, she sort of cursed herself for not taking the chance with him when she had it. Over and over.

"And this final promo button here," Ani said.

Raffi scooted closer to read the small text.

Their legs were touching suddenly. A light area of pressure. But the heat of him spread through her body like wildfire.

Ani's breathing grew heavy as she melted into the feel of his leg against hers.

The laptop suddenly felt too warm on her thighs. Or maybe it was the way he was so close now, the scent of him, like fire-light drifting through a dark night.

He pointed to something on the screen, murmured some-thing low and distracted, and she couldn't process a word of it. She could only feel.

She wanted to throw her laptop aside and straddle him again, wanted his hands squeezing her hips, wanted to kiss the breath out of him, wanted—

Raffi scooted away. "The time. We should probably go," he said softly.

That one registered.

Ani, yanked out of that dream of closeness, cleared her throat. "Right. Thanks, yeah."

He hadn't kissed her. Maybe she'd misread him. Maybe as they grew closer, he only felt sisterly affection for her. The fountain, the near drowning, it might have made him feel more like a big brother than a boyfriend. Because he wasn't making a move. Raffi—the consummate flirt, the playboy, the silver-tongued tease—would not kiss her.

She grew sad as she rose, put away her laptop, and went to the bedroom to get dressed. Her spirits buoyed only slightly by the prospect of putting on the prettiest dress she'd ever owned.

17

Raffi

ANI WAS AN absolute vision. She always was, even soaking wet and coughing up fountain water. But the look on her face right now, wearing the dress he had bought her, was something new. She glowed like she felt taken care of, adored, and he hoped he might have had something to do with it.

"So, it fits," she smiled shyly.

"You can sure say that," he said, unable to stop himself from sounding like he was salivating. Like really, man, rein it in.

"Thank you so much, again. I don't deser—"

"Do not even finish that sentence. Yes, you do."

And now Raffi also knew exactly what garments were under that dress. A matching white bra and panty set. Lace trim on both. He tried very hard not to study it all too much because he didn't want to be gross, but she had handed him the pile. They had fallen out. And he had pulled them out of the dryer and folded them on the guest bed. There had been time for his eyes to roam and his brain to imagine.

"Let's go check out this engagement party," Raffi said, and ushered her toward the door.

They arrived at the Napa Harvest Inn, which sounded much quainter than it was—a sprawling hundred-acre property with luxurious villas dotting the landscape. He could already hear the band playing.

Ani slid out of the car with so much elegance, considering that she'd had a near-death experience just hours before. He remembered it again, seeing her body sinking in the water, and he was gripped with a sudden urge to hold her and never let go. He'd first had that thought while she napped on him during the movie. He didn't think his brain absorbed one single second of the film because he was too focused on the feel of Ani snuggled against him. And also, at several points, willing his boner to disappear by thinking of the unsexiest things possible. Palm Sunday church service with his grandma. That time Raffi's nemesis stole the soccer ball from him and immediately scored a goal. His spiteful childhood piano teacher who was always eating egg salad sandwiches while he practiced. They all worked like charms, until he felt Ani's breath rise up and down, felt her cheek against his shoulder, her lips pouty, so kissable.

He'd wanted to kiss her many times but felt, after what she'd been through, that perhaps he shouldn't push. She seemed into him, he thought. Maybe? She certainly trusted him to handle her underwear. She'd fallen asleep on top of him. She hadn't moved when she woke up to find his arm around her. These were good signs.

But a kiss was something else entirely. He wasn't going to do it just yet. The moment wasn't right, with them just arriving and Ani about to work.

Didn't mean he couldn't be close to her now, though. Raffi rushed to Ani's side, closed the car door for her, and held out his arm like he was courting her. To his pleasure, she took it, and they walked arm in arm toward the music.

"Does your family do engagement parties?" Ani asked. "You know, your broader family?" she added quickly.

He didn't want Ani to feel that his family was a sore subject. To that end, he should probably stop being an emo jerk every time they were brought up. He regretted his mean laugh earlier when she asked about his parents' relationship.

"Don't feel bad about asking about my family," he said. "I promise I'll be less grumpy about it. I like talking about even the hard stuff with you."

"Thank you," she said quietly, and he may have imagined it but she moved a little closer to him.

"But yeah, my second cousin and their whole branch of the family is into that. A bunch of siblings have all been lucky in love, so I've been to my fair share of engagement parties. Usually just as big as the wedding."

She nodded. "We only had one in my family, and I was thirteen or so, but I remember thinking how romantic it was. My uncle—or, like, second cousin once removed? I always forget—he and his bride seemed so enamored with each other. They're still going strong. I like that whenever I see them together and he's telling a story—he's a fantastic storyteller by the way, that whole side of the family is—she still looks at him like he's the funniest, most amazing man in the world."

"Fuck, that's sweet."

The sun was setting, styling Ani in golden light as they walked past row after row of grapes.

"Yeah, it is." She paused a moment. "My parents are like that, too. I didn't want to, you know, rub salt in the wound, but it's been kind of nuts growing up with parents who are still so obsessed with each other. I feel like they often put themselves first, above me and my sister—"

He liked learning this about Ani's family, even if it was in stark contrast to his own. He wanted her to be happy. And he was curious about her sister, since, well, he had a thing about siblings.

"So, you have a sister."

"Yeah, younger, actually. The more successful, prettier version of me. Ani 2.0."

Raffi stopped walking, and because they were linked, Ani jerked back. "Don't say that," Raffi said, serious.

"What?" She shrugged. "It's true. She is a corporate lawyer—not a *paralegal*, mind you—a very fancy lawyer who works a thousand hours a week. She got married first—my *younger* sister—to an Armenian man, and she'll probably be having kids soon. Every Armenian parent's fantasy."

"That's great for her, but you're chasing a different dream right now. You hated law. Do you wish you were a lawyer?"

"No."

"You like what you do, right?"

"Honestly, I love it."

"There you go."

"But I'm not successful."

"We talked about this, Ani jan. *Yet*. You're not where you want to be, *yet*."

"Okay Mr. Growth Mindset."

He smirked. "It's true, though. You have high expectations for yourself, that's great. And you're working toward them. I think that's fantastic."

He did. He loved her drive, and her work ethic inspired him to be better. Somehow, seeing her striving made him want to push all the more, too.

Raffi started walking again along the crunchy pebbles, satisfied that he'd made his point. He was also pleased to feel Ani's arm brushing this way and that along his again as they took their strides.

Ani dug into her purse and pulled out her phone. "Yeah, but I don't look like this."

The background of her phone was a photo of her and her sister at a party of some kind. Both of them dressed up, hugging, smiling, and they seemed like they genuinely liked each other. Ani's sister was undoubtedly hot—her hair and makeup were done, but overdone, in his opinion. You could see more of what Ani really looked like. Her sister was taller, but Raffi liked Ani's petite stature. He loved how she fit into him. Plus, there was some look in her sister's eye, or maybe it was the angle of her jaw, that simply didn't attract him.

"She's very nice, but she's no you."

Ani rolled her eyes, hard. "Oh, come on."

"It's true. You're a natural beauty."

Now Ani stopped dead in her tracks. "You can't be serious. I don't think anyone's called me that in my life."

"Well then, they missed out on a chance to give a compliment to a natural beauty. You can't tell me you don't know you're gorgeous."

Ani's cheeks blushed so quickly, so scarlet, Raffi's heart burned with joy. He'd made her do that.

What else could he make her do?

Then she picked back up. They were nearly at the tent

where the band was playing. "You're just saying that," Ani muttered, which Raffi could hardly hear over the boom of the bass.

"I'm not," Raffi replied. "I told you my policy, right? I'm transparent. I don't lie, and I don't flatter. I do compliment, however, when compliments are due. And you, Ani Avakian, are gorgeous."

He stopped just outside the tent while he delivered this line, with Ani's eyes locked straight onto his, her sun-blessed skin glowing with neon hues. Her neck arched toward him.

He could kiss her now, he could really kiss her. A quiet gravity began to pull Raffi and Ani together, the distance dissolving between them ever so slowly. He watched Ani's eyes darken with anticipation, while he steeled his nerves, not truly believing this was actually happening, when a loud "Opa!" was shouted from a group of men directly behind them, clinking shot glasses and downing cloudy ouzo.

The moment was over.

Raffi shook himself, pretending the almost-kiss didn't almost-happen. His voice came out somewhat hoarse. "Greek engagement party?"

Ani seemed distracted, like she was still a few seconds behind. She took a deep breath and turned on a smile. It was her business smile, though. "Yep, the soon-to-be Athanasious couple, I believe. That's why this band is so special; the members are Greek Armenians, so they can do the American stuff and Armenian songs, too. Plus Greek ones, as we might see."

A little bitter at having failed at kissing her, Raffi tried to shake it off and led Ani through the doors of the tent and into the world of the party. The music blared, playing an impressive cover of "Uptown Funk," while guests chatted and laughed and hugged and danced. The tent glowed with hundreds of lights, creating a floating effect, and at the center of each table stood a massive flower arrangement. He realized they were surrounded by people who looked quite a bit like them, although somewhat different. Alternate versions of his parents, cousins, aunts, uncles, grandparents, and friends everywhere. He and Ani were more or less indistinguishable from the other party guests.

"If we get a drink, would that be unethical?" he asked Ani.

"The soon-to-be Athanasious apparently invited me to go ahead and have a glass on them. I think, in all this expense"—she gestured around—"it would be okay if we took two."

He followed her to the bar, where she had a glass of champagne—so classy, of course she did—and he had an old-fashioned. They landed near some high-top tables where they could view the band, the guests, the whole spectacle, but not be in the way.

The engaged pair danced in the center of the floor, surrounded by friends and family, doing a call-and-response singalong to "Call Me Maybe." Everyone was pushed so tightly together, gyrating and smiling, as if a gale had swept them all together and they were tickled by the happy accident. He felt a tinge of loneliness then, but when he glanced down at Ani, at her long lashes studying the scene, the sadness receded. This was . . . interesting.

Once Raffi had stopped attending Armenian celebratory events with the sole purpose of finding a woman to sleep with, he found he was only crushingly lonely at them. So he left behind the Armenian banquet scene all together, unless he was forced to attend a friend's or cousin's wedding.

What a different world this all would be with Ani by his side. He was seriously considering it, wasn't he? Not just Ani as someone to get to know a little better, not as someone who was just a plus-one, someone he casually liked. But as someone to be with. Attending these events. Being in the center of the dance floor. Her in a long white dress. A jolt shot down his spine, but it was more thrill than fear. And that thought amped him up still more.

"The band has a great vibe," Ani said, near shouting over the music.

"Agree," Raffi said. "Dance floor's packed, young and old. That's how you know they're good."

Ani smirked. "You're an expert in barahanteses, aren't you?"

A reference to his attending many such dance-centered events, ones he was realizing he missed.

Raffi shrugged. "I've been to a fair few. Not lately, though. Haven't been in the mood."

"Really, why?"

How much could he tell her? "Felt hollow after a while. I'm not a big dancer anyway."

No, he was. He used to be. But the truth died in his mouth.

Ani watched the dance floor, her fingers skimming the rim of her champagne glass. "Me neither. I got rejected in a really embarrassing way my sophomore year in high school and I just sort of stopped. God, that sounds stupid. You'd think I'd be over it."

She said it like it was something small, but her voice

dipped at the end. Raffi said, "It doesn't sound stupid. What happened?"

Ani gave him a look. "You really want to know?"

He did. He honestly did. He'd stand here and listen to her tell the entire story of her past, from her very first memory until right now, if she offered it. "Yes, I really do," he said.

Ani threw her head back and sighed. "Ugh. Well. I wasn't unpopular in school but I wasn't popular. But. Everyone knew I had a crush on this boy named Adrian, like a stupid, tell-everyone-about-it, write-his-name-in-your-notebook crush. I guess the hottest girl in school also liked him, and he rejected her. So at homecoming, I thought I looked cute, it was a sports theme and I had this tennis outfit on, really feeling myself—"

Raffi would like to see her in this outfit now, but part of his stomach was also in knots because he sensed danger looming for poor Ani. He almost didn't know if he could take hearing it.

She continued, still casual, almost dismissive of her memory. "And all these girls started coming up to me telling me Adrian thought I looked super hot and wanted me to ask him to dance. That he was too shy or something. Which checked out because he was a boy of few words. They were like, all these girls I didn't talk to that much, and they seemed excited for me. And then 'You Belong with Me' came on, and I loved that song, and it seemed like a sign because, you know, it's about the shy girl with the popular guy—"

Raffi found he was holding his breath.

"So I went up to Adrian, who was standing with a group of his guy friends, and I was insanely nervous, near shaking. I tapped him on the shoulder, and he turned around, along with the five or six guys, and I asked him in this squeaky voice if he wanted to dance. Aaaand he stared at me for a second, assessing, this look in his eyes like he had no idea who I even was. So he sized me up and then just said, 'Sorry, no,' with a backdrop of his bros covering their mouths and going 'Ohhh!!!' and 'Rejected!' And I gave this fake smile and said, 'That's okay!' all chipper like—"

Raffi's heart squeezed hard, and he felt a little sick for fifteen-year-old Ani's pain. It looked like real, living pain, too, by the look on her face. That son of a bitch Adrian didn't know shit.

"And as if that wasn't bad enough, I realized that the popular girl and her clique were all watching the rejection going down, and when I turned around, they were all pointing and laughing and giggling. I cried and called my parents to come pick me up early and—ugh. It's so silly, though. It happened forever ago."

His fingers flexed, and his jaw tightened. He knew high school was ruthless, that kids could be cruel, but hearing it now, knowing it had happened to her—it made something dark and protective stir inside him.

How dare anyone treat Ani that way? How dare they make her feel small?

Raffi shook his head. "Don't minimize it. That is absolutely cruel. Give me this girl's name, Adrian's too. I have a couple revenge ideas. Tit for tat, nothing crazy. A little shaming, a little humiliation—"

Ani laughed. "Raffi, we were all kids. It seems silly to still be mad at a fifteen-year-old. Besides, I think she has, like, triplet babies and lives in North Carolina or somewhere out there."

"Still . . ." Raffi breathed, feeling gruff and fiercely loyal to this beauty by his side.

Then the band began to play a slow Greek ballad Raffi was not familiar with. It was pretty, though, with its use of the bouzouki, the Greek guitar. His uncle was an instrument aficionado and occasionally played it, along with the guitar, the duduk, the saz, and sometimes the sitar.

Raffi had been to Santorini on one occasion, to visit his mother when she refused to come home for Christmas, and they had something that resembled an almost good time. He remembered one sweet moment, when they sat at a restaurant with some live music in the evening, eating fresh fish, overlooking the caldera. He wanted to go back there with Ani. And to Hayastan, the motherland. To Beirut, where his parents had immigrated from. If she would have him.

As the music played, he felt something larger than himself, pushing him to take a chance. A risk. Whispering in his ear that it would be worth it if he just let himself try. A voice that had been dormant so many years reawakening because of Ani, for Ani, about Ani.

He'd be a fool not to listen.

Raffi put his glass down and his hand out. "May I have this dance, Ani Avakian?"

She stared at him, incredulous. "Are you being serious?"

"Dead serious. I would love nothing more than to dance with you right now."

"You're not doing this just because of the story—"

"Partly, but I wouldn't ask if I didn't mean it. Nothing would make me happier."

He kept his hand out, hoping he'd feel hers in it soon. Then

Ani rested her flute upon the table and took his hand. When she touched him and he felt her softness in his palm and against his fingers, he knew he'd made the right decision. Ten years away from the dance floor, from depriving himself of moving his body to music. But today, right now, with Ani, he'd begin again.

He squeezed her velvety hand and led her to a corner of the floor. The band members played their mix of traditional and nontraditional instruments, and the lead singer crooned a sad, sweet melody that was clearly about love. And then Raffi ushered Ani into his arms, one hand on her waist, one holding her hand. Waltz style for tonight. Nothing fancy. He didn't want to show off at a place he wasn't even technically invited to.

In position, it was like new life was breathed into him. His hand, his muscles, they were ready to bend and sway with the music. Called off duty too soon, ready to return at a moment's notice.

Raffi leaned into Ani's ear and whispered, "Follow me."

Her face flushed sugary pink. "Gladly," she breathed.

Then he took off, slowly at first, with an inch of room between their bodies. He moved simply, rotating with calm, left-right taps, to which Ani followed along beautifully, no instruction needed. He caught her eye, and she looked away quickly with that private smile. He loved it, he loved catching it, he loved being the reason for her mirth.

And oh, how he'd missed this, the rhythm of his feet, the bending of his core, the filling of his whole body with music and letting it fly. He'd starved himself from this joy of his, and why? Suddenly it seemed so stupid to self-flagellate by taking away one of his life's greatest pleasures. He could have been feeling *this* all along. Then again, maybe he was just waiting for the right partner to bring him back.

The song grew in power during the chorus and Raffi followed suit, extending the length of his steps, taking Ani for a ride all along the edge of the dance floor. Her eyes lit up in surprise. He threw her out for a spin, and goddamn, the woman followed all his cues, turning and then pressing back into him. Closer now, much closer. Their bodies touched, torsos end to end. Raffi kept the pressure of his hand tight on her lower back.

"Okay, Fred Astaire," Ani said, so close against him he could feel her vocal chords reverberating against his chest. "So you can dance."

"That don't impress you much?" he asked, mirroring Shania Twain's accent.

Ani let out a loud laugh, then quickly buried her face in his chest.

"You, Raffi jan, are hilarious. And continue to surprise me in all the best ways—nineties pop-country references, ballroom dancing?"

He'd say it now. He'd tell her. She shared with him; he'd share with her.

He slowed their clip and then spoke. "I used to dance, you know. I stopped after Sev."

Ani looked horrified. "Oh God, I didn't realize. I would have never told my silly little story."

"No, no, yours is legit, are you kidding? I'm happy you told me."

She gave a small nod. "So, you took classes?"

"Yes, and competed."

She blinked, her lips parting slightly, like she was seeing him in a new light. "Wow, okay. Surprise after surprise. Were you good?"

He shrugged. "I was getting good. Sev was always so supportive, came to my competitions. He and Mom. We kept it from Dad. Not manly enough, you know."

He couldn't believe he was telling her this. He hadn't told *anyone.*

"I had no desire to, after Sev died. None. And not just competing—dancing at all. It felt polluted, cheapened."

Because it had been about more than just some dance classes.

Yes, his mother had suggested them, but Raffi had been too scared of his dad finding out. So she brought in backup.

Raffi took a deep breath and shared with Ani. "It was Sevan who pushed me, who reassured me. Who made it 'okay,' even though it was something we were doing without Dad knowing. Sev dragged me to my first lesson, clapped me on the back, and said, 'You're going to kill it, trust me.' And he'd been right."

Dancing had been the one place Raffi let himself be something other than what their father expected. It was where he felt weightless, where his body moved without thought, where he didn't have to live inside the rigid, unspoken rules of their family. It was freedom, and his mother, but mostly Sev, had given it to him.

Raffi continued. "But then . . . Sev was gone. The idea of dancing without hearing his voice cheering from the crowd, without him rushing out to the floor afterward, congratulating me like I'd just won an Olympic medal—it felt wrong."

Like moving his body that way, trying to reclaim that joy, would be an insult. Like dancing without Sevan to witness it, to validate it, would erase part of what had made it meaningful in the first place.

He couldn't say it out loud yet, could barely tell himself. But then Ani looked at him with so much support in her eyes, with a quiet understanding, that it nearly undid him. She wasn't pitying him. She wasn't rushing to fill the silence. She was just . . . there. Listening. He felt like this was right, telling her.

Finally, she said, "I can imagine. So when did you start again?"

Raffi paused. A quiet breath, then: "Um. Now."

Ani stumbled at his words and stepped on Raffi's foot. He didn't mind. She barely seemed to notice in her shock. "Wait. You mean to tell me you haven't danced in—am I getting this right—ten years?"

"Yes."

"But you're dancing now. Why?"

Raffi exhaled, feeling the weight of the moment pressing against his ribs. The dance floor was full, the song rolled along in its romance, but in his mind, they were the only two people under the glittering lights of the tent.

Be brave, man, he told himself.

"You."

The word hung between them, fragile but unshakable. Her eyes locked on his.

Raffi continued, "I felt like if I danced with you, I could do it again."

She whispered, "Oh, wow."

"Good 'Oh, wow'?"

Ani nodded, quick little bobs. "Yes, absolutely. Thank you—thank you for sharing that with me. I feel like this could not have been easy."

"Honestly, it's been shockingly easy, dancing with you. Opening up to you."

Then the smile she gave him. Her eyes so full. "You're something else, Raffi Garabedian."

He loved hearing his name out of her pretty, kissable mouth.

"Oh yeah?" he asked, feeling a little nervous. Not wanting to fish for compliments but wanting, very much, to hear her thoughts on him.

"Oh yes. Your kindness, your humor, your generosity. Your rock-hard pecs."

Now it was his turn to laugh, but really, he was lit up like someone had flipped a switch in him. A thousand watts shining on the marquee of opening night, letting everyone know something new was happening.

"Well, coming from you, that means a lot."

"Coming from me?" she asked shyly.

"Ani," he said seriously. "I want you to know, I—I—"

He hadn't said these words in forever, not since Kami, but this time, it felt so different, not just lust or infatuation. It felt *real*.

He stalled on speaking but suddenly remembered Audre Lorde's words, buried in his memory, a passage he had flagged and committed to memory. Like he knew, one day, he would need them: "What is most important to me must be spoken, made verbal and shared, even at the risk of having it bruised or misunderstood."

In Ani, he saw the woman who challenged him, who made him laugh, who shared her gifts with so much humility. He saw her in his too-short winery T-shirt, he saw her straddling him and bringing him back to life, he saw her private smile, he saw her under the water. And he had to tell her.

"—I really, *really* like you."

Her eyes searched his like a lifeline, like his words were saving her somehow. Her brows pulled together, her expression a mix of seriousness, vulnerability, and shock. The fairy lights of the tent surrounded her lovely face like a halo.

The bridge of the song began, the lyrics desperate and pleading.

"Raffi, I—"

His chest tightened. Every muscle in his back drew taut, bracing for her response.

"—I feel the same way."

And that was it. The confirmation he needed, the verbal key to his long-locked heart. Not an end but a beginning.

Raffi, still holding her, placed their joined hands against his heart. Let her feel it pound. Let her know how wild she drove him.

If he didn't kiss her right now, he might die.

He leaned down, pressing his forehead to hers. Her eyes fluttered closed, taking in the moment.

"Please . . ." she pleaded.

The word cracked him open.

Shock, joy, and want all collided in one sweeping rush that

left him dizzy. Their lips hadn't even touched and already he felt undone.

She asked. And God, if she asked him for anything, he'd give it. Gladly.

His voice came out low and edged with restraint. "Ani, baby, I'm going to kiss you now."

She took a huge breath, like she was gasping for air. "Yes. Yes," she begged.

She hardly finished her sentence before Raffi tilted his head and pressed his lips against hers. The softest, sweetest lips he'd ever tasted.

He'd needed this. He'd needed her. Her and no one but her.

His hand slid from her back, up to her neck, threading her hair in his fingers. She moaned into his mouth, and he felt himself nearly blacking out at the ache in her want.

It couldn't be real. Every kiss that had happened before this was a nonevent, simply skin on skin, but this—her lips, her mouth, her moans—set his entire body aflame.

He pulled back momentarily so he could see her pretty face, her sparkling eyes.

"Raffi," she whispered, "that was—"

God, her voice, he could listen to it all day long. Soft, breathless, laced with the remnants of whatever spell they'd just fallen into together. Their hands were still clasped against his heart, and he knew she could feel it racing.

He kept his voice low, warm. "You have no idea how long I've wanted to do that."

Her breath hitched, and something about it settled deep inside him, the way her reaction to him felt just as intense as his to her. He wanted to give her more—not just this, not just touch, but all of it. Everything. The kinds of things that stayed, that mattered.

"I loved it," she said. Then the music ended, and it was quiet while the band introduced a new song, so he could hear exactly what she said, no mistaking it.

"But we can't do that again."

18

Ani

FOR A FEW moments, Ani had been transported to a celestial realm heretofore unknown, held safely in the arms of her dark-eyed prince. His dancing, and even more, his confession about not dancing for ten goddamn years until Ani. When he asked her, called her *baby*, she was done. She would have done any damn thing he asked. It was good they were in a public place because who knows how far they would have gotten before she stopped it. The way he kissed her was a revelation; it sent her to new heights. But then the music had changed, and she remembered.

Talar's warning. The whisper network, all practically shouting "Stay away from him!" It was clear he had changed, yes, but he still hadn't been in a relationship in who knew how long. She didn't want to be some trial run. Not to mention, they did work together, and it was her policy not to date people she worked with. It was a small wedding world, and she would not be burning bridges or gaining the kind of reputation she didn't want.

But the way he held their hands against his heart . . . Oh, it had been beating so furiously. She wanted to believe, wanted to trust, that he wouldn't destroy her.

He dropped her hand at her words.

"Is it Kami?" he asked, his face tight and worried.

"Ka—no. Not at all."

Relief washed over his face. "I didn't know if maybe things changed when we kissed. You remembered her—"

"The thought of her did not enter my mind."

Entirely true. Which was such a lovely, freeing thing. If nothing else, Raffi had given her that gift. Helped pry her loose from the depths of Kami's clutches she'd allowed herself to be held in.

"Then what?" he asked.

"Raffi, we work together. We're going to be working together for a while. We can't have this little"—she searched for the right word—"dalliance while still maintaining professionalism."

She wanted to add: "I can't put my heart out there for you to take and smash as you please. As you've done so many times with others in the past. How can I trust you to have truly changed?"

Even the word *dalliance* didn't feel right. The way he kissed her seemed bigger than that. She could see the hurt in his eyes when she said it, like a flame dimming, like something in him closing off just slightly.

Raffi walked back to the high-top tables where they'd left their drinks, and he downed his in one gulp as she followed him. "I know how important your work is to you," he said. "So, maybe you have a point. But"—and here he stared straight at her, his stance strong—"you can't deny we have something here."

Following his suit, Ani drank her champagne all too quickly.

"I agree, but what is it? Just lust? You're going to sleep with me, then what?"

There, she said it. Because if this was just a fleeting thing for him, a moment that would fade the second the heat burned off, she needed to hear it now—before she let herself believe in something more.

"Ani—" He groaned.

"That's your MO, isn't it? Who's to say you won't get bored of me after one night together?"

"How could I? That's what you're scared of?"

"That's what you've been doing, isn't it?"

"Not always," he said. "I've wanted to date, in theory, I just hadn't found the right person. Until now."

Ani shook her head, her inner armor not allowing his words into her heart. She loved hearing Raffi speak about her like this, she did, but the danger was too great. She literally, *literally*, had just gotten over Kami after two years of pining over her and sabotaging her own love life.

Yes, it was true that Raffi wasn't what she thought he'd be. Not at all.

The reputation, the rumors, the warnings—she'd expected someone who took what he wanted without a second thought. But the man in front of her? He listened. He paid attention. He didn't push. Even now, with his heart laid bare, he wasn't demanding anything from her. He was standing here, waiting, letting her decide.

But putting her heart out there—trusting Raffi with it,

trusting a man who until very recently had no desire for a relationship—it felt too terrifying to risk.

Ani pulled at the edge of the tablecloth on their high-top table and kept her eyes down. "That's—big. That's a lot for me to take in. But I also meant it, I can't do this right now." A ripple of courage urged her to look up at him. The shine of his eyes had dulled over, and she knew she was crushing his hopes. But she had to press on. "I've had a rough two years in the love-life department. She really wrecked me. And if that kiss is any indication . . ."

Say it, just tell him.

". . . the damage you could cause me could be much worse."

Raffi stepped back and took a deep breath. He stayed quiet for what seemed like forever.

Please say something, please say something, she silently pleaded.

Finally, he exhaled, nodding slowly. When he looked at her again, there was something softer there—no resentment, no frustration. Just understanding.

"Okay," he said, his voice quieter now, steadier than she expected.

Then a gentle, "Okay, Ani jan. Let's get you back home."

And when he gave in like that, her heart very unexpectedly broke. She mourned—for what, though? For what could have been? No, she had to shut that away. The path with Raffi was almost certainly a path of ruin.

With that, they walked back to the car, then drove to his home, where she packed up her things with minimal conversation and left.

19

Raffi

OVER THE NEXT few months, construction at the winery went smoothly, with Chris's team working with effortful precision to get every last detail in place. The dome looked incredible, the sandstone along the floor blended seamlessly into the garden, and the fountain was progressing so quickly that even if they had to do the wedding next week, they could more or less pull it off.

Not only that, but Ô had had many new inquiries about wedding hosting. Raffi had conducted tours, shown the construction progress to prospective brides and grooms, and even booked three more weddings for the fall, after Kami and Grace's. Ô was on the path to success.

And yet Raffi was deeply unhappy.

He stood in The Parker's cold, gleaming empty gym, staring at himself in the mirror. He added twenty more pounds to his deadlift bar, pushing himself to a new high, hoping that the physical stress would help him deal with his mental stress. That's how it worked, right?

Since the engagement party, every day he woke up, got

dressed, and wished for a text or call from Ani. He'd send her progress photos. She would give them a thumbs-up response or, if she was feeling very charitable, a "Thank you. That looks great." He told her about the new bookings, thanking her profusely. She replied kindly but professionally. Once or twice she'd communicated that Sanan would be heading up to the site.

Raffi stood in front of the bar, let it hit his shins, and mentally prepared to lift.

Living this way was torture. Raffi was in an entirely new state of being. Before meeting Ani, he was fine. He was sad in a different way, he could admit to himself. The only thing that mattered before was making the winery a success, because his father, rocky as their relationship was, was the only person from his childhood who was still close to him. His mother wasn't an option.

She wasn't gone in the traditional sense, but she might as well have been. When she came home—briefly, elegantly, effortlessly detached—it was like a stranger waltzing into their home. After Sevan died, the woman who used to fuss over their meals, who used to sing old Armenian lullabies to help them fall asleep, who used to pull him and Sev into tight, smothering hugs—that woman disappeared. What was left behind was a ghost of a mother who never stayed long enough to be real.

He at least saw his dad and talked to him regularly. Sometimes, on their best days, they even made jokes and laughed. In those rare moments, Raffi felt like maybe there was something real between them. Something salvageable. And he wanted his father's approval, to usher their relationship into something a little more friendly and a little less hierarchical.

A relationship that wasn't built solely on expectation and obligation. He still very much needed that.

But now he'd been flung into longing, hard and deep. He had not realized he could even feel this way about another person. Yes, years ago he'd been obsessed with Kami, but he wasn't sure, in retrospect, how deeply they'd ever connected. With Ani, he wanted to be around her constantly, wanted to know everything about her, wanted to touch her everywhere. He had gotten one tiny taste at the engagement party, and his mind had just exploded.

Every day he woke up and wondered how he could possibly get through the day without Ani. He was well and truly fucked, in every sense but the literal.

He needed to tell her how he felt. But only if she was up to listening.

Raffi grasped the bar and pulled, the gnarled edges of the metal scraping against his legs. He exhaled deeply, heat surging up his neck, as the weight successfully reached his thigh. A new personal record; he'd done it. Now he needed to do that five more times.

He placed the weight on the floor when his phone pinged. He practically dove for it, hoping it was Ani. It was not, but it was close. Kami had group-texted Ani and Raffi in a chain she'd horrifyingly named "Kami's Ex Krew, Hehe." Frickin' Kami.

> Can I swing by next week to see how the construction is going? Ani said it's nearly there but I want to see in person!! I'll be in Napa next Thursday afternoon anyway. Lmk!

Just as Raffi was wondering if this meant Ani would come, too, she appeared to read his mind through the ether and responded, Great. I'll be there.

Raffi was confident about the progress, so that aspect of the meeting didn't worry him in the slightest. But getting to see Ani? That made his stomach flip.

He'd been dying to be near Ani again, aching for it like a man starved. And now that he had the chance? He was both delighted and scared shitless. Because at some point, he had to pull her aside, look her in those impossibly perfect eyes, and tell her exactly what she meant to him. Not in some half-assed, offhanded way. No, he had to lay it all out there. Tell her that she'd knocked the wind out of him, that she'd taken up permanent residence in his head, that his world was starting to rearrange itself around her.

He just had to steel himself that her answer could still be no and assure himself that he could somehow survive after her rejection.

One week to pull himself together. He picked up the heavy bar and began again.

20

Ani

MORE THAN THREE months without Raffi.

She missed him so much. At first she'd felt a hollowness she did not expect. Drained of her excitement and drive. Because it wasn't just the kiss, or the way he could level her with a single whisper, a single look. It was him. His stupid, thoughtful questions. His rough hands handling fragile things with impossible care. The way he listened, really listened, like everything she said mattered.

And the worst part? She hadn't expected to miss him this much. Hadn't expected his absence to sit in her bones, making every second stretch on unbearably long.

At least, through all these feelings, there were momentary distractions. Brief and never quite enough, but distractions nonetheless.

She buried herself in work, because if she stopped moving, even for a second, the missing would catch up to her. So she pressed on, throwing herself into wedding prep—work for other weddings plus *the* wedding, creating custom invitations, finalizing flowers, and working with vendors to create a lounge area and custom lighting, all remotely so that she wouldn't run into Raffi.

Today was the day Kami wanted to see the construction progress. So Ani would have to go to Ô and wonder how she could look Raffi in the face for the first time since that earth-shattering kiss. After telling him they couldn't do that again.

She felt her decision was both prudent and stupid. It was smart to guard her heart, smart not to get involved with someone she had to work so closely with.

And absolutely idiotic to deny herself a person whose very presence made her want to burst with joy. Who wanted to be with her, too.

And today she'd see him. She decided she wouldn't even think about it. Besides, Ani had been up to something else the last few weeks, and it had finally borne fruit this morning.

To distract herself from the wedding and Raffi, Ani had been doing some work to get answers about where that couple who stiffed her had landed.

A month ago, Ani made another fake Instagram account, this time pretending to be a real estate investing guru, and had bought a bunch of bot followers for pennies. Knar and her husband had mentioned their interest in real estate investing many times, so this seemed like a more promising trap to set. Ani committed all the way, publishing fifty posts, many of them regurgitation of the same information she'd discovered elsewhere on the internet. Her catfish was ready. Dr. Sam Huntman, Your Real Estate Investing Guru. Yesterday, Ani sent a friend request to Knar along with a professional-sounding DM.

And today? Today Knar had accepted her request. Ani bumped back against her kitchen table, staring wildly at her phone.

"Why are you smiling like a fiend?"

Sanan had come over early, about twenty minutes before they had to leave, which normally would have delighted Ani, getting to chill and pretend she wasn't about to see the most gorgeous, sweetest man she'd ever met *who she had rejected*.

Ani snapped the phone to her chest.

Sanan continued, "I'd say it seems like you have a crush, except those eyes weren't crush eyes; they were devious eyes."

Sanan was . . . right on. Ani couldn't tell her, though. She didn't want her assistant feeling sorry for her, or worse, offering her money or something like deferred payment for Sanan's work. Or resigning. Shit, she wouldn't be surprised if Sanan resigned. Ani wouldn't want *her* boss to be an incompetent insolvent whose business was hanging by a thread. Things were slightly less dire at the moment since she'd received Grace's first payments for her wedding planning and project-management services. She still had two more payments to go, according to the contract, but Ani could breathe a bit easier now.

"Long story," Ani said. "But I do need to check out something. I'm so sorry, can you give me a second? You can eat all the manti in the fridge. I also made hummus last night. Pita's on the bottom shelf."

"You said *all* the manti, so I'm going to take you up on that," Sanan said, already heading toward the refrigerator.

Ani ducked into her bedroom and scoured Knar's Instagram page. She saw a photo of her, that same sharp bob, and her husband, Giro, with his signature massive gold cross necklace—the scammers who indirectly got her into this Kami-Raffi mess. If they had just paid her, Ani's life would be so different.

Then a snap of fear stung her, thinking that she didn't actually want to reverse taking on Kami's wedding, meeting Raffi. Sure, the wedding kept piling on new types of awkwardness, but there were plus sides, too. Big plus sides. She'd shrugged off the dead weight of her lingering Kami feelings, and she'd kissed someone new for the first time in two years.

Not just any kiss.

An astronomical kiss. She wanted more, she did, but—there were too many "buts" about it. The one thing she knew was that she'd never take back meeting Raffi. So the Avedissians sticking her with fifty thousand dollars' worth of debt was somehow not the worst thing in the world.

But *they* still were the worst. On to snooping. Knar had posted recently, and—interesting—all of her photos included lush tropical backdrops and lots of rattan furniture. Guess that was her style. Ani tried to find a coffee shop or a restaurant, anywhere that had been tagged. Maybe if there was a place the Avedissians frequented, she'd have a chance of confronting them.

It only took inspecting five photos to find a tag. It had been posted just two weeks ago, and it was a photo of Knar and a friend in front of a lavish spread, with similar outdoor greenery in the background as the other photos. Ani clicked on the restaurant name. She had to zoom out to identify the city, and the map was loading, loading. And then she saw it.

Bali, Indonesia.

Bali? They had moved to Bali? Or were they just vacationing there? Ani scoured the rest of the photos, and it seemed that immediately after the wedding they had absconded to Bali. So maybe they hadn't moved but they were on a very, very long vacation/hideout in Indonesia. She couldn't serve them in Bali, much less get there. She didn't have a casual thousand dollars to spend on a twenty-hour flight to have a public tiff.

Well. That was the end of that trail. Her stomach twisted, a tight, helpless rage coiling in her chest.

She wouldn't be seeing that money anytime soon. Probably ever. A hard-earned lesson, sure. But hard-earned lessons didn't pay her assistant. Didn't keep her business afloat. Didn't undo the hours she'd poured into their wedding.

She hated that there was going to be no justice here. No confrontation. No legal recourse. No cathartic, dramatic reckoning where she got to stand in front of them and demand what she was owed.

Just this. Just staring at their smug, sun-kissed faces through a phone screen, while everything she'd built dangled in uncertainty, its fate resting in the hands of her ex-girlfriend. Who she hoped like hell loved what she saw on-site today.

Ani slunk back into the kitchen to find Sanan polishing off the last of the manti, straight from the Tupperware.

"Okay, let's head to the winery."

"You got it," Sanan said.

TIME TO SEE *Raffi*.

Ani stepped out onto the winery's parking lot, once again nervous as hell. This time, as she and Sanan approached the walkway that had the rock moat, Ani noticed it was gone.

"They got rid of that plywood eyesore," Sanan said.

"Yes . . ." Ani said, thinking that she hadn't been on-site in way too long.

They rounded back toward the garden, and Ani held her breath, waiting for the moment she would see Raffi. Her heart pumped hard, and her vision fuzzed around the edges in anticipation.

Then she spotted him, standing in his paradise like a lost prince, casually suited as always, staring at the open valley.

He turned when he heard Ani and Sanan making their way into the yard, and Ani's mouth burst into a huge smile. She hadn't meant it—the action was entirely involuntary—but the sight of him made her body sing. His hands, his lips, so strong and soft at the same time. The scent of him, cultivated and fresh. Why had she rejected him again? Something about her fragile heart? Oh God, she saw why she had kept her distance. She was an absolute goner around him.

They approached Raffi, and Chris emerged from the other side of the garden, too.

"Hi, Raffi," Ani said, catching his eyes, then looking down. "Chris, hi." She smiled politely.

She wanted to hug Raffi but didn't think she'd be able to let him go. He looked at her for a long moment, a trace of a smile playing at his lips. As she held his gaze, it felt like he was weighing something, turning it over in his mind, and every second he stared, Ani grew warmer and warmer. She finally broke away and released a breath.

She glanced around, realizing she hadn't scrutinized the work at all yet. "This is incredible. So much progress in so little time. Never seen anything like it."

Raffi clapped Chris on the back. "Told you he was the best."

Chris waved it off. "Yeah, yeah. I had the time so why not be on track to finish ahead of schedule?"

"I like that," Sanan blurted out awkwardly. She blushed red.

Ani said quickly, "It's true. You've made all of our jobs easier."

Chris smiled. "I'm going to have to leave if you all keep complimenting me."

Then heel clicks sounded from the side of the garden and Kami appeared, Grace-less but with Galia, her younger sister. That was a nice surprise.

"Hi, Galia," Ani said with a wave.

"My first time here. Wow. This is totally amazing!" she replied, staring around her.

Kami stepped into the garden wearing a wide-brimmed hat and a long gauzy taupe dress that split down the middle to reveal knee-high boots. She was pretty and her outfit was hot, Ani remarked to herself, and yet she felt no longing. Not even a twinge. Not being sucked in by Kami, it felt like a superpower. Like she'd been deprogrammed from some years-long hypnotic spell and could finally see clearly. And what a beautiful, liberating, long-overdue sight it was: Kami was just a person.

"Hiiii, everyone," Kami beamed. "Can't wait to see the—"

Then she gasped when she caught sight of the dome. "It's so perfect." Then her face fell. "But . . ."

Her eyes started to well with tears. Raffi stepped forward and put a hand on her arm. Envy surged hard in Ani. But no, that was stupid; she knew how Raffi felt about Kami.

"What is it?" he asked Kami.

"Kam?" Galia asked in concern. Ani's envy was quickly replaced by worry.

Kami began to shake, her face turned red, and her eyes filled with tears. Oh no. "Why isn't it more . . . white? Didn't I ask for white? I thought I specifically asked for white. It's just not white enough!" she whined. "Why did you make this huge decision without consulting me?" Her tone grew angry.

Somehow, whether by proximity or some other force, Kami was taking out all her annoyance on Raffi, like it was his call. Ani had seen this side of Kami a few times, when things didn't go her way at, say, an airport, and she wasn't able to use her charms (or platinum card) to fix the situation. Not pretty. Ani was about to walk over and say that the lack of white tiles was completely her doing when Raffi spoke.

"You're absolutely right, Kami. I thought white would be perfect, too, at first."

And Ani stopped dead in her tracks. Was Raffi about to throw her under the bus? What in the actual hell?

He continued. "But then I realized this amount of white stone, facing this way with the sun"—he pointed upward, helpfully—"would completely blind all your guests and ruin the photos." Raffi spoke slowly, calmly, rationally. Not only had he not sacrificed Ani as the scapegoat, but he took responsibility as the person who made the decision, taking the fall for it while Kami was in a state to blame someone.

And on top of that, his measured response seemed to be calming Kami down. Just when Ani thought she couldn't like him more.

"Oh," Kami said. "That's . . . that's a good point. I wouldn't want that."

"That's right. That's what I thought, too." Then, and only then—when the tension had fully ebbed from Kami's shoulders—did he glance over at Ani, his voice shifting ever so slightly as he added, "I didn't see it until Ani pointed it out to me."

Ani felt the warmth in his gaze, the quiet pride in his expression as he said her name.

She stepped forward, ready to take this. "Also, Kami, the good news is, this place is going to be absolutely decked out in white flowers. So you'll get all that bridal white, plus the natural earth tones of the stone and dome. Honestly, with the flower order you guys put in, you're barely going to even see the stone." She gave her a reassuring smile.

"Okay, that makes me feel better," Kami said, seemingly placated but still in the process of getting over it.

Ani whipped out her phone and pulled up the mock-up she'd shown Raffi. She held it in front of Kami. "Dang it, I see what you mean," Kami said.

Galia chimed in, "I like it the way it is. I mean, it's perfect. I don't get what the problem is."

Kami turned to her and laughed. "Of course you don't. You're just a kid."

Galia turned away as if slapped, and Ani felt for her. She squeezed Galia's shoulder. "Not for long. October birthday?"

Galia nodded sadly, apparently still stung by her sister's words.

Kami piped up. "Walk me through what else needs to be

done? But I have to leave in like ten minutes. Galia and I have a lunch with an old friend at Farmstead. We're going to put some makeup on her and try to get her to pass for twenty-one so we can all partake in the vino."

Galia came back to life at this, being included again in her sister's afternoon.

"Fun," Ani said, not quite hiding her bitterness. She was somewhat envious that Kami could do whatever she pleased during the work week, since her businesses were mostly run by managers she had to check in with only occasionally. A lip gloss company, a boho accessories drop-shipping company, a Pilates equipment company that simply put her logo on some standard Pilates reformer machinery. What a life. Then again, the less effort put in, the less there was to be proud of. That was how Ani saw it, anyway. Although she thought Kami was probably plenty proud of herself.

"Did you say Grace was in LA?" Raffi asked.

"Yes! Her promo stuff is really ramping up. They dropped a couple teasers, and the trailer is being released this week. I'm so excited for her."

Raffi, Sanan, Chris, and Ani all shared various exclamations of interest. It was pretty cool. They were all now one degree of separation from Robert De Niro.

Ani walked Kami through more of the setup and wedding details, then Kami and Galia headed out. Ani realized, after speaking to Kami, that she had more venue-related tasks to see to so she could ensure they had everything absolutely finalized. She had a list from her vendors of items she had to check on. This was good, as Ani wanted more time with Raffi.

Raffi, Ani, and Sanan walked through the grounds together while Chris got back to work, and Ani kept her tone and her inquiries very professional. She almost hated herself for it. She wanted to joke more, open up, show him that she still cared about him. But she was scared, especially in front of Sanan. It probably wasn't her imagination that while Raffi reflected her professionalism, there was a sadness in his eyes.

About fifteen minutes in, when the three of them walked into Ô's kitchen, Sanan's phone buzzed. She read it, then her head popped up to Ani.

"Um, Ani, mind if I—" She indicated that she needed to pull Ani aside. Ani excused herself, and the two of them stepped aside.

"Ani, I'm so sorry, I know we still have a whole list of things we need to do here, but my mom texted me that my dad isn't feeling well. Maybe he has food poisoning, but it could be something worse. I don't like to seem unprofess—"

"Sanan, oh my goodness, of course. Don't even worry. We can head back."

Ani was slightly sad about having to leave, but she was not about to keep Sanan from her family.

Raffi's head perked up at Ani's words.

"You're heading out?"

"Sanan's got to go; we carpooled up here."

Raffi nodded, thinking. "You know, I'm going into the city later. I could drive you back after running through the task list."

"Really?" Ani asked. She did have more work she needed to get done here. And they came in Sanan's car anyway. Sanan had insisted on driving because she obeyed the speed limits more judiciously than Ani—"No offense, boss."

"It'd be my pleasure," he said, and Ani's body warmed instantly at his words.

Sanan gave a string of apologies, which Ani dismissed and assured her everything was completely fine. She asked Sanan to keep her updated, then Sanan gave her a quick, tight hug and ran off.

Raffi and Ani were left alone in the kitchen, where they had been alone months ago, Ani laying her dress out and doing her best not to flash her cheeks. There was a heaviness in the air, something charged, ready to spark at any second.

"We—we have to check the number of outlets," Ani said.

"Seventeen," Raffi responded immediately.

Ani shook herself from her shy stupor. "What? Really?"

Raffi smirked. Oh, there was that devilish smile of his. "I'm kidding. I don't keep tabs on the number of outlets in all rooms of the winery."

"I was going to say: Add savant to your list of skills."

Raffi stepped closer to her, and her breath hitched. "Oh yeah? What are my other skills?"

Ani's throat felt like she'd never had a drink of water her entire life. "Don't make me list them."

A moment passed between them, and he appeared to be fighting a smile. "Just checking to see if you . . . remembered."

Of course she remembered. She'd thought about that kiss every single day, if not every single hour, since they'd been apart. And now he was standing close to her, so close, and she could step up on her tiptoes and feel that kiss again, his arms around her, drawing her in.

"I remember," she whispered. Then she added, "But I have

a big to-do list. I wasn't expecting to discuss the, uh, situation at the engagement party so soon."

Raffi shrugged. "Hey, I was just riffing off you bringing up my skills. Seemed a shame not to mention it with such a great setup."

She really had teed that one right up for him.

"True, true. Okay, step one—help me count these outlets, and let's do our best to, you know, remain professional."

Raffi put his hand on his heart, and she remembered the beat of it, so hard and fast. "I am the soul of professionalism."

She took a chance and bumped him playfully with her body. She loved seeing the surprise on his face, loved the feeling of his body against hers.

"Mm-hmm," she said, then got to work.

They spent about an hour going through Ani's checklist, and it was easier to keep their eyes on the tasks at hand when they were outside because Chris and his team were there, hammering, sealing, polishing.

When they were nearing the end of their discussion on electricity, Ani's stomach gave a great angry growl so loud it could be heard even over the sounds of the construction crew. Damn, that was humiliating. Ani gave a half smile to cover her embarrassment.

But instead of smiling back or brushing it off, Raffi's face appeared concerned. "When's the last time you ate?"

She had to think aloud on this one. She wasn't sure. "I don't know, I guess I had an egg for breakfast and meant to have more but got distracted."

He stood by her side. She could smell his desert-wind cologne, and she had to stop herself from closing her eyes and taking it in. His voice was sweet. "Ani jan, you have to eat. I'm taking you out."

She began to protest but couldn't quite form the words, because she realized that actually, yes, she would love that.

21

Ani

RAFFI TOOK ANI to a restaurant attached to one of St. Helena's boutique hotels that happened to be open at this odd, three p.m. hour. It was a lovely, and frankly romantic, spot. Outdoor seating surrounded by thick green vines, a fountain gently dripping, shade and sun playing across their faces.

When Ani saw that they were being directed to a U-shaped booth and they'd get to sit near each other instead of across the table, her breath hitched. She'd be so close to him. Maybe their arms, their elbows, would touch.

Once seated, Ani ran her fingers along the cool pressed-cotton menu. "Hey, I wanted to thank you. For earlier."

Raffi appeared confused. "For—?"

"For not blaming me, with Kami, when she was whining about the white stones."

Ani put a hand over her mouth, realizing the judgy verb she'd used. "I didn't mean to say 'whining'; that's not fair."

Raffi laughed kindly. "Ah-ha. So you see it now, right? She *was* whining. I'd even use 'tantrumming,' and it might still be accurate."

"Weddings cause a lot of stress . . ."

"Don't tell me that's the first time you've seen a Kami tantrum."

Ani paused, remembering. "Well, there was this time at LAX when she thought they lost her bags but they were actually at a different carousel."

"Five or six years ago at a family friend's gathering, Kami broke down and sobbed in front of everyone because her great-aunt put her homemade kuftes on her vegan boyfriend's plate. This lady was ancient, like ninety, and did not understand the concept of not eating meat. But Kami made this statement about how disrespectful her family was to outsiders and ran off crying."

Ani nodded. She didn't really want to put down Kami, but at the same time, this was sort of therapeutic. Kami had dumped her, disappeared off the face of the earth, then snapped her fingers and expected Ani to plan her wedding for her two years later. Granted, Ani had willingly agreed to do it—she had to—but what kind of person would have the audacity to ask that of her? And who would know better, the little things that grated on her, than one of her other exes? "Sounds about right."

They both stared at each other for a second. That was that. A good mini-trash-talking sesh about Kami.

Then Raffi said, with the hint of a smirk, "Don't miss those sneezes, either."

Ani slapped the table and laughed. "Oh my God, the sneezes! Does she think she's a tiny woodland bunny in a Disney fairy tale?"

"Ah-chi! Ah-chi!" Raffi mimicked Kami's high-pitched sneezes.

A man at a table in front of them turned around in disgust, which only ignited their laughter. She honestly hadn't thought anyone else had noticed—no one had ever said anything—but Kami's sneezes were so comically fake and cutesy, they always secretly annoyed her.

Between fits of laughter Ani said, "There's no way that's her real sneeze, right?"

Raffi wiped his eyes. "That is one hundred percent an affect."

"I hope when she's alone she sneezes like a bear. Like an Armenian dad at six a.m. on a Sunday, waking up the entire neighborhood."

"Your dad does that, too? I think my dad wakes up the entire county of Napa with his."

Ani tilted her glass in his direction. She knew the issue of his dad was sensitive, but Raffi had just offered up this humorous tidbit, so she kept it going. Besides, they had talked enough about their ex. "They need a sneeze-off."

Raffi smiled warmly at her. "We'll have to make it happen."

Ani returned it, then buried the smile in her glass.

They both drank wine from a nearby winery Raffi said was owned by decent people, and Ani felt the drink go to her head far too quickly, having only had that egg at breakfast and a slice of bread from the table.

Raffi didn't seem to be tipsy like her, but he was studying her closely. She turned away from his gaze, reddening and remembering their kiss for the thousandth time. The press of his body, how protected and adored she felt. How he had shielded her from Kami's wrath without a second thought.

A heavy silence fell over the table. To break it, she said, "So, what're you doing in the city?" at the same time Raffi started talking, but she couldn't hear what he said.

"Sorry." She shook herself. "You were saying?"

"I don't have anything to do in the city tonight."

"You don't?"

"I don't."

She didn't quite understand why he had said otherwise earlier. He seemed so serious. Had he meant . . . "So you're not going to drive me home?"

Raffi laughed. "That's your conclusion? No, Ani baby, of course I'm going to drive you."

A delicious warmth spread through her at the term of endearment.

She could hardly speak, but managed, "Then—?"

He spoke quietly, deliberately. "I mean, I wanted to spend more time with you. I don't mind driving you back home, because that's an extra hour plus we get to spend together."

Her mouth made a little circle. "Oh . . ."

Then he reached out and clasped her hand on the table. Strong and warm.

He looked at her meaningfully, and she held her breath, not entirely sure, but hoping, hoping.

"I have to say something. Would you let me say something?"

Her heart pounded. She wanted to hear it. Whatever it was. "Yes," she said, zeroing in on him entirely.

He looked down, then up at her, shifting in his seat. "I'm going to start talking and—" He cut himself off, then restarted. "Ani, I can't keep pretending I'm not completely wild about you. The last few months have been hellish without you in it.

I realized you're starting to mean a lot to me, and I don't want to keep that fact to myself anymore. I always thought— Well, instead of scaring the shit out of me, I'm thrilled by it, by the prospect of you, anything that has to do with you. Everything about you."

He couldn't possibly mean this, could he? This wasn't normal flirting; this was a serious declaration of *like*. This man, who she was starting to adore, was telling her these beautiful words, and she wanted to let herself feel it all the way. She was almost there, every last hesitation almost dissolved.

He continued, his eyes intense, dark, and searing.

"And to make it crystal clear, I'm not just talking about the physical, but believe me, I want to do things that . . . well. Let's just say things that are incredibly amot."

Ani felt the heat between her legs instantaneously. He thought about her body and wanted to . . . do things to it. She wanted that, too. Very, very much.

Raffi continued, "But not just that. I want to be with you. To see where this goes. For the first time in a long time, I *feel* something. For you. Brilliant, funny, fearless you. I want to try being together. Date you, spoil you, be there for you in every aspect of your life the way you deserve."

Ani's mouth dropped open. She had to force herself to close it.

Raffi Garabedian just asked her to be his girlfriend.

He'd addressed it, too, that she feared he only wanted to sleep with her. That he didn't have intentions beyond the physical. "Date you, spoil you." Oh my God, that was such a turn-on. The closed gates around her heart swung open. The most gorgeous guy she'd ever seen in her life turned out to be a total sweetheart who was interested in her. Very interested in her. The girl who got rejected by Adrian Lamont and publicly humiliated. The older sister who all the aunties looked at with pity at Talar's wedding. The woman who thought she'd never fall for someone ever again. She'd fallen for *him*. Northern California's most eligible Armenian bachelor. And he felt the same way. It wasn't blood rushing through her veins but liquid ecstasy, metallic and sparkling and filling her body with the warmest glow.

"Is that a good jaw drop or a bad one?" he asked nervously.

She put their combined hands in her lap, scooted closer to him, and stared at him in adoration. She wanted him to know how happy he had just made her. "A deliriously good one."

"Yeah?" he said, the relief obvious.

"Yes. Yes." She couldn't stop smiling.

A beat passed when they basked in each other's adoration.

"I do have one, uh, stipulation, though," he said.

Well, now she could stop smiling. The worry rose in Ani again, and she straightened in her seat. "What's that?"

"If you're not—if you don't really feel it, or don't think we could have anything together . . . if you're still pining for someone—"

"I'm not."

"—just say it. Just tell me no. If you don't think this has potential, you and me—if your gut feeling is saying no, then please, you have to tell me now. I can't . . ."

He trailed off, like he was getting choked up. He was the one who was worried. He was afraid of something; of what, exactly, wasn't clear yet. She stayed quiet to let him speak.

He stared down at the table, straightened a fork. "I can't go into this with all this hope just to have you leave me. I'm not sure I could take being left by the one person I've started to care about."

This whole time, she'd been bracing for the crash—so sure that if they ever actually got together, he'd eventually walk away. But here he was, sitting next to her in a booth, admitting that his biggest fear was *her* leaving *him*.

He had meant every word. No ego, no performance.

And it startled her, honestly. The depth of it. The vulnerability.

Ani picked up their still-clasped hands from her lap and kissed his. "Raffi jan, I can't guarantee that down the line we won't realize we're not compatible and break up. You know that, right? Neither of us can."

He stiffened, and she really felt for him. He'd been hurt so much. She'd never accounted for *his* fears before. But now that he'd shown Ani that side of himself, she could do her best to allay them. "I *can* tell you that right now I am one hundred percent enthusiastically in—"

Now he brought their joined hands to his mouth and laid several kisses on hers.

Ani continued, "To the point where I'm not sure how this is real. Because you're *you*, and I'm just me. Average—"

Raffi cut her off. "No, nope. No talking about my girlfriend in that way. You are exquisite, Ani jan. A treasure. And I'm not wrong about these things."

Girlfriend. Ani reddened, knowing he could see it, liking that he could.

"One thing I wanted to ask—you mentioned you didn't want to date . . . vendors." He gave her a smirk and continued. "I understand that. If you wanted, we could keep things completely private, at least until the wedding is over. What do you think? Would that be okay for you, or is there some other arrangement—?"

He remembered, not just in passing. He understood how much her work mattered to her. Ani's entire body felt light, fizzing with something too big to name, something that made her want to grab him by the collar and kiss him stupid.

"That's perfect," she said, interrupting him, a ridiculous grin stretching across her face.

He was so easy to be with. That was what struck her most. No tension, no second-guessing, no exhausting mind games—just Raffi, giving her space when she needed it, teasing her when she could take it, and standing by her in all the right ways.

Ani smiled. "You are something else, Raffi jan." She hesitated for a second, then sighed. "I was so wrong about you. Every time we're together, you're so sweet, so thoughtful. Generous. Not just more than I expected—but more than anyone I've ever known."

He squeezed her hand and lovingly ran his thumb along it.

"Plus, your phenomenal six-pack you so conveniently showed off after getting drenched."

He threw his head back and laughed. "Finally, someone appreciates my true talent—being aggressively shirtless."

Now it was her turn to laugh, and even after it faded, the glow of it lingered between them. Ani looked up at Raffi, their hands still joined, the warmth of his thumb brushing over hers.

The golden light of the restaurant flickered in his eyes, and she found herself wanting to memorize every inch of him.

"So let's date?" he asked.

"So let's date."

He tilted her chin up, and a slow, shivery heat bloomed in her chest. "I've been dying to do this again," he said.

"Same."

He kissed her, and just like the first time, the world liquefied. His lips savoring hers, his hands framing her face, reverent and sure, as if memorizing the shape of her, of them. *I am dating him. We're dating.*

He dropped a hand to her thigh and let out something of a growl. Oh yes, she wanted more. Too bad they were—

A cough sounded from above. "Your dishes, madame et monsieur." An amused waiter set down her sea bass fillet and his lamb roast.

"Thank you," Ani said, embarrassed by how heavy her breath came out.

Raffi mirrored her thanks as the waiter walked away. Ani noticed the deep berry-red stains on his mouth. Her thumb brushed gently across his lower lip, smudging the gloss she'd left behind.

His mouth parted slightly beneath her touch, and his eyes grew darker.

She ran the pad of her thumb once more across his lip, slower this time, and she could practically feel Raffi's body vibrating with want.

His hand, until now, had been on the top of her thigh, resting partly on the fabric and partly on her flushed skin. But then he slid his hand underneath the skirt.

Ani gasped.

"Yes?" he asked.

"Yes."

He ran his hand slowly up her thigh, stopping short of Ani's underwear, his fingers grazing her skin so, so gently.

"God, your skin is smooth," he groaned.

She managed, "Something else is, too," before she saw stars. She wasn't sure when the last time was she took a breath. He had to be feeling the heat emanating from between her legs.

Raffi sucked in a breath, sat back in his chair, and slowly removed his hand.

His gaze flicked to hers, then to the artisan ceramics on the table, the soft clink of cutlery around them, the waiter approaching another table with a decanter. They were in a public place where their chances of getting kicked out for lewd behavior were high. Right.

When he looked at her again, his voice was laced with restraint.

"If we weren't sitting in a restaurant where the bread has its own biography"—his jaw flexed—"I'd already have you undressed."

Ani looked down at her food, which objectively appeared delicious but at the moment held no interest for her. She agreed with him, but all she wanted was his hand back. Higher, higher.

"I'm not really hungry anymore."

Raffi was adjusting his pants, and Ani didn't dare glance down because she guessed what she might see and she didn't think she could make direct eye contact with any of the waitstaff after that.

"Same," he said, "but eat up. You're going to need your strength for what I have planned."

She let out a sound, a type of squeak, and that elicited Raffi's wolfish grin.

Then, so sweetly, he wrapped an arm around her and kissed the side of her head. He picked up his fork and said, "Come on, let's try our best."

They ate, Ani vaguely registering a citrusy tang and a pleasant basil pairing with her fish, but mostly focusing on calming her breath enough to swallow and stop her imagination from running wild.

When she had eaten enough, she turned to Raffi, who seemed to be in a similar battle of forcing down food while not getting too horny in a Michelin-starred restaurant.

She leaned into him and whispered, "You know, I don't really need to be home tonight."

Raffi clanked his fork down on the plate. "Okay, fuck this, let's get out of here."

He whipped out a sleek black leather wallet and threw down a few hundreds, vastly overpaying.

"That's more than—" she started saying, but Raffi grabbed her hand and led them out of their booth.

"It's fine. I can't do math right now. All the blood is gone from my brain."

Ani's must have been, too. She didn't remember details from the short walk to his car, but suddenly they were inside it.

Raffi seemed to have calmed himself somewhat in that time. "It's seven minutes to home. Do you think you can handle it?"

She gave him a look. "Can *you*?"

His response was an impish smirk, and she wondered what he had planned.

They began the drive. Ani's heart pounded. She was in

Raffi's car. They had kissed again. They were dating. They were about to do . . . well, whatever it was she wanted to do at his house. And truth be told, she wanted it all.

While Raffi kept his eyes on the road, his hand wandered over to her side. He rested it on her leg and, with one finger, tapped the inside of her thigh. "Open these for me."

Without hesitation she complied, spreading them wide for him to do as he pleased. She'd been waiting for his touch there again.

"There you go," he said.

She couldn't even speak, just absorbed his low, gravelly voice and waited with a shaky breath of anticipation for what he was about to do.

He dragged two fingers up her thigh, heading exactly where she needed them, then he swept them up, across her mound, and back around the other side, down her other thigh. Ani's head rolled back, and a moan escaped as he began again, teasing her, *not* touching her in the place she needed specifically. But he'd get there eventually. Right? Raffi drove on, eyes on the road, placid face, betrayed only by the slightest uptick of his mouth. How long, had he said? Seven minutes? No way he could keep his hands off her sex, being that close to it, for seven minutes.

But Raffi did. His fingers, rough and warm, grazed and tantalized near it, but not on it. She turned to him. "You are evil," she muttered.

"I know," he said.

When they pulled into his parking lot, after what felt like hours of brushing his fingers *just* shy of her clit, Ani was a heaving, horny mess. Panties soaked before he'd ever made contact. On the one hand, she couldn't get out of the car fast enough, but on the other, his patient touches had anesthetized her, stitching her in place in those long seven minutes.

As if reading her mind, Raffi waltzed over to her side, opened the door, and drew her into his arms like they were newlyweds. She wrapped her arms around his neck, inhaling the indigo-blue scent of him.

Raffi unlocked, then kicked open the front door and carried her immediately to the couch. She couldn't pull her gaze away from him, the intensity in his eyes, how his pupils grew black with desire.

He sat her in his lap and snaked a hand through her hair, pulling her in for a kiss. Hungry, frenzied kisses between them.

He broke away, his voice rumbling. "Last time you were here I didn't get to do this. I wasn't sure if you wanted it."

"I want it," she purred, reassuring him.

He ran his lips lightly along her neck and she shivered at the sensation. Then his tongue slowly circled her ear and her pleasure amped up so high a moan, unbidden, escaped her. His voice was low, feral. "I can tell."

He locked his mouth onto hers and they made out, nothing more, for what seemed like an hour. Ani hadn't noticed until this moment that she'd been rocking her hips, needing to release some of the pressure built up between her legs. She felt him, too, his hard mass under his pants. Sizable. She started pressing against him with more insistence.

"All right, baby, slow down. You need more?"

"Please, yes," she groaned. She was sure, absolutely positive, she'd already ruined his pants just by grinding on him. She'd never felt so turned on in her life. Ever. She could tell he was raring to go, too, but he also took his sweet damn time and she loved that. She didn't want it to be over; she wanted to savor every bit, draw it out as long as possible. So did he, it seemed.

Raffi began unbuttoning her shirt. "Let's get this off."

Self-consciousness momentarily struck her. What if he didn't like her body? What if she wasn't good enough—

Then he unclasped her bra in one pinch and she felt it peel off her body. Ani watched him stare in awe, gripping her hips, at first gently and then tighter. Ani's breath hitched while he took her in.

"God, you're beautiful," he said, like he'd never seen anything so perfect.

Then she did something she didn't usually do and began unzipping her skirt. She wanted to show him.

He murmured appreciatively, "Yes, let's see more of you. I want to see all of you."

She stood, missing the heat of him instantly but enjoying stripping her last few remaining pieces of clothing down her legs. First her skirt fell, revealing dark violet satin panties—the ones his fingers had skimmed over and over. She was nearly naked and he was fully clothed, and somehow this made everything even hotter.

He grabbed her ass, taking it in both his hands and pulling her closer to him. "You wore these for me? Or is this your everyday?"

"For you. It may have been wishful thinking."

"Well, someone listened, that's for sure."

Raffi pinned her to him and kissed her, but this time with his hands seeking farther, stroking. Ani kept moaning into his mouth as he touched her, then up to the ceiling, emitting animal sounds she didn't know she could make when his mouth began to explore the rest of her.

He laid her down gently and covered her with his body, kissing, rubbing, while she gasped.

"I want to see you, too," she said, tugging at his shirt button.

"All right, Miss Wedding Planner," he smiled, sitting up and pulling off his shirt.

Oh yes. There it was again. Broad shoulders with taut muscles, those pecs she'd been face-to-face with before. Rippling abs along his torso with those V lines pointing south. Hers now. To touch, to taste.

She ran her hands along his chest. "Goddamn, Raffi."

"I've been thinking the same about you."

He leaned back over her, their skin rubbing against each other. The way he looked at her, touched her, ravished her, she felt like an absolute goddess. The self-doubt had disappeared, melted away under his touch, leaving her polished and gleaming.

Then he swept back, pulled off her underwear, and threw it aside.

"Fucking beautiful," he rasped, and began kissing her from her belly on down, lower, lower. When he made contact, she thought she might actually black out. He was savoring her, kissing her like he'd been wanting to do this for centuries. Ani whimpered so loudly when he ran his tongue over her clit that she clapped her hand over her mouth.

"No need to be quiet. No one can hear," he said.

He continued, harder, hungrier, using his fingers alongside his tongue. Ani's hips bucked as her body filled with ecstasy, as it got tighter, more frenzied, more craving of a release. But it wasn't enough. She wanted to be filled with him.

With shaky breaths, she begged, "Please, Raff. I need you . . . in me."

He pulled away before climbing on top of her, using his hand to keep her pleasure steady. "I'm sure you do, but not tonight."

"Wha—?" she gasped, barely able to articulate it, her need was so intense.

"I want you to know, for sure, what I'm in this for. Not just to have sex with you. Until you believe that, until you won't wake up with regrets, no sex. No nothing for me. I'm going to keep my pants on. All night."

Through the haze of her lust, the meaning of his words filtered in. He wasn't going to—? She had felt his generosity before, but this was something else. All right, Raffi, message received.

"Ughhh," she groaned. She knew he was looking out for her, and it was so sweet, so damn sweet, and she knew he was right, but her body begged to be connected with him in that way. She'd endure it, though. She'd accept his blissful torment.

"Not to worry. I'll be taking care of you. You think you're only getting a single orgasm tonight?" he said with that devilish smile.

"I haven't even—"

He stroked her hair. "I know. Let's change that."

22

Raffi

FOUR. HE'D GIVEN her four orgasms. Three with his mouth and a surprise one when he had her perfect breasts in his mouth and she ground on him while he flicked her sensitive peaks over and over until she shuddered atop him.

Sex—or not sex exactly—with Ani was unlike anything he'd ever experienced before. He'd never even made out with a woman for more than a minute before stripping her naked and sleeping with her. Maybe when he was still a teenager, unsure of what to do next. But now, he was sure as hell of what to do next but wanted everything slow and never-ending with Ani.

True, his balls had swollen and ached and he'd had to take care of himself, but he didn't want Ani to feel any bit of burden with it. Let her see, not through pretty words but with actions, that he was going to be there for her exactly how she needed. And he had a feeling that if they went any further last night, or even today, that it'd be too soon for her.

Although when she begged for him, her huge eyes half shut in rapture, her pouty, kissable mouth pleading "in me," he got far too close to losing his resolve. To ripping off his pants and sinking into her, fulfilling them both. But some higher part of him allowed him a couple of spare brain cells to think, and to abstain.

And above all this, what was different was that after what they'd done, he hadn't felt out-of-his-skin jumpy, wanting to move on. No. He wanted more. Not just sex. Kissing her, holding her, talking to her. Being there for Ani in every aspect of her life.

He had decent blackout curtains, but the morning light still found a way through, thin slivers that heralded the dawn of a new day.

A beautiful new day.

One with Ani by his side, as his girlfriend.

She was here now, her warm, naked body tucked tight against him. He kept his boxers on in an attempt at modesty. A vain attempt, because he was already hard as a rock, pressing into her gorgeous ass.

He wanted to get up to shower, rub one out so he had a chance of making it through the day without being ceaselessly entrenched in sexual fantasies. Eh, who was he kidding? One orgasm wasn't going to relieve that.

Ani began to stir, and when he kissed the inside of her neck, she gave a soft "Mmm" and a little smile appeared across her lips. God, she was an angel. An actual angel.

"How'd you sleep?" he said into her ear.

She moaned. "Like I was buried in a cloud. Best sleep I've gotten in ages."

Raffi realized then that he had, too. Deep, heavy sleep with vaguely pleasant dreams he could no longer remember. Just contentment.

"Good," he said, running his fingers along her hair, her neck, down her back. Her skin tightened and she shivered once, and he loved that he had that effect on her, that he could give her that feeling.

"Mmm, what time is it?" she murmured.

Ani reached over and grabbed her phone from the nightstand. She studied her phone while he buried his face into her back and nuzzled it.

But then her body stiffened. Something was wrong. "What is it?" he asked.

"I think—" Ani scrolled, read, concentrated fully on her phone.

"Did you miss something important?" Raffi worried. He didn't want to be the reason she forgot a meeting or whatever other engagements she might have. His heart started beating fast. She was not answering him. Raffi sat up.

"Get your phone," Ani said. "See if this is showing up on your news app, too."

Now Raffi was actually concerned. "Ani, what is—?"

But he'd grabbed hold of his phone and saw someone familiar on his news homepage. Grace. Front and center. Worry about Ani transformed into curiosity. Far preferable.

Rising Star Grace Zhang Charms in Viral Video with De Niro

Even though he already knew the answer, Raffi asked, "Is that Grace Grace? Kami's Grace?"

"Sure seems like it. Cloaked in newfound fame. Might be a

fifteen-minute cycle, though. I guess we'll find out. Should we see what it's all about?"

"I'm going to make us some sourj; you pull up that video."

"You, Raffi Garabedian, make sourj?"

"My medzmama taught me well," he said. "And I prefer it. The American stuff is so weak, giant watery cups of thin coffee."

"Well, well. Let's see what you have."

"Prepare to have your mind blown."

"Okay, Mr. Cocky," she smiled.

He shook himself and climbed out of bed. "Can't have you saying that word. Not now. Not yet."

"Which word?" She put on a mock coquette voice and positioned herself seductively. "Cocky?"

"I'm running away to the kitchen now," he said, leaving a flood of her giggles in his wake.

Raffi gripped the handle of the jezveh, remembering his medzmama's words when he was twenty. "I'll be leaving you soon, too, I feel it. So at least let me give you this gift. Always make sourj. Every morning. Always for guests." He'd never known his mother's mom, but he had known his father's. Medzmama. A stern, hardworking, religious woman who was about zero parts nurturing but still meant a lot to him. He'd failed Medzmama by not serving Ani any sourj last time, but he was distracted after nearly losing her to drowning and then nearly kissing her on the couch.

He turned on the burner right as Ani strode in, wearing one of his plain white T-shirts. The outlines of her nipples were visible, and the bottom of the shirt barely skimmed her ass. Why did everything she wore have to look so sexy?

"I've got it," she said, waving her phone, oblivious to how hot she was making him by just standing there.

Raffi curled her into him and rested his head on her shoulder as they watched.

Robert De Niro and Grace—Raffi still couldn't believe he was seeing someone he knew chat with De Niro—were sitting in some kind of interview room, each on a plush chair across from each other. This seemed to be a clip from the longer interview. De Niro read from a card. "Your favorite food?"

Grace looked away thoughtfully. "I don't love food."

The camera cut to De Niro's face. His eyebrows shot up, his mouth twisted slightly, the kind of expression that said, "Are you kidding me?"

"You don't love food?" he finally repeated, his voice loaded with the kind of skepticism that could crush a man.

Not Grace, though. The camera cut back to her, where she appeared nonchalant, matter-of-fact. "Chewing is messy," Grace said, wrinkling her nose. "I just wanna, like . . . swallow it."

De Niro raised an eyebrow, intrigued now. "So we're talking maybe smoothies?"

Grace smiled. "Mmm."

De Niro asked, more animatedly, "Maybe oysters?"

Grace now pointed to him. "Mmmm!"

And that was the clip.

Ani set down her phone. "So Grace is a little bit of a weirdo and the internet goes wild?"

Raffi shrugged. "Guess so. Wait, look, scroll down, what's that?"

Ani read, then tapped. "I guess there's already a remix of it . . ."

They listened to an electronica version of the interview with Grace's "I just wanna, like . . . swallow it" as the chorus.

"Catchy," Raffi said, struggling not to laugh.

"I have a feeling this is just going to be contained to the internet," Ani said. "But it's still great her star is rising. Good for her."

Raffi agreed, grabbed the jezveh off the stove before it bubbled over, then poured two small Armenian cups for them.

He handed Ani hers on a saucer. Ani sipped, closed her eyes, and let out a contented hum.

Raffi leaned in close to her. "Get used to that. Any time you're over, it's twenty-four seven bottomless sourj."

Which he hoped would be very often.

She beamed at him, then ran her fingers along the edge of the carved copper cup holder. "I love this set."

"Handmade in Armenia. Belonged to my medz."

Ani turned the piece slightly, inspecting it like she was memorizing every detail. "It's beautiful. It stands out here. All this modern design, then bam, we're dropped into a nene's house from the eighties."

He let out a low chuckle. "I know. There's barely anything Armenian in the house otherwise. Which . . . I don't know. I think I did that on purpose."

Ani looked up at him, curious but quiet.

"I love Armenian design," he continued. "Warm tones, intricate, ancient patterns. But for a long time, 'Armenian' meant 'family.' And, well . . . you know how that's gone for me." He scratched his jaw, suddenly feeling a little exposed. "So I got the whitest, most impersonal place I could find."

Ani's face softened. Her fingers left the copper cup holder

and drifted toward him. She laid a gentle hand on his forearm. Raffi immediately broke out in goosebumps at her touch. Every brush of her fingers felt like a balm over the past.

"I'm sorry," she said, her voice low. "That you had to carry that kind of weight."

He laid his hand on hers. "It's honestly okay." And he meant it. "I have a feeling that can change too."

"Me too." She smiled.

And speaking of weight, they hadn't had much of a chance to talk about *them*. And Raffi was wondering. "Ani jan, how are you feeling? About, you know, us."

"Us?" She took another sip. "I feel perfect." She leaned over and kissed him. "You?"

"The same," he said, kissing her again.

Too good, honestly, he thought. "I didn't know I was allowed to feel this happy," he wanted to say.

"Ready to go, I see," she said, eyeing his lap.

"Ugh, ignore that. That's going to be a permanent state for a while."

Ani giggled. "Maybe not that long."

He couldn't even let himself entertain the thought of burying himself between her legs, because he might lose his resolve.

Raffi finished the last of his coffee and turned the cup over in its saucer. "Since you're in town," he asked, steering the topic away from their bodies, "should we head over to the winery and check on the worksite?"

"I was going to suggest the same. We sort of disappeared yesterday, and I wonder what Chris and his team got done."

Raffi stared at her lustfully. "But only after I get my breakfast in bed."

"Not going to refuse that," Ani said, beelining to his room.

RAFFI DELIVERED HIS stretch goal of three, and now they were cleaned up and on the way to Ô. A few minutes from the winery, after pleasant and flirtatious conversation, Ani turned to him, somewhat seriously.

"Okay, almost time to turn off the relationship. Think we can do this?"

Raffi picked up her hand and kissed it. "Of course, Ani jan. That was my last, until you say it's okay again."

She squeezed his hand in thanks.

"Although," Raffi added, "it's going to be damn near impossible to behave myself anytime we're together."

Ani laughed. "C'mon, you love a challenge, though."

Raffi threw his head back. "You've got me pegged."

Ani's eyes went big.

"Not," Raffi said, "like that."

And they both laughed until they reached the winery.

His winery. Ô. Which was usually empty, especially at ten a.m., but was now crawling with people, mostly men, dressed casually, holding . . . very large cameras. The sound of Raffi's car attracted them, like vultures to a fresh carcass. They turned, then raised their cameras, loud clicks filling the air like locusts.

Raffi's hand jumped immediately off Ani's, and he hoped that no one had seen them from this angle.

"What the . . ." Ani said.

"Seems like Grace's fame isn't an online-only phenomenon." Raffi scowled.

"Holy shit. Do I look sexed up? I don't look sexed up, right?" Ani sounded panicked.

"No, baby, not at all. Trust me, I held back after you did your hair. You look polished and beautiful. Paparazzi ready."

"How are you so calm about this?"

He wasn't. His entire body was buzzing on high alert, ready to protect or defend Ani if need be. He did not trust reporters in the slightest. He remembered how a couple of them had come banging on his door, wanting to report on Sevan's death. The party had been at the house of a major donor for the mayor, hosted by the donor's son, so it was newsworthy. He wouldn't let them near his girl.

"I'm not. We don't have to say one word to them, okay?"

Ani took a deep breath. "Okay."

Because he had the top down on his convertible, the questions started before they even got out of the car.

A cacophony of voices erupted around them.

"When's Grace and Kami's wedding?"

"Who are you? What're your names?"

"Can you tell us anything about the wedding? Any theme? What's their song?"

"Is De Niro invited?"

"You're doing a lot of work back there. Is it going to be done in time?"

Raffi silently waded through them, Ani close beside him, keeping their heads down. He turned around briefly to check on her. Ani was smiling politely, but he could see the fear underneath.

Suddenly, the doors of the winery swung open, and, oh no, it was his father. Moushegh was there, gripping the edge of the door, shouting in Armenian. Then English. "Get out of here. You scum. Get off my property. I will call the police!"

"Dad," Raffi mouthed, but his father's eyes were nowhere near him. Raffi didn't know much about the world of online celebrity journalism, but he knew this could be bad. He did *not* need the image of Ô tainted by the angry bear that was his father. They didn't need this type of publicity.

Then Ani spun around to face the hungry crowd. "Hi, everyone. My name is Ani Avakian, I'm the wedding planner. This is Raffi Garabedian, the co-owner of Ô winery. We're grateful for your attention today. Unfortunately, we don't think Grace will be making an appearance anytime soon, but we are thankful for your interest. I will share that the work Raffi and I have been managing will be done in time for the wedding, and it is going to be stunning. To maintain the couple's privacy, we won't be answering any other questions at this time. Thank you!"

She capped her speech with a sweet smile and turned back, her face immediately morphing into a combination of worry and relief.

There was more clamoring from the paparazzi behind her, but slowly, more and more cameras fell to their sides as they realized they didn't have anyone famous to capture. Thank God.

Ani, once again, was fucking brilliant. He had to tell her, he had to—

They reached his father at the door, and Raffi and his dad had an awkward silent moment, then Raffi ushered Ani inside, followed behind her, and shut them all in.

Oh God. Meeting the parents. Parent, anyway. Far, far too soon. But then again, in Armenian relationships, meeting the family often came early on. That was the norm. Even so, this felt different. And not in a warm, sentimental way, but in the way that made Raffi's shoulders tense beside her, his movements just a fraction stiffer than usual.

Because Moushegh was hardly a peach.

Raffi didn't want to subject Ani to him, not yet.

"Those damned reporters," his father growled in Armenian. "Defiling our property. No shame, no shame at all!"

Raffi cleared his throat. "Um, Dad, this is Ani. Ani Avakian. Ani, my dad, Moushegh."

Really driving home that there was an Armenian woman before them who could understand every word.

His father shook himself as if he hadn't really noticed until now the presence of *a lady*, as Moushegh sometimes said.

"Ani, eh?" his father asked. "You speak Armenian?" he asked in Armenian. God, the first question. He was already sizing up Ani for future wife potential.

"I do," Ani said. "Not perfectly," she said with a perfect Armenian accent, "but I understand it well."

"Lovely girl," his father said, and Raffi about wanted to die. "What are you doing with my son here?"

Ani held her breath, and Raffi quickly answered. "She's the wedding planner. We've been working together."

"Ah, yes," Moushegh said. "I recall now, seeing you the day Kami Mardian was here."

Moushegh lurched over to the window and peeked out. "The cockroaches appear to be leaving. Whatever you said to them, Ani, my girl, seems to have worked."

Ani was standing near enough to him that Moushegh tapped her on the shoulder twice. Ani didn't seem to mind; her smile was genuine.

"Thank you. I'm relieved it did."

Speaking of relief, Raffi wanted to get Ani away from his dad as soon as possible because who knew what would come out of Moushegh's mouth next.

"Ani, we've got a lot of work to do. Let's head out back."

"Oh, okay. Nice to meet you, Mr. Garabedian," Ani said in Armenian.

"Please, call me Moushig," his dad said with a smile.

Oh no. Dad liked Ani. He wasn't sure if this was a good or bad thing. Probably a good thing, but it still made him feel uncomfortable. His dad wasn't *kind*. Raffi didn't want Moushegh inflicting any of his negative vibes onto his girl.

His girl. He liked that.

It was a little after ten now, and Raffi felt he'd lived an entire lifetime since waking up. From coffee to the video, to diurnal activities, to surprise paparazzi, to his dad meeting his brand-new girlfriend. It was too much. He breathed out a great sigh when they were entirely out of Moushegh's earshot. Raffi steered Ani into a storage closet, mostly empty but with some spare bar towels, bottle openers, extra menus, and the like. The faint scent of oak filled the air as he closed the door behind them.

"Sorry," he said. "Needed a little quiet alone time with you before jumping into the next thing. And who knows what's going to be out there."

"Pirates?" Ani ventured.

He smiled and pressed a kiss to the top of her head.

"You were amazing, by the way. How did you do that? In the car you were practically shaking, talking about your sexed-up hair, and two seconds later you were addressing the press like the president of the United States."

She shrugged. "Figured it might help take the attention off your dad. Journalists don't like getting yelled at, I imagine. I used to follow a lot of celebrity gossip back in the day, and I remember reading that the paps would get even for celebrity bad behavior."

"Well, you were fucking fire. Water, really. Cool, smooth, placid as hell."

"Thank you . . ." She blushed pink, and it was so damn cute. God, he adored her.

"But Raffi," she said. "We should be extra careful now. I don't think the press is interested in us at all, but you never know how big Grace is going to get. If they dig into her history, then Kami's history, and find out that you *and* me both dated Grace's future wife? They might get interested. So let's sort of lie low? Do not look at me adoringly like you were two seconds ago."

"You could see that?"

"Oh yes, and I would like much more of it at a later date."

"Good. You're getting it." He kissed her quickly to keep his arousal at a minimum. They had things to discuss in this closet. Not things to do. Even though he really, really wanted to do things.

"And also," she started biting the edge of her nail, then whisked her hand away. "This wedding is now a lot more high stakes." She looked downward. "As if it wasn't already," she muttered.

That was odd; what was high stakes about the wedding as

is? That it was Kami's and Ani felt some sort of obligation to make sure it went well? Or that she was dating the guy who ran the place?

"What do you mean by that?" Raffi asked.

For a millisecond, Ani's expression mirrored a frightened doe's, but it zipped by so quickly he wasn't sure he'd seen it at all. Then she appeared unconcerned. "You know, that I'm trying to break into luxury weddings and this could be my chance."

"Ah, right." He felt bad, suddenly, about his comments when they first met about her lack of elaborate weddings on her website. What a dick. "You're going to crush it."

"Well, let's hope so. The press around Grace? It can be a really good thing," she said, beaming. "Because I think we can pull it off. Disastrous if we can't. But seriously, it could mean big things for us both, if we do it right. And I believe in us."

His hands alighted to both her shoulders. "I believe in us, too."

Raffi bent forward, drawn like a tide, and kissed her. A quiet agreement, a whispered promise between them, that Raffi was sure, in that moment, nothing could break.

23

Ani

DESPITE HER BELIEF in herself, things were *not* going according to plan.

A few weeks later, Grace's star had only grown. The trailer for *Mafia Princess* had dropped, and the internet had exploded—fans dissecting every frame, memes flooding social media, and hashtags trending worldwide. Every magazine and newspaper seemed to feature her, whether it was a glossy cover story or a breathless think piece about her meteoric rise, with headlines like "Lights, Camera, Zhang: The Overnight Stardom of *Mafia Princess*'s Leading Lady." Even the phrase "Zhang effect" was taking hold, with people talking about how social media could cement stardom before a movie was even released.

Ani and Sanan had held a call with Grace and Kami during which Grace had briefly discussed it. She didn't mind the paparazzi but preferred they not be on the premises the day of the wedding. That was something new Ani would have to figure out. This might be the one and only time she had to.

Ani was at her parents' house in San Mateo with her sister,

Talar, and Talar's husband, Nshan. Her parents had made lunch together: eech, tabbouleh, and vospov kuftes because they were currently on a vegan diet. "We enjoyed it so much at Lent," her mother had told her, "that we decided to make it permanent." So apparently they had fish on Fridays and were vegan all the other days. And of course they cooked all their meals together in true romantic fashion.

The five of them gathered comfortably in her parents' family room, sitting on the long L-shaped couch, eating lunch and watching an Armenian soap opera Ani's mom had gotten into. Ani, regrettably, could hardly understand the Eastern Armenian dialect, so her mother acted as a live translator.

"That means 'celebratory,'" her mother said. She held up a notepad where she'd written down words that were new to her. "See, I am studying *Eastern* now. Your mother is going to be a master of both our languages."

Her mother worked at Nordstrom in the cosmetics department, but because, as she claimed, she had no children in the house to cook for and no grandchildren to watch, she had no choice but to watch copious amounts of Armenian TV in her spare time.

Ani had almost finished her plate when she got the call.

"Hello, is this Annie Uh-vak-ean?" the voice of an older woman demanded.

Ani stood and bumped into Talar's knees on her way out of the room, Talar rubbing them dramatically and putting on a mock-hurt face. Ani replied, "Yes, this is. May I ask who is calling?"

"This is Jeannie Tilde," said the voice, "of Tilde Florists in Napa Valley."

Ani swallowed hard. Jeannie herself, the legendary owner of the fanciest florist in Napa, was calling her. And she sounded *pissed*.

"Jeannie, an honor to hear from you. Could I please ask why you're calling?"

Her pulse was already racing. Had Kami gone rogue and called up the florist requesting changes? Ani paced down the hall to the bedrooms, absently viewing family photos on the walls.

"Well, I wish I could say I returned the sentiment, but after I heard what had happened from Madison, I had to call you up myself to talk to *the* most unprofessional wedding planner I've ever encountered."

Me? Ani wondered. *Was Jeannie talking about me?* She quickly racked her brain for any interaction with the florists that could have been construed as inappropriate. She had called them a week ago to confirm their mega-order, had spoken with Madison, and all had gone well. The deposit was paid, the details were correct, and her conversation had been cordial. So why . . . ?

Ani drew up her courage and said, "I'm sorry, Jeannie, I'm not sure what you're talking about. Maybe there's been a misunderstanding?"

Jeannie scoffed. "You're damn right there's been a misunderstanding. What planner calls to confirm the details and then a week later *cancels the entire order*?!"

Ani's stomach dropped, a cold wave of dread washing over her as she gripped the phone tighter. Her palms were slick with sweat, and she could feel her heartbeat thudding in her ears. Canceled? How could the order have been canceled? She hadn't spoken to them or made any type of contact in a week.

"I . . . Wha—" Ani started to say, but Jeannie wasn't through.

"After we spent significant time and expense ordering the absolute bushel of flora that was requested. Do you think it was easy, securing ranunculus at this time of year?"

"Jeannie," Ani dared to interrupt. "I'm so sorry, but I didn't cancel the order—"

A photo of Ani, Talar, and her parents in a photo studio from the early 2000s, complete with questionable millennium fashion such as Ani's dress over a pair of jeans, stared at her as she attempted to process this conversation.

"Sure you're sorr— Wait, excuse me, what? Yesterday, Madison spoke to a young woman who said with conviction that the entire Mardian-Zhang order was to be canceled, lock, stock, and barrel. 'Your services are no longer required.' Those were the exact words."

Ani's mouth dropped open but nothing came out. A young woman. Who . . . ? Because it wasn't her. Her mind raced, scrambling for answers.

Was it Sanan? Maybe there'd been some miscommunication and Sanan thought she had to cancel? But no, that didn't make sense. Sanan would never do something like that, even accidentally. She dotted her i's and crossed her t's. Or . . . Kami—had she spiraled again, panicked about some detail, and canceled everything in a moment of impulsivity? Ani's chest tightened at the thought. Linen colors were one thing, but there was no way she'd cancel the entire flower order. Ani would check anyway.

Or, with the paparazzi lurking around lately, was it someone else entirely? Someone trying to sabotage the wedding, to stir up drama for a headline? The possibilities swirled in her mind, each one more unsettling than the last. This was insane. This was movie shit; this was not real life.

"Jeannie, please believe me, I'm not sure who made that call, but it wasn't me. The wedding is on and your flowers are going to be the crown jewel of the whole affair. It's going to be nothing without you."

"Absolutely right about that." Jeannie let out some kind of huff, but she sounded less angry.

"I know it, believe me. I'm going to talk to my, uh, associates, and see what happened here. For now, will you accept my deepest apologies to you and to Madison, and can we please ensure that everything is back on, exactly as planned?"

There was a brief silence on the other line. Ani held her breath.

"I'd like to, but I'm just not sure anymore. Something feels fishy."

You could sure as hell say that again, Ani thought. But this was not okay. Not in the least.

"Listen, Jeannie, I'm in the Peninsula, but I can be at your shop in about two hours. I'll come by and I'll have answers by then and we can figure this out."

Silence again. "I'll be here," Jeannie said, then promptly hung up.

Shit. Shit, shit, shit, shit, shit. Ani wasn't exaggerating or puffing up Jeannie when she said the flowers were going to be the wedding's showpiece. Flowers were *essential*, and there was no possible way to book a reputable florist for a wedding happening in two weeks. She quickly texted Sanan, sure that this had nothing to do with her but hoping her assistant might have some info.

Ani turned and was met with Talar, leaning against the wall under a photo of their parents kissing at their tenth anniversary party. Ani had apparently been born nine months later. A fact she did *not* need to know.

"Trouble in wedding-land?" Talar asked.

There was no point in denying it; Talar seemed to have heard enough. "Uh, you could say that. Sorry I have to take off so soon."

Ani's phone buzzed. Sanan had no idea what was up and seemed very concerned. Ani would give her a call soon, hopefully once everything was smoothed over, if she managed it.

"Well, don't be sorry, 'cause I'm coming with you."

Ani wrinkled her nose. "No you're not. You've always got stuff to do. This one trip is going to take the rest of the day."

"Oh, yes I am. I never see you anymore. I'm busy every second of the weekday, and you're always busy on weekends. This is a rare Saturday when you don't have a wedding and I don't have a crushing caseload. I need sister time."

Ani sighed. She wanted sister time, too. But she had been hoping, because she had to head to Napa anyway, that she could see Raffi. Now that wasn't going to happen. She and Raffi had never stipulated that they keep their relationship a secret from their own families, but considering Talar's views of good-for-nothing Raffi Garabedian, Ani wasn't exactly eager to introduce them.

Ani had seen Raffi once last week, luckily. He'd come to San Francisco, taken her out to a ridiculously nice restaurant where the staff came out with dishes in a way that felt perfectly choreographed, and she was surprised to find she enjoyed their take on haggis. They'd had a romp in bed that evening that still consisted of Raffi keeping his pants on. And Ani had grown impatient. She wanted to show him she trusted him. Tonight in Napa could have been an impromptu sex night, but now it seemed she'd be missing him entirely.

Because Ani couldn't deny that she'd been deprived of sister time for far too long.

"You're right. Now we have to break it to Mom and Bab."

ABOUT TWO HOURS later, as Ani had promised Jeannie, the two sisters walked into Tilde. Talar had assured Ani that she could back her up as her lawyer, and even though Ani said that was not necessary for this diplomatic mission, Talar still put on her meanest litigator mug.

Jeannie appeared, short, thin, and fashionable, with her arms crossed and her brows knitted.

"Jeannie," Ani said, and extended her arm. "Ani Avakian, here as promised. Let's clear this up."

Talar stayed behind, suddenly entranced by the floral artwork surrounding her and forgetting the whole deal about being Ani's legal representative.

Alone with Jeannie, Ani apologized profusely and said, truthfully, that she was still looking into the incident. She gushed over Jeannie's floral artistry like she was getting paid by the compliment, then silently prayed while the older woman weighed her words.

"I can see you've got conviction," Jeannie said. "Still, in my thirty years in the business, this has never happened to me."

Ani's heart seemed to stop. No flowers. Maybe *she'd* have to do the flowers. By hand? Oh God, that would take all night, if not longer. She could make a decent arrangement, but they wouldn't be nearly as good. Then, an idea sprouted.

Ani pulled out her phone, tapped around, and pulled up a page.

"Jeannie, here's *Entertainment Tonight*. Front page is Grace Zhang, who is my client, who would love for *your* flowers to be at *her* wedding. There are literal paparazzi stalking the winery venue weeks before the actual wedding date. This wedding is going to be all over the news, and we might even get a feature in *Vogue*."

"Grace Zhang, eh? Haven't heard of her," Jeannie said, squinting at the phone.

"She rose to fame pretty recently, but the press is all over her. You'll be seeing her name around," Ani assured her, a smile on her face but inwardly losing hope.

Madison popped out from behind a corner. "Did you just say that mega flower order was for Grace Zhang? Like *Mafia Princess* Grace Zhang? Are we seriously doing her wedding?"

Jeannie stepped back and stared at Ani. "*Vogue*, you say? I haven't had a feature there in a while; we *are* due."

Ani nodded. "A very strong possibility."

The older woman considered Madison, who had pulled out her phone while humming the Auto-Tune version of "I just wanna like . . . swallow it," and gasped. "Oh my God, Grace is riding horses in Malibu with her fiancée! Iconic."

Jeannie tapped her leg while staring at Madison, considering. "Well, it was a large order. And we did already call in some special favors. Would be a shame to lose out on that."

Ani nodded again, eagerly. "It would, it would." Madison loudly agreed as well.

She felt a presence behind her. Talar, no doubt, catching up to them.

"All right," Jeannie said. "We can do it."

Ani's smile grew huge and she restrained herself—with great effort—from looking too enthusiastic. "Yes? It's back on?"

Apparently her—and Madison's—excitement was contagious because Jeannie had some sort of mini-smile on her face, too. "It's back on."

"Oh thank God," said a man's voice behind her. A man who sounded *a lot* like Raffi.

Ani whipped around. It *was* Raffi. Standing right next to Talar.

"What're you doing here?" Ani asked, shocked.

"What're *you* doing here?" Raffi returned. He appeared surprised himself, but thrilled, like he had been given an unexpected gift.

"Who is this man, and how do you two know each other?" Talar asked, an impressed tone to her voice as she sized up Raffi. She didn't know him well and obviously didn't recognize him out of context here in the flower shop. But she clearly thought he was hot and was jazzed that her sister was consorting with a guy like this. Little did Talar know . . .

Jeannie, seeing that these questions had nothing to do with her, turned on her heel and waltzed to the back of the shop.

"I asked first," Ani said.

Raffi appeared like he wanted to hug her but then clocked Talar, undoubtedly remembering her from the photo on Ani's phone, and shifted from one foot to the other instead. "The florist called me and left me a message that I didn't really understand, because I thought it sounded like she said the entire flower order was canceled, but that seemed too ludicrous to be true. Anyway, I was a few stores down when I listened to my voicemail so I figured I'd pop in. And if anything was really wrong I'd give you a call right away."

Sweet of him. Try to sort it out himself but knew this was Ani's territory. God, it was difficult being this close to him and *not* being able to hold him, kiss him. She could smell his cologne very faintly and wanted more of it. How would she introduce him to Talar? She'd better figure it out because she owed Talar an answer to her question.

Ani avoided Talar's question a little longer and said, "And we're here because you're right, someone did apparently call Tilde and cancel the flowers. Which is insane. I have no clue who, or how it could have happened." Although she did wonder, with Raffi's father so displeased by the queer wedding and so disgusted by the paparazzi and reporters . . . she could imagine him taking steps to ruin it. But canceling the flower order? That felt more of a mean jab, less "shut down the whole thing."

Raffi's jaw tightened. "This isn't good."

"No," she said. "It's not." They were so close, so very close, to the wedding, and someone was playing around trying to sabotage it. To screw around with her future. If this wedding didn't end up the perfect fairy-tale dreamland she'd promised, she was toast—and not the cute, artisanal kind. Photos ruined, no magazine features, and worst of all, now there was the threat of *bad* press.

"Do you have any idea who it could have been?" Raffi asked tentatively.

Ani wasn't about to blurt, "Your dad!" but in truth, that was her only lead. "I'm—I'm not sure. Someone who doesn't like the idea of a queer wedding maybe?"

Raffi pressed his lips into a thin line. "Hmm. I hope not. My first thought was that this was related to Grace's sudden celebrity. Either an enemy or someone trying to make a great story."

Ani thought. "Someone who wanted the *Mafia Princess* role but didn't get it?" Canceling flowers did feel like the petty kind of thing someone who was trying to poke at their nemesis would do. It was possible, but that theory, a fellow celebrity, would be a tough one to track and confirm.

Talar stepped forward. "I'm sorry, Ani, do you mind introducing me to your new . . . friend?"

"Uh, sure," Ani said uneasily. "This is Raffi. He runs Ô winery."

Raffi extended one elegant arm, but Talar's hand flew to her mouth as it dawned on her, apparently, exactly who this Raffi was. The one Talar had explicitly warned Ani about. Telling Ani stories about his racy, reckless past.

"Nice to meet you, Talar," Raffi said, prompting Talar, as his hand was still outstretched.

Ani gave her sister a discreet nudge. Talar, her eyes still glued to Raffi's face finally reached out and shook.

"And you're . . ." Talar started. "Here to help with the flowers?"

"Yes," Raffi said. "Though as usual, Ani figured out how to solve the problem without help. Speaking of flowers, you should have seen her a few months ago when this man refused to sell me his rare plants. I was about to get into a fist-fight with the guy when Ani swoops in and sweet-talks him into selling us his entire stock. Still not over that." He shook his head, smiling fondly.

"And by the way, they're growing perfectly, thanks to the instructions you left me."

Talar looked between them, and Ani's heart ticked up a couple notches. Ani wanted to tell Talar. She really did. But she needed to prep Talar first about how Raffi had changed.

"You're Raffi Garabedian?" Talar asked, truly puzzled.

Raffi gave a magnificent smile. "I am. You've . . . heard of me? All good things, I assume," he said, laughing at himself.

Talar gave a weak smile. "Indeed."

Just then, Ani's phone rang, which was a huge mercy considering she didn't know how much longer she could endure the awkwardness of this interaction. But then she saw who it was. Kami. Ani flashed the phone to Raffi, frowning, which he returned.

"Have to take this. Give me a sec."

Ani picked up and said hello.

"Aniiiiiiii," Kami wailed, then hiccupped.

She must have heard about the flowers, too. "Don't worry, I sorted everything out with the florist," Ani said confidently.

"What thing with the florist?" Kami asked, her voice still

thick but less whiny. Woops. So this call wasn't about the flowers.

"Nothing at all. Everything's great. But what's up?"

Kami took a deep breath and sputtered. "It's my dress! I'm at the final fitting and it's all wrong. They messed up. It's like they made the pins bigger instead of smaller and I'm swimming in this and they say they can't make all the changes on time and I neeeed youuuu," she cried out the last two words.

"It's not that bad," Ani could hear Galia say in the background.

"It is!" Kami stammered.

Kami's voice was so loud on the phone she was sure Talar and Raffi could hear it. In fact, she knew they could. Talar rolled her eyes and wandered off, admiring the floral art. Raffi appeared gravely upset. She didn't blame him. This was more of the job of a relative, not the wedding planner. At the final fitting, Ani would have to examine every inch of Kami to see how the dress was fitting. A close-quarters job that she didn't want to do. Plus, she had *just* gotten to Napa. She would say no. She would say. No.

"Kami, I'm sorry, I can't come. I'm in Napa." *Fixing a near disaster you don't need to know anything about.* "With traffic I wouldn't even be able to get there for another hour and a half at minimum."

Kami sniffled. "Can you come anyway? I'll wait."

Shit. Ani caught Raffi's eyes, which had darkened. He had heard that and was waiting for Ani to run to Kami again.

"No, I can't," she said simply.

Kami sobbed openly on the other line. "What am I going to do?"

Ani took a deep breath and thought. She didn't want to completely leave her bride in the dust. "Send me photos, lots of them, of all the parts of the dress that aren't working, and send me videos, too, of you standing and moving around in it, and then of you walking in it, back and front. Tell me which parts they say they can't fix. Also, remind them that you can pay extra to get it rush altered," Ani added, remembering that Kami had the benefit of being able to throw money at the situation. "Can you do that? Then I'll send my recommendations."

"Ohhh . . . kay . . ." came Kami's shaky voice. "But you are coming to the house in two weeks, right?"

Ani stared off in confusion. "What house?"

"We rented a house in Napa for the hinoum and the wedding and . . ." she hiccupped, "we got you a room in it so you can stay."

"Oh," Ani said. This was actually very considerate because it would have been a huge pain to drive from San Francisco to Napa for the engagement party and then the wedding. But she had been hoping to stay at Raffi's, although they hadn't discussed it yet. And she couldn't tell anyone she was sleeping over at his place anyway. So now she couldn't refuse this. Shit.

With hesitation, she said, "Of course, that's really thoughtful of you guys."

Kami's voice was still thick with tears. "Okay, well, I'll see you then, and I'll send some photos now." She sounded so sad, let down by Ani—Ani remembered that well, the guilt Kami would pile on when she didn't get her way, and Ani would immediately reverse it and jump to do whatever Kami asked.

But not today.

"Great," Ani said. "I'll let you know as soon as I have suggestions."

She hung up and stared at Raffi, who appeared crushed.

Ani called to her sister. "Tal, can you give us a few minutes?"

Talar's eyes pinged back and forth between them. She shrugged her shoulders but appeared anything but indifferent. "Sure, whatever you need to do," she said, sarcasm icing the edges of her voice. Ani could deal with her sister's suspicions later. Right now, she needed to talk to her boyfriend.

24

Raffi

RAFFI FELT LIKE something was crawling all over his skin, and it wasn't just the warm Napa day getting inside his clothes, making him sweat. He loved running into Ani, and this should have been the happiest of coincidences, but instead he felt small somehow.

First, Ani couldn't properly introduce him to her sister. Then her sister figured out who he was and looked at him like he was a kind of war criminal, but then seemed confused that he wasn't, actually. The fact that someone was maybe trying to sabotage the wedding? The wedding that Ani's and Raffi's futures were riding on? It felt big and uncontrollable, and the thought gave him a sick feeling in his stomach.

Then that call from Kami, that'd been such a punch. Kami demanding Ani's presence. He'd been so proud of his girl when she said no, but then the alternative? Almost worse. Kami sending a bunch of up-close photos of herself, her body in no doubt some sexy dress, if he knew Kami, to *his* girlfriend. His girlfriend, who'd just gotten over Kami. He didn't like it. It wasn't fair, and this shouldn't have been Ani's job.

And then, as if things couldn't get worse, he overheard the part about Ani staying over at a house Kami rented. He hadn't asked Ani yet, but he had been waiting to tell her that she could come stay with him for those three nights. Now it was too late. Kami was keeping Ani close to her, just how she liked it. Who knows what Kami might try, feeling emotional the night before her wedding? Would she go and sneak into Ani's room?

In Armenian, Kami meant "strong wind," and that's exactly what she was living up to now—she had swept into their lives like a tempest, upending everything in her path.

They had agreed to date, he and Ani, but they weren't acting like it. And that was what scared him. Not a future with Ani, but *no* future with Ani.

He shoved his hands in his pockets, faced his girl, then looked down, embarrassed. "I'm going to be honest with you, I'm feeling pretty bad right now."

Ani stepped closer to him, one eye on Talar. "I know, I can tell, and I don't blame you."

Now he could look her in the eye. "You don't?"

She appeared so sympathetic, he wished he could kiss that beautiful face. It killed him not to be able to. "Of course not. I didn't introduce you to Talar properly, and I am guessing you heard most, if not all, of that conversation. The house . . . I don't want to stay there. I wanted—well, to be honest, I wanted to stay with you. If it wasn't, you know, an imposition."

The tightness in Raffi's chest unknotted. He should have known that. Of course Ani would prefer to stay with him. Where the hell was his confidence? He needed to trust Ani and their relationship more, but it was still so new. It was easily battered before it even got a chance to grow properly.

"It's never an imposition," he said. "You could have stayed."

"Well," Ani said, "I was thinking maybe I could sneak out one of the nights and stay over anyway, then sneak back in the morning. No one has to know."

Raffi's heart warmed, but he shook his head. "You don't have to lose sleep for my ego."

"No, but I do want to lose sleep because of what we'll be doing at your place."

Despite himself, he growled. He felt it. They were getting closer. She trusted him more and more. She might have implied sex. Did Ani imply sex?

"I'm not sure how I'm standing here not kissing you, Ani jan."

"Then do it," she challenged.

But Talar. "Your sister?" he asked.

"I'm going to tell her anyway," she said.

Raffi was stunned for a second, then the full realization of what this meant hit him. This wasn't just about telling her sister; it was about letting the people she loved most in the world know that he was important to her. That their relationship was important. After weeks of secrecy, of stolen moments, this felt like a seismic shift. It was trust, and it left him breathless. In an instant, he scooped her into his arms, then cradled her face as he kissed her long and deep.

They were interrupted by a voice saying, "Wow, okay. I guess we're skipping the explanations and going straight to the PDA. Nice."

Talar stood there, hands on her hips, sizing him up. Raffi

let go of Ani entirely, but then she grabbed his hand and held it.

"Explanations, right. Talar, meet my boyfriend. Raffi."

Talar's eyebrow raised so high, Raffi was actually impressed.

"You can't—this is—we talked about this, Ani."

Talar was the first person they told about their relationship, and it was off to a harrowing start. He supposed he deserved this, though. After everything he'd done, all the damage he'd caused, shouldn't he feel some shame? Shouldn't his bad behavior bite him back? He just wished Ani didn't have to get hurt in the crossfire.

But when Ani squeezed his hand, Raffi's anger and fears ebbed. In her touch, he felt her steadiness, her quiet conviction. She wasn't shaken. She could handle a few probing questions—because what they had was worth it. The two of them, together as one, were strong.

"Raffi and I have spent a lot of time together. A lot." She looked at him meaningfully, and damn if that didn't hit him right in the chest. A lot of time? And it wasn't enough. He wanted more—more of her quiet mornings and her loud opinions, more of the way she made him feel like he was the only person in the room, even when they were surrounded by people. He wanted to be the one she turned to when the world got too heavy, the one who made her laugh when she didn't think she could.

His thoughts were interrupted by Ani's voice, steady and sure, like a beacon. "Whatever you heard, maybe that was him once, but it isn't now. Raffi, I hope this is okay to say."

He nodded, then looked toward the door. "It is. I feel like I should go so you two can talk about me behind my back," he joked.

"No, stay." She turned back to her sister. "Tal, we were going to keep it secret until after the wedding, so we could keep people's attention on the actual wedding and not us. We're supposed to be just working together. But I don't want to hide it from you. I adore him. He's . . . everything to me."

He felt a great weight lift, as if something in him had been unlocked. Ani had been melting the cold hardness in him for months, but there had still remained an icy gate that Ani just smashed open with her words. Sharing their relationship for the first time. He didn't know it had meant so much to him. To have her tell one of the most important people in her world that they were together.

He realized it now. He wanted it all—every second, every breath, every damn heartbeat.

Raffi wanted to marry this woman.

Talar shifted uncomfortably, sizing up Raffi. "I have to admit, you're different from what I thought you'd be, praising my sister like that. Ani really does have a magic touch. I should bring you into some of my negotiations."

Ani held up her hands. "No, thanks," she said. "Done with that world."

"So." Raffi cleared his throat, feeling a lightness in his body, so light it was turning to near pleasurable delirium. "Should we grab a bite? If you have time?"

Talar smiled cautiously at him. "We have time."

The three of them strolled to a café, ate enormous chocolate chip cookies and drank iced lattes, and enjoyed the warm Napa afternoon. They showed Talar the winery and the finished work he and Ani had helped bring together. And slowly, while chatting with his girlfriend and her sister under the September sun, he felt himself being pulled into their world. Into a second family, one where he might belong.

All they had to do was make it through the wedding, then he could shout his love to the world.

25

Ani

THREE DAYS BEFORE the wedding, Ani drove to the address Kami had given her for the house her family had rented in Napa. It was ten minutes of a windy, hilly drive off the Silverado Trail, and Ani wasn't sure what to expect because she couldn't see many homes beyond all the thick oak trees and wiry bushes. Just a couple of gates with houses hidden far beyond them. Her phone's map showed that it was a twenty-minute drive from the rented house to Raffi's place, which wasn't too bad. She had swung by his place first for sourj and kisses.

Things had been going well. Things had been going *so* well. The construction at Ô was finished and looked stunning, even better than she could have imagined. Ani had double-checked with every single vendor to confirm that no other orders had been botched, and even gave them specific security instructions to ensure that nothing could be changed without Ani's explicit consent. Her brides were happy, the dress crisis had been averted, and they were not panic-texting her about anything.

Ani, of course, was still stressing because she hadn't figured out who was behind the sabotage. Who had canceled the flower order? Had Kami's dress alteration fiasco been a random error or an intentional scheme? (Luckily, Ani barely needed to help Kami with the dress issue after Kami apparently told the seamstress, "Money is no object. Just make this dress fit me ASAP!") And what was with those menus?

Three weeks ago, the menus had arrived at Ani's place printed incorrectly. Not just typos. The full menu had been turned into a middle-school joke. If she hadn't been freaking out, she would have been amused by the "chunky fish Jell-O shots" appetizer and the "deep-fried mystery nuggets" main course. But this silliness was not her brides' doing. Luckily, Sanan had been able to personally go down to the printers and oversee the creation of the correct menus.

Not knowing who was behind this made Ani's stomach turn, and it wasn't just the twisting road. She had a feeling that whoever they were, they weren't done yet.

As Ani rolled up closer to the address, she heard something other than the crunch of her car tires over the gravelly path. Talking, clamoring, commotion.

Then she saw it. A massive group of reporters and paparazzi stationed outside the gates of Kami's rented home. They turned Ani's way, flashing bulbs at her beat-up car. They were going to be sorely disappointed. No Grace here.

Ani had to roll down her window to type in the gate code, and immediately the questions blew in.

"Wait, you're the wedding planner, right? How's everything going?"

"You nervous about the big day?"

"Is the construction finished?"

"Are both brides wearing white?"

Ani gave them a big smile. "Everything's going great. Construction's finished. Brides are happy. To be honest, I don't know what Grace is going to be wearing. It'll be a surprise for us all. Pardon me, I have to get going."

Ani punched the numbers, careful to shield them from view. The gate yawned open, and Ani drove in. That was totally fine, a pleasant-ish experience with the press. She willed herself to feel optimistic that all future interactions with the press would continue that way. Because they had to.

Thanks to a check from Grace and Kami, Ani had just paid Sanan for her work, but between that and the most recent personal loan payment, which was mostly interest, Ani's bank account was back to dwindling. Three more days, and the final, largest deposit from Grace and Kami would arrive. Then she'd be okay. Well on her way to solvency.

There had been no need to tell Raffi about it because, well, money was so touchy to talk about, especially so early in a relationship. But if Ani was being completely honest with herself, it was also because she was ashamed and didn't want Raffi to ever think of her as less than. Nothing he did made her feel that way, but this secret debt felt too huge, too mortifying to share, even with him. Especially because he likely could easily pay it off for her, and she didn't want to be someone's charity case. She'd rather tell him *after* the debt had been resolved.

As Ani drove up to the house the building revealed itself to her, and she realized calling this a "house" had been a mistake. This was a mansion, styled in French seventeenth-century style. Well, at least it would be easy to sneak out of and get lost in.

Ani grabbed her luggage and lingered a moment longer outside, where it was quiet. Breezes ruffling the olive trees, Napa's sun absorbing into her skin, the smell of that fall crunch in the air.

Then the door burst open and Kami appeared, jumping toward Ani and wrapping her in a huge hug. "You're here! I'm so excited. Isn't this place darling?"

Darling is how Ani would have described a well-appointed cottage, not this ten-bedroom castle. But perhaps it was a difference of opinion.

"It's massive," she said.

"Which is good," Kami replied. "The whole family is staying here. Phew, so much family. But they can't wait to see you."

Ani's stomach tightened. She felt, starkly, that she did not belong here. She should be with Raffi right now.

Ani blindly followed Kami inside, which was—wow—impeccably designed with antique furniture and a mix of classical and provocative art along the walls. The place was swarming with relatives and the sounds of people shouting, laughing, and chatting. She said hello again to Kami's mom and aunt, then to Kami's father, uncles, grandparents, and cousins until her head spun. Were any of these people behind the wedding sabotage? It just didn't seem likely. She couldn't imagine an auntie, even a mean one, intentionally trying to ruin her niece's wedding. It wasn't the Armenian auntie way.

"So many photographers outside, this is crazy!" Kami's mom said, but didn't seem upset.

Kami said, "I know, right? I love it, though. They follow us everywhere, and people are going nuts for Grace. I even told them about my lip gloss line, and sales are up fifty percent. Just from one mention!"

Her mother hugged her. "This is fantastic, Kami jan. You have a good head for these things."

Many of her relatives made sounds of agreement.

Well, Ani supposed she was happy that Kami didn't hate all the press and wasn't having second thoughts about being with Grace or wanting to call off the entire wedding. Ani had feared that possibility, but it didn't seem to be an issue. Kami didn't even have an Instagram—only because her spiritual healer had told her it was too much negative energy beaming into her soul—but she didn't mind being splashed all over *People*. She supposed it made sense. Instagram was work. Being paparazzi-ed was passive. And maybe her spiritual healer approved of it.

One of the aunts called out in Armenian, "There are a hundred light switches for the kitchen, and I can't find the one that lights up the countertops. Someone help me!"

Ani was *more* than happy to heed the call and rushed over to the auntie. Ani flipped switch after switch and finally found the one the auntie needed.

Then, seeing another chance to escape, Ani muttered that she needed to unpack and pulled away.

Galia found her then, and Ani, although wanting to go to her room, was relieved to see her familiar, friendly face. They hugged.

"Hi, Galia," she said.

"This is intense," Galia said, gesturing all around.

Ani gave a small nod. "It's a lot."

"You know how it is, though: What Kami wants, Kami gets," Galia said, frowning.

Before Ani could address that, Kami herself swung back into the picture like a boho Bloody Mary, appearing at only two mentions of her name. If she had heard, she made no indication of it. Kami squeezed Ani's shoulder. "Let me show you to your room."

The room was lovely, one of the prettiest she'd been in. Decorated in impeccably girly French antique style. But Ani still did not want to be there.

"And," Kami said with a secretive smile, "it's right next to mine. Look! There's even a door connecting our rooms!" she said with glee.

Ani couldn't hide the look of horror on her face for a split second, then washed it away into a fake smile.

"So I can come in here and cry to you about all my bridal problems." Kami laughed.

Oh God. This was going to be a nightmare.

Ani smiled. "I need to get ready for tonight. I'm going to settle in and then head over to the winery to prep for the hinoum. I should be on-site a few hours before everyone else gets there."

Not a lie. There was a ton of stuff to prepare for the traditional Armenian ceremony that was being held at Ô tonight. Sanan would be meeting her there, too. Sanan's relatives lived in Santa Rosa and insisted she stay with them. Ani had a little bit of time at the winery before her assistant would arrive.

Now, to get away from this place where she didn't belong and back into Raffi's arms. At least until the guests arrived.

26

Raffi

RAFFI WAS DIRECTING the caterers toward the kitchen when he caught sight of Ani. She had donned a long leather skirt and a black shirt with frilly sleeves. It was an enticing combination of sexy and girly that he would have great difficulty attempting to ignore.

She practically skipped over to him, and they met in a hug. Raffi couldn't help it, he picked her up a bit. No one currently bustling around knew them. It was fine.

"Hello, sexy," he said to her, keeping his voice low but not keeping the hunger out of it.

"Hey, Raff," she said, and he had to keep his shit together. Raff. That's what she called him in bed. Good God. Today was going to be harder than he thought, in more ways than one.

"Not sure how I'm going to make it through the night with you in a *leather* skirt. Are you trying to torment me?"

"Maybe," she smiled. "But it's *pleather*."

He pinched her ass. "Pleather, leather—I'm not convinced you didn't wear it just to short-circuit my brain."

"Then my work here is done."

Ani smirked, then slid an arm around his back as they took in the scene. The construction was finished, and the fountain was filled since the last time Ani was here. The water rippled peacefully, lending the entire garden an even more calming effect. The florist had been by and showered the space with flowers for the hinoum, more restrained than they would be for the wedding, but still impressive. Although it wasn't dark yet, string lights ornamented the grounds and gave everything a romantic, intimate feeling.

"We did it, Raffi," Ani said. "Well, really, Chris did it."

Raffi chuckled.

"It's better than I would have ever thought."

"Me too," he said. "I'm just glad I listened to you."

"Or we'd all be covering our eyes right now and cursing the sun."

He smiled, then said gratefully, "This really is going to help us get so many more weddings at Ô."

Ani nodded, considering. "I'm serious—once people see wedding photos in this garden, it's going to be *the* spot in Napa. Nothing else comes close."

A shiver ran through him. She believed in it, the space they helped create together. "Damn. Well, we'll see."

She looked up at him. "Time to get to work."

AN ARMY OF Armenian drum, dhol, and zurna players marched into Ô, with big camera bulbs flashing behind them, announcing Kami's arrival. Kami was brought in on an ornate palanquin, held up by four of her burly cousins. She was dressed in a mix of traditional Armenian garb, with a red-and-white flowing headpiece and a modern red, white, and gold dress. Oh, she must have been loving this, Raffi thought. True queen status.

The Armenian folk music blared into the night, and Raffi was thankful they were far away enough from neighbors that they wouldn't get any noise complaints. And then he stopped worrying for a moment and enjoyed the spectacle.

He loved the sound of the instruments; it brought him back to Armenian Sunday school, the Armenian dance classes he took there years before ballroom dance.

Grace was already on-site and had been waiting for her bride to arrive. When Grace herself had been driven to the property, Raffi witnessed the reporters and cameras go into a feeding frenzy, the likes of which he'd never seen before. They stepped all over each other, shouting like mad, all trying to get the perfect shot of her. He had to say, Grace handled them with, well, grace. She gave them one look over her shoulder and a closed-mouth smile that he was sure would make the papers the next day.

Now, a couple of paps had climbed the walls of the winery and snapped photos of Grace and Kami holding hands while the band played around them. He'd hired security for the wedding, as instructed by the couple, but not for this event. Raffi was regretting not going ahead and doing it anyway, but he thought if Kami and Grace were okay with it, he would be, too. Maybe they wanted to tease this event so they could get more cash for selling the private wedding photos. And the shots of Ô would be stunning at least.

Kami's mom breached the circle and fed a spoonful of honey to Grace and then one to Kami. She handed them walnuts as well, which, if Raffi remembered correctly, were supposed to ensure a sweet and happy life for them.

Raffi glanced over at Ani, standing too far away from him on the outskirts of the crowd. He wanted to do this with her. Have a hinoum. The whole shebang, too. He could imagine Talar at the front door of the Avakian family home with a saber, not allowing Raffi in until he paid the traditional bribe. Usually it was the brother of the groom who played this role, but he thought Talar would do formidably.

God, he wanted this with Ani. Three more days. Tonight, tomorrow, then the next day was the wedding and they could really be together, no more hiding.

Grace's family had entered the circle and were pretending to barter for Kami. Grace's brother was promising chickens, lamb, and a whole cow. It was a good joke because that's what was on the menu for the feast tonight. This was Kami's family's big chance to showcase Armenian culture, while tomorrow there would be a tea ceremony, and at the wedding, there'd be Californian and Malaysian fusion food to honor Grace's.

After some dancing and cheering, the guests took their seats for dinner. Server after server stepped out of the kitchen with enormous trays of roasted meats from a well-known Armenian caterer. The air filled with spiced lamb, pilaf, and fire-kissed vegetables.

Raffi stayed on the periphery, although technically Kami had invited him to sit and eat as a guest. Raffi's father was there, though, seated next to Kami's father, no doubt talking business. Raffi didn't feel like he could just hang out and socialize while so much was happening at the winery, so much potential for things to go wrong at any second. Besides, Ani wasn't going to relax for even a moment, so why should he?

Ani was chatting a hundred miles a minute with some *vendor*, which he was certainly not—not a vendor but her boyfriend. Ani caught his eye and seemed relieved to find him.

"Raffi jan," she said formally, though with a hint of endearment, since they were in front of the vendor, whoever he was. "This is Dillon. He mentioned that someone tripped over one of the patio lights and the plug broke off but it's still in the socket. Do you know how we could fix that?"

Shit, he didn't. But this seemed like a solvable problem and not a party-ruiner. They had so many patio lights he hadn't even noticed. Ani didn't seem overly worried, either, so they'd take the time to fix this without freaking out. Raffi mentally patted himself on the back for keeping so levelheaded in the face of a setback.

"I'll take a look and call the electrician."

But Raffi did not get a chance to call the electrician.

Suddenly, several guests started screaming, and then more screams joined in. A cluster of guests were jumping up and Raffi ran in that direction, now fully freaking the fuck out—what was it? A fire? He didn't see or smell anything. Or was it a rat? God, that'd have the wedding shut down faster than he could say "health code violation." But then he saw it.

Arching over the guests, looping, twisting, and turning like an inflatable tube man outside a car dealership, was a small plastic hose, mercilessly soaking all the guests at his winery.

What. The fuck.

It was one of the fountain tubes, the newly installed fountain tubes that had been working perfectly until this very second.

He saw Ani rushing toward it now, getting splashed by one chaotic swoop, her hair sticking to her face, and she and Raffi raced together, then grabbed it at the same time, wrangling the tube and trapping it underwater in the fountain.

Raffi didn't register that he'd gotten wet, too, until he and Ani stared at each other, panicked, not speaking, just taking huge, terrified breaths.

Then, *pop pop.* Flashbulbs flared from over the fence. Raffi scanned Kami's guests, all uproarious about the unwanted waterworks. Fancy Armenian ladies, like cats, did *not* like to get wet without permission. Or at all. His mother had never once stepped foot in a pool their entire childhood, although she was more than happy to sit at the perimeter of one. He spotted aunties with their furs doused, men with their toupees plastered to their heads, and younger guests with makeup running down their faces.

How the hell could this have happened? Chris was flawless in his designing, there was no way he'd let something like this slip. He wasn't rushed toward the end, not that Raffi could recall. Then Raffi remembered the flower predicament. And how Kami's alterations went wrong. Could this be related?

Raffi asked Ani as quietly as he could, while still being heard over the din, "What the hell do we do?"

Ani's eyes were massive, terrified, and he thought that for once, maybe she didn't know, either. "I—I need a second to think—"

Then, her gaze roamed over to Kami and Grace, who had

escaped the impromptu shower. And Kami? Kami was standing up, laughing. Then Grace was laughing. Kami was trying to shout and say something over the ruckus, but it was hard to hear her.

"Hold this down," she said, then Ani bolted. Raffi had no idea what she was doing or how to help other than keeping the wiggle-happy hose in place, so he just stood there, hand plunged in the water. Sanan rushed up to his side then, also half-doused, and grabbed the hose from him. "I've got this. You might be needed elsewhere. I'll figure out what to do with this thing."

"Thanks, Sanan," Raffi said with sincerity. He took his hands out, dried them on his pants, and looked for Ani.

Ani had grabbed a mic from somewhere and handed it to Kami.

Kami's voice boomed, and between her giggles, she said, "Calm down, everyone! This was obviously a gift from Anahit, goddess of water, healing, and . . ." she waggled her eyebrows in Grace's direction. "Fertility."

The crowd quieted and calmed somewhat.

"We'll get you all towels. But stay, eat, and enjoy a rare blessing from an Armenian goddess!"

Raffi scanned the crowd. It worked. He supposed that if the bride was happy, if she called it a blessing, then everyone had to go along with it. Raffi twisted his mouth. He supposed Kami's woo-woo tendencies and her charisma did come in handy.

Ani jogged over to Raffi and Sanan now, a roll of duct tape and a napkin in her hand.

"Let's get that tube stuck in place," Ani said.

"I can do it," Sanan said. "You guys should go get the towels."

Ani nodded. "Good point. Thanks, Sanan. Let me know if it doesn't work."

Once Ani and Raffi were inside, Raffi could tell, even though Ani's mind was working analytically now—likely trying to figure out what to do in the fastest, best order possible—she was *not* happy.

"Ani, baby, look at me. It's going to be okay," he said, not sure if that was true but wanting to reassure her anyway.

"We'll see," she muttered. "Do you have towels?"

Now Raffi smiled, trying his best to lighten her mood. "You bet. After the fiasco at DePietro's, I bought enough Ô towels to handle a damn tsunami."

Ani gave him a weak smile. "Good thinking."

Raffi and Ani distributed the bushel of brand-new towels, and it proved to be enough to cover everyone. But the last table Raffi approached was his father's, and he saw Moushegh there, rubbing his ankle, Kami's aunt by his side.

"Raffi jan," the aunt said, "Moushegh had a fall."

"Dad—" Raffi said, with concern at the same time Moushegh roared, "Damn it, Sima, I'm fine."

Sima repeatedly shook her head no. *No, he's not fine.*

Ani materialized then, and Raffi could see a small smile on his dad's face. "Ani Avakian, yes?"

"That's me. Can I help you in any way?"

Moushegh tapped the side of his glass. "Another Johnnie Walker, perhaps?"

Ani laughed good-naturedly, but Raffi could see she was trying to hide her concern. "Certainly," she said in Armenian, and picked up his tumbler.

Sima, angry at Moushegh's rebuffing, and seeing that all seemed to be well, walked away.

"Dad," Raffi said.

"I do not want to hear it," Moushegh said.

"How'd it happen?" Raffi asked.

His father sighed. "The water was everywhere. I tried to get up to move away and then suddenly I was on the ground."

Raffi nodded silently. "Will you let me look at it, at least? I'm actually trained for it, even if I haven't been practicing lately."

Moushegh angrily shook his head. "Not here, not here."

"Okay, but later?"

His father pursed his lips. "Fine."

"We'll get out of here soon. I have a feeling the party's going to wrap up earlier than expected."

Then Ani returned with a whiskey for Moushegh and one for Raffi, too.

"Thanks, but where's your drink?" Raffi asked.

Ani smiled. "I never drink on the job. Though . . . I may have had a sip of yours."

"Good on you," Moushegh said to Ani, then took a swig.

Ani occupied the empty seat next to Moush egh. Uh-oh. Why was Ani sitting next to his father?

"You know," Ani said quietly to Moushegh, so low Raffi could barely hear. "My grandfather was Toros Avakian, fighter in—"

"My God," his dad said, his voice softening with recognition. "Toros Avakian. He fought in Artsakh, didn't he? Under Monte—back in the nineties?"

Raffi blinked. His dad knew her grandfather. The way

Dad's voice shifted, like he was speaking the name of someone sacred, made Raffi sit up a little straighter.

Ani nodded, seemingly thankful for the recognition. "As you may know, he was injured from it. Went everywhere with a cane. But he loved that cane so much—it was made of cedarwood from Beirut—it became part of his silhouette, his presence. He even asked to be buried with it."

Moushegh made some noises of discomfort, then said, "Well, such a fine cane, I'm sure. And such a man. He could wear that cane with pride."

"Some might say you're such a man." Ani smiled at Moushegh.

And then something wild happened. Moushegh smiled back and said, "I wouldn't dare compare myself to war heroes, but—"

"But," Ani said, a full sentence to sit there, for him to consider. Then, she touched Moushegh lightly on the shoulder and added, "I have to go now, clean up this mess somehow."

"You do that, my girl," Moushegh said, entranced.

Both father and son stared in her wake. Then Moushegh turned to Raffi, his expression stern but with a flicker of softness underneath. He jabbed a finger in Raffi's direction, his voice low and gravelly. "You better not do anything stupid. A woman like that doesn't come around twice."

27

Ani

ANI WOKE UP in Kami's Napa house to many, many texts. This was never a good sign, and before Ani had read anything, she had a sinking feeling in the pit of her stomach.

She decided to read Talar's text first. **What the hell? Is this true?** There was a link, and it was from the *Daily Mail*. God help her.

Ani clicked it and held her breath.

The title read, **Grace Zhang Pre-Wedding Drama—EX-GIRLFRIEND Wedding Planner to Blame?**

Oh no, no, no, no. Ani read quickly.

> No one's star has been rising faster than Hollywood's latest darling, Grace Zhang (27). The stunning actress has captivated audiences worldwide, with her viral video alongside legendary co-star Robert De Niro making waves across social media. And now, the world has been watching with bated breath as she prepares to tie the knot with entrepreneur Kami Mardian (30).

As fans eagerly await every detail of Grace and Kami's upcoming nuptials, they were excited to catch a glimpse of the first major event: a traditional Armenian pre-wedding ceremony. This intimate gathering, honoring Kami's Armenian roots, was held last night at the picturesque Ô winery in Napa. But what was supposed to be a night of cultural celebration and elegance quickly turned into a soggy disaster.

In a shocking turn of events, the *Daily Mail* can exclusively reveal that the wedding planner is none other than Kami Mardian's ex-girlfriend, Ani Avakian (30). Yes, you read that right—Grace Zhang's picture-perfect wedding has been orchestrated by the very woman who once held Kami's heart!

Nothing could have prepared guests for the unexpected drama that unfolded. Just as the guests sat down for dinner, a rogue water hose suddenly burst to life, drenching the exquisitely dressed attendees in a torrent of water. What was meant to be a serene celebration turned into an unplanned—and very unwelcome—water fight.

Was this just an unfortunate accident, or something more sinister? Guests were left whispering in dampened disbelief, with many speculating that this could have been a deliberate act of sabotage. Could Ani Avakian have used her position as the planner to exact revenge on her former flame, spoiling her special day with Grace?

While the soaking incident left everyone in a state of shock, Grace, ever the poised starlet, laughed it off with a grace befitting her name. But behind the scenes, tensions are said to be at an all-time high, with Grace and Kami reportedly questioning the decision to involve Ani in their wedding plans.

Will Grace and Kami's wedding day be as star-studded and flawless as we all hope, or is there more drama on the horizon? One thing's for sure—this is one Hollywood romance that's anything but boring.

Stay tuned for more exclusive updates as we keep you in the loop on all the latest developments in this unfolding saga!

Reporting by Basil Wentworth.

Ani set down her phone and stared blankly in front of her, at a white antique wardrobe, for about ten minutes straight.

Ani had never been written about before. She'd never had any press, never been in any paper—not even the high school newspaper—never been talked about in any way. She'd had no desire for fame, and now she saw she was right for thinking that.

The main thing she was worried about was whether or not Grace and Kami were indeed questioning firing Ani. The rest, she could take. Because she knew the hose wasn't her fault. It was some kind of freak accident that she in no way could have predicted. There wasn't a checklist item for "secure the fountain hoses." So she wasn't upset at herself for that. But that Grace and Kami might believe this gossip rag, that *she'd* done it on purpose, and that now they'd sack her? That would be bad.

She had to woman up, walk over to Kami, call a meeting with her and Grace, and talk things through transparently.

Okay. One step at a time.

It was nine a.m., and she heard voices outside, so she hoped she could find Kami there. Ani took a deep breath, her fingers trembling slightly as she buttoned her blouse and smoothed her hair. She put on a brave face and walked out the door.

She rounded the corner and froze. The entire family was there—Kami's parents, sister, uncles, and aunts—seated around the table, their plates piled high with eggs, pastries, and fruit. The moment Ani appeared, the room fell silent.

Oh God.

She could feel the heat rising in her cheeks, her pulse quickening as she forced herself to take another step forward. "Good morning, I—" Ani said, her voice about as steady as a dinghy in a storm. "I just wanted to apologize for last night. Have you, by any chance, seen any articles about it? Because I'd like to, um, refute them."

Kami caught Ani's eyes for a second, then looked back down at a piece of mango she was cutting and kept going at it. Oh no, Kami was clearly pissed and blamed her. She believed the article. Dear God, this was it. She was going to be fired.

Kami's mother narrowed her eyes at Ani. "Oh, we read it. I hadn't put it together until they reported it. Ani . . . how *could* you?"

"I—I didn't—" Ani began, her vision clouding with sudden tears. How could she convince them? There was no way. They'd already made up their minds.

The silence in the room was the loudest sound she'd ever heard.

Then, suddenly she felt arms attack her from the side, and Ani startled, shocked that she was going to be dragged into a physical fight. But then she realized the arms were a desperate, hard hug, and someone was crying onto her shoulder. Galia?

Galia stared up at Ani, her usual sparkle gone and tears streaming down her face. She pulled away, wrapping her arms tightly around herself like she was trying to hold herself together. "Ani, I am so, so sorry," Galia choked out.

Ani blinked, her mind struggling to catch up.

"It was me," Galia said, at first to Ani, and then to the rest of the room, her words spilling out in a rush. "It was me! I cut the hose. With scissors. I didn't know it would go crazy like that! I just thought maybe I could get it to spray Kami when she walked by. I'm so sorry."

Ani froze. What the . . . Galia? No way. Galia was so fun, and yes, she was a little mischievous, but this? She wasn't prone to full-on destruction. Ani tried to reconcile her ex's younger sister, sarcastic and fun, seemingly carefree, with the one standing in front of her now, tears streaming down her face, shoulders hunched under the weight of her confession.

Ani didn't appear to be the only one shocked by this. Kami and Galia's entire family started talking at once, but Ani ignored them all, keeping her eyes only on Galia, who seemed to want to say more.

"Why?" Ani asked in a low voice.

"Because," Galia said, suddenly angry, "Kami gets everything. She's the prettiest; she's the golden child. I'm the ugly one no one cares about. She bats her eyelashes, and whatever she wants, she gets. I just needed her . . . I just needed something to not be perfect for her, for once."

Ani couldn't speak. Galia was young, only seventeen, but this was still so wildly immature. And yet there was something in her words Ani could relate to. Talar, too, was the golden sister—effortlessly smart and successful, while Ani had felt like an afterthought, the one who had to work twice as hard for half the recognition. She understood that ache, that desperate need to be seen, to matter. But where Galia had lashed out, Ani had turned inward. She never would have resorted to sabotage. Hell, she planned her own sister's wedding, even though the event had been painful for her in some ways. She felt more like she was losing a sister than gaining a brother. She felt she was behind and would never find love. But she gave Talar the best wedding possible despite everything.

"I didn't think about you—" Galia said, her voice trembling as she fought back tears. "I didn't think they'd blame you for it. I swear, it didn't even cross my mind."

That, Ani could believe. No one in the Mardian family seemed to think about anyone else but themselves. There was a lot of noise and talking among all the relatives, so Ani took a chance to ask Galia now, in a lower voice. "The flowers, the dress, the menus—was that you, too?"

Galia nodded her head sadly.

Fuck. "Galia." Ani closed her eyes and pinched the bridge of her nose, forcing herself to breathe through the frustration clawing its way up her throat. She was still the wedding planner, still a professional. And Galia was seventeen after all. "What you did weren't harmless pranks—they were reckless and made a lot of people's jobs harder. So much time and effort spent to undo them. I really, really wish you had thought twice before pulling something like this."

Galia started to stammer something, when Kami brought over her phone. She seemed to have Grace on speaker. Ani held her breath. Hopefully Grace believed Galia? Or was Ani about to be fired anyway?

"Ani," Grace said, seemingly calm except for a slight hint of irritation in her voice. "Sorry about that story this morning. I didn't think about how the press would spin the whole ex-girlfriend thing when we hired you. I mean, I've never had press like this in my life, so I wasn't thinking it was a possibility."

"That's, um, that's okay," Ani said. She wasn't getting fired? It didn't seem like it.

"I'm going to call them myself," Grace said. "The *Daily Mail*. And tell them it wasn't you, and that the wedding is going on as scheduled, with you continuing to plan it."

Ani let out a huge breath. She felt lightheaded with relief. "You'd do that? Thank you, that's really generous of you."

When Grace hung up, Kami threw her arms around Ani. "I'm sorry I didn't believe you."

Ani wrestled out of Kami's grasp quickly. "It's fine."

"And you, Galia," Kami said pointedly, "are in *so* much trouble."

Kami's mom also rounded on Galia, and Ani actually found herself feeling sorry for the little sister, who was clearly acting out based on some family dynamics.

"Hey," Ani said to Kami and her mom. "I know it's not my place, but go easy on her, okay? She's still in high school. And maybe, I don't know, she has a point?"

Ani walked away without waiting for a response. She didn't want to have to elaborate. Let them figure out what she meant.

She needed Raffi. Now. Needed to talk to him—hell, needed to see him.

When she picked up her phone, she knew Raffi had seen the article, because there were three missed calls from him and a bunch of texts.

> Baby, oh my God, I'm sorry. You okay? Let's talk.

> Call me back when you can.

> I'm thinking of you.

> And I want to murder that reporter at the Daily Mail. I hope this isn't evidence.

> Let me know you're okay?

> Please.

She called him back right away.

"Ani," he said, sounding out of breath.

"I'm fine, I—thank you for your texts. It's, it's—"

She wanted to tell him it was all cleared up now, but she burst into tears instead.

"Shit, okay. I'm going to get you. Now. Give me the address."

She sniffed. "There are paparazzi everywhere out there."

"I don't give a fuck. I'm coming. Address?"

She could hear his front door slam and then his car beep.

"I'm texting you." She really did need him, too. Then she

had a thought. "Put the top on, on your car. I don't want them getting a clear shot of you, or us."

"Whatever you want," he said, and she heard clanks and clunks from the background as he was no doubt doing as Ani asked.

"Drive *safely*, okay? Seriously. I'm okay, I'm okay."

"I'll do my best," Raffi grunted.

Ani sat on her bed, her mind reeling. Thank God she'd be with Raffi soon. She'd be safe and comforted and okay.

Just the mere thought of Raffi's arms around her, his voice low in her ear, telling her it was going to be fine, that he had her? It sent a sharp tug low in her belly, a warmth curling under her skin.

And suddenly, she didn't just want to be comforted. She wanted to feel wanted.

Ani tore through her closet, ditching comfort for something less family-friendly, sleek, and slinky, with far skimpier undergarments than strictly necessary. She ran a brush through her hair, swiped on some lipstick, then grabbed her bag.

Just then, the door between her and Kami's rooms opened and Kami stepped in while saying, "Knock, knock."

Ani's cheeks flared. Kami hadn't actually knocked. What if Ani was still undressed? Her ex felt so entitled, she didn't even think it'd be a problem. Ani simply stared at her.

"Oh my God, I just wanted to give you a real apology. I am so, so sorry I ever doubted you for even a second. You've been, like, crucial to this whole thing. I can't believe I thought you might have done that. You're the best."

Kami threw her arms around Ani and nuzzled her neck. "Also, wow, you changed and someone looks pretty hot." Ani froze, a sharp current of anger spiking through her. This was it. A step too damn far, and she wasn't going to have it anymore.

Ani pried Kami's hands off her and stepped back. She folded her arms. "Listen, Kami, hugging me like that, touching me in the many intimate ways you have been, speaking to me the way you have been—it's not okay, and I don't like it. I'm not your friend, and I'm not your girlfriend. So please, you have to stop that."

Kami stared at her, open-mouthed. She started to speak, but Ani interrupted her.

"I am, however, your wedding planner. And I'm going to create, for you and Grace, the most flawless goddamn wedding you could have ever imagined. Utter perfection. And you are going to love it and cherish the memories for the rest of your life. But our relationship, you and me? It has to be strictly professional. You broke my heart, which you seem to be unaware of, and honestly that's fine, you're allowed that. I even got over it, finally. But you're not allowed to act like we're best buddies anymore. Because we're not. I hope—I hope you can understand that."

Kami stood there in dumbstruck silence, nodding.

"Now, if you'll excuse me," Ani said. "I have to go. My *boyfriend* is coming to pick me up. Call me if there's a wedding-related matter."

And as Kami's jaw dropped for the second time this conversation, Ani walked out the door.

28

Raffi

SHE WAS IN his car, safe, kissed, and beautiful. Ani insisted on ducking while they passed the mob of reporters, and Raffi threw one of those Ô towels over her just to be sure. They'd made it out and no one had followed them. Ani was catching him up on everything, talking a mile a minute.

"—and then *Galia* comes forward and says she did it! The whole thing. The flowers, the dress, the menu, the hose. She cut it with some kitchen scissors!"

Raffi muttered angrily, "Jesus Christ, that family is trouble. Swear to God. If anyone needed an example of why not to spoil your kids, there you go."

And then he had a clear image of himself and Ani, raising a family. Teaching them respect for others, to work hard, to stay humble. It seemed so natural. They were such a great team together. *One thing at a time, bro,* he told himself. He didn't even know if Ani wanted kids. And he wanted Ani alone to himself for quite some time before potentially delving into that world.

"And then I have to tell you what happened with Kami," Ani said.

She explained how Kami came to her room seconds after she'd finished changing, did the usual huggy compliment-bombing, and Ani was not having it. Raffi's face split into a huge smile. "You actually said, 'I'm not your friend'? Damn, girl."

"I actually did."

He was proud of her, so proud.

"Badass move by my badass girlfriend."

She squeezed his hand hard, her smile unable to leave her face.

She sighed loudly. "It feels great. Can't believe I didn't do this sooner. Who knew one piece of negative press could bring this out of me."

He rubbed the top of her hand with his thumb. "Seriously, Ani, you okay with all that? I read it, and I'm not kidding that I was this close to booking a nonstop flight to London to find that reporter."

Ani chuckled, then said, "Yes, I'm okay. I wasn't before, but I am now, because first off, it wasn't true. I didn't actually try to ruin the hinoum. Secondly, the person who did admitted it. And thirdly, Grace is going to call them up and fix it."

"Damn, that Grace is a class act. Maybe she'll eventually rub off on Kami," Raffi said.

"One can hope."

Raffi held up Ani's smooth hand, kissed it, and rubbed it against his freshly shaven cheek. "Glad you're all right."

"More than," Ani said, her voice softer now and edged with something he couldn't quite place.

Then she shifted in her seat, crossing her legs slowly, deliberately. Raffi stayed quiet a moment, his pulse kicking up as he waited to see if she'd share what was clearly on her mind.

Then she did.

"I have an IUD, you know."

His breath caught, sharp and immediate.

Damn. All right then.

Raffi had frozen, and he knew Ani could feel it in the way he was holding her hand. He tried to be relaxed, but it wasn't working.

"And, um," he said, concentrating hard on keeping his voice steady, "why are you telling me this?"

"Just in case," she said, her voice smooth, dripping with meaning, "this piece of information might be interesting to you."

Oh God. She was ready.

Heat shot through him, sharp and dizzying. Every muscle in his body went tight, his pulse hammering in his throat. He wanted to play it cool—really, he did—but the way she was looking at him? The way she'd just said that?

Jesus Christ.

Well, he'd been prepared in case this blessed day should somehow arrive.

He swallowed hard, forcing himself to breathe and not completely lose his mind. "I have something to offer in return, in that case."

"Oh?"

"That I've got a clean bill of health over here. I haven't so much as glanced at a woman besides you since we met."

"Is that right?" she asked, smirking.

"Chris and I went out sometime in March, and all I could think was, none of these women were you. That was the problem with them. Not Ani."

Her smirk deepened. "And yet it took you forever to kiss me."

His hand slid along her arm, the feel of her sending shivers down his spine. "Far too long," he murmured. "I'm not wasting any more time."

Raffi shifted gears, punched the accelerator, and got them to his home in record time.

Once parked, Raffi dashed to open Ani's door, picked her up by the bottom, and carried her upstairs to his bedroom.

He gently sat her on the bed and she blinked at him, clearly surprised he didn't immediately pounce. God knew he wanted to—had wanted to for months—but instead, he crossed the room.

"I have something first," he said. "It's nothing big. Just . . . I wanted to give it to you now."

Raffi grabbed a black gift bag from atop his dresser and handed it to Ani. She tilted her head, curious, as she reached inside. She pulled out a small photo frame—brushed silver and gold—and stared at it.

It was them. The second time they met, at Ô. Right where the dome now stood. Caught in that split second when they were looking at each other, like the rest of the world had gone a little blurry.

"I know we have a number of selfies," Raffi said, suddenly self-conscious, running a hand through his hair. "But this one . . . this felt like the moment I knew, or started to know.

And we're lucky enough to have it captured, so, I just wanted you to have a copy. I've got my own here, too."

He gestured toward the photo's twin, sitting by his nightstand.

Ani choked up. "I remember this. The way you looked at me. I—I'd forgotten the photo even existed until now. I love it."

"I want you to know that almost from the very start, I felt you were special."

Ani kept her eyes on the photograph a beat longer, then gently set it down and threw her arms around him.

She pressed her lips to his ear, making his heart race. "Thank you, my darling Raffi," she whispered. "I love it . . . and I really, really can't wait anymore."

The air between them shifted—gentle turned urgent.

This was it. Raffi climbed atop her. She unbuttoned and ripped off his shirt while he stripped her naked, relishing the moment his hands touched skin.

She was open for him, blooming for him. The curves of her breasts and hips, her smooth skin from her navel to the bud between her legs—she was utter perfection.

He wanted to worship. Get down on his knees like the supplicant he was and pray to this goddess before him. This perfect woman who'd shown him sweetness, shown him what it meant to feel loved.

"To be clear," Ani said, watching him watch her, "I want to have sex with you." She lay back, parted her legs wide, and he almost lost it.

Raffi unbuckled his belt and tore off his pants, his erection springing up to make itself known. He crawled on top of her.

"I'm not sure how slow and gentle I can go with you. I've been waiting for this for a while."

"I'm not delicate," she whispered, her voice thick with lust. "I can take you."

That was all the invitation he needed. He pulled off his briefs and let himself free, rubbing the length of him at her wet entry. His eyes rolled back in his head, and a groan escaped him at the same time Ani moaned.

"Holy shit, you feel like heaven and I'm not even inside yet," his voice rumbled.

Ani's hand reached down to find him, running his inches back and forth, and he caught her looking down at what her hand was gripping. "Raff, oh my God."

"I know," he said, unable to stop himself from smirking, but only for a quick second, as it was extinguished by all-consuming lust, the feel of her hand on his sensitive skin.

"Let me taste you first," she said, and he momentarily saw stars as she shifted down to meet him. "You're not the only one who's been waiting a long time."

And with that, she took him into her mouth and Raffi felt the pleasure ring throughout his body, from his scalp to the tips of his toes. He clawed at her hair while her mouth worked him, and he had to summon every ounce of restraint not to come, not yet. *Don't you dare come, Raffi.* She deserved a real fucking, after waiting for him so long, and he would give it to her.

"I've got to have you *now*," he said, pulling himself out.

He hooked his hands under her arms and jerked her back to the top of the bed. "On your back so I can see your pretty face."

Ani let out a surprised puff of pleasure.

Then Raffi held himself at her entrance, nipped at her neck while she gasped, and slowly, carefully, guided himself inside her. My God, the feeling. It was her. There was no one else but her, and there never would be ever again. Ani was it, the end, the beginning.

Then came her choked voice, "More. More . . . *please*."

Her *please* was so insistent, how could he do anything but oblige her?

He pushed in harder, and she was so tight and warm around him, he could hardly take the sensation blaring inside his body. He rocked into her and she gripped him desperately, her body trembling under him, a symphony of moans pouring into his ear.

As he slid in and out of her, he was there, yes, and he was transcended, too. The way she stared into his eyes, wanting him the way he wanted her. She was entirely there for him.

This was not just sex; it was trust.

"Baby," he said. He needed to tell her.

She moaned in response.

"You're more than sex. You know that, right? You know I'd do anything for you. Whatever you ask. I'm yours."

She gazed back at him, those giant pools of brown and black sucking him in, straight to her heart. "I know. I know. And I'm yours," she said, breathless.

"My girl. Mine." He thrust into her, and the combination of being buried inside her and knowing she was his was almost too much.

No way he'd be getting off before her. "What's your favorite way to come?" he asked.

"Top—on top," she panted.

Arms around her back, he flipped them, never losing his lock inside her.

She ground on him in a familiar way, like she had before, except this time they were tied together. Her hair skimmed his face, anointing him with the scent of orange blossoms. Her moans grew louder, faster. They started to turn to sobs as she rubbed hard against him, her insides clenching him so tight that his vision blurred and he gripped her ass with both hands. Knowing she was close was pushing him over the edge.

"You're almost there, baby. Show me," he encouraged.

She sobbed out, "You're making me—oh God, Raff. Raff . . ." He felt her from inside, convulsing, heard her wails, and when she collapsed into his arms in spasms, and he knew he'd given her that feeling, that was it. His muscles locked up, and months of tension released as he pumped his love and longing, his gratefulness and belonging, for this woman.

He held her, spent, more in love than he knew was possible. He closed his eyes, his body tranquilized. He ran gentle fingers through her soft, thick hair and kissed her temples and cheeks.

Ani's voice was breathless as she murmured, "That was incredible. I've never— I don't think I've ever come like that."

"Same here. You are a marvel, my Ani."

They rested there, wordlessly enjoying soft touches of each other's skin.

After what could have been five minutes or fifty, he asked, "You want kids one day?"

She laughed, surprised. "Kids? I mean, yes. One day." She stared at him suspiciously. "Why?"

"Just checking. Because I definitely do." *With you, only with you. The first woman who has ever made me have that thought.* He'd be brave enough to tell her that eventually. To tell her he loved her. He was too chickenshit now, though. What if she didn't love him yet? He couldn't take it. He needed a little more time, more reassurance.

She sat up on one elbow, appearing amused. "You proposing to me, Raffi?"

He brought her in for a quick kiss. "Not yet. And you won't have to ask when I propose. You'll know. It'll be worthy of you."

She blushed and covered her face. "Oh my God."

He whispered, somewhat worried now, "That doesn't scare you?"

She strummed fingers across his jaw. "Not in the least."

The ease flowed through him, followed by a new rush of blood. They spent the rest of the morning and afternoon together, in bed, blissfully unaware of the rest of the world still at work.

29

Ani

ANI WALKED THROUGH the doors of Kami's family's mansion, so sore between her legs, she was sure everyone could tell. No one could, of course, but she felt like it was written all over her face: fucked into oblivion.

Oh my God, Raffi was a sex god. It wasn't just his technique; it was how *intense* he was about everything. She could practically feel his possessive thoughts about her as he drove in again and again. *Mine. Mine.*

They'd spent hours together, and still she could have more. A lifetime more. Wow. *That* was a thought. A big thought, and she liked it. Oh, she held on to it like a precious creature, stroking its soft ears and whispering to it, encouraging it to grow and thrive.

He must have put that into her head when he asked her about kids. An irrational part of her brain almost wanted to yank out her IUD with her bare hands and tell him to go for it. Obviously not, but as she'd told him, *one day.*

She took a deep breath and slunk into her room. They didn't need her today, so she'd spend it prepping for tomorrow. The actual wedding. Today, the tea ceremony was run by one of Grace's family's planners. It must have been over by now because Kami's family was back at the home, from what Ani could tell. And tonight, the family wanted to lie low, inviting Grace's close family over for a private chef dinner right here at the house. Everything was taken care of by the house staff, so Ani could hide away. Relax and plan.

She woke up to a knock on her door, not realizing she had fallen asleep. The sun had set now, and Ani tried not to sound groggy when she asked, "Who is it?"

"Grace," came a voice.

Her client. Ani jumped to the edge of the bed, straightened out her clothes, and called, "Come in."

Grace entered and Ani rose. Ani meant to give her a quick hug, but Grace held on a bit tighter, then let go. "I'm so sorry," Grace said, "about the article today. That's horrible, and you should not have had to go through that."

"Oh. Oh, that is so nice of you to say."

Ani thought Grace had come to give her a rundown of the tea ceremony, or check in on some last-minute items for tomorrow. But no, Grace was there to share her kindness.

Grace continued, "I called them and let their celebrity editor know it wasn't you who cut the hose. That we all had it under control. That we all trust you and you have been so on top of everything."

Grace looked like she wanted to say more. Ani's chest tightened, and she braced herself. "But?" she asked.

Staring down at her feet, Grace said, "They were pretty interested in you. Being Mimi's ex, planning the wedding. I didn't— I'm really sorry to drag you into all this. Fame is fun in some ways, but it also sucks. Especially when it hurts people around you."

Ani gave a half smile, trying to put on a brave face. "It's not your fault. I appreciate you sharing with me."

Grace nodded. "Anyway, just—be careful, I guess. They're snooping around us and you're not excluded, even after my call. The very snobby editor made sure to tell me that he couldn't keep sizzling news out of his paper, were he to uncover anything juicy. He actually used that word, 'juicy.' Ew. So I'm not sure how I can help, but I wanted to give you the heads-up. Let me know if I can do anything. Seriously."

Ani bit her bottom lip, trying to keep her worry from seeping out. "Sure. Thanks, Grace. Don't worry about me; just get some good rest tonight so you can enjoy your big day."

Grace gave her a smile and left the room.

The rest of the night, Ani planned, checked, double- and triple-checked everything for the next day. Nothing would go wrong. Everything was prepped and in perfect order, but Grace's words rang in her head and she had trouble sleeping.

ANI WOKE UP the morning of the wedding before anyone else. She wasn't sure she'd slept at all. Maybe an hour or two. Her body ached and protested at her insistence on getting up. But it didn't matter, because there was a huge day to plan, and she was going to give it her all.

She showered, dressed, put on professional makeup, and checked her watch. Right on time for everyone to wake up before the hair and makeup team arrived. Ani knocked on doors, was cheerful and firm, and ushered everyone to the kitchen to get a few bites to eat.

Ani strode to the front doors as the doorbell rang and opened them to the makeup team and the photographer and videographer. The hair and makeup crew got started exactly as planned. *One hour of sleep be damned*, Ani thought, *I've got this*.

She wove through the bridal party, grabbing muffins for people and giving opinions on shades of eyeshadow. She and Kami made eye contact and smiled politely. Ani, feeling a little bad about how harsh she was the day before—even though she knew she needed to be—told Kami, "You don't have any makeup on, and you already look radiant."

Kami gave a demure smile and said, "It's the cryogenic face mask I put on this morning."

As Ani made her rounds, she felt the air shift around her. Not as many animated conversations. More hushed, whispered. Then, glances in Ani's direction. Stolen glances. Ani made eye contact with Kami's bridesmaid cousin, who promptly snapped her gaze back down to her phone. Something molten formed in the pit of Ani's stomach. She wanted to know, but she really didn't want to know. Not here. Not today.

Then Kami called for her, sounding cautious, even nervous. "Ani?"

Kami had been keeping her distance from Ani but not in a passive-aggressive way, more in an I-am-sort-of-scared-of-you-now way.

Ani approached her ex and sat on the edge of a chair while Kami's hair was being twisted into tight ringlets that would later be set loose. "Just so you know," Kami started, "I don't believe it at all. Okay?"

That was when the dread truly took hold of Ani. A chill shook through her, and Ani shivered, anticipating, terrified.

"*Daily Mail* again?" Ani asked.

Kami nodded.

"Can I see?" Ani asked, figuring it was already up on Kami's phone.

Kami held it up. Ani took a deep breath and read the headline:

EXCLUSIVE: Grace Zhang's Wedding Planner on the Brink of Financial Ruin!

Reporting by Basil Wentworth

Oh God, no, no, no, no. She'd expected a headline about her and Kami's past, possibly about her still pining for Kami, or photos of her and Raffi hooking up. But not *this*. This was the secret that no one but her and the banks knew. And it was true.

The truth of it, the bare-naked truth of her shame, splashed all over one of the world's largest tabloids, was almost too much to bear.

But she had to read what the article said.

"Just give me a second," Ani said. She trembled on the way to her room and shut the door behind her. She found the article, saw her face plastered in between Grace's and Kami's, and read.

The *Daily Mail* has uncovered exclusive details about Ani Avakian (30), the wedding planner behind freshly minted shooting star Grace Zhang (27) and entrepreneur Kami Mardian's (30) highly anticipated nuptials. While the world waits for what promises to be the wedding of the year, it seems that Ani's personal life is far from the picture-perfect image she projects.

Our in-depth investigating revealed that Ani Avakian is teetering on the brink of financial ruin. The wedding planner who so far has only serviced more modest clientele is reportedly $50,000 in debt, having resorted to personal loans just to maintain her lifestyle.

Questions are swirling about how Ani's precarious financial situation might impact the high-profile wedding she's been entrusted with. Did Kami Mardian, her former flame, hire Ani out of pity, making her a charity case rather than the best choice for the job?

As the big day approaches, many are wondering whether Ani will be able to pull off the event of the year, or if her money troubles will cause yet another disaster for the happy couple. With the pressure mounting and the eyes of the world upon her, Ani is undoubtedly feeling the heat. Based on her online portfolio, a wedding of this grand scale is far out of Ani's comfort zone. Will she rise to the occasion, or will her financial woes lead to yet another headline-worthy snafu?

One thing's for sure—Grace Zhang's wedding is shaping up to be far more dramatic than the role she

> plays on-screen opposite Robert De Niro in her upcoming film *Mafia Princess*. Stay tuned as we continue to bring you the latest updates on this unfolding saga.

She felt like this reporter had reached through the phone and stabbed her. The humiliation nearly overcame her.

A charity case. Her modest clientele. Her inability to handle a wedding like Grace and Kami's. That was all true. Even if Kami didn't know it when she hired her, there was no denying it was true.

At least one thing she could defend. Her lifestyle? *Please, Basil,* she thought, she didn't have a lifestyle. She lived in a beat-up apartment with a roommate, driving her fifteen-year-old car, and the fanciest thing she did was style cheaper outfits to look nice. She owned a dress that was more expensive than her entire wardrobe put together, but that was Raffi's doing, not hers.

Raffi.

Hopefully he wouldn't see this article. It wasn't the biggest news of the day, not by far. It's possible he could have missed it.

However, the Armenian community talked, and she was sure at the very least it'd be widely circulated. He'd find out. He'd find out she'd kept this secret from him.

After everything they went through yesterday, how they were both, she felt, on the brink of telling each other they loved each other, of proposing a lifelong commitment, that she still held back from him. Didn't trust him enough to share. What did it say about her and her relationship with Raffi?

And before she could answer that question, she received a text from Talar. She couldn't open it. Could not even look at it without feeling the shame of her sister knowing what an incompetent person Ani was. Not today. She would not talk to Talar today.

She realized, then, that she would have to tell Sanan, too. She wanted to crunch herself up in a ball like a scrap piece of paper. But there was no hiding. The phone was already in her hand. Ani dialed.

"Boss, everything okay? Sorry, not *boss*. Ani?"

Ani, despite herself, gave a small smile. "Sanan, not really, but it's not about the wedding."

"Oh." A pause. "Then what?"

Sanan hadn't seen the article. Ani put Sanan on speaker and began to text her the link.

"Just texted you. Read it, and I understand if you don't want to work together anymore."

"Wha—!" Sanan sounded panicked. "Why would I ever? Wait, what is this?"

Ani waited, since it seemed Sanan was reading.

"I'm confused," Sanan said. "How can this be true if you've been paying me? They're direct deposits. Can't fake those."

"I couldn't not pay you, Sanan jan," Ani said. "I—"

"Wait. Was this because of the Avedissians? I remember the day of the wedding, I overheard you asking them for a check, and the bride was so angry, she scribbled something off and threw it at you. Was it that? They always gave me this feeling, kind of a shady couple. They openly told me about the many ways they cheated on their taxes."

Ani nodded, impressed, despite the mood she was in. "You got it. That check bounced."

Sanan groaned. "Ani, I am so sorry. I wish you'd told me. I

could have taken a hiatus. You know I'm still working in customer support. I didn't need—you didn't need to pay me. I would have taken an IOU."

"You are too sweet, Sanan. That's exactly why I didn't say anything. I couldn't let you work for free. You deserve to be paid for your time, for your effort. No matter how bad things got, I wasn't about to take advantage of your kindness."

Ani heard a deep sigh on the other line. "Well. I appreciate you trying to keep everything going even while all of this was weighing on you. I do still want to work with you, Ani. I love working together. I want to keep going and going until I can quit CS. You're an amazing boss, and I feel like you always have my back."

Now Ani was going to cry—because of Sanan's words, but also because everything was starting to hit her at once.

"You are the best, Sanan," she said. "Let's forget all this today and pull off the biggest, baddest wedding of the year." Ani tried to rouse herself with false enthusiasm, but it wasn't working.

"You got it, Ani," Sanan said.

After they hung up, Ani lay back on her bed and stared at the ceiling. An ornate white and crystal chandelier blinked down at her. That was one mercy, that Sanan still wanted to work together. Didn't hate her for keeping that secret from her.

She had been worried about Sanan finding out, but *Raffi*. What he must think of her, if he even saw?

Then her phone rang. Probably Talar, pursuing a new avenue after Ani ignored her texts.

It was Raffi.

Ani bolted upright. Shit. She wasn't sure how to explain

herself. For the first time in a while, she considered declining. That *not* talking to him would be easier than talking to him. Then that thought made her panic. Did that mean she and Raffi were on shaky ground? Did that mean she didn't really love him? She didn't know. Why wasn't there someone out there who could just tell her all the answers?

On what she imagined must be the phone's very last ring, she picked up.

"Hi," she said wanly.

"Ani? You okay? Can't believe I'm making a call like this again. I'm not kidding, as soon as the wedding is over, if you want me to, I'm flying to the fucking *Daily Mail* office and punching Basil Wentworth in the face."

Ani traced a finger along the edge of the duvet. "I think they all work from home now anyway," she said, feeling small.

"Ani," he responded, frustration in his voice.

She took a deep breath. "It's true, you know," she said. "The article."

"What? Which part? What do you mean?"

Ani sighed, fell back on her bed, and closed her eyes. "That I'm in debt. Less so now, since Grace and Kami paid me half of the planning and project-management fees. But that was the real reason I took on the wedding. Not because I was hung up on Kami. Not because I wanted to do a luxury wedding. Because I needed the money."

Silence on the other line. "Why didn't you tell me?" Raffi said finally, but he didn't sound angry. Or accusing.

Just . . . sad. Like it hurt him to know she'd been carrying this alone. Curious, too, like he was trying to piece together how she could trust him with so much—but not this.

Ani's eyes snapped open, and she sat up. Her chest tightened, heat rising to her face—not just from frustration but from the awful, twisting shame of it. "Because. You wouldn't understand. Fifty thousand is nothing to you. It's crushing to me. Crushing. It's been weighing on me like a backpack full of lead for almost an entire year. And it's all because I was too trusting, too ignorant to see the truth of the situation."

Ani had heard him swallow when she mentioned that the amount of money was nothing to him. She knew it was true. "How did it happen?" he asked.

So Ani recounted the Avedissians' deceit, including how she tracked them down but discovered they're in Bali so that was a dead end. It was on her to make up the money herself.

"I'm going to be honest. I'm feeling a little embarrassed buying you that dress, taking you out to those dinners. What did you think of me? God. Meanwhile, I could have just . . ." Raffi said.

Ani's eyes narrowed. "Do *not* say you could have just given me the money. I know you could. I didn't ask. I could have asked Talar, too. I never did. The article makes me out to be some poor, dumpy little wedding planner charity case, and I will not turn into that."

"Of course not, Ani. Of course you're not." He sounded firm, and so sure of himself. But instead of building her up, it only made her feel smaller. Like she had tricked him somehow into thinking she was some great person when she was not.

Ani looked at the time. She couldn't burrow away in here any longer. "Listen, I have to go. I just need—I need a little time to think."

"About what?" Raffi asked. "About us?" He sounded panicked.

"I have to go. We'll talk later, okay?" she said, and hung up.

She was feeling absolutely miserable. Like the ground had been yanked out from under her, and she had to pretend she wasn't still stumbling. Undeserving of her sweet boyfriend, with his gentle steadiness that never wavered, even when she was at her lowest.

She had been publicly humiliated, been dragged through the mud, and had her name splashed across headlines like some kind of cautionary tale. And today, she had no choice but to step right back into the public eye, bruised ego and all, with nowhere to hide.

But none of those feelings mattered, because there was a wedding to tend to, and her job—her reputation—depended on perfection. So she would push down everything, put on her best face, and do what she did best—make something beautiful, even if she felt like a disaster inside.

30

Raffi

RAFFI WAS NOT doing well when he pulled into Ô in preparation for the wedding festivities. The place was surrounded by reporters and paparazzi again, and this time? This time Raffi was not feeling so charitable. He whipped out his phone and looked up the local police station number.

"I want to report trespassing on my property."

Raffi gave them his address, explained that the reporters and paparazzi, while keeping out of the winery itself, were still camped in the entrance and parking lot, which were technically Ô's property. And he wanted them out. Onto Highway 29, outside the gates. The gates were open, but they were not invited. The police administrator told him they'd see what they could do.

This would have made him feel better, but instead the dull sense of fear in his stomach rose up and morphed into anger when he saw the cameras turned toward him as he approached. This was *their* fault.

"Which one of you is from the *Daily Mail*?" Raffi asked with a false smile.

There were murmurs in the crowd. They parted to reveal a tall, skinny male photographer, wearing a fedora. "You Basil Wentworth?" Raffi asked.

The name had been burned into Raffi's mind, and he was itching for a fight. He felt his fingers twitch with anxious excitement.

"No, Mr. Garabedian." Raffi flinched at how the reporter knew who he was. "Just the photographer."

Goddamn it. Well, one less reason to be thrown in jail today, he supposed.

Raffi stepped forward and said in a low, dangerous voice, only vaguely aware of the cameras being raised around him and the photographer, "Well, do me a favor and tell Basil to go *fuck himself*." Raffi punched a finger in the man's chest as he emphasized those last words.

Then he turned on his heel and walked into his winery. He should have been feeling better, and maybe the anger had somewhat dissipated, but the anxiousness, slow and spreading, still remained.

He needed to see his girl. Was she still his? Goddamn it, he should have waited until after the wedding to sleep with her. He just couldn't wait, could he? Now she was feeling insecure again after this news about the debt. It was obviously a very big deal for her, and he wanted to be there to support her through it. If she would just let him.

An hour flew by as he threw himself into work, ensuring all the details Ani had left for him were exactly as she wanted them. He would do his part, at least, to keep this wedding running smoothly. One by one the vendors arrived, transforming the space from peaceful to opulent. When flowers arrived as planned, they enveloped the space in showy, romantic beauty that almost sent a shiver through him. They truly were a work of art. He breathed a sigh that that hurdle had passed.

In the next hour, police came by and negotiated with the photographers, reporters, and Raffi to get everyone to a happy medium. Thankfully, Raffi had a map of his private property and was able to kick out the opportunists to the sidelines. They landed on the edge of the highway just outside his property lines. Their best shots now would be of Grace and Kami (and Ani) behind tinted windows. He'd protected Ani from more photos, which wasn't everything, but it was one small step.

Good luck, fellas, he thought as he strode back up the hill.

Shortly after, the limos arrived for Kami and Grace's first look photos. And with them, he knew, would be Ani.

Raffi stood at the entrance of the winery, waiting to welcome everyone in, with the ulterior motive of keeping a lookout for Ani.

The brides—his ex and a now-major celebrity—exited, but he did not feel a thing until he saw Ani emerge. Her mere presence filled him with a fizzing energy, but it was extinguished when he read the pain on her face. How she would hardly meet his eye. Then panic rushed into his heart, and he had to go get a glass of water to keep from feeling faint.

When he returned, he watched Ani flutter about, straightening Kami's veil, ushering bridesmaids here and there, and chatting with the photography team. She had set up the first look about thirty yards away from the winery, and Raffi couldn't help but follow.

Ani stood behind a tree, out of the way of the photographers, watching Kami and Grace. Raffi stepped up to her, and she turned when she heard him approach.

"Hi," she said sadly.

And with just that one word, Raffi felt the hope inside him crack—small at first, like the hairline fracture of glass, but spreading fast, threatening to shatter. The fragile belief that whatever had been weighing on Ani, whatever had made her say she needed time to think, wasn't about them. Wasn't going to pull them apart.

And now, here she was, standing in front of him, her voice steeped in sadness, her eyes holding so much heaviness—and that hope felt dangerously close to slipping away.

But he wouldn't let it.

Whatever was breaking, he'd mason it back together with whatever he had. Patience. Reassurance. Love.

He just had to figure out what, exactly, needed fixing.

He reached out and held her hand. She held it back, but there was a limpness to it. This contrasted so strongly with how she had rushed around Ô right before this, getting everyone and everything lined up perfectly.

"I want you to know you're rocking it. Today is going to be perfect because of you."

She shrugged. "We'll see. There are still hours to go, and so much could go wrong."

"Well, if it does, it won't be anything you overlooked, I know that."

She smiled at him, somewhat more warmly now. "Thank you."

Then the photographers climbed back up their way and Ani said, "Sorry, have to get ceremony-ready now."

"Of course," Raffi said, letting them all walk past, nodding to Grace and Kami, a small polite smile on his face.

Ani disappeared from sight into the depths of Ô, and Raffi forced himself into motion. Double-checking sound, lighting, catering—things he could control. Because if he stopped moving, even for a second, the weight of uncertainty would settle too heavily on his chest. He needed some time to talk to Ani, really talk. But when? Tomorrow, maybe. Or tonight—toward the end of the night, when the pressure had eased and the night belonged to the party instead of the planner.

When she could breathe. Then, he could finally ask her what was breaking inside her—and how he could help piece it back together. So, for now, Raffi continued to busy himself.

Soon, the guests arrived, filling the space and remarking on the otherworldly beauty of it all. They seemed seriously impressed, and he loved that they were not just talking about his winery but about all the design work Ani had put into the grounds and the wedding details. Ô had never looked so alive. Raffi was thankful for the wedding photographers snapping away, documenting all of Ani's work.

His father appeared at the doors of the winery, and when Raffi gave Moushegh his arm, he was surprised his father actually took it and allowed him to usher him to a seat. That was a step. His dad didn't thank him, or say a word, but it was okay. He wondered if it was what Ani had said to his dad that inspired this change.

The ceremony began, and Raffi, both guest and *vendor*, stood toward the back. Ani had a headpiece she was whispering into, ushering bridesmaids down the aisle. Then Grace and her parents, then Kami and her parents. It was a nice touch, he thought, and he liked the idea of both parents walking their child down the aisle.

The two brides stood under the impressive dome, the lush Napa hills as a backdrop, with sunlight painting the scene perfectly. Raffi couldn't help but see Ani's touches all over the ceremony. The placement of the dome, the stones the guests' chairs sat upon, the fountain—now fixed—gently bubbling behind them. The chairs, flowers, vines, and flowing linens lending so much splendor and romance to the scene. Ani really knew her work.

The ceremony itself was equal parts touching and eye-rolling, as there was far too much talk of crystals and The Goddess for his personal taste—although to each their own, he had to admit—then Kami and Grace were pronounced married and had their first kiss as newlyweds.

There was a cocktail hour inside the winery while the event staff had to pull off a miracle in one hour to transform the garden from ceremony space to dining area. His staff, along with the rentals staff, flew into action, taking down the ceremony site in under a minute while others rolled out the tables onto the grass. Linens parachuted and landed on tables, followed by flatware, stemware, and more flowers, flowers everywhere. Ani dashed about, ordering this and that in her unrushed yet presiding manner.

She was doing this; she was making the wedding of the year a reality.

Right on time, the space turned into a charming, luxe evening among the vineyards, flowers bursting from every corner. As the sun set, they invited the guests to their assigned seats to begin dinner.

From across the way, Raffi spotted an older Armenian couple tap Ani's shoulder and say something to her. Almost like a speech, they had a lot to say. Their eyes seemed sympathetic, though, not angry. But Ani's face absolutely fell. Just for a moment. Without realizing it, Raffi started walking in her direction, wanting to help. Then Ani rearranged her features, gave what was pretty obviously a fake smile, replied, and dashed off into Ô. Damn it. She likely had to prepare the wedding party for their entrance. Raffi didn't want to interrupt that. But whatever had transpired, he wanted to assure her it would be okay.

That's when he heard his name. "Raffi?"

He turned. It was a woman who looked . . . familiar. Pretty Armenian brunette, and seemingly pregnant. Hand running over her stomach, she said, "Wow, I haven't seen you in years. It's Nareh Bedrossian. Formerly of KTVA, now with Hye Media. You called me 'Reporter Girl.'"

Then it dawned on him: He'd hit on this woman years ago at an Armenian event called Explore Armenia. Mortifying. He had not been his best self back then, to put it mildly.

He shifted uncomfortably, wondering if his smile looked more psycho than polite. "God, yeah, hi. I think I've seen your segments, the one on Armenian lacework in Berkeley? My grandmother used to love Armenian needlework. Great reporting."

Nareh's eyes widened, surprised he remembered it. "I loved that one."

Another memory slammed into him. He'd cornered Nareh in a hallway outside a bathroom. A *bathroom*. And asked her out in a way that, in hindsight, was less charmingly confident and more . . . cringey-skeevy. His entire body seized with regret so intense he wanted to peel off his own skin. All the years that had passed, all the ways he'd worked to be better, and yet right now, under Nareh's polite but penetrating gaze, he felt like that same oblivious idiot. He didn't want to let his past actions stand between them, unspoken.

Raffi ran a hand through his hair nervously, then cursed himself for messing up his expertly gelled coif. "You know," he said, gathering courage, "I am really sorry about how I acted back then. I'm so glad you turned me down. I was still figuring stuff out."

Nareh appraised him with a somewhat confused smile. "You *have* changed, haven't you?" Then the confusion melted away into genuine kindness. "Well, I want you to know, it's totally okay. I've long given up on the idea of obtaining perfection. We all mess up. As long as it's not a pattern and we grow from it, it's fine."

"Good rules for living."

A beat passed. He saw her catch the eye of a tall woman dressed in striking black lace, who waved in her direction. Nareh beamed, then turned her attention back to him.

"So, have you?" she asked.

"What?"

"Figured it out?"

Just then, Ani appeared by the door of the winery, speaking into her headset as the music quieted.

"I think so," he said, staring at Ani. "I really hope so."

THERE WAS DANCING, eating, and now the toasts had begun. He'd had an idea after his conversation with Ani this morning, and Kami had given him the green light, so Raffi was preparing himself.

He still hadn't gotten a chance to talk to Ani, who was so busy that he could only imagine how exhausted she was. He was dying to be with her but would not do anything to jeopardize her work when it was all so time-sensitive. He saw her across the way, chatting with the caterers, when it was his turn to make his way to the mic.

Raffi crept up to the front, trying not to make any noise and disturb the speeches. Then, as he passed a table, he overheard a woman exclaim to her daughter, "That is Raffi Garabedian, the owner of this winery. Isn't he handsome? So rich, too. You need to find a way to talk to him."

Raffi shuddered. Those words were not meant for his ears, but the auntie likely had one too many glasses of the Ô chardonnay and couldn't temper her volume. He hated that the world didn't know he was taken, didn't know that he loved one woman, Ani Avakian. He couldn't exactly shout it out yet, that was his and Ani's agreement. But he could do this.

He reached the front right as the penultimate speech was winding down. The bridesmaid handed him the mic, and Raffi looked out into the crowd. Deep breaths. There she was. He stared hard in Ani's direction, waiting for her to see him.

And she did. All the way across the garden he could see how large her eyes grew when she spotted Raffi, standing in front of the dome they'd created, with a microphone. He took another breath away from the mic, then brought it close.

"Hello, everyone, my name is Raffi Garabedian, manager of this winery and longtime family friend of the Mardians. First, I want to thank every one of you for being here. This wedding today, between Grace and Kami, is the inaugural wedding event at Ô winery, and I know I am full of pride to be able to host such a significant event.

"But I have to say, none of this would have been possible without the incredible vision and hard work of one very special person—the landscape designer and wedding planner, Ani Avakian. Ani, I've known you for several months now, and I suspected you were talented. But what you've done here today goes beyond anything we could have imagined. Just look around us. I haven't ever seen anything more perfect, have you?"

A ripple of murmurs spread through the crowd, the kind of quiet, appreciative hum that signaled agreement. Heads nodded, and glasses lifted slightly in an unspoken toast. Raffi glanced toward Ani and caught the way her eyes flickered, a shy smile on her face.

"You took Grace and Kami's hopes and dreams and brought them to life in ways none of us could have imagined. You have a true gift, and we are so grateful to have you," here, he coughed, "in our lives."

Raffi steadied himself. "Kami, Grace, I wish you all the happiness in the world. I hope you are reveling in this dreamland around us."

Kami shouted happily, "We are! It's perfect!"

Raffi smiled and concluded, "Everyone, let's all raise our glasses to the marvel that is Ani and to the wonderful couple. Cheers!"

His heart was hammering hard, and he spotted Ani wiping a tear from her cheek. He never wanted to make her cry, but he thought maybe it was not a sad tear.

Maybe it was hope.

He wanted nothing more than to make his way down the middle of the dance floor and sweep Ani off her feet, but he felt a sudden hug crush him from the side. He looked down. It was Kami.

She released him and began talking a mile a minute. "Oh my God, Raffi, that was so sweet. I was a little nervous when you said you wanted to speak, I thought maybe you were going to plug Ô, but instead you plugged Ani. Cuuuute. I mean, she did do an amazing job. You both did. Look at this place."

She stared around her, and Raffi, despite wanting to get away, did the same. The sun had set, leaving behind a deep indigo sky streaked with the last traces of twilight. Overhead, strands of fairy lights draped from tree to tree, casting everything in a golden glow—soft, warm, and impossibly romantic. The lantern-lit stone pathways wound through the garden, around the fountain, like glowing ribbons, leading guests toward the heart of the celebration. It looked truly special. Ô's garden had always been striking, but the changes they'd made had elevated it to a whole new plane. He couldn't keep that thought to himself.

He coughed. "You and Grace, paying for all these updates to Ô . . . It's too much. I want to make it right. It was a big lift, no question—but the difference is huge. I've already got weddings lining up, all because of the work you insisted on."

Kami waved him off. "Mama and Baba gave me a budget, and it was massive, so we could have had the wedding anywhere, but I thought it would be so much more special to have it at an old friend's place."

Raffi's heart squeezed. Kami, for all her faults, did not hold a grudge against him, even after he'd been sort of a cold jerk to her for years. She seemed to think the best of people. She was a big part of the reason that his father's dream of owning a successful winery would come true. Perhaps it was time for him to release his grudge, to stop punishing her for not knowing how to show up for him all those years ago. It felt like the right moment. Like letting it go wouldn't mean losing anything. Perhaps even gaining a little.

Raffi tugged at his sleeve when he said, "Can I tell you something? It's kind of embarrassing."

Kami stepped a bit closer, expression open. "Sure. Anything."

"That night." He cleared his throat, the fear of that day wrapping its claws around him as he remembered it all again. "When Sevan died. We were broken up, and you sent me this—this short text. I felt so let down by you. So alone. I know it's too much to put on one person, but I just—with all of our family's history, I guess—I expected more from you. Sorry to put this on you on your wedding day, but it's just that, well, if you ever wondered why I've been curt with you all these years. That's why. And I am sorry for it. I do wonder how we could have been friends, if things would have been different."

Kami's eyebrows raised in concern and sympathy. "Oh, Raffi, honey, I am so sorry. I—I was so stupid about it. The thought of Sevan—what happened to him. It terrified me. I had no idea what to say to you. I was scared to say anything, so I said as little as possible."

Raffi nodded. He understood that. She hadn't been the only one after all.

Kami continued, "Honestly, people aren't my strong suit. Like, I don't understand how to communicate the way other people do, or what I'm even doing wrong. Sometimes I think I'm broken, but Grace . . . She makes me feel whole." She smiled in the direction of her bride. "So please accept my way-too-late apology."

Raffi shook his head. "Of course. If you can accept mine for being so cold to you for so many years."

Kami smiled and said, "Honestly, I hadn't noticed much. See? Broken. But sometimes it works out for the better."

He hesitated, then added, his voice soft, "Kami . . . you're not broken. You just have your own way of seeing the world. And maybe not everyone gets it, but—" He glanced toward Grace, trilling her fingers toward Kami in an adoring wave. "The most important people do."

She gave him a tight hug. "Thanks for saying that." She released him, and her head tilted slightly as she considered him. "Not such a grump after all, huh? Kind of a romantic, actually!" She winked, then bounded off toward Grace.

Raffi felt a tightness in him release. A knot that had been wound so tight, for so long, he hadn't even realized how much space it had taken up inside him. He had been holding that in for a decade, and all he had to do was talk to Kami. It was that simple.

Now the guests were beginning to fill the dance floor, signaling the last few hours of the party. There was still one person he needed to find. One conversation left unfinished.

And now he could finally talk to her.

31

Ani

RAFFI STRODE THROUGH the sea of guests, heading straight to her.

She was shaking, she realized. His speech, his public declaration of her capabilities and his belief in her—it meant so, so much. The validation she never knew she needed.

And the wedding had gone well. Better than she could have expected. At this point, it was nearly over, all the difficult parts were done, and there was almost nothing left for her to do that was crucial. She should feel relieved, and part of her did, but another part felt crushed. Still wounded from the article, from the aftermath she'd already felt today at this wedding.

Raffi was in front of her, a vision, so tall in the sexiest suit she'd seen him don yet. The tie had a subtle abstract design that made her think of legs slipping through silk sheets. He smelled of desert winds. He looked at her like she was the only woman in the world.

"May I?" he asked, holding out his hand.

The music was a slow Armenian song, and the whole scene

was so similar to their first kiss. She couldn't resist. She was scared—scared of what she wanted to say to him—but she couldn't keep from touching him, having him hold her close. They weren't supposed to make their relationship public until after the wedding, but it was just a few hours until it was technically "after the wedding." So why not?

But when she placed her hand in his, he walked her away from the dance floor, away from the wedding itself, around the corner to a quiet side of the villa. They stood on a small trail, with a soft light above them and endless vineyards on all other sides. They were alone.

Raffi wrapped his arm around her waist, and she curled into him, feeling the familiar sensation of being calmed, protected. But then little alarm bells flared inside her, telling her that her sense of peace was false, that she should still be anxious and worried.

"Raffi," she said into his shirt, into his strong chest. "Thank you for that speech. For saying those words in front of everyone."

He ran his hand up her back, into her hair, stroking it down toward her shoulders. "I meant every word. I had to hold back, actually. Made sure I mentioned the actual brides instead of gush about you the entire time."

She chuckled, but mostly relished the feel of his hand against her. Her entire body prickled at his touch.

"What did you mean this morning?" he whispered. "When you said you needed time to think?"

He sounded nervous. She felt for him. She didn't want to hurt him.

"Just that—" she started, but she couldn't finish. Two worlds warred within her, one shouting, "What are you doing? Everything is perfect! Don't ruin this!" and the other shouting that mantra she'd heard in her head since she could remember, the one that had quieted lately with Raffi, but the one this morning's article had brought back, surging strong as a monster of the deep: "You're not good enough."

"I'm not sure you should be with someone like me."

Raffi stopped dancing but still held her while he stared at her. "What?"

"You read that article. It was true, all true."

"We all make mistakes, it's just—"

"This was too big. Too stupid. Too careless. I want to be with you, I do. I'm just mortified. Next thing everyone's going to think is that I'm some gold digger, being with you."

"Who would . . ." But then he trailed off, having realized the answer. He continued, less sure of himself, "I mean—people do often talk about that stuff, but they're wrong. You know I'd set straight anyone who said that."

Ani leaned against the warmth of his chest, savored it. This might be the last time she felt it against her cheek. "Do you know," she asked, "three separate people came up to me today? Distant family friends, people I know on the periphery. They came up to me and asked if I needed financial help. Three totally unrelated people."

Raffi muttered under his breath, "Fuck." Then, he stammered, "I thought I—I saw an older couple talking to you. Saw the way your face fell. That's just—they were just trying to—"

She said it then, with conviction. "I'm not good enough. Just admit it."

He shook his head vigorously. "No. No, I never will. That's bullshit, Ani. Somewhere in there, you know it."

She didn't say anything, too sad to reply, not sure if she believed him or not.

He asked, "Who did this to you? Who convinced you that you were less than? Was it that fucking high school dance?"

That was an easy yet monumental question. "No, no, it wasn't just that. It's . . . been everything."

"Tell me."

Ani pulled herself out of his arms. She didn't want to be held or comforted while she shared this. "Everyone, since I was little. Talar was the cute sister, the pretty sister, the smart sister. I was forgotten. My parents didn't really see me, even though they're great, I know. But it always seemed like they were more into each other than being parents. They never paid attention to the things that really mattered to me. So between that and mediocre grades, middle-school bullies, that fucking dance. Being a shitty paralegal. Being a wedding planner for *modest clients*, having that in print now. A lackluster love life until Kami, then being dumped by Kami. I mean, I'm over it now, but—I don't know. All of it. Years and years and years."

Raffi stared at her, and she thought he might have tears in his eyes. They shone in a way she'd never seen before.

She continued, "And I feel so stupid saying any of this to you—you, who's had actual tragedy. You, who despite all that, have come so far."

"Have I, though?" Raffi asked.

"What? Of course you have. Listen, Raffi, I, I—"

She was about to say it, make the break, when Raffi interrupted her.

His voice, while steady, had a sharp edge to it, just barely there. "Ani, if you leave me now, I'm not sure my heart can take it. Do what you want, what you think is right, but I'm fragile when it comes to you." He took a step closer, his hands flexing at his sides as if he wanted to reach for her but didn't dare. "If you leave me now, I'm not sure I'll ever be able to come back."

She stared at him, angry. That was not what she wanted to hear, to be guilted into being with him.

"I don't want you to be with me just because of some default. Because you're too afraid to be away from me. I want you because you want me."

But before he could respond, there was a rustle in the bushes. An animal? Or worse, a reporter? Then a bright flash blinded her, followed by the sound of a shutter. She spun around, arms instinctively crossing over her face as if she could somehow shield herself from the already-taken photograph. This was all she needed, to be splashed across the *Daily Mail* yet again, her face plastered beneath some lurid headline, this time painted as a strumpet, a drama-causer, a woman caught in another mess of her own making. Her pulse roared in her ears, drowning out logic, drowning out everything.

She couldn't do it. She had to leave.

"Raffi, I'm sorry," she said and broke away to rejoin the wedding, forcing herself to avoid Raffi's presence and act like nothing was wrong. She could not wait until this wedding—the one she'd been anticipating for more than half a year—was finally over.

32

Raffi

THERE WAS NOTHING for him to do. Raffi woke up in his bed in a cold sweat. He felt he'd had nightmares all last night but couldn't remember them distinctly. Not that it mattered; he was pushed into a living nightmare. One where Ani ran away from him and wouldn't answer his texts or calls.

He couldn't believe it. He'd finally found someone he loved, but he couldn't hang on to her. They may have had a chance to work things out during the wedding, but then he had to go and ruin it and basically *threaten* that he'd never get back together with her if she dumped him, that he couldn't take it. What the hell kind of scared little boy sentiment was that? He knew he was stronger than that. Fuck. *Fuck*.

He puttered around his house, having no motivation to work out, no appetite. His inbox was begging to be attended to, but he had no desire to do so.

Then his phone buzzed, and he was a fool to even think for a second it would be Ani. It was his book club group chat wondering how the wedding went. He could have ignored it or sent back a generic "Great!" but decided maybe he needed some advice. He wanted to take action. He knew that if he told Mad, Bad, and Dangerous about what happened, they wouldn't shame him; they would help him. He texted them back, I blew it. Not the wedding. Ani.

Immediately texts rained in, asking him what happened, and when he told them the last thing he'd said to Ani—wincing while he typed it—and then about the photographer in the bushes, there was quiet for a moment. Then several sad-face emojis and more than one "Oh no . . ."s. He told them he knew he'd made a mistake but wasn't sure how to make it up to Ani.

Then there was a knock at his door. That was strange. No one ever came to his door. Ani. Maybe it would be Ani. He threw down his phone and ran toward the door, hoping despite himself. But then he saw the outline. Someone very tall, large. Not Ani. He slowed his pace and his heart rate slowed, crushed once again. An idiot twice over this morning, thinking she'd reach out to him in any way after what he'd said to her.

When he opened the door, he found his father standing there. With . . . a cane. Holy shit. That was new.

Raffi stepped aside and let his father in. His dad carefully walked over to the dining room table, pulled out a chair, and sat, taking in the view. Raffi joined him. The two men sat in silence.

"The wedding went well," his dad said in Armenian.

Was this an olive branch? Interesting.

"Yes, it did. And judging by the number of emails in our inbox, we're going to have a very full roster."

His father raised an eyebrow, just slightly. "How many did you receive?"

Raffi pulled out his phone, checked the winery's inbox,

which he had only glanced at earlier, scrolled, and had to click to the next fifty emails before he reached the end. "At least seventy," he said. Raffi clicked on one and skimmed it. "People want to travel in for it, too. This couple is from Washington."

Raffi's dad nodded slowly, thinking. "We raise the booking fees, and if we have a wedding forty or so Saturdays of the year, we'll be in the black."

"And if we do more than forty, we might make a decent profit."

"People will also want to get married on Fridays and . . . Sundays." His father crossed himself at this blasphemy, but Raffi knew despite his religious objections he wouldn't turn down those Franklins.

"This is good," Moushegh said, nodding.

Raffi realized this was it; this was the moment his father acknowledged that Raffi did, in fact, have a good idea, that he had succeeded. He wasn't going to get much else, not now, not with their relationship so damaged over the years. But it was a start. A tiny flame of warmth that had been long dormant now sparked. Although somehow, even with that, he still felt run through, clawed at. What was this all without Ani?

"This is all good," his father repeated, "yet you look like shit."

Raffi almost laughed but just said, "Thanks."

"Is it because you ruined things with that girl, Ani?" his father asked.

Raffi snapped to attention. "How do you know?"

Moushegh tapped a knuckle on the table. "I'm no idiot. I was watching you all night. Yesterday, compared to the hinoum, something big had changed. And I'm sure you're to blame."

"I mean—not entirely, but partly, yes," Raffi said.

"Don't put this on her. It's time to man up."

Raffi rolled his eyes. "We've talked about this. You and I don't agree on what that means."

"Raffi. Let's put that aside for a moment. Do you love this woman?"

Raffi took a deep breath. It felt so vulnerable to talk about this with his dad. Raffi didn't *share*. So tentatively, he said, "Yes."

Moushegh nodded. "It is time to show her that whatever you did, you are sorry. That no matter what, you are there for her."

"Dad, I—"

His dad wasn't done. He charged on. "Men don't beg. Except—*except*—when it comes to women. When it's a woman you love, you must get down on your knees and grovel." Then he stared at his shoes and his voice softened. "I should have done that with your mother years ago. Now it is too late."

Raffi's heart seized with sadness. His father's regrets about his mom. The things they'd said to each other. How his father never ran after his mother and brought her back. He could have gotten on a plane and gone to her. But he hadn't. And he regretted it. That meant so much.

"Mom's coming home for Christmas. She texted me." He ventured a look at his father, who seemed to be considering this, slightly lightened. Raffi said, "Maybe not too late?"

His father nodded once. "Maybe."

Raffi felt a surge of hope. If his father, stalwart that he was, after years of acting one way, after so much loss, could change in his older age, then maybe Raffi hadn't completely ruined things with Ani. Maybe, even after his mistakes, after what had gone wrong between them, it wasn't too late for him, either. There was still time to fight for what mattered.

He knew it. He just felt it. This was not his and Ani's final chapter. They were meant to be together, to grow old together, on one pillow, as the Armenian saying went. It was on him to fix it.

"For now," his father added, "concentrate on turning this place from a bachelor pad into a family home."

"I'll think about that." Raffi smiled. He couldn't help it.

There was so much he and his father disagreed on, but this was one definition of masculinity he could get behind. Being there for his family. Supporting, loving, no matter what. He realized that this was the kind of care his father had always wanted to show his mother, but somewhere along the line he had decided that working hard and providing money was the only kind of support he was "allowed" to give. And it led to so much misery in their family, especially after Sevan died.

But now his father, in his own way, seemed to be trying to tell Raffi to do better than him. And he would. He would.

"Got any kebabs in the fridge?" his dad asked.

"For breakfast?"

"Son, it's always kebab time."

Raffi laughed, a genuine laugh that eased his cracked heart the tiniest bit. There was still so much work to do, and he wasn't sure where to start. Maybe his book club would have an idea.

33

Ani

IT WAS TWO days after the wedding. This morning in her apartment in Russian Hill, Ani found her bank account so full that she immediately paid off her personal loan, then made a credit card payment. She still had twenty thousand to go, a number which, after all that, should have been demoralizing. Would have still felt totally out of reach. Except . . .

Her inbox had been blowing up since Kami and Grace's wedding, all the leaked photos, all the times she'd been tagged on Instagram. Grace had done her a *huge* solid and given Ani a full-on shout-out on her social media pages, which absolutely flooded Ani's DMs.

She couldn't believe it. She was getting so many requests she couldn't keep up with them all. All that negative press in the *Daily Mail* had been for nothing. It had completely vanished after the wedding and concentrated instead on the happy couple. That photo of her and Raffi that the paps had caught had never materialized. Very strange.

Last night after Grace's Instagram post and the subsequent rush of interest in Ani's services, Ani wrote Grace and Kami a heartfelt thank-you email and sent best wishes for their honeymoon and life together. And she meant it.

So now she had it. She had exactly what she wanted. Credibility, the path to success, and the ability to charge more (and dig herself out of this debt hole probably much sooner than later). It felt good.

But she also felt like a dry husk of herself. She regretted, more than anything, that conversation with Raffi. Why had she sabotaged herself like that? Why hadn't she let herself believe she deserved happiness and goodness? He'd proven himself to her over and over, and that was how she'd repaid him.

Then he said he didn't think he'd ever want to get back with her. Those words had been on her mind for two days, and she'd shoved the framed photograph of them into the back of a busy desk drawer. She hadn't heard from him since her sudden departure, and would she ever again? She wanted to tell him she was sorry, but would it just crush her further?

Ani pulled herself out of bed right as she got a FaceTime request from Talar. Oh God. She had sent Talar a quick "Talk later" text the day after the wedding, and she supposed today was technically "later." She could just imagine how she looked. Well, her sister had seen her literally at her worst, so this wouldn't be anything new. Ani picked up.

"Just waking up?" Talar admonished.

"'Hello' is customary," Ani grumbled.

"It's eleven a.m. I've been wanting to talk to you about—"

Ani wanted to face this head-on. She interrupted, "I messed up, Tal."

Talar's face immediately softened. "What happened?"

"I assume you saw the second article?"

Talar nodded. "And it's bullshit, right?"

"No. Not really."

Talar stared at her. "Which part isn't?"

"I am—actually, I was—in about fifty thousand dollars' worth of debt."

"What the—"

Ani quickly recounted the story of the scheming Avedissian family.

"Ani," Talar said angrily. "Why didn't you tell me? I could have given you money. You should not be paying twenty percent interest. Do you know how insane that is? When I could have just helped you?"

"No," Ani said, that old flame building inside her. The one of shame. "I needed to do this on my own, entirely. And I have. I'm almost out of it now, and if I just do two more luxury weddings, which I easily can now, I'll be in the clear."

Talar propped up the phone and clasped her hands together in a prayer position. "Ani. Please, please, please let me *lend* you whatever else you currently owe. I cannot in good conscience let my sister pay those fucking vultures twenty percent APR."

"Twenty point nine nine, actually," Ani smiled.

"No time for jokes! Let me. Please. An actual loan. Not a gift. Not charity, okay? Just good business."

Ani thought about it. There was a time when she would have been too proud to even consider this. Bootstrap everything, earn it through hard work, or don't earn it at all. But she had done so much. She'd dug herself out of the worst of it. Her sister was just saving her one, or at most two, shitty monthly payments. She wasn't being pitied. Just helped. And that was okay.

"All right. Okay. Fine."

Talar breathed out in relief. "Thank God. I'll wire you today. Pay those fuckers off, I'm serious. Don't give them another cent of interest."

"But Talar?" Ani said, her voice unsteady, her throat tight. A familiar weight pressed against her chest. "I just—do you know the reason I didn't tell you about the debt?"

"Uh—" Talar was at a loss, and she appeared uncomfortable.

Ani's pulse drummed in her ears. She swallowed hard and took a deep breath, forcing air into her lungs, trying to steady herself before the words tumbled out. "Because you guys—you, Mom, and Bab—won't just let me be the big sister. I feel like I have to be perfect, that I have so much to live up to. You, your constant success, Mom and Bab's ideal relationship. Making a mistake this big, it felt like confirmation that I was the dunce of the family."

As soon as she said it, a wave of vulnerability washed over her, leaving her raw and exposed. She wasn't sure how Talar would take it. In fact, Talar didn't say anything.

But then Ani saw the tears forming in her sister's eyes. "Is that how I've been making you feel?"

Now Ani felt her own eyes getting hot and wet. "Yes," she whispered.

Although they were close, the two sisters never talked about anything too heavy, preferring to stick to lighter topics, inside jokes, and the like. They especially never discussed *their* relationship.

On the screen, Talar's face crumpled. She blinked rapidly, then tears slipped down her cheeks in shimmering streaks. She wiped at them with the sleeve of her sweatshirt. When she finally spoke, her voice was thick with emotion. "I'm sorry, Ani. I know I can be a little—you know, a little domineering." She let out a short, unsteady laugh, then pressed her lips together, shaking her head as more tears escaped.

"With Mom and Bab all caught up in themselves, I felt like I had to be loud and bossy and successful to be noticed by them. When you said you feel this pressure to be perfect, I feel that, too," she admitted, her voice breaking. "And I'm sorry that you got caught up in my, I don't know, my personality. I sensed it but thought it was fine, and now hearing you say that, I just— I'm so embarrassed, so sorry. I care about you. And I miss you. I'm sadder than—"

She broke off, covering her face with one hand.

Wow.

Ani stared at the screen, momentarily stunned. So the way Talar acted was also in response to Mom and Bab. It all made sense.

But more than that, Talar had apologized. Without deflecting, without getting defensive, without brushing aside Ani's feelings. She had acknowledged the hurt she had caused, even if she hadn't meant to. That alone was staggering. God, she was lucky to have a sibling like Talar.

A lump formed in Ani's throat. She had spent years feeling like the little sister, like the one lagging behind, never quite catching up. But now Talar wasn't standing above her, looking down—she was beside her, admitting that she, too, had been struggling in her own way.

What had that last part been about, when she cut herself off? Was it because of Ani? Or something else?

Ani studied her sister's face, the way her eyes shone, her breath still uneven, as if she was holding back. "Are *you* okay? Besides me. And thank you for saying all that. I care so much about you, too. So that's why I'm asking . . ."

Talar gave her a sad smile. "I'm figuring things out. I'll fill you in soon, I promise."

"Okay," Ani said, holding her gaze, making sure she knew she meant it. "But you know I'm here for you, right?"

"Yes," she said, her voice a little steadier this time. "Definitely."

Just then, Ani got a text from Kami. She saw it flash over her FaceTime with Talar but didn't have message previews on. Then another one came in quick succession.

"Hey, Talar, can I call you back?"

"Sure," Talar said. "Ani, I love you."

Ani sat with that for a moment. It wasn't that they never said the words—they did often, in passing, in casual goodbyes—but this felt different. It was so unexpected but so needed. "I love you, too, kourig," she said. "Sister."

She hung up and let out a deep breath, taking in the emotions and holding back the tears. She'd kept them all in for so many days. She wanted to let them go but wasn't fully able to. She couldn't just have a good cry.

There was always something more to do. Always another call to make, another thing demanding her attention. If she stopped, even for a second, she'd fall behind. Or have to face her feelings, which was too terrifying. And now Kami needed her.

So instead of breaking down, she swallowed hard, wiped

at her eyes before anything could spill over, and got ready to talk to her ex.

Ani tapped on her messages and read what Kami sent. Hey girl, can you give me a quick call? Nothing bad I pinkie promise!

Ani's stomach clenched.

Nothing bad. That was supposed to be reassuring, but the fact that Kami even had to say it made Ani uneasy.

Nevertheless, Ani hit call before she could second-guess herself.

As soon as Kami picked up, her voice burst through the speaker, fast and breathless, her words tumbling over one another like an avalanche of energy. "Hi hi! First of all, don't freak out, it's nothing bad, I swear—I know I already said that, but in case you thought I was lying, I double swear. So anyway, we're packing for St. Barts right now but I wanted to call you before I got there since we're doing a phone detox on our honeymoon."

Ani let out a small smile, despite her nerves not being assuaged in the least.

Kami took a dramatic, audible breath on the other end. "I want to say I'm sorry for, for . . . I don't know. Treating you like a best friend or someone to flirt with, or like nothing was wrong. I honestly didn't know how hard the breakup hurt you. I should have, but I didn't, and that's on me. I know I can't undo that, but—" she exhaled, her voice quieter now, more hesitant. "I'm sorry anyway. And look, we don't have to be friends. I get it now. I wanted you to know that."

There was a beat of silence, like she was bracing herself for Ani's reaction.

She took a moment to let Kami's words settle. Ani had already felt lighter after she confronted Kami, but things had been awkward between them ever since. Hearing Kami say all this now? She felt a knot inside her loosen.

"I appreciate that," Ani said, her voice steady but softer than before. "I really do. And honestly? I feel better now. Just having this conversation, knowing you see it—helps." She hesitated, not wanting to overpromise anything. "We don't have to be best buds. But . . . who knows what the future holds?"

There was a pause on the other end, then Kami let out a small relieved laugh. "Yeah. Maybe the four of us could even go on double dates together!"

Ani was too surprised to mask her voice. "What do you mean, 'double'?"

Now she could hear Kami's sly smile over the phone. "Oh, you know exactly what I mean. This is how I figured it out—one sec. I got these sneak peeks from the photographers—"

A message dinged from Kami.

A photo.

It was in black and white, her and Raffi dancing in near darkness under the single bulb. It captured both their faces. Hers nuzzled into Raffi's chest and him looking down at her protectively.

Ani's breath hitched. It was one of the most incredible things she'd ever seen. And one of the most painful.

The photographer must have been snapping them silently before the flash went off, during their argument. So it hadn't been a reporter. She'd run away for no reason.

Ani was barely able to speak, but luckily, Kami did for her. "So that's who you meant by 'my boyfriend.'" Kami's voice practically crackled with excitement through the phone. "I love this for you, by the way. I totally see it."

She could hear the grin in Kami's voice, the sheer delight radiating through the speaker, even while Ani's heart was breaking.

"And let's just take a moment to appreciate," Kami continued, undeterred by Ani's silence, "that my wedding is the reason this happened."

Ani let out a noise between a wheeze and a groan. "Kami—"

But Kami gasped dramatically, cutting her off. "Hey! So it's a good thing I broke up with you two!" She burst into giggles, completely pleased with herself.

Despite Kami being Kami, Ani wasn't upset with her. She gave a sad little laugh through the phone. Then Kami recovered herself. "Okay, okay, Grace is giving me a look. But before I go—Ani, seriously. Thank you for the best wedding in the universe. Pure, utter perfection."

Ani's throat tightened just a little. "You're welcome, Kami."

They hung up, and the room was quiet.

Ani glanced down at her phone, then kept staring. She couldn't look away from the photo.

It felt unreal, seeing them together. She ran her thumb over the screen, as if that might make the moment tangible again, might let her slip back into it.

And suddenly, she could feel it. Exactly what it felt like to be in his arms, the steady rise and fall of his chest, how safe and loved he made her feel.

Her breath caught, and regret curled deep in her stomach. She cursed herself for letting her insecurities eat her alive and ruin this thing with Raffi. Let them whisper that she wasn't enough, that he would eventually see all the ways she fell short. That this—they—couldn't possibly last.

But it was real, and she didn't want to let it go.

She had to try. He never told her *not* to talk to him again. So screw it, she had to try.

There was no time for texting. She'd already had two good calls today; maybe the third would be extra lucky.

Ani tapped to his name in her favorites and pressed call.

She waited for the ringing to start, but instead, it went straight to voicemail. Oh no. Was there no service? Maybe she had no service.

She waited a few seconds, then tried again. Straight to voicemail.

She texted him. Hey. Just to check, because she had a bad feeling about it. The text, which normally showed up as blue, showed up green.

He'd blocked her. *No.* He'd . . . blocked her?

The pain in her chest seemed more expansive than anything she'd felt. Her eyelids were heavy, all her limbs leaden with heartbreak. She couldn't move. He had really meant it. He said if she left him, then that was it, and he'd followed through.

But then, what had been real? She could have sworn he was in it for the long run. Was he so afraid of being hurt that he'd rather block her and never speak to her again than try to talk and work things out? It didn't seem right. But then, her phone didn't lie.

She realized none of it—the success, the weddings, the esteem—meant nearly as much to her now without him. She needed him. And he wanted nothing to do with her.

Then, she felt the tears begin, and this time, she could not stop them.

34

Ani

AFTER THE MOST epic cry and a day full of chocolate and romance movies, during which she threw popcorn at the screen when the couples got their happily ever afters, she decided to pretend she was all right. This had always worked out for her before, so she was doing it again.

Two days later, sporting dark bags under her eyes from spending her nights tossing and turning, she was sitting at a divey café on Polk Street. It wasn't her usual spot, because she hoped she wouldn't run into anyone she knew. She had work to do, and wanted to get out of the house, but she didn't want to speak to a single soul except the person behind the counter. There was a hollowness about her; she knew why it was there but there was nothing she could do about it.

Ani stared at the inbox on her tablet, and her eyes went fuzzy. The burst of emails should have excited her, but since the realization that Raffi had shut her out, she couldn't find it within herself to feel joy in her work. *Come on, Ani, you can do this,* she told herself and opened an email.

It was from a couple wanting to plan their big bash at Ô. Of course they did, because that was where Grace Zhang tied the knot. She scanned several more emails, and half of them wanted to hire her and have their wedding at Raffi's winery. She hadn't thought about this. Would she simply have to decline those weddings? Or have Sanan go to all in-person meetings at the winery so she didn't have to?

A strong wave of nausea passed over her, thinking about how to navigate this. She felt almost dizzy, then realized no, that buzzing was from her phone.

Ani pulled it out, and there, before her, was an actual bona fide text from Raffi.

Holy shit.

She didn't know if the text would be good or bad. An essay of anger or apology or a "don't contact me," but she had to know. Even if it was horrible news, she had to read it.

It said: Ani. Call me? Please.

Please. *Please* was good. *Call me* was good. Very good! He wanted to talk.

Ani quickly stood, stuffing her tablet into her bag and leaving her latte on the table, and dialed as she stepped out of the café and onto bustling Polk Street. Raffi picked up on the first ring.

"Ani," he said, and his voice sounded like a salvation.

That was all she needed, one word, and she melted, remembering everything—the way he held her hand to his heart, his kisses, the way he told her over and over that she was worthy.

"Raffi, oh my God. I thought you'd blocked me. I tried calling—"

"You tried calling?" He sounded shocked with a mix of anger. Not toward her, she sensed, but perhaps toward himself. "No, no, I didn't block you. I didn't get any of your calls. Shit. I had no idea you were trying to contact me."

Relief hit her. He hadn't blocked her; he didn't even know she'd tried to call. But then . . .

"Why wouldn't they go through?"

His voice was quick, desperate. "I'll explain. What are you up to right now? Do you want to—can you meet me?"

"Yes!" she nearly shouted. "I'll be wherever you want. I'm near my place. Where are you?"

A couple of people walking by turned toward her as she spoke. But it didn't matter. Her heart was pounding, and she felt her blood rushing through her body, felt truly alive for the first time since the wedding.

"Fuck. Still in Napa. Should've flown into SFO. I'll drive to you. Be there soon as I can."

It would still be a whole hour if he sped like a bat out of hell. Too long. "I can't wait," she said. "I'm coming to you. Let's meet in the middle."

"Which way are you taking?"

"Golden Gate, up through the North Bay."

"Okay. Marin Headlands. Meet me there."

That was definitely a farther drive for him than for her, unless she ran into traffic, which was probable.

"That's not halfway. I'll be in Larkspur before you even get to Sonoma."

She heard a car door slam. "We'll see about that," he said.

"Raffi," she warned. "Drive safe. I want to see you. Alive."

He grunted, then said, "All right. For you."

She smiled, thinking his old car probably wasn't equipped

to handle high speeds for extended periods and thanked the stars he wasn't a Ferrari guy.

"I'm going to see you soon," she said, almost to herself.

"You sure are," he replied, and she could hear him smiling.

When she hung up, the noise of the street rushed back in her ears, like it had paused the entire time she was talking to Raffi.

Ani ran the five blocks home in the warm September air. Early fall was in some ways the most marvelous time of year in San Francisco. The fog had receded, and with it the cold, so everyone was outside, enjoying the weather in shorts and bare shoulders. Ani thanked herself for wearing flats as she sprinted down Polk Street and hopped into her car.

She was going to see Raffi. He wanted to see her. He sounded so happy on the phone, about the fact that they would be reunited. She let herself hope and hope and hope.

35

Raffi

RAFFI DID MAKE it to Marin Headlands before Ani. She got stuck in bridge traffic. When she called to tell him, they stayed on the phone this time.

"I'm parked," he said as he got out of the car.

"Be there in a minute," came Ani's beautiful voice that he absolutely knew he'd never tire of hearing.

What a day to be here. The fog had cleared so there was a full view of the Golden Gate Bridge, the Presidio, the Marina, and downtown San Francisco. There had been an unexpected rain shower a few days before, so the hillside was blanketed with greenery.

He breathed in and out, the ocean breeze layered with the warm fall day. Ani wanted to see him. She was rushing to see him. It would be okay. He was ready to grovel anyway.

After the last couple of days he'd had, he should have been tired, but instead, he was energized. He'd had a group FaceTime with MBD Book Club and spilled all the details—okay, not *all* the details—and Lana suggested in her quiet monotone voice the very answer to what he could do to mend things with Ani.

Her car pulled in next to his, and the second the engine was off, he hardly had a chance to take her in, his love, because Ani jumped out of the car and sprinted into his arms. Oh my God. He was holding her now. He hadn't expected—

It took him a moment to breathe her in. Her soft curves pressed against him, her arms found their way inside his jacket, and her cheek buried against his chest. He held her tightly. He couldn't believe she was here, they were touching, she was happy to see him. Four days ago he thought he'd lost her for good.

"Ani," he said. "I'm so sorry. I've missed you so much. I shouldn't have said what I said. I will always come back to you, as long as you want me. I'll be here for you. Always. I am never letting you down again. You have my word."

She was shaking her head. "No, no. I'm the one who's sorry. Everything was going great, and I let my insecurities get to me—"

He wouldn't hear of it. He hadn't been sure he'd ever see her again, and an apology was the last thing he'd ask for. He didn't need it; he understood where she had been coming from.

"That article was horrible, I don't blame you—"

"No, I still should have trusted you. Trusted myself."

He looked down at her, held her face in his hands. She stared up at him with so much adoration. "I want to make damn sure. You're telling me you want to be together?"

"Yes, Raffi, yes. I love you." She laughed, then said it again. "I can't be without you. I love you."

Raffi held her so tight and kissed the top of her head. "I've been wanting to tell you the same thing for a long time, Ani jan. I love you in a way that I can barely control. No one has made me feel this way in my life. No one. It's you. Since I met you, Ani, it's always been you."

Tears slid down her cheeks, and Raffi wiped them away with his thumbs. She did the same for him. He kissed her cheeks, her eyelashes, then her mouth.

The kiss deepened, Raffi pressed against his car and Ani melted into him. They didn't stop until a tourist family full of children brought him back down to earth. He heard a toddler boy say, "They doing kissing?" and he and Ani pulled away and started laughing.

"But Raffi," she said. "Why was your phone off, or whatever? I thought you blocked me and never wanted to talk to me again."

He nuzzled her head, hoping the gesture could take away her past pain. "I'm so sorry that you ever thought that. Fuck. I never wanted to make you feel like that. I was on a plane."

"Plane?"

"I've been out of the country."

Ani appeared puzzled, rightfully. Raffi dug into his inner coat pocket and pulled out a check, then handed it to his girlfriend.

She read it. "Sixty thousand . . . ? What is this? I thought I told you I didn't need—"

"Look at the name," Raffi said.

The check was from the Avedissians. Those fuckers who scammed the love of his life.

"You . . ." Ani began, but was at a loss for words.

"Went to Bali," Raffi finished. At Lana's suggestion: "Why don't you just go to Bali and find them yourself? You've got connections." "I found them. And made them pay. As you can see, that's a cashier's check, so this one isn't going to bounce. Fifty thousand plus interest."

Ani gaped at him, open-mouthed. "How did you get them to pay—?"

"Good question. And by the way, we have to go back there. I hardly got to see it, but truth be told, I didn't want to experience it without you." Raffi took out his phone. "Here's how I did it."

He showed Ani a video of his dad, Moushegh, sitting in front of a roaring fireplace, gripping a cane with both hands, glowering at the camera. Dad did look incredibly intimidating. Raffi dragged the player forward a bit. "There's a little intro, then we get here," he said.

In Armenian, his dad roared, "And if you do not pay, the entire force of the Armenian mob will rain down on your sorry asses, sending you back to hell, where you belong."

Ani let out a choked laugh. "What? Oh my God, he *is* in the mob?"

Raffi smiled. "No, he's not. But if everyone thinks he is, why not a little threat to help out a woman in need? I'm sorry I told him about the debt; I know it's a tough subject. I hope that's okay. He really likes you. Was happy to make this video if it meant lending you a hand."

Ani stared at the screen, her eyes wide and unblinking, as if she couldn't quite believe what she was seeing. A laugh bubbled up in her throat, equal parts disbelief and joy. "He's really convincing. So this actually worked?"

He nodded. "It actually worked. And they gave me an apology full of excuses, but I won't sully your brain by repeating them. Suffice it to say, they're sorry now."

Ani shook her head and looked at the check, her smile growing brighter. "Wow. *Wow.* Thank you. Seriously."

Raffi shrugged. "It's not exactly a grand romantic gesture, but it was the best I could do."

Ani stared up at him, a huge smile on her face. "It is *incredibly* romantic."

She stood on her tiptoes and kissed him.

He pulled back and groaned. "We live too far away. I can't be away from you."

"I know . . ." she said.

Raffi had a plan, though. "But I've figured it out. I'll move back to the city. I'll hire more people at Ô. I can commute."

In truth, he loved living in Napa, but he loved Ani more. So if he had to head back to the city to be close to her, he'd get a new place tomorrow.

He continued, "I'll go anywhere you need me to be. You feel more like home than home ever did."

Ani gave a particularly adoring smile, her cheeks pinkened. But then she shook her head. "I don't know, almost all the wedding requests I've been getting are for Napa and Sonoma County. *I* might be the one who has to move."

Raffi froze. She would move to Napa? That would be . . . that would be beyond amazing. He could still be near his father in case he needed him. He'd still be able to run the winery daily and would get that mental peace from living in the country.

"You'd really do that? . . . With me?"

Ani hesitated, her fingers twisting the edge of her sleeve as she looked down, then back up at him. "I've been thinking about it . . . I want to, but I can't move in with you."

Raffi stared down at her, trying to read her face. She was smirking, though. "Why, baby? Too soon? I get that. I don't want to push."

She shook her head. "No, it's not too soon."

Encouraged by that, he continued, "You know I would make my home yours in a second. You can decorate it any way you like. Even if you wanted to turn my place into a pink coquette paradise, I'd be down."

She smiled. "I'm more of a minimalist, so you don't have to worry about bows and ruffles. But no, decor isn't the issue. My very strict parents would absolutely kill me if I lived with a man before I was, uh, engaged." She blushed hard at that word. "I sort of made the promise to myself, too. I mean, I'm not asking anything—besides, I still have two months left on my lease, and I could always find a little apartment in downtown Napa—"

Now Raffi laughed as he held this perfect woman in his arms. The woman who had changed everything for him. She thought he wouldn't want to marry her today? Oh, he did—only she deserved a real planned proposal. "Ani, Ani, Ani. Don't worry about that. I've got a plan."

Raffi kissed her again, feeling the waves of excitement for the future flow through him. He knew that they were creating a foundation upon which they would be building a life together, a brand-new one with him and her at the helm.

Epilogue

Ani

IN TRUE GRACE fashion, she continued to be a class act and invited Raffi and Ani to the premiere of *Mafia Princess*. And in true Raffi fashion, he had rented a stretch SUV limo for just the two of them from their hotel in West Hollywood to the Fox Bruin Theater. Which is where they were now, in a line of cars waiting their turn to pull up to the entrance.

It had been a month and a half since Ani and Raffi had reunited in Marin, and it had been the best month and a half of her life. She'd been booked solid with weddings, as had Ô, and Ani was planning the majority of them. Everyone wanted a taste of celebrity at the now-iconic winery where Grace Zhang walked down the aisle. Which meant she and Raffi still got to spend plenty of time together.

He'd met her parents twice, and both times had gone wonderfully. Her mother had googly eyes for Raffi, and Ani caught her dad slapping him on the back jovially. She and Raffi had even attended a banquet together and danced all night in front of what felt like the entire Northern California Armenian community. Nothing said "official" more than that, she joked with him, and he wholeheartedly agreed.

She stared out onto the scene of cameras flashing and no longer felt any fear about them. The stories about her completely died after the wedding. It seemed no one was actually that interested in the wedding planner, so no further stories surfaced. She happily retreated into obscurity—at least from the celebrity point of view. Ani was no longer obscure when it came to wedding planning. She smiled at the thought, proud of herself.

Raffi kissed her neck, and Ani closed her eyes to take in the full sensation. She leaned into him, savoring his touch.

Then Raffi reached a hand under the slit of her deep burgundy dress. He dragged his fingers up her thighs like he had several months ago, and he still took her breath away.

"Do we have time?" Raffi asked, his voice gravelly.

Ani gasped as he made contact, but their car moved forward. They were nearly at the front.

"I don't—I don't think so," she managed. "See—" She motioned toward the glass, torn between wanting him and not missing their chance to get out of the car.

His hand slowly retreated, and he reached up and tenderly kissed her cheek instead.

"Probably for the best," he said. "That hair and makeup need to stay intact."

"Oh yeah?" she asked. He was grinning at her like he had a secret.

"I do think, though," Raffi said, sliding down the seat and onto the . . . floor? "We do have time for this."

My goodness, Raffi was dutifully committed to oral. She

glanced out the window and noted they did probably have a few minutes. And after all, she wouldn't mess up her hair. He was so thoughtful. Ani braced herself for the parting of her thighs.

But it didn't come.

Then she saw it. He wasn't just on the floor. He was down on one knee, reaching into his jacket.

Her heart stopped, because time had already folded in on itself, as this man, this impossible, wonderful man, looked up at her like she was his entire world.

He pulled out a dark blue box and asked, "Ani, since the moment you crashed into my life—literally falling into my arms—you've challenged me, pushed me, and made me want to be better, not just for you but for myself, too. There's no one in the world like you. No one who sees me the way you do."

He exhaled, then stared straight into her eyes. "I want to spend the rest of my life trying to be the person you deserve, to love you the way you've loved me, and to build a life together that's as wild and beautiful as you are. You are my one. My forever one. Will you do me the honor of marrying me?"

She hadn't even looked at whatever was inside the box because she was too focused on Raffi's smoldering eyes staring into hers with so much love.

"Yes, Raffi jan, yes. Yes, *yes*. I'm yours. Every day from now until forever."

She threw her arms around him and he kissed her carefully, still thinking about her makeup, although she didn't give a damn anymore. She'd just been proposed to. She was going to marry Raffi. This was a dream. This was the most beautiful dream.

She pulled away for a moment and looked in the box. Then she threw her head back. "Raffi! I can't. That's too big!"

Raffi smirked. "That's what—"

"Don't say 'That's what she said'!"

They both giggled. He slid the ring onto her finger. A perfect fit. She watched it shimmer in the low lights of the limo. She may have cried a little.

"It's fine. It's lab-grown anyway. Half price, and I love a deal."

She pushed him playfully. "Stop. This is too much. But goddamn, it's magnificent."

He held her and stared at her with so much devotion. "Ani Avakian, my fiancée."

"Raffi Garabedian, mine," she said.

A moment later, their car pulled up directly to the theater.

"And now we get to take post-proposal photos on the red carpet."

"You're really something, Raff."

He laid his head against hers and whispered, "This is just the beginning. We have our whole lives together."

With one more kiss, Raffi opened the door to the dazzling beams of the Fox Bruin Theater, to loud joy and kinetic excitement. Raffi held her hand as she stepped out, and even among the sea of strangers and reporters, she felt entirely safe, powerful, and loved. Ani marveled at how her life had changed so quickly in less than a year. Because of him *and* because of her. Because of them, together.

Acknowledgments

A THIRD book! I thank my lucky stars (in the form of my agent and editors) for this opportunity. Katelyn Detweiler, a hearty thank-you for always being my champion and for loving this book. I still cannot believe how quickly you read the first draft. I am so grateful for your support. Thank you to Sam Farkas for expertly managing foreign rights, and to Denise Page and the rest of the team at Jill Grinberg Literary Management. It's wonderful working with you all!

Angela Kim and Cindy Hwang—wow, together we can build quite a concept, right?! I am so grateful we had the chance to go back and forth, refining this idea until we polished it to the ultimate one! Thank you for giving me this chance to write such a fun book, for your insightful edits, and for giving a voice to Armenian culture in the romance space.

I love working with everyone at Berkley. Thank you to Katie Ferraro and Elisha Katz for your expert help in getting the word out about this book. Thank you to Christy Wagner for your copyediting expertise. Thank you to Jamie Thaman and

Amy Carbo for polishing up the manuscript. Thank you to Megha Jain for helping bring this story into the world.

To Katie Smith, Katie Anderson, and Lila Selle, thank you for creating such a beautiful, romantic cover. And to Alison Cnockaert for the lovely interior, thank you.

To Jesse Q. Sutanto, thank you for reading an early outline and bringing the drama to this story. You are the plotting goddess, and I bow down.

Rebekah Faubion, thank you so very much for getting pumped about this idea early on and for your immensely useful edits to my outline and first chapters!

Elizabeth Reed, my romance queen, thank you for reading my alpha draft and for your tremendous feedback, which helped me improve Ani and Raffi's relationship. I am so thankful for you!

Alyssa Jarrett, thank you so much for reading my revised first chapter, for helping me push the rivals-to-lovers dynamic even further, and for your general support of this book! It is so appreciated.

Robert Nazar Arjoyan, thanks for always reminding me I could easily crush my word count goals. Thank you for reading the alpha draft and providing your eagle-eyed edits. I am so grateful for our friendship. Հիմա քո հերթն է եկել:

Annie Mare, thank you so much for your generosity in reading my beta draft and for your incredibly thoughtful comments that elevated this book. I am so grateful!

Saniya W., thank you for your deep, thoughtful read of my book. Your suggestions steered this book in a totally new and wonderful direction, and I am so thankful for your help!

Elyse Moretti Forbes, my dear friend, I'm so grateful for your friendship and constant support, in addition to your astute edits to my manuscript! Thank you for reading and always being there.

Mary Antoinette Chua, thank you for all your social media support! I could not navigate IG without you!!

To my friends Doctors Cathy Chuang and Bahram Sohrabi, thank you for dispensing your medical profession knowledge, particularly in the area of "how soon after being shot with an EpiPen can one get a boner?"

To the Berkletes, who saved this book when I had zero ideas of what plot points to add, thank you so very much for your hilarious, brilliant ideas, particularly Danica Nava, Katie Shephard, Sarah Hawley, Isabel Cañas, Eve Chung, and Tori Anne Martin. Your ideas became some of my favorite scenes in all of *Our Ex's Wedding*. And to all the Berkletes, thank you for your friendship, your advice, and your ability to be there in moments of panic!

Thank you to the dedicated librarians and booksellers who have done so much for my books and supported my authorship. Special shout-outs to Abril Bookstore (Parev, Arno!), Book Passage, Christopher's Books (Hi, Jackson and Tee!), and Books Inc. (Hi, Summer! Hi, Jerry!) for all you do.

To Yuri, thank you for always being there for our family and helping take care of V so I could write. I love you!

To my family, thank you for your continued loving support of my writing. But please don't read this book. Or at least skip chapter 21, the first half of 22, and definitely all of 28. We'll all be happier this way, trust me.

Tamar Voskuni. ;) Thank you, my dear sister, for being my constant support, the one who always understands and always inspires me. I don't know anyone as badass as you, and I feel lucky to be your sister! I love you!

Ryan, the core idea of this book is about you, us. The concept that one person can wander into your life and change the entire course for the better. I felt unmoored until I met you, so thank you for this beautiful life of ours.

To my little D and V, thank you for giving me the motivation to be the best I can be, for you two. The love you radiate into our lives is like nothing else I've known.

And to you, the readers. Thank you for picking up this story about two Armenian Americans in the diaspora, finding their way to each other. Because of you, I'm able to share these stories with the world, so thank you, all readers, for your support.

Author photo by Clouds Inside Photography

TALEEN VOSKUNI is an award-winning writer who grew up in the Bay Area Armenian diaspora. She graduated from UC Berkeley with a BA in English and currently lives in San Francisco, working in tech. Other than a newfound obsession with writing Armenian rom-coms, she spends her free time cultivating her kids, her garden, and her dark chocolate addiction. Her first novel, *Sorry, Bro*, received starred reviews from *Kirkus* and *Booklist*, was favorably reviewed in the *New York Times*, and won the 2023 Golden Poppy award for best romance. She is also the author of *Lavash at First Sight*.

VISIT TALEEN VOSKUNI ONLINE

TaleenVoskuni.com

𝕏 TaleenVoskuni

TaleenAuthor